These Unrighteous Vows

Sienna C. Jones

To my Grandmother,
Glenys Jones.

To those who can face the storms alone,
but cherish the thought of having someone
who cares enough to be there.

ALSO BY SIENNA C. JONES

'In death, I will find you again,
and there we shall dance beneath the moon.'

THE GODDESS OF SOMMSIA

Holder of the Sommsia Realms

Fire, Sunlight, Warmth, Healing

THE GODDESS OF AUTUMNIA

Holder of the Autumnia Realms

Nature, Death, World-Warping, Change

THE GODDESS OF WHYNTIOU

Holder of the Whyntiou Realms

Weather, Memory, Water, Storms

THE GODDESS OF FLORA

Holder of the Flora Realms

Rebirth, Renewal, Late Awakenings

PROLOGUE
THE WARS OF THE DEEP

Death was an exquisite thing for one's mind to dwell on.

It was a thought that was sweet, malicious, kind; it was a thought that may either have one staring up at the ceiling at night, counting every little splinter of a crack that swept across the plaster distracting away from the consuming whispers of their mind... or it may have one asleep with not a single worry treading across their frail mortal skin.

But either way, death wasn't something that usually seemed to entangle itself in the crashing waves that wiped away the memories of the past.

The shadowed water thrashed against the withering cliff sides with a silhouette that had the lost souls turning. Bodies, lives, spirits all lurked in the water's depth, turning with every breath the old King of the East once took.

His body was old, his olive skin aged and wrinkly... except it wasn't like the wrinkles on any other elderly mortal or immortal, it was like the wrinkles the beloved curse left behind after haunting one's spirits for several eternities at a single moment in time. Immortality was not kind to him—it had never been kind to him. It was a heavy haze that followed his every breath, a constant agony that pained his old lungs. Yet, because of the amount of wealth it layered onto his jewelled shoulders, the King of the East cherished every little inch of power he got, and he was overjoyed with the power that managed to blindly soothe his aching breaths.

"She is alive?" his words were haunting, low. A thrum to them that matched the thunder that echoed through the crackling skies since the moment the Realms *last living hope* had perished alongside everything else the curse nicked. "How can that be? You said the curse was sure to kill her." His words formed into a slithering twine of venom, arrows shooting straight towards the heart Adonis Evermore was rumoured to once hold.

"She was not meant to survive," he gravely replied, his eyes not once daring to look away from the dark marbled tiles before him. They were cracked, with human handprints engraved into them as if they'd died here just yesterday. "It was said that the moment the curse entered into her heart, she would become one that I could experiment on. One that I could use to capture the magick of the Gods—for you, Your Highness."

"So, why are there reports of her activity in the Kingdom of Aeonia? Especially when she is meant to be back and beneath the Realm of Harlia—as you said?" the King of the East demanded through a thick growl, his fists smashing down onto the throne wrapped and wielded in thorns. Adonis swore that he could see those the curse had captured wielded around every prick, and when it bled, their tears finally flowed.

With fear crawling through the depths of his eyes, Adonis looked up, ignoring how the windows began to rattle. A thick and quick-witted lightning bolt struck the burnt land metres before the palace, and Adonis swiftly closed his eyes with a clench of his bruised jaw. He knew the curse had just claimed another one of its many victims. It wasn't a sheltered fact that all the Realm's population had been halved since that fatal night in

Harlia—but unfortunately, that was not his problem to deal with, not as he looked back to the merciless King. Adonis swallowed the thick venom of terror that murmured at the back of his throat, pushing away any potential panic that the King, who somehow glared at him, could potentially taste.

Taste but never see—except that didn't stop him from drinking the blood of those who were meant to be sitting in school learning basic maths and literature.

The King of the East was blind, but that did not stop his other senses from tracking Adonis' every move. Adonis could tell from the way his white pupils moved with his every movement. He had a great scar that stretched down the centre of his chest, leading to the bottom of his abdomen. *It mimicked the electricity of lightning*. Rumour has it that he had received that miraculous scar in the same moment he went blind… when the bolt of lightning meant to murder him, struck him in all of his manacled wickedness.

Attempting to take away one of the Gods worst consequences.

Some say they can still hear his roar, his scream, his cry echoing through the Forgotten Realms that now lay burnt to the crisp after the curse confirmed that they would *stay forgotten*. Others say that it's in the nights when his agony ripples across their flesh. A forever reminder of what had occurred during the sleepless nights of the Great War.

A reminder that he will reach them soon enough—that those who managed to escape will never actually *escape*.

Adonis shook his head, but his actions were mere quivers. Useless against a King who had a bloodthirsty hunger for fear. "I'm not sure—"

"You aren't sure?" the King mimicked through a cavernous cackle that sent the seas thrashing and the wind screaming. "Then tell me why, boy, why have I been told by several trustworthy sources that there has been activity in Aeonia for the past several rotten months? You told me a month ago, through the form of a flimsy letter, that she was 'bolted to the table' by your side—that you, *boy,* had everything under control."

Adonis nodded, his vision not daring for a single second to give way as he kept his gaze steady. He could feel the King breathing down his back, the curse slipping from his tongue and forcing Adonis to stay still. The many blades in the curse's hands begging to slice his flesh to oblivion. "It was an illusion of some type—it had to be." Could the King smell lies too? Adonis didn't want to know.

"I would've thought you were smarter than that, boy—GUARDS!" Adonis flinched as his voice echoed through the large abyss of the throne room, and the storm beyond began to fasten too, as if those watching over him, *if there were any there,* were too trapped inside of their fear. "Consume his soul."

With widening eyes, Adonis quickly shook his head. A weak whimper scattering from his lips as the darkness from each corner of the room warped into the silhouettes and figures of guards. Was the death they were sure to bring all a mere deception too? Adonis longed for that to be the case. "No! NO!" he bellowed in a crumbling tone as he looked for anywhere to flee out of, but the darkness continued gaining on him, squirming around his fingernails, and nipping beneath his bones until true tears of shadowed oblivion ran down his already bloody cheeks. The journey here hadn't been a nice one, leaving Adonis covered in the blood of those he'd had to murder to survive. He'd *had* to. "NO! I can help you! Please—*please,* let me do something," he breathed, "*anything—*"

The King of the East laughed as he turned his thin, bony fingers in a circle across one of the few visible spots of whatever substance the throne was made of. With a flashy grin, he ignored the blood that pooled at his feet from the several thousand wounds to line his skin. It had been centuries now since he had felt any true touch of pain. The last time probably would've been when he watched his family burn at the stake. "What could you possibly do for me, boy? You are merely a mortal in my eyes."

"Mortal or no mortal, I can still help you!" Adonis gasped as the darkness began to bend around his throat. He could feel it slithering into his heart with every breath he took. The curse was already in the process of wiping away yet again another soul to a place unheard of. Adonis prayed for their peace. "If you spare me my life, I vow to you that I will find Althea Evangeline and bring her heart and soul to you on a silver platter—" Adonis struggled against the darkness that weaved across his skin, his fragmented movements trying with everything in them to squirm him out of its quivering and deathly hold.

"And how exactly will you do that?" the King questioned through an echoing laugh; cruel sounds erupted from the depths of his cursed soul as he cocked his head to the left, forcing any surviving nature or wildlife beyond to burn from the insides out as his magick caressed his own spine. "I don't think you and your little pet will be much of a match against her. If anything, it would be far more enjoyable on her end to watch a squirmy little thing like you... die."

"Yes, but I have—I have an insight!" Adonis gasped, and the King cocked his head to the left. He wasn't sure where he was going with this, but at this point, he was grasping at anything.

"Hmm? And what's that, *Adonis?*"

"Kylen Noxwell, King of Lorundio," Adonis stated with a firm breath. His features were poised, his breaths uncanny to the ones his lungs had been scorching several seconds earlier.

"And what can that child of a king possibly have to offer someone like me?"

Adonis cleared his throat, breathing easy for a splinter of a second as the ghosts of his past finally loosened their ungodly hold on him. He was so close—so *close*. "Nightshade."

"Nightshade?" the King echoed sceptically. "Boy, if I find

that you are making a mockery of me, I will make your death one that is severely painful—and I always keep my word."

"*No*—no. Nightshade was the Noxwell's Kingdom speciality back when his parents ruled. It was a poison they brewed in the dungeons of their castle. It was long forgotten, but I dare say that everything is still there, untouched. If I—we get our hands on it, we can use it to our advantage."

"Isn't that where the King of Aeonia lies in his own filth nowadays? In the depths of those dungeons?" the King of the East laughed maniacally. "Then they would obviously know of the drugs they are growing—especially something of that deadliness."

"No," Adonis choked as his vision wavered. The darkness was tightening on him, threatening the circulation of his skin and bones. "That old ruination of a king lies in the areas that Kylen Noxwell knows of—that boy doesn't know of these other sections," Adonis explained, his words bending to his advantage.

"And how do you—a boy from Harlia, know of this?"

"You forget that I am one with the birds. Nature. My crows keep track of what's being spoken, and what they think I need to know gets reported back to me. By gaining access to Kylen and the nightshade, I can use both against Althea; and I will bring her back to you."

In all its inevitable glory, silence spread across the floor like wildfire. Adonis straightened his spine. His lips and expression were firm as he looked the king in his dark, cruel eyes.

He tutted a sound that sent pain through Adonis' bones, but he didn't dare break his stance. "Very well. You have until two moon cycles from now. I want Althea Evangeline here, and I want the power she holds." He paused, narrowing his gaze as he thought aloud, "While you are at it, bring me a batch of night-shade as well. I remember the rumours about it; I know that that has an effect against the curse—it will be fun to experiment on her and on the boy she left empty… bring me Kylen Noxwell too."

Adonis let out a sigh that had been held captive by his lungs, nodding his head quickly as he got to his knees and bowed. "Thank you, Your Greatness. You will not be disappointed."

☾

The wind howled beyond, and as the days turned into weeks, Adonis Evermore clasped onto the cursed ship, looking towards the lands he had never dared to travel to.

The sky was dark, but the seas he left had been darker.

Adonis had never wanted to see the seas that the King of the East dumped his victims' souls into. But now he had, and he was sure to do everything in his power to ensure that he didn't end up there himself.

He would do anything.

The

Lost

ONE
ALTHEA

They noted her frail bones as if they could physically feel how she was withering away as each second ran out of her scarred hands. They noted the Markings that lined her arms, caressing them in the dead of the night while she stared at the memories that had escaped from her seeping mind. They noted her breaths and the beat of her controlled and imprisoned heart, all as if it brought them such malicious joy to make such a mockery of her.

To make her out to be a bloody fool.

The old, weathered cell that was eyeing her every movement had a shadowed slither of darkness running through the air. The darkness of the spirits reached for her with loose hands and over-calculated movements, but the girl did nothing more than simply watch it as she steadied her breaths. She'd gotten used to this process long ago; now... it was effortless. Her tired eyes skimmed through the air with not a single thought to her mind as she allowed her eyes to slowly open and shut; the repetitiveness of *each and every day* earned her bones to grow dreadfully weak.

There was one single flickering *light* in the old, weathered cell in which she sat, and that was placed in the middle of the small, squared, white roof that was both a hallucination and a deception of a lie. Because she knew that it wasn't *actually* real —an inevitable *manipulation*, and Althea knew this because every time she reached for the round light, her hand would always go straight through it without an utter thought. Leading her to want to go insane because she didn't know just what was real and what was not—*was she even real anymore? How was she to know that?*

Everything about this old room with what looked to be *real walls* and *real floors* seemed to be a mere figment of her imagination, and yet somehow... against everything she had ever known, it was all real at the same time—because how else could she be here? Knowing and understanding that she was trapped?

While nothing inside the weathered cell seemed to be real or physical in any way, the force of it kept her imprisoned—and she didn't know what was possibly *worse*...

Being contained to a single cell.

Or realising that she was in the abyss of her soul... *and it was like a merciless desert.*

Althea Evangeline, the girl who once was, had stared at the same ordinary wall before her for three-hundred and thirty-two long days; and she knew that that was accurate because there were three-hundred and thirty-two ignorant lines engraved into the prison wall at her left. The one that was one of four that kept her trapped within the walls of her very own frail soul—*or what was left of it, that was.*

She couldn't comprehend in the slightest how her own soul was keeping her a prisoner within it. Althea obviously understood that the curse had a large part to play in this eternal agony, but still... it was *her* soul, and she was meant to control it, was she not?

However, one of the few things that she did know during these long days was that this world was so tiring—*so cruel.* Her eyes were seconds away from closing for good every time she blinked—but *every time she went to give into the darkness,* the visions of what would happen if the curse was to fully claim her soul always flashed before her burned mind... as if there was still an element of her soul that was alive and *fearful.*

The curse would have full control of her magick. They would butcher the world with the magick of the Gods... *leaving all to die...*

Despite the factor that the door before her wasn't an actual or physical wooden door, Althea could still see where the splinters had finally given way after all of her weak attempts to feel the rain melt her burdens and caress her sins once again. Ultimately leading Althea into a downward spiral to wonder just what parts of her soul were physical and which were not. As of that moment, it felt like a clutter of confusion, and she felt like a belittled child with no knowledge of anything.

It was a difficult concept all around to understand that the flesh she wore wasn't real nor a lie. She was a figment of her mere imagination, and yet she felt as if she was physically stuck within her own body, with the ability to tear at her skin.

Althea didn't know what she was anymore.

Or where she was.

She had lost beyond everything.

Even her mind.

The clock from somewhere beyond the old room ticked, and Althea glanced up as she heard the final arrogant tick of the day. The one that was awfully louder than the rest. The one that had her head turning up and her eyes burning through the cement that surrounded her, wondering what it would feel like if she were to approach the door and actually find it open for once.

For such a small place within her soul—*her mind*, she felt as if she was freezing to death... as if the cold air around her was going to be the one thing to drive her to pure insanity and beyond. Everything was so dreadfully cold, so ice-like that every time Althea held her hands to her arms she felt like her flesh was about to wash away with the memories of her tears.

"Remember me, Althea, don't let them take away who I am, who you are~"

The final echo of the clock rumbled out, and Althea's eyes peered down to the deathly pale hands that were *so ghost-like*. Maybe she was a ghost; it would help her understand why she had a ghostly mind with no thoughts in it whatsoever.

"I am not insane, not insane, not insane."

Althea ran a steady finger down her veins before releasing one of the many sighs that haunted the depths of her once lively lungs. Her scars were still there, her Markings too. Her flesh looked relatively normal, other than the fact she looked awfully pale.

With a small heave of her chest, Althea reached forward, her fingers curling around the charcoal that had been mockingly left behind by the cruel shadows every time they dared to pay her something of a visit. It crumbled beneath her touch, but enough was there for her to coat her fingers with it, watching as her very touch left a fingerprint of pure *darkness* behind, the only shade that didn't appear to be washed out by the abyss.

With a small breath that wasn't actually a proper breath, Althea finished writing the message she had written herself just hours before—a message that had her mind craving sleep. Peace. Anything that was close to freeing. *Or anything that was close to real life.*

In soft, delicate letters, the words: HAPPY BIRTHDAY ALTHEA, were written across the aged floor that was already covered in drawings of forgotten and lost memories. They were memories she knew the curse was wiping from her, yet never knew exactly when—would her birthday be taken next? Or did they know that this was torture, knowing that she was aging without actually aging? Her eyes scraped over each and every letter, a delicate pain in her heart that had her mind aching beyond compare.

There was a tremble to her gaze, one that appeared as she reached forward and brushed the dust away, the very sight of her name becoming too much to bear.

"Don't let them take your name away from you—"

Now her hands were completely covered in the sins of the darkness, the ash coating her flesh as if it was toying with reality an inch before her mind. Was she their pet? Their entertainment? She heard them cackle in the depths of the 'night'; they always seemed to be watching. Except, of course, the darkness lasted no longer than a splintering second as it was flustered away into the depths of the *wind,* leaving her hands to look just as they had seconds ago. They wanted her to react—*to weep—to scream*—they wanted her to do anything other than just stare, because they knew how she longed for something of control.

Was this a punishment? A punishment set on her for all of the wrongdoing she had done?

Or was this merely her punishment for being born? For giving her mother a burdened life to cradle before allowing it to drown.

Althea didn't know anything anymore, not as she tucked her long white curls behind her ears, sighing heavily as if the constant lie that echoed through the melodies of the air wasn't driving her to the brink of insanity. Her heartbeat could be heard in the distance—and yet, at the same time, it was heard at the ends of her fingertips. It was a constant echo that repeated, all until her mind couldn't take it anymore. But Althea couldn't react—she wouldn't risk reacting, as the spirits were watching her every move.

And Althea knew that they were using the beat of her own trapped heart as leverage.

She could feel the spirits, *the lives of the cursed…* laughing at her, watching her. Mocking her for the way she no longer fought against the darkness every day. They called her *weak,* a *fool,* a *disgrace of a daughter.* They wanted her to pity herself, to allow the tears that she felt torturing her heart to win the battle that she had grown tired of so long ago. But the truth was that each time Althea did try to fight, each time she did try to *breathe*, they took something from her.

They took her *mind*.

Her *memories*.

They made her forget the reasons why she was fighting.

Why she hadn't given up and allowed the spirits full control of her body altogether.

At first, Althea hadn't realised that that was what they had been doing; it took her until the fourth night to realise that her mind was full of visions of a boy she could remember and yet not name.

She could remember his *eyes*, the curve of his *jaw*, the bump of his *nose*...

But everything else was like a haze that she had seen from the window of her tower in the Kingdom she too could not remember the name nor lost details to.

Althea wanted to know why her heart hurt when it came to those distant memories. Why her heart pained for a girl she no longer wanted to care for. In fact, she wanted to slit her throat and watch as her own blood ran across her skin as she fell to the floor lifeless, only for the darkness to take her away instead. *She* was a girl that deserved to live while also toying with death— true death that she knew would find her sooner than later.

Althea didn't want to forget anymore.

As it was, she was barely holding on.

She leaned her head back against the cold white wall, picking up the charcoal once more before scribbling out the plan she had been hoping with everything in what was left of her heart to be true and not another deceptive lie.

Althea had hoped that the man in her mind who had a mixed bundle of emotions to his memory would save her—the girl who always claimed to never need saving. She knew that on any regular day that she was strong and did not need someone to save her—*but today wasn't any regular day.*

She hadn't lived through a regular day for a long time now.

The curse and the spirits… they wanted her to give up. To give into this emptiness and float away in the wisp of the wind as if she never truly existed.

That was their plan.

To see how long Althea Evangeline laughed in the abyss before she slowly allowed insanity to claim her life.

But Althea was stubborn.

And she *had* hoped that the man who was somewhere in the world she too was beginning to forget would realise that the only moment he would inevitably be able to access some entry into her soul would be on the day that she was born.

But that memory of a boy hadn't appeared right as the clock struck twelve, and that was the only opening she knew of in the multiple realities of the Realms.

Althea shut her eyes slowly, feeling as the world in her mind slowly formed.

She imagined herself opening her eyes… truly opening her eyes and not the eyes of her soul. The boy who did not have a name, would appear before her with a gentle smile, one that she knew would be able to calm the seas on a stormy day. He would step forward, his hands rising to cup her cheeks before wiping away the tears she had still not been able to spill because of how numb her heart felt.

His touch would be soft and gentle, and she was sure if she focussed enough, she would truly feel some warmth.

One that she knew would be able to calm the raging seas.

TWO
KYLEN

The sea wanted to welcome his body into its depths. To taste the pure blood that ran through his haunted veins. To feel the agony that coated his heart in a cruel blanket. It wanted to swallow him whole so that his life in all of its glory would not be remembered—*so that his life would not be burdened anymore.*

Because that was all *he* wanted.

And the sea and him were beginning to share a soul.

His eyes were fixated on it all; watching with a lost gaze as the waves and skies mourned alongside his dull heart; watching as the sea remembered the nights he had taken for granted—the nights where he had danced with *her* in his hands, wishing that tomorrow would never come as he knew that blood was bound to follow. Except it wasn't only that the sea was remembering. It was also recalling all of the *taken-for-granted* years that Sayah had spent her precious time teaching him the ways of the sea.

It remembered it all.

Every.

Little.

Thing.

Kylen Noxwell looked down at his calloused palms, looking down to the dark and *healthy* skin that glowed with a glistening gleam despite it all.

It was a joke.

One fucking sick joke.

His hair got caught in the wind as he turned. It was slightly longer and curlier—the scent of the sea hiding within each lock because of all the long hours he spent out here, sitting on the edge of the ship with his legs hanging overboard. Practically teasing the world and the monsters below the surface to taste his burdened skin.

But it was time.

And he knew that.

Kylen needed to return to his Kingdom; it had only been a month, but still, it had been too long. And he knew that. The King of the East had officially declared war, and Kylen *did* need to get some of that anger, pain, and ache out of his *lively* veins. His current victim had withered away too much, and he knew he had to wait a month or two before he revisited him—else the King of Aeonia would die before Kylen could fully get *Althea's* revenge, *Sayah's* revenge.

But those were two names he no longer allowed himself to hear.

Because each time he did, he killed something—*someone*.

Rising to his feet, Kylen turned and walked across the bare deck as the rain began to fall from the weeping clouds. His cabin was dull and quite gloomy—the lack of the siren's touch evident through the way everything was left frozen in place; books were scattered across the floor, bed, and desk: all of which opened onto pages that were no use to him.

In the very beginning, before he had fully moved on from the stage of denial, Kylen had spent so many long hours simply reading. Trying to learn how he could possibly revive a soul of the torturous curse. Yet he found nothing on it—the curse was almost completely unspoken about, the only partial mentions of it being within the myth of Astaria, but even then, it was brief.

Time had passed in slow stretches, eating at his skin as his eyes grew weary of the words he'd read so many times. And when he'd finally started to give up on it all, the cruel world decided to force another burden into his tremoring hands.

So now... he too was left to figure out how to resurrect someone from the dead, as well as cure one's soul from the curse because Kylen Noxwell would be damned if he didn't get Sayah Linix back—or *Althea Evangeline*.

It felt as if Kylen had been tortured and forced to flee back through time. To visit the past he so desperately wanted to forget —*to visit that time all those years ago when he had spent so many long hours under the cold moon, looking for answers regarding anything on the curse and his brothers.*

Now he was looking for answers on just about everything.

Sayah was dead. *She had been murdered.*

Althea was dead. *She had been murdered.*

And the very whisper that the wind carried of their name sent his anger spiralling, his heart burning.

The only things Kylen had really learnt about were the curse's origin and the myths of Harlia. Perhaps if Althea were here, he would laugh with her at the girl known as Astaria—one of the lost Gods who was too taken away too soon by the curse. Or if Sayah were here, he would mock Erwin and his nameless brother because of the stupidity of their greed that had turned their world into a withering graveyard. One where the darkness was always watching, feeding on a new soul each time the lightning struck.

He never intended to sound so cruel, so angry. He didn't want to push away the only ones he had left, and it hurt his already wounded heart to realise that that was exactly what he was doing. But Kylen didn't know what to do anymore—*how he could stop these incredibly consuming emotions.*

His soul was hurting.

His mind was screaming.

Without even realising it, Kylen subconsciously entered the rough harbours of his Realms before leaving the ship there to drown in the depression and emptiness that was his Kingdom. What a lie it was.

The people that were once loud and joyous towards him and his every breath now stayed silent as they slyly watched him out of the corners of their eyes. They didn't dare talk to the King who was rumoured to scowl at anyone who looked his way. They didn't dare cross the path of the King who was rumoured to take their lives if he so felt like it.

Kylen figured that he should care—that he should try to do better.

But Kylen didn't know if he could.

He was tired. So inevitably tired.

The walk through his kingdom was slow; however, since it was the same path he walked every time, it went in an utter blur. The halls of his castle weren't any better. They were just as ghostly as anything, holding onto the whispers of the past and breathing down his spine as if they wanted him to suffer. To feel something, anything that wasn't sheer rage.

Only three out of the six ghosts that had once waltzed down these halls remained. Two out of the five that were once deemed as his family. His court. But even then, one was a whisper during the days and the other a whisper during the sleepless and dream-less nights.

Neither Khatri nor Atticus spoke to him or interacted with him in the slightest.

Whether they were afraid or simply didn't care for him anymore, he didn't know. They just pretended that he was also a ghost and ignored his presence entirely. They forgot that he existed, all because he preferred to be drowning himself in liquor and quietness instead of dealing with life itself. Was that truly such a crime?

So, since he hadn't seen either of them in weeks now, one could only guess how his feet abruptly halted with such shock, worry, *and idiotic fear*, when he found Atticus sitting inside *Kylen's* quarters, waiting for him beside his study with a flimsy old letter in his scarred hand. He didn't look at him at first, and Kylen couldn't help but notice how aged he'd become.

The storm beyond the window seemed to quicken and harshen; the rain pooling against the glass panels was beginning to send a rattling eeriness through the depths of the air, chilling Kylen's breaths and the blood that had long ago been 'cured'. The storms hadn't stopped since his boat had entered the harbour of Lorundio after his wondrous visit to Harlia. Constant rain. Constant thunder. And constant lightning. Sayah had said it was because the world was mourning for the last of its Gods—but Kylen found it easier to block out any memories of that fatal time.

The two locked eyes for not even a second before Kylen peered down to his feet, moving to hang his coat on the rusty fishhook before clearing his burning throat with the anticipated question that had his bones riveting. "Who is dead?" Kylen asked, his mind reminding him of all the guilt that was buried within his bones. "I take it that it's not you—*or perhaps I am truly going mad.*"

Atticus sat up from where he leaned against Kylen's desk, moving to approach him before halting and abruptly sighing as if there was an invisible war on his tongue. "No one," he breathed, "but that's not to say that no one is *going* to."

Kylen looked up to him then, swallowing the anxiety that laughed in the echo of his bruised heart. "What is it, Atticus?"

"The King of the East is heading towards Aeonia."

Aeonia... no one had dared so much as to even whisper that name here in months now.

The thunder mocked him in all of his power as the crows that stood perched outside of his window laughed at him in glee. Laugher was a common thing, apparently. Especially to those who had once still cherished the ground they walked on as if it wasn't constantly throwing daggers after their heart. "What does that have to do with us? That kingdom is a ghost town, and he will probably end up leaving mere minutes after arriving." Kylen's voice was rough and yet so small in comparison to the rhythm of his heart.

Hearing any news of that kingdom threatened them; it made Kylen's body go rigid. It made his stomach plummet, and nausea aimed arrows at his throat. He didn't want to recall the time that he was there, trapped within the palace walls after learning of what he had to do to survive this war while being a literal child. "Even if he were to go there," Kylen continued, "what would he find? An empty and haunted throne? Good luck with that—nothing but bad luck comes from that place, and I for one, cannot wait to watch it burn."

Atticus chuckled—and that laugh was nothing at all close to pure. It was dry, firm, almost as if he was also one of the ones to mock him nowadays. "That's the thing, *Kye*, that throne is not empty anymore. In fact, it apparently hasn't been empty for the past several months, and before that, *she* was apparently seen up west searching for a little someone the two of you came across last year."

"Someone has claimed it?" Kylen asked as he glided past his brother and towards the desk he had previously been sitting at. He ignored how his reflection showed him a complete stranger compared to the boy he was a year ago. He didn't need a reminder of all that he'd lost from his control. It wasn't that Kylen had chosen to partially ignore what Atticus had said about the throne not being empty; it was that his ears had grown very used to selective hearing—and now he heard what he wanted to hear, and the rest, it was buried six feet under. "About time. Want to bet on how long until that kingdom breaks out into another war—perhaps an apocalypse—that could be amusing to watch the blood splatter."

"*No*, and no one has—*well*—" Atticus stuttered, earning Kylen's furrowed gaze to lift once again. The words were on the tip of Atticus' tongue, and yet he seemed to be tongue-tied. "A girl with long black hair and cursed magick has claimed the once abandoned throne. They can not only sense such curses, but they have also caught glimpses of her *darling blue eyes* haunting the dead of the night."

Kylen's hands halted as they searched through the paper on his desk, his fingers quivering over the wood as he focussed his withering gaze on the maroon wallpaper that was beginning to peel off his walls.

Dark hair and cursed magick...

A girl he had seen die eleven months ago had dark hair and a *deathly* cursed magick.

Not to mention the eyes that followed him in all of his nightmares.

Kylen lifted his eyes and slowly turned towards Atticus, already in the process of shaking his head as a thousand words stormed his vision. "*No.* You don't mean—"

Atticus cut him off before he could finish. "Kylen, I have sent several guards to Aeonia in search of confirmation. Not all of them returned, but those that did... they confirmed that *Althea Evangeline* is alive—but not the Althea Evangeline we remember."

THREE
ALTHEA

The spirits were creeping in on her—their many eyes piercing through hers as Althea did everything in her strength to hold back the many breaths from escaping. The outer world must have been lacking any entertainment for them to chew on because now they had decided to spend their time taunting her, the girl who was nothing more than a prisoner to her own body.

"*Aaaaalllllltttttttthhhhhhheeeeeeeaaaaa~*" one of the many voices murmured. Every little breath that left her true, physical lungs—every little breath that wasn't under *her* control, slithered down her twisted spine, causing her to straighten her body against the taciturn walls in a weak attempt to escape their clasp.

The cell door began to tremble; the quivering locks that were nowhere to be seen thrashing against unknown metal and causing the rattling to scrape through her brain as if it wanted her to fall victim to insanity. It was such an ear-piercing screech that every muscle within her body felt on the edge of bursting. With a quick breath, Althea slowly rose to her feet, preparing herself to stand trial against the evil that held her hostage.

Because really, that was only what a soul could do when it was spell-bounded to its own mind.

Darkness began to suffocate the room the moment the door opened a fracture from their presence, and the lost spirits flooded in almost instantly, spilling against the unkind air as Althea locked eyes on the girl who looked near identical to her.

Except she had *dark hair*, *dark blue eyes*, and *dark veins* creeping along the skin that was sickly pale.

Althea figured that this was what she looked like in the real world.

Like a walking corpse.

"Oh, my dearest, *dearest* girl; *we've missed you*." The words were like spiders waltzing across each sound. Such daggers aiming for her hidden heart as the girl of curses looked her up and down with a gaze that was sure to send her death threats.

While Althea could only hear one voice leave the cursed girl's lungs, she knew millions hid behind it. Tiny little screams of the cursed begging to be let out of hiding.

Althea—*the true, hidden-away prisoner Althea,* knew not to react. She knew not to blink nor choke. She merely had to pretend that her soul wasn't pained. She had to forget the girl she once knew—the one who would try with everything in her heart to torture the girl of curses before her.

Because she knew what would happen then.

Althea would be digging herself a grave if she were to so much as to lift a finger the wrong way towards the curse before her, and if this was the stage before death, Althea didn't know what death would be like for someone who died from the curse.

She had always heard of all the cruel stories escaping her father's lips about those who died from the curse. They were left to wander through broken and fragmented Realms for eternities on end while their souls rotted.

And that didn't sound very appealing.

The spirits challenged her with a raise of their brows,

wanting her to fear them so that she would eventually allow them to claim every last inch of her soul. And while they were keeping her prisoner… Althea had found that she had *something of control.*

She could feel the spark and mockery of pure magick that flourished beneath her palms.

The spirits wanted *that magick,* but even if it drove Althea to some form of Hel, she wasn't going to give it to them. Although partly it was because she was stubborn, Althea also knew that so many could get hurt if the spirits consumed the whole soul of a literal God.

That was one of the little things that she hadn't forgotten.

But she figured that the spirits had allowed her to keep those daunting memories because they knew, *in all of their wickedness,* that those memories were more like nightmares.

"*You know…*" the spirits began to taunt, a cruelty to their voice that hid the snickers within. "It's quite a bore to be alone in that little old castle. There are no souls, no *living, breathing soul,* that would keep us entertained—*although the King is rumoured to give us a little old visit next month or so*; perhaps then, when we are in the midst of battle, we will allow you to hold a touch of control so that you can feel the true bruises of your marked skin —we truly have painted it a beautiful shade of purple."

What King? Althea wanted to ask, but again, she knew better not to.

Her mind teased her with the memories and emotions of three kinds, except none were clear. Three versions of a King had run from her mind.

One was *punishing*—except there was a feeling of lost time tied to them. Severe emotions too. It felt as if she wanted to feel something like platonic love for him—*except she also wanted to loathe him.* Her skin ached at the very thought of him; it had her fingers quivering at her sides. Discomfort rocketed through her bones as she willed her mind to redirect her to the next king.

The second was kinder—but this memory had been burdened with emotions consuming Althea's body and soul. He held a connection to the boy in her memories, but whether that was him or not was a mystery to her. All she really knew was that this boy brought war to her mind. One that she wanted to shield herself away from.

The third king… *Althea had only heard of him.* She knew that because he was no more than a mere word floating through the severed abyss in her mind.

"Oh, don't tell me you are still giving us this silly old silent treatment?" the spirits queried through the shadowed girl who stood before her lips—*the version of Althea with black hair and flesh that was rotting alongside death.* The version of Althea that was the one the real world had to witness. Althea watched as they tilted *her* head to the left, and the long locks of darkness fell over her bony shoulders—drastically different from the white hair that fell over her own. It was as if she was looking into a mirror—one that showed her something crueller than she could've ever imagined.

The spirits stepped forward, and Althea stood tall. She lifted her eyes up and away from the sliced Markings, holding her breath, her lungs suffocating as she stared at her mere reflection with a look of boredom. A look that she knew got under their skin.

Well, *her* skin.

"I can feel that your anger has dampened into something more like sorrow. It's quite… *comedic* to watch someone who is nothing of a human feel such emotions," the spirits chuckled. "You must learn, if you truly dream of escaping our security, *that emotions are nothing but dark burdens.* They are nothing but—"

The spirits' words halted on the tip of her cursed tongue, the darker version of her eyes catching onto something that had their irises darkening even more. Their head turned towards the weathered door behind them; however, to Althea's dismay, their bodies stayed facing her... as if they had turned that version of her body into an owl. Althea tried not to grimace or flinch in disgust as she watched, so she flickered her eyes in any which direction to try and look away. It was unsettling, truthfully.

"It seems as if the shadowed saints have heard our wondrous pleas and thrown us something to toy with... We'll see you... *soon*, Althea—"

Before the final word echoed through the empty air, an ear-piercing screech of a blade gliding through it cut their many taunts off—and *that* blade decapitated the cursed Althea's head that fell to the ground before disappearing into mere black smoke. This was different.

Althea looked up from the severed head swiftly, looking towards the still standing body that was beckoned by the wind before it brushed the last of it away. Althea gasped, her heart stammering heavily as the departed cursed body revealed a small child that looked no older than six behind it. Was this real? A dream? A hallucination—*Althea swore that she was halluci-nating*—she had to be hallucinating. "Hello," the girl whispered, her voice awfully calm despite Althea's panicked expression. "Hello, Al—"

This was a *new game*.

This was an awfully new and awfully cruel game.

Who were the spirits to taunt her with life when Althea already knew that it never dared to exist in this abyss? Her soul was basically as good as dead, was it not?

"Who are you?" Althea asked despite her mind's plea to stay silent. Her tone lacked any emotion, almost as if she was the mental soul that the curse possessed. Her voice felt so rough—so *raw*. She hadn't spoken for months now, and yet something about the girl before her brought the words right from her bruised lungs. "I don't know what memory you've come from, but I am pretty sure that I don't know you—"

"That makes sense," the girl muttered with a shrug of her

shoulders, a laugh caressing her lips as if this was any other day. "We have never actually met, *Your Highness*—oh, but goodness me, it is an honour—*truly, Miss Althea.*"

The way she spoke sounded so lively. So true. Was she an illusion of someone *alive?*

"I'm afraid that I'm not alive," the small girl with long brown braids replied, smiling up at her with a grin that met the eyes as if her words meant nothing to her. Althea furrowed her brows, confused about how she had heard *her* thoughts. Not even the darkness had been able to—sure, they could sense them. But they had never been able to understand it all.

The girl sighed before nodding once to herself, a look of defeat playing on her features as she anxiously picked at the 'skin' on her hands. She was nervous, Althea observed, and the girl looked away as she collected all of her words together before speaking, at last, not caring for a single second about the panic that was wielding a noose around Althea's bones. "Because I am not one with the spirits and curses consuming your soul, I am… merely just a visitor; I can hear everything you think. *I can feel what you feel,*" she explained; her fingers were toying with the edge of her braid, yet her eyes refused to look away from hers.

"*Who are you*—why—*how* are you *visiting* my soul?" Althea asked quickly as she stared the child down, the heartbeat that sounded to be in the air before her quickening as the panic rose once again. "My soul is as good as dead, kid. Why would you risk yourself to visit a literal graveyard?" She knew that her tone was cruel, that her words were bitter for no reason. But Althea felt adamant that this was another one of the curse's taunts.

It had to be.

"Because I am too dead, *Althea*—can I call you that? It's weird to call you Your Majesty as I think of you more as my *sister* than a *Queen,*" the girl rambled with a flutter of a laugh.

Althea felt her head slowly tilt to the left as she tried to understand what this child was preaching so profoundly. What it was that had her now avoiding Althea's burning gaze. "Who are you?" she asked again, and the girl flashed her a charming smile against all odds.

"Your future *dead* sister-in-law. That is if you can tolerate my brother for that long." A brief *and easy* laugh left her lips. One that brought a hum of a melody to her mind, but she couldn't find the specific memory it was from.

Her brows became lost to the creases of her forehead as Althea twirled her white hair around her finger tightly. It was a habit she'd always had, though found that now it helped her differentiate herself from the curse. As the cursed, manacled version of her had black her—but her, the real her, had white hair. She kept her eyes steady on the girl's brown ones, noting the exact moment she realised that Althea was still beyond confused. Did her features make it obvious? Or was it her mind? "I am Elara Noxwell," Elara breathed, offering her a comforting smile as she reached a hesitant small hand towards her.

She smiled an awful lot, Althea noted. What was possibly so joyful about the afterlife—life altogether, that made someone smile *that* much?

Althea watched as her hand went straight through the glistening, invisible barrier that had kept her concealed in this abyss of a cell. Not so much as *reacting* at all to the enchantments Althea knew the curse had put on the barrier of this room.

Noxwell.

That name rang numerous bells that all sang a melody in her heart... and yet none of them revealed why it had her heart racing beyond reach. That name was familiar, on the tip of her tongue. It whispered secrets to her mind while knowing that, for whatever reason, she wouldn't remember it when she would go to take her next breath.

Elara's expression changed to one that was softer, realisation dawning on her own cheeks as she nodded once. "They took your memories, didn't they?" her question was quiet—like it was afraid of the overall truth.

"Not all," Althea retorted quietly as her cheeks darkened with a blush. She felt ashamed, turning into the exact victim that the curse wanted of her. "I tried to be tolerable when I became aware of what they were doing to my mind—my past, but it seems as if they'd already taken a fair... portion of everything."

"So, they still took one of the most important ones first; how sweet of them," Elara pondered through a sneer, and her features changed drastically—not to mention that there was something like grief to her tone.

Althea dropped her gaze to the child's still extended hand, watching as it tremored through the air. "Why are you here?"

"To take you to the afterlife so that *our* family can help you get home—*where you belong.*" Elara had features that Althea knew she recognised. But she presumed that they'd been on another being that she had once known. Her eyes—the bump of her nose—she knew it all, and it was driving her insane. Althea felt her chest tighten, despite the darkness that she could feel screaming at her. *Breathe,* she beckoned herself, yet of course, her demands went ignored. "You are Althea Evangeline, for the God's sake, you are not a bloody prisoner." And she knew that she wasn't. She had promised herself that she would never be a prisoner to another force of evil again—she wanted to get back the life she was owed. *"But please,* we don't have much time; come on."

The air turned, and Althea didn't know why she listened or why she obeyed the smiling child before her. Still, her hand linked with hers, feeling the warmth that seeped into her ice-cold skin as if she had been deprived of it all her life. Althea figured that if this all went to utter shit, the moment she got free, she would find it easier to escape this mess altogether. She didn't know how she should react—what she should do or what she could say. She merely stepped forward hesitantly, feeling as the impossible barrier wavered across her skin, the child's very touch being the key for her to *break free*.

Althea's eyes widened the moment she stepped outside of the doorway, a laugh on the edge of her lips when she heard the sudden spike in the spirit's screams as they realised just what had happened. Elara immediately tugged at her hand to start running, barely giving her a second to react or to think what the sane thing was to do.

The curse must have sensed something or another. Perhaps it was whatever magick Elara had used to be able to break her mind free of her soul, or perhaps it was Althea gaining a sense of freedom altogether—but either way, they were coming for them, causing Elara to flinch.

Althea, however, had grown used to this torture long ago.

Elara's brown eyes flew past Althea's head as they took each step through the light. Looking towards the darkness that Althea could feel trailing after her every step, the same darkness that was filling her cell to the brim as if it wanted to finally kill her and risk losing the strength of her magick. While she had been confined in her little prison for so long now—she had seen enough through the small crack of a window to know that everything in her soul was just a nothingness glow. All pure whiteness.

"WE NEED TO RUN FASTER!" Elara tugged her hand forwards again, and Althea followed her with a blind eye. Her expression slowly took in the abyss that the cell had held her to. Everything was so light. Like she had been trapped within a blurry dream this whole time—it was obscure, pure insanity. It caused her heart to ache, but Althea looked over her shoulder and towards that little old cell one last time. If she had it in her, she was adamant that she wouldn't leave this abyss before she used every little inch of force from her magick to burn it down —*burn everything down*. She would do anything in her power to try and feel something like revenge after staring at the same

crack on the wall for so long. She deserved that much... did she not?

The little old cell, however, was alone.

One little room that stood tall amid nothing.

That sight had her heart thrumming and her anxiety running miles. Why was it true that she was the only thing to exist in her soul—shouldn't it be full of memories, of colours, of magick? It didn't make sense, and that caused her to feel nauseous. It made her truly feel like she knew nothing at all. Althea glanced back to where they were running so hurriedly towards, skimming her gaze over the young, dead girl who held such determination in her own narrowed eyes. *Her heart was already trusting this child...*

And yet Althea still did not know why or how this child looked to be one she had met in her dreams before—but she willed her to belong to a good and trustworthy memory.

FOUR
KYLEN

He wished with whatever it was that was somehow still alive in his heart that time was on his side for once. That the world he had once looked up to with bright eyes was no longer out for his grief-stricken soul. But instead, was *wanting*—and *willing* to heal all the severe cracks that his soul now held in melting hands.

However, of course, that was just a malicious joke; he was never one with luck on his side. It was unknown to him.

Kylen looked to the dark streets ahead, ignoring the crackle of the air that was threatening to push him back the way he came. He watched with furrowed eyes as the puddles of blood and water reflected the glisten of the candles that just barely lit up the streets. Kylen could hear the murmurs; the wind brought it to him as if he was one with nature.

Perhaps he was.

After all, he had never had the freedom, the ability, or the chance to use his true Elemental magick without the burden to his name. And now, he didn't want to so much as take the tiniest glance into it: because that was what he was meant to be doing with *Sayah*. They'd both been mourning for the same girl who his heart had unknowingly bled for—and yet she'd still organised to spend weeks on end with him to try and move on. She had seen his scars, the way they were still bleeding despite the wounds having healed long ago, and yet, she'd said that once the memorial and funeral were over, they'd go explore his abilities as a way of healing.

But then she died.

And Kylen was still standing in the doorway of Sayah's bedroom, staring at the body surrounded by blood, frozen in the delicacy of time as the world continued spinning.

So, Kylen didn't know what magick he truly held—and he was in no way looking to figure that out *today*.

Or *tomorrow*.

Or *the next day*.

He chose to pretend that it wasn't there instead.

That was the easier option.

The one that didn't hurt his heart.

A dark, skinny crow swooped down at him, nicking at his icy flesh before aiming for the castle that he'd left still standing, and as if the crow was the bearer of bad news, he swore that a sense of deja-vu washed over him—because such a strange reminiscing magick flooded over his features, and Kylen's gaze was trapped to the bird that flew into the beyond.

Disappearing into the night.

The people of *his* kingdom looked to him with curiosity burning against the tip of their noses. Except they were looking away not even a moment later as if his sight was pure poison—a lethal, deadly poison that would have their hearts faltering if he so dared to stare at them in the wrong way. Kylen's people feared him; they were petrified of him—and the anger that was beyond his control, which stirred in the pits of his stomach, crawled at the gravities of his spine.

It was good in some respects as it initially meant that he didn't have to speak to those who exhausted him. It meant that he didn't have to fake his healing because the world already knew that nothing could heal or save him now.

He had managed to survive his parents' *deaths*.

His siblings' *deaths*.

Althea's *death*.

Sayah's *death*.

But that didn't mean that he was going to start living again.

The thrum and rhythm of the music he loathed with every inch of his body strummed through the air with a cackle. The sound of chatter and laughter lined every little bump of the melody as it circled his every heartbeat.

Kylen could sense Atticus creeping through the shadows, following him with eyes he no longer recognised to ensure his safety; after all, the whispers kept track of him for Kylen.

They told him that Atticus wanted to trust him to act with his head—but he knew his heart was taking control. *And the curse that was no longer his to hold* was already prepared to turn one's skin inside out if they so dared to cross his path at the wrong time.

Kylen approached the buzzing bar with shadowed memories curling around his every step, threatening the ground beneath him as the people standing tall outside the bar, drinking, and smoking their lives away, all fell silent. The crowd parted for him. All gazes were hesitant and far too fearful to hold his. Kylen didn't pay anyone any notice; he simply looked towards the male who had his back turned to him, yet Kylen knew that this male before him was more than aware of his presence.

He, too, had been subconsciously tracking his every movement.

Khatri held his glass against his bruised chapped lips, barely sending him a second glance before he swallowed the bitter taste of grief away. "Look who's returned from the *dead~*" He cooed, his words awfully bitter. "I didn't believe it when the people of *your* kingdom began to whisper that they had seen your ship approaching. I didn't believe when they began to sing that the king had decided to come back and play the role of leader that had been murdered *so-so* long ago."

Kylen kept his stare ahead strong, his gaze unwavering. He would not give Atticus the satisfaction he sought from where he stood behind him in the depths of the people. "Hello, *brother*—"

"*Brother*?" Khatri barked through a laugh, turning to him with a quizzical expression full of mockery. "Oh, is that what we are? *Are we brothers*?" His eyes were bloodshot. His skin was bruised and slightly scarred because of all the fights he had gotten into over the past eleven months.

He was truly unrecognisable.

Kylen tipped his head down, looking towards the people he knew to be listening in. "Can we speak outside, please?" He didn't want—he didn't *need* any prying ears to come after him.

"No," Khatri sneered as he turned back towards his glass. Raising his hand up and gesturing with two fingers for another two drinks. Kylen reached forward, but before his unsteady hand could reach Khatri's shoulder, Khatri had already shoved it fiercely away. *"Get the fuck off of me."*

Atticus didn't wait; he appeared behind the two no more than a splinter of a second later, his eyes turning into an expression of pure venom as he shot Khatri a torturous look. The air around them dropped in temperature as Khatri looked between the two faces before scoffing loudly, such disgrace shining heavily in his drunken eyes. "You two are fucking unbelievable," Khatri murmured with a growl. He went to place his glass back down onto the bench; however, it sounded as if he had slammed it instead, and the very echo had the entire pub quietening.

"Khatri, you're drunk," Atticus stated, and Khatri chuckled such a bloodthirsty sound.

"Oh really? Thank you, Captain Obvious. I see why Kylen gave you *Sayah's* old role as Captain."

The air Kylen toyed with seemed to deepen at that, and he

looked away, beckoning back that taste of dread that again coated the back of his throat. The thoughts—*memories*—all of what was in his head was becoming far too much for him to swim through. Leaving him drowning in his sorrows as he tried to breathe through it. Kylen parted his lips, but it wasn't that that had the words flowing into the air—he had to physically pry them off his tongue, "Khatri, I need to speak to you."

"So, I've been told," Khatri replied, turning away once again.

Kylen looked to Atticus, restraint coating every inch of his lips as he huffed. Why didn't he understand the urgency of this? Atticus looked to his feet as he flexed his fingers in circles at his sides, subtly concealing the words that they spoke into a bubble that Sayah had taught him how to control so long ago; how Kylen wished that day had been just yesterday.

Then perhaps he would actually pay attention during those lessons.

Khatri rolled his eyes as he also sensed the glistening magick that Kylen chose to pay no notice to as it spread around them. Instead, Kylen cleared his throat before looking down at him with an expression that was beyond lethal because he no longer had it in him to be that smiley named king, the one which the world was constantly throwing things at and yet he always still grinned as if there was no tomorrow.

I guess that's because in my mind, there wasn't.

"So, were you going to write me a little fucking letter too? Telling me that *my girl*—Althea *fucking* Evangeline is alive? Or were you just going to wait until my birthday and say 'hey, by the way, your wife is alive'?" Kylen demanded, and this time he allowed his voice to be rough. With everything he has ever wished for, he wished the words would choke and suffocate him so that he no longer had to put up with the misery this world had. He wished that whatever form of superiority was out there would tie a noose around his throat and throw him from the balcony that was still coated in Althea's sweet memories.

Because at least then, he would catch a break.

Khatri murmured something inaudible under his breath, a chuckle that noted each withering bone inside of his body as it escaped into the alcohol-infused air. He looked up at him, a blood-chilling gleam of light reflecting in the darkness of his eyes.

"Not your wife. None of the above."

Kylen spat such a horrid sound before shaking his head, looking away as he ran a hand through the curls on his head. He could feel whatever magick it was that he possessed coming to life, cursing such foul words Khatri's way whilst begging to taste his metallic blood.

But Kylen ignored that magick. It truly made him sick, if anything. He wanted nothing of the magick that had been suffocated by the curse for so long.

"Why am I not surprised? I mean, honestly, who am I to expect that *you* would tell me anything about the girl I have mourned for?" Kylen asked with a raise of his brows, staring the man down as if his gaze was a stranger.

"The *murderer* you mourned for, you mean," Khatri corrected as he allowed his gaze to drift away. "Why would I tell you about the life of the girl I want to kill?" he asked, and Kylen felt his blood nip away at his soul. "You do realise, *Kylen*, that if *dear old Althea fucking Evangeline* is alive… then that means that there is a chance that she truly did kill our beloved Sayah."

Murderer.

Kylen couldn't handle the way Khatri spat each word at him. It was as if the words were venom. Pure, unbreakable, intoxicating venom. But Kylen knew that there was a possibility of truth behind those words. He knew it because it was what the shadows of his heart kept spitting at him too.

If Althea was alive, then that meant there was a good, quivering, aching chance that she had truly killed Sayah—but that question there still coated his tongue as if it was ice.

"You remember our beloved Sayah, don't you? Or did Althea —*the one who was acting like a stranger a year and a bit ago*, mean more to you than her?"

Sayah had been his family. The one consistent person by his side.

He would give anything to see her again and to tell her that he was so sorry for not being mentally there those last few days.

Kylen had been a ghost—yet Sayah still held him when he couldn't find himself getting up to attend Althea Evangeline's memorial service.

Kylen parted his lips to reply, but instead, he found that his words merely ran dry, leaving his tongue to shrivel up and die as amusement covered Khatri's face. Why couldn't he see how torn up Kylen was about this? Sayah was basically his mother—they both had meant so much to him in completely different ways. Nevertheless, he had *loved* them both.

"Exactly," Khatri muttered.

No.

Not 'exactly'.

Kylen stepped forward as his fists curled at his sides, but as if Atticus was the bloody *God* to save them all, he stepped forward; already pushing Kylen to step back and shrink into himself as his eyes searched for a drink for him to drown in. "How did you find out that she—*if she even is*—alive?" Atticus asked civilly.

"Oh, unfortunately, *she is*," Khatri cooed as a matter of fact. He had that 'know it all' look on his face. His features were awfully arrogant and ignorant. "They have seen her new famous black curls roaming the lonely halls of that wicked old castle multiple times now. Not to mention, her magick is scented throughout the Kingdom—and trust me when I say that *Zaire knows the scent of the magick that killed Sayah*."

"—*Zaire is in Aeonia?* Did you go to Aeonia?" Kylen asked through a whisper of a breath. He hadn't heard a mention of

Zaire for months now, and he also knew for whatever reason that the two biological siblings, *Zaire and Uzziah*, had stopped replying to Atticus' letters months ago too. Leaving him completely in the dark too.

No matter the fact that he was basically family without being blood.

"Oh, Gods, no. Zaire, yes, but I? No. I also sent some guards, however, but *Atty* probably already told you that," Khatri said with a click of his tongue, spitting Atticus' nickname to make a mockery of them all. How did it become like this? Just yesterday, they were boys pulling pranks on the people of his kingdom that adored them, and yet today... today Kylen didn't recognise any one of them.

Kylen felt like his heart was threatening to rot the last of his deceptive health. He turned away, his heart stammering rapidly as he pushed past both boys once deemed as his brothers. His eyes were wide as the crowd sent murmurs down his spine. Their words begged for darling fresh air to ease his soul—but even then, that still wasn't enough to *calm* his soul.

He had to go.

He had to go there—

If Althea was alive, then why had she not come to see him?

If Althea was alive, then how come her magick was laced around Sayah Linix's corpse?

Kylen's steps quickened as he sprinted down the streets of the kingdom he once knew and loved. His heart was in his head as his eyes furrowed against the rain that dared to hold him back. He encountered the stables in the midst of the storm scattered minutes later. The sky was dark, and the *crows* followed his every step as if they could feel him losing the wits of his mind. His eyes caught onto the dark animal before him, looking towards the black horse that welcomed him with a bow and bob of his head. *Did he remember the day they'd ridden back to Kylen's kingdom together? Only to be greeted by the corpses of his family.* Kylen grabbed one of the cloaks from the rusty hooks on the wooden wall, throwing it over his shoulder and head before going to climb up the horse that stared at *the presence he could feel but not give into.*

Kylen took a breath, releasing the fog of his lungs into the air as he looked over his shoulder and into the eeriness of the night. He never won these battles, no matter how quickly he tried to fight them. "You cannot stop me from going," Kylen breathed, his words creating a thick cloudiness that filled the elements of the air.

Atticus shook his head with an exhale of a laugh. "Who said I'm going to stop you?" he asked as he also approached and grabbed one of the many cloaks off the wall. "I know this would consume you beyond measure if you were to wait around, and quite frankly, I don't think either of us wants to be here for that."

"It isn't safe for you," Kylen warned, casting him a look as he climbed onto his horse. Atticus met his gaze, and it was evident in his eyes that these words had caught him off guard. Even if Kylen was cruel now—surely his brother knew that he still cared for him. He was family, after all. "You said some didn't make it back—it isn't safe for you—*and I don't want to lose anyone more.*"

"And is it any safer for you?" Atticus countered, his eyes burning into the side of his head as he climbed onto a white-haired and brown-spotted horse. Kylen no longer cared for himself. He wished death on his soul more than any other, but that didn't matter; that was the way of life, was it not? "Someone has to be the one with some sanity to stop you from allowing your emotions to blind every inch of you."

Kylen tutted as he beckoned the horse to start moving. His eyes were awfully dark as he placed the cloak over his head. "My emotions aren't blindsiding me," he argued, although his soul pleaded differently, and so did the burn of his Marking on his back.

"Oh, aren't they?" Atticus quipped, and he copied Kylen's actions, throwing the cloak over his head. "Then my mistake; you must just be an all-round idiot."

The horse beneath him began to quicken his steps, and Atticus flowed by his side as if they were in sync. "I am not an idiot," Kylen stated jaggedly. "My emotions aren't having any toll here—"

"Then tell me, Kye, how are you going to react when you go and find that Althea is actually physically alive?" Atticus hummed into the night as the stars hid behind the trembling clouds. "The same Althea whose magick was scented when you walked into Sayah's grave?" Atticus abruptly prompted. "Will you look at her, see that she is lively, and go to kill her out of inevitable rage? Or will you see her and allow the shock of her heart being lively before *you* make you vulnerable for a second too long?" Kylen finally met his stare. "Brother, I don't mean to pry, but if Althea is truly alive, then we will need to think for a minute. We are going to need to think and figure out what we could possibly do next."

The rain met with his cloak, but he felt Atticus' magick seep over his frozen flesh, creating a layer that blocked the rain from causing him any more pain.

Kylen didn't know how to answer.

He didn't know what he could possibly say.

If Althea was alive, then Kylen had no idea how he would react.

How was he, in all honesty, to know?

Atticus crept closer to his side, but Kylen didn't bother sending him another look. He knew the expression his face held, and he didn't need Atticus to feel any pity for him. Kylen merely kept his eyes directed to the world before him, looking towards the shadows of the night as he grumbled, "Fine. You can come."

FIVE
ALTHEA

The quivering of her eyes was so scarily focussed on the hand holding hers. Studying with such intent how young and *lively* the hand looked as it flexed across her burdened skin. The skin that looked something like the skin of a corpse. Elara didn't look to be harmed, to hold the power of death whispering and caressing her past; she looked lively and youthful.

Except Althea knew that that was all a deception.

This hand was a hand of a dead girl.

Nothing but a flake of a memory that was leading her through the beyond.

Althea's eyes travelled up as she heard a punishing screech. Multiple words flew at her as if their ignorant threats were of any use to her now. Althea found that the air around them was moving quickly, whisking against her features and causing the hair on her body to turn on end. She looked towards the abyss they were running through, noting as the light *that wasn't harsh enough to blind them* began to wield around the two lost souls in a tunnel-like form. It looked as if it was capturing them—claiming them as the curses and spirits' next victim. Elara—the girl on her hand whose name was ringing an unclear melody within her mind, beckoned her to keep running as if the hesitation in her heart was heard by all. It was so unsettling to her how Elara was being the lifeboat Althea had been searching for... for what felt like the past several months—*lifetimes.*

Elara.

Elara.

Elara Noxwell?

There was an ethereal ring to that name. One that sent chills throughout the mist of her soul—whatever was left of it, that was. *Who was to say that her fleeing her own soul wasn't giving in to actual death?* Althea would truly love more than anything to give her bones *and soul* a nice cold wash in some glorious icy water so that she could shed herself of the sins that insisted on drowning her in life—or whatever version of that this abyss was.

Althea's eyes fled over her shoulder, looking at the drastic metres of dark shadows that were flooding in after them, seeping across the ground that was covered in a thin layer of water as if it was helping with quickening their steps. The thick, shadowed darkness took the shape of hands, all of which had nails that wanted to scratch their already corpse-like skin to shreds... to brush away the last crumbs of their existence.

"Just a little further," Elara breathed through a huff as she looked down at the broken compass in her hand. It was spinning rapidly, not revealing whether where they were heading was north or south. *Should you really be trusting this girl?* The question repeatedly asked in her mind... And as always, Althea was stuck for an answer.

She was wordless.

Just as she had been for the past several months.

It was like Elara's words had formed the very *portal-looking doorway* before them—the one that was a rip in the abyss of her soul, allowing multiple bright, vigorous, and yet indulgent and securing colours to flood through the cracks that this rip was opening. A wooden door appeared, although Elara didn't give Althea any time to hesitate, to *rethink*. Instead, she forced her to quicken her steps as the old, brown, frail door opened before them, revealing three blurred faces that were all waiting on the other side of the 'portal' with arms extended towards them. "*Hurry!*" Althea heard someone scream—however, their voice sounded like they were ten feet underwater.

Althea felt rushed tingles run down her spine; the hair on her arms and legs stood on end as she heaved a quick, uneasy breath —so unfamiliar to the breaths she used to shed when she had genuine inevitable power wielding together in her hands. Althea looked over her shoulder for what felt like the hundredth time, and almost instantly, she held her breath as the darkness mocked her, holding it as she inched her way out of the curse that was about to rip them *both* to shreds. She could already practically feel the skin leaving her bones, leaving her soul to truly rot. *Go to Hel*, she wanted to spit at them. But she knew that they were already in it.

"Ready to jump?" Elara quipped in a quizzical tone as Althea looked down at her brown eyes with one daring confused look. *Where were they jumping to? Could she even remember how to jump?* It had been so long since she had even moved; this all felt like a dream to her—perhaps it was, and she would wake up soon...

"I guess so?" Althea offered through a small breath, her words barely audible. Although, she had no idea what it was that she was offering. The only thing she did know was that she was willing to make any jump if it meant that she wouldn't have to drown in this emptiness any longer. *She couldn't bear it.* Even though that emptiness had been frozen in her heart for many years now—she had never thought that her soul would be the exact replica of that emptiness... and yet it had been for all these lifetimes now.

A disgrace to the name her father held.

Althea's feet left the floor as she pushed herself into the air, ducking with such strength as she fled through the doorway. Almost immediately, she felt the horrible feeling of forceful nausea warp across her flesh and mind. *Wind*—the deception of it, seemed to thrash against her face as she fought back this nausea, all as if she had smashed her head and body into the barrier that dared to hold her back.

Althea, Althea, Althea, Althea, Althea, Althea, Althea, Althea—

At least now she understood what Elara meant when she said jump.

She meant jumping through *time*, *realities*, and *Realms*.
Worlds.

Althea hit the ground with an ear-crackling thud—but it took her no more than a second to gather herself up with a deep inhale before *realising* that what she had landed on was strangely awfully soft for something in the supposed *underworld*. Althea dug her fingers into the gentleness beneath her as she willed her vision to clear; it had become blurred the moment the wind decided to swallow her whole. *Whose faces were those? Did she want her vision to clear if that meant engaging herself into more potential trouble—?* "What—" As Althea squirmed in an attempt to beat the nausea, beautiful, luxurious, *soil* got uncomfortably stuck under her nails. She removed them from her hold on the ground, and whilst her eyes at last cleared at that... it was revealed to her silent mind that what she was kneeling on w*as, in fact, soil and grass.*

She didn't care whether it was a lie or not—a deception of a cruel nature—it was enough to make Althea's heart skip several beats at a time because it looked real enough. It was full of pastel colours, a translucent glow waltzing through the air her lungs seemingly still breathed in, and that was more than what she had been able to see for months now.

It gave her the strangest sense of ethereal hope.

The grass swayed through her fingertips, and Althea allowed the trembling gasp to leave her lips as she almost dared to weep. This was real—she had escaped. She was no longer trapped—

But then, someone awfully loud shouted an order to another, and Althea glanced up as two bodies ducked past her sides and towards the door that was beginning to shake with the darkness that was begging to escape. One by one, the four *human*-looking people ran to the same wooden doorway she had leapt through, doing everything that they possibly could to shut the door on the manacled dark hands that were slowly creeping through the cracks.

Raise your hand. Raise your hand. Raise your hand—

"*Look out!*" Althea bellowed without so much as a second thought. She held up her right hand, feeling as though the magick she had unwillingly suppressed for so long now rejoiced that she was allowing it to come out and play. *To burn.* Such crystallising twines of arrows aimed for the middle of the deceptive wooden door of Realms. An array of blues, purples, oranges, and pinks, all colours that were earnest, twirled through the windy air and forced the door to slam shut with a loud screech. It hit the door with such strength before it slammed, cutting off the few shadowed hands that had managed to follow her through such depths. The two children, who had both been holding back some portion of the door, stepped back, jumping into their parent's arms as the darkness seeped into the soil beneath them. The door disappeared and became lost through the midst of time.

Again, as if curiosity was Althea herself, she looked up with wide eyes, hesitantly rising to her feet as she took in the four *new* starstruck faces that watched her without a thought appearing to float through their mind. Their faces were all so very different, *judging* her in all very different ways. Althea held onto the fabric of her clothes as she inched herself back. It had been so long; how was she meant to sanely act in front of other people whom she knew had something of a soul?

She had been deprived of any interaction for so long now.

How was a girl with no mind meant to know any better?

The male, *the father*—she figured, stepped forward, and Althea took an automatic step back, feeling as the grass flattened beneath her bare feet, a sensation that almost had her smiling. *Is it real, or is it not?* Althea flicked her eyes down to the smaller child at his hip, the one who hid behind his father before catching sight of her quizzical, concerning gaze, and against all cruel odds, *he* smiled a gentle grin towards her. One that tried to reassure her into believing that they weren't going to hurt her... Did he take her as an ignorant fool? She wouldn't believe that they were harmless even if they gifted her with all of the lions and tigers in the world. She couldn't believe it—she wouldn't believe it. Not after all Althea had been forced to learn.

The father cleared his throat as he took in her sceptical expression, an assessing haze shining heavily in his wise eyes. He had brown hair and fair skin, not to mention the freckles that had claimed his cheeks and forehead as their own. He had a beard to him, too; one like Althea always knew her father desired to grow and yet never could.

"Hello, Althea," the male greeted, his voice surprisingly calm for such an outlandish conversation. Althea realised that he also sounded as if he would be one of the old, polished gentlemen she imagined would read and study in the large libraries of this world throughout their days; the type of men she imagined teaching the world of literature as she eagerly read about them in her many books. "My name is Willix Noxwell." *Was he expecting her to answer? She didn't know the Noxwell's —no matter the fact that it sent an illusion of a kiss to her breathless lips.* Althea didn't say anything in response; she merely stared the male down as her hands slipped down to her bony, cold elbows: clinging to herself for guidance. She was the wisest here, after all. "It's truly an *honour* to meet you—"

"*An honour?*" Althea queried as she broke her silence, and

while her voice wasn't exactly to its usual tone, there was still a bite to her words, "That's truly something."

The woman—the one who held kind eyes and a soft, undefined jaw stepped forward. She was around Althea's height and wore clothes that hugged her curves and brought a vibrant warmth to this new… variation of an *abyss*. Her skin was far darker than the males, and her eyes held a fierce warrior-like glow to them. This woman seemed like one she would like to know—a woman who she knew would have plenty of stories to tell. However, she most definitely didn't look to be dead. As she, too, wore a smile that no dead soul could bare to wear anymore. "Hello, dear girl—"

Her mind was howling at her to remember. Telling her that she was being ridiculous for not knowing who these faces belonged to. But her mind felt beyond empty as her eyes flickered from face to face, looking over the shared expressions that she didn't know how to feel about. *Am I going insane?* She wondered, and the answer in her hands didn't seem too kind.

"She doesn't know who we are," the boy, the smallest, with a gracious smile on his lips—a smile that was now dropping, noted from where he held his mother's hand tightly. *Fear,* something she had both missed and had enough of. "Mother, why doesn't she remember us?"

Althea allowed the question to float through the air before swallowing away her fear and admitting, "The spirits took my memories away, child."

She hated how weak she sounded. That *realisation*—that *pain*—it all brought an ache to the heart she could still hear beating somewhere in the midst of the air, and yet she no longer felt any physical ownership for.

Elara's face was covered in panic, her hands fidgeting anxiously before her as a thousand thoughts ran through her mind. She already had known this, yet now Althea knew that she was realising the complications of it all. "Will she *remember*?"

Elara asked faintly: a distraught expression bleeding over her features as her words ran quicker than her ears. "She has to remember—"

"She will," Willix stated, as a matter of fact, his eyes holding Althea's stare as he calmed his daughter down with a careful nod. "You will remember, just with time. I want you to know that we will *never hurt you.* We will protect you if anything," he offered, his words sounding so sincere that Althea was left fidgeting there uncomfortably. Did they really take her as an ignorant fool? She had known one too many strangers that had said that to her, and what did they do? Exactly the opposite of that.

But... there was no denying, never once had she had an older male look at her like this—a look of respect that didn't strip her of her dignity, her security. Never once had she spoken to someone that didn't treat her as if she was nothing at all. A deception that she knew all too annoyingly well.

"I'm sorry—" Althea blurted as she glanced over both of her shoulders, looking for any way that she could get herself out of this mess. She felt as if the walls of the afterlife were caving in on her, the heavens above threatening to collapse. All this time, she had been trapped, but now, after waiting and staying silent, she had a chance at seeing the world again. Something she never thought she would want to jump at. "I'm grateful for you helping me and all, but I don't tend to hang around with strangers that I just met," Althea explained wearily, her eyes slyly looking around the otherworldly grounds that she was standing on. She wasn't sure where she was, but either way, it was truly breathtaking.

Except that didn't mean she wanted to hang around in it any longer. And whilst her soul seemed to recognise these people... her mind did not. It was a torturous feeling, one that had her fumbling against her very words. She felt stupid. Oblivious. As if she was everything her father spat at her when the storm was at its peak.

There were beautiful, large, exceptionally crafted, willow trees swaying in the distance; the frail leaves and long branches waltzing in the melody of the wind that Althea could not hear but instead feel brushing against her physical *and yet not physical features*. To the left of her, towards the large mountains that looked to be shimmering in the distance, was a waterfall, one that would presumably lead her to the small little stream that ran past the right of her feet. It made her giddy to think about dipping her toes beneath the calm surface, feeling something so pure and right.

"You haven't ever met us, Althea," the woman was quick to say, pulling her attention back to her as Althea looked to her hesitantly. "Well… physically, you haven't, but *mentally*… we have always been with you. Watching after your heart and soul as the world took you for granted," the woman, who was far curvier and shorter than her tall and lean husband, spoke with a delicate yet uneasy smile. Willix turned to his wife with a nod, beckoning her to continue her words as if Althea didn't feel tongue-tied on her behalf. A touch of reminiscence was on her lips as she sighed greatly, and she turned her stark gaze back onto Althea. *Was that meant to make her feel better?* It didn't. It made her chest heave and her heart tremble. "If it had been our way, we would have met long ago, sweetest little thing. We would have travelled with our eldest when he met you for the first time, and we would have brought you back to our home so that you wouldn't have had to go through all that you did alone."

Her words felt like direct daggers to her heart—triggering a strange burning sensation as Althea took in their *sweet* features. The Markings on her arms burned, but long ago, Althea had grown quite exceptionally talented at hiding her true emotions under a cold mask that had even the curse daring to look away. Althea took in Marilla, slyly blinking away all that she had said while she tried to figure out who *they* reminded her of. Was it the boy in her dreams? The boy that had walked by her side in the battles of her mind. The same boy that had raised Hel in order to get her back. Of course, that was what she had made up, but it felt nice to believe in the weakest of dreams rather than no dreams at all.

Althea tilted her head, her tongue numb as she lowered her gaze to her feet. The woman's words *must have triggered something in Althea's mind*—or perhaps it was because she had now created some distance *of the Realms* between the curse and her... as her mind was currently finding the missing pieces to her darling yet cursed memories and piecing them together against all bloody odds.

It did—it had to have brought back something in her soul because *that face—those features*... the ones that followed her into the depths of the shadows and held her hand as they existed outside of them... was beginning to turn into the soft sound of rhythmic laughter that noted the bones in her spine before splintering each and every one of them.

But the laugh that was echoing throughout the existence of her soul was a sound that had her heart tightening as a weep threatened in the base of her lungs. A weep that could set her steps alight if she so craved the ashes that would sweep against her toes.

"My name is Marilla Noxwell, this is Huntio and Willix, and well... you have already met Elara," Marilla pointed out through a light chuckle. Althea looked to each of their faces, holding her arms tighter to her chest as she nodded once. Was it obvious that she was trying with all of her will to not look as perplexed as she felt? Or did they see right through her as if she was the archer?

"*We are Kylen Noxwell's family.*"

There it was.

That *rhythm*.

That *movement*.

That *melody*.

That absolute *heartache*.

Althea knew that name. It appeared as if she knew it more than what her mind had let on. That name had danced across her heart before holding a needle and thread in preparation to sew it back together before murdering it all over again. That name had been the illusion of time that kept the sanity from creeping its way out of her lungs and leaving her to drown in the midst of hallucinations.

Kylen Noxwell.

He held the name that belonged to the face that chased her through the nights.

The face that held so much emotion in her heart because she now no longer knew what to think of him.

Althea's eyes must have drifted to her feet in thought because now she rose them, looking towards the faces and eyes that stared at her in anticipation for any reaction at all.

"You are *Kylen's* family."

SIX
KYLEN

With every little inch of Kylen's once *cursed* heart, he could say with full confidence that he couldn't wait to watch these streets *burn*. He could already picture it, watching from the distance as the castle went up in flames. It would be glorious. He hadn't missed these roads of fatality one bit—the way the wind howled with the torturous screams of all those who had been beheaded in the kingdom's square, the way, if you looked hard enough, you could still see the faint outline of where the piles of bodies once lay.

Kylen clung to the shadows, holding onto the scent that was holding a bare blade against his lungs. The scent was one he knew with everything within him—one that had roses rotting across his skin—the thorns burying into his flesh and creating such horrid graves.

He felt like he was going insane.

But he wasn't—

Kylen wasn't insane.

Atticus appeared without a word at his side, gliding past him before halting his steps abruptly. Kylen looked to his own hands then, noting how his magick began to spread along the trembling ground, mimicking the art of the shadows—except his was all merely a wicked illusion. *Because he no longer had the curse.* He was imagining it all.

Kylen shook his head, and he forced himself to release a sigh that dared to send the rats scattering away to their deaths. The king, who was dressed in all black, went to try and say anything that would be of reason when Atticus quickly beckoned him forwards with a wave of his hand. "Let's go to the somewhat *'lively'* areas of this town and see what the people there have to say." *Town.* Kylen had forgotten how this kingdom was more known as a town rather than a kingdom. It was because of the fact that a kingdom nowadays had to have living people wandering through it to be a kingdom.

Despite Atticus' words being a mere statement as he walked, Kylen could still sense the questioning there, awaiting his approval. So, he nodded… feeling so utterly useless compared to the man he once was.

The man he was expected to be.

Aeonia was healing, and Kylen could see that—but he didn't know how to feel about it exactly. The curse was still present; he could feel the way it whispered and cooed in the corners and the alleyways. It danced through the nights, following every step of a soul who had finally become free of this… *sin.* Of course, the curse was ultimately deemed as gone now. It was rotting beneath the soil of Harlia, the Kingdom that had apparently never been a true myth in his mind—but apparently, everything was a mere lie these days because the curse was no longer decaying beneath that soil anyways. *So, what was the truth?*

Kylen so desperately wanted to know.

The beloved curse was rumoured to be in the very castle that Kylen caught a glimpse of every few scattered steps. He argued to Atticus that they should go straight there and meet the curse with a dazzling smile, but his brother was rather adamant about his decision, as he decided that he found joy in pinpointing the risks to Kylen as if he was nothing more than a child.

This Realm was so empty that it was causing every inch of his soul to want to flee. Tiny little splinters of the wind ran across Kylen's fingers as he tightened his hold on his cloak. The darkness was playing tricks in his mind; because everywhere he turned, he swore that he could see a man that he didn't want to remember. The male who took his girl away and left nothing but the dust of burdened memories in his trembling hands.

Atticus halted silently at his side, his eyes travelling towards the fog that surrounded the grounds of the palace of death. The figure that he swore was following him disappeared again, and just like that, he forced *Adonis*, the myth of dragons, out of his mind. The walls of the palace were much larger than what he partially remembered, although as he stepped closer towards it, he noted how it was beginning to crumble, falling victim to the night that someone his heart missed dearly had *left so bare*.

Did he want Althea to be alive? That was a question he didn't think he could ever answer. A question that he was sure would be left written on his headstone for all future generations to dwell over.

Atticus cleared his throat after several unbearable seconds of silence. Had he realised that he had pissed Kylen off? Or did he just want to be insufferable? "Should we go into town and see if anyone knows anything?" his brother asked for the second time, asking the question that Kylen had forgotten to audibly answer the last time.

"We already know what they will say," Kylen retorted in a snarky tone, his voice awfully hoarse. He laughed, a laugh so cruel and distressing that it had Atticus' eyes darkening on him. "They say that the King *who had once tried to kill them all* was now recovering behind the castle walls after having had his soul returned to him after so-so dreadfully long." Sarcasm, in all of its glory, dripped from his voice as his eyes stared ahead. That whole myth, whisper, rumour—*was utter bullshit*. Why on the Realms name did they believe that the king who would've happily murdered them all—and basically did murder them all—had been possessed by the spirits of the curse? And worst of all... why did they want to believe that?

Wouldn't they prefer watching him bleed out on the cold tiles before them? Life draining out of him as each second passed on...

Kylen knew that that was the option he would—*and did,* choose. He didn't regret spending minute after minute torturing the cruel flesh that coated his skin. He wanted him to bleed. To pay. It was his favourite part of his nights to enter the dungeons that reeked of corpses. It earnt his soul to flood with a feeling so strange yet so glorious as he watched the old King's eyes widen at his very presence, shaking his head as if that very action could rewrite history.

Sayah would be disgusted.

Althea would be proud.

Or perhaps it would be the other way around.

Atticus placed his hand on Kylen's shoulder, urging him to turn around and face him—but Kylen could not bring himself to do so. He didn't want to look at the boy who no longer had any light behind his eyes. Where was the boy he had once travelled the seas with? Was Atticus still there? *No.* That boy had never returned from the dead, and Kylen was beginning to think that he had that effect on people. *Death.*

"I want to go to the castle," Kylen insisted for the second time, the exhaust from his lungs fogging up the cold winter air before him. "I need to see if any soul resides in that castle, *as the people say.*" Kylen didn't give Atticus a chance to respond; he merely instead began to walk forwards, ignoring the way the shadows begged him to turn away and flee from this miserable kingdom of the past.

He felt eyes on him—many pairs of cruel despicable eyes

that all pointed to the one weak spot that had the ability to rip his already burdened soul into two. Kylen tried not to let it affect him—to not let the shivers that tingled every inch of his skin see his sins. He held his head high, feeling as the wind brushed through his many curls as he looked towards the scars of the night with determination shining sinisterly in his creased eyes. Kylen went to take another step around the sharp corner when that determination hiding within his gaze was quick to crumble.

He had barely made it around two corners of the old, rickety, and crumbling building before his body had collided with *another*—and almost instantly, the air around him and within his lungs froze as *she* took three steps back.

The air darkened, and Kylen's lips parted as he stumbled a few steps back. His eyes connected with *hers* as if, in every lifetime, they would always be drawn to each other. Almost instantly, Kylen found that he could not look away from the ones that were a shade deeper than he remembered so profoundly. *Stories filled those dark blue eyes,* but not stories that he was seemingly a part of anymore. Althea looked at him with her lips slightly pursed. Her skin was far lighter than it was tanned. Her eyes were dark, but he swore that he saw a lifeboat with Althea's soul swirling within the middle of them. Althea didn't flinch nor react the way he did—she didn't have the expression of seeing a ghost as he prominently did.

The face before him was one that he mourned for, one that he had begged the night for—but as quick as it was there, it was gone, disappearing within a blink of an eye, leaving Kylen to wonder if he had made it all up. *Had he truly gone mad?*

Atticus caught up to his side no more than a hurried splinter of a second later, his face dropping almost instantly into a concerned expression as he took in his brother's frozen features. *Had he just seen a ghost?* "Kylen—" Atticus quipped as his hands caught onto his face, lightly tapping his left cheek to get him to say something—*anything*.

"She was just here," Kylen uttered as if he was afraid that her very mention would take her away from him forever. Was she even real—was that a hallucination? His voice was a bare whisper against the thunder that was threatening to silence them all. Kylen turned to him with something lost in his soul, shaking his head as a chuckle of a manic laugh burned through the bottom of his lungs. It had to be her. She'd looked like everything he had ever prayed on, everything he had ever pleaded for. "Atticus—*she was just here.*"

Atticus rose a hesitant brow, looking around at nothing but empty and haunted streets that met his view. Kylen knew that he could not see what had stained his mind, but nonetheless, he looked into the abyss too—begging whatever God that was left out there to lead him to the soul of Althea's breaths. "Who? Kylen?"

Kylen inhaled deeply, preparing his soul for the word that was about to echo through the clouded air before him. A word that the Gods screamed and tore each other apart for. A word the cursed of the underworld sang as if she was their lord and saviour. "*Althea.*" It felt like a lie. One that wanted him to feel like a fool for believing in such nonsense. "Althea," he repeated, hoping that it would sound firmer—except it did not. It sounded like anything but firm.

Kylen took multiple staggering steps forward as his steps quickened into a run, leaving Atticus behind as he sought the night to show him the face he dreaded and yet longed for.

The *real* people of Aeonia looked to be both humans and the evil from his dreams as he ran past them—but none of them looked as haunted and manacled as the face did that he could still see in flashes of his vision. *Althea's face.* Kylen's head turned in every which direction, searching for the eyes that didn't look to recognise his. He ran his hands through his hair as he halted his steps, slipping against the bloodstained stones of the kingdom square as his chest throbbed such terrible sighs.

Althea. Althea. Althea.

She was going to be the death of him.

And he didn't know how many more series of deaths he could survive through.

He wasn't going insane. Was he?

No. Kylen had definitely seen her.

He had seen her, and she had been as real as these past few months—then again, they had been drowned in liquor... If anything, they were a mere blur. But still, she had been real— that was the body of his Althea, and he knew it. Kylen looked from one judgemental *real* face to the next; his expression scattered as he tried to think—*breathe...* he just needed to breathe. Breathe. Breathe. Breathe.

Again, as if there was a magnetic force wrapped around his body, Atticus reached his side, looking at him as if he was insane. Giving him the same look that every other soul had given him over his years of living. They all looked at him as if he wasn't just like them—they singled him out for being young or for thinking with his heart instead of his head.

Atticus said something to him, his lips sounding out the words, except Kylen could not hear them as the only thing his mind was throwing at him was his very own curse.

Althea. Althea. Althea. Althea.

Oh, how he felt to be drowning—but even then, that memory was swarmed with Althea's breath. Althea's touch. Everything was haunted by her, and he felt to be on the brink of a meltdown as his chest heaved and heaved and...

Kylen took a step back—and Atticus must have said something regarding the real Aeonian people around him because he looked around. Noting how every little beading eye there was, was pictured on *him*. He took in Aeonia then, looking and realising how much it had changed and evolved... for the better or for the worst? *That was still the question.* There was a strange buzz to the streets that had Kylen feeling as if he had misplaced his kingdoms. Aeonia had always been the kingdom of death. Every corner you walked, there was a body; blood splattered onto the walls as if it were the glistening rubies a queen wore at her coronation. Kylen still distinctively remembered the smell— the way it had his nose turning up at every corner, yearning for the scent Sayah had drowned him in when it came to her weekly Thursdays of cooking and baking.

Now... Aeonia reeked of death, except there were people buzzing in and out of markets that were surrounded by the glow of the candles he could only presume an Elemental had cast. It was like a fucking night market. And sure... that was a normal occurrence in villages, kingdoms, cities, et cetera... but *Aeonia had never been a kingdom with people walking freely through it.* It wasn't a normal Kingdom.

"I guess now is the time to try and figure out if Althea is alive," Atticus seemed to murmur, and Kylen felt the bile swirl around the insides of his throat. *Did he not hear what he had said just minutes ago?* Kylen looked to him, and Atticus held his crumbling expression. "It's not that I don't believe you, Kye, but I just don't think we can entirely rely on *your* word at the very moment."

Did he think that he was the Insane King too?

How could he—he was his brother?

SEVEN
ALTHEA

As if every little memory that had been taken from her impeccably fragile mind was now out to get her again, all of the voices and all of the visions flew back into her soul with a breath of *fresh* air. It felt like her past was consuming her body and soul with every breath that dared to aim straight for her stammering heart as she remembered a life she hadn't truly realised had slipped from her hands.

Kylen Noxwell.

Kylen Noxwell.

That name alone brought back a world beyond her understanding. A world that brought a thousand memories that felt so natural to breathe through, so natural to feel every little emotion to.

A smile that was delicate and secure appeared on Willix's lips, and Althea's chest heaved as she stepped back. She couldn't believe that she had remembered something that she'd never realised to have forgotten. *It felt surreal.* As if this was another of the curse's cruel games that she was spellbound to.

Althea's hands rose to her chest as she felt memories overcome her. They were now consuming her movements, her actions, holding such control over the mind that begged for his touch. *His embrace.*

She felt as if a life she hadn't been able to live flashed before her broadened eyes. Memories of a girl who had been wronged in every which way swarmed her gaze. Althea could feel her pain, her bruises, her wounds, all of it—and yet never once had that girl justly ever blamed those who had wronged her. Her heart held her back from doing so. Because she was good—after everything?

It was the same heart Kylen Noxwell seemed to want to love and yet always managed to pick the threading of. That was what the new wave of emotions she could feel tugging her mind in the opposite direction was. While she did want to remember every-thing—this felt like far too much to breathe through.

Althea's chest heaved again, and this time as she lifted her eyes from where they had fallen, she found herself looking into the windows of the past. *Her unrighteous past.* The blurred memories still forming were clouded with a frost that was slowly departing, leaving a warm shimmer to flicker away from the 'fire' that was burning with envy.

First, her eyes laid witness to Kylen.... and this was when he was a sweet, *harmless* child. His eyes were gleaming, his lips *hopeful.* She saw him wearing his father's suit upon arrival to Aeonia. It was quite baggy on his small frame, and the sleeves were rolled up to the point where it made a fourteen—thirteen... (she wasn't really sure; her memories were still blurred) year old boy look even younger. It honestly made Althea want to chuckle —but it wasn't a manacled laugh that was full of a cold bitter-ness, it was elusive, easy. From the moment their eyes met when they were children, Althea knew that they were going to be great friends. If only they'd had the opportunity to be.

Kylen walked up the steep steps of the Palace of Aeonia,

smiling at her graciously; Althea returned that daring grin as she curtsied her nerves away. She had never known another child that was fully unaffected by the curse *(or so she thought)*, so meeting Kylen was a breeze that she never wished to part with.

No matter how painful it was to now reflect on.

The next memory was of Kylen... *again*—except now he was grown. *Did the spirits take away her memories to save her from this terrible ache?* Kylen was dancing with a girl. Her head was resting against his quivering chest as he looked down at her with something almost like regret. *It was regret*—she reminded herself. He had known what trouble he was leading her towards, yet he still led her there with a blind eye. That look in his eyes as he gazed beyond the sea was one that was treacherous, as if he could see into what troubles and burdens the next few days would bring the two of them.

Althea hadn't known this then, but he had pressed a kiss to the top of her silver head. A gentle, whisper of a kiss, as he looked down to her with a noose slowly weaving around his flesh. She must have been too consumed by the thoughts that were realising that maybe this boy wasn't so bad, that his eyes were kind, his touch addictive.

But then again, Althea had already realised that long-long ago.

Marilla's hands reached for her cheeks, except her eyes were still trapped within her memories, drowning in a puddle the size of the ocean as each struggling movement, breath, and quiver seemed to have her sinking deeper and deeper beneath the surface.

Next, she saw sweet, kind, Sayah. Her eyes were soft as she watched Althea use her magick on the little lake back when she'd had her first and last Queenly visit to Lorundio. Now she desired to see more, to feel the whisper of freedom press gentle kisses to the edge of her nose. Sayah looked so at peace, so inevitably happy despite what the world had thrown at her. Her eyes were warm—*they were always warm*. Her complexion radiated her golden aura as Althea's magick consumed the both of them before the very vision was gone.

And it was clear at that moment then that she wanted to see the siren more than *anything*. She had been her *friend*, one of the rather few that had earned her to smile.

After that, Althea saw glimpses of Kylen's once lost brothers. She watched as Khatri and Atticus acted as if they had already accepted her as one of their own—and then when something of the sort like death greeted her, Uzziah, at last, defended her name, a gesture so unlike the one she would've expected him to play when she had still been *alive*.

Althea wasn't sure how she saw all these cruel reminders of *what she had lost*, but perhaps it had something to do with what the spirits wanted her to see.

Althea had never wanted brothers growing up.

Nor sisters.

Nor siblings.

She didn't want anyone to feel the burdens of the same pain she was left to deal with, as she had always known that she would've taken all the pain the world threw at her if it meant keeping those she loved safe.

Even her father.

For him, she would've done anything.

Because even on the coldest of nights, she could still remember the man who would walk to her room and make sure that the windows were shut and the blankets were on. He would kiss her head and wish her sweet dreams as if life would always be precious.

But then she had grown up, and the life before her shattered at her feet.

Yet there was something about the relationship she was beginning to form with each one of Kylen's brothers... *and even Zaire*, that created a relationship of a sibling with her. And that had Althea missing their company against all dreadful odds.

It made her loathe being alone—and that said a lot since she used to long for it.

Althea watched as another merciless memory that this time did not belong to her played across her mind. She watched with a mourning heart as Zaire slowly crept through the cold streets of Lorundio, heading towards the kingdom's square that was as frozen as a lake on a winter's day. Althea realised then, that this memory felt different. *It had her bones threatening to crumble as she leaned into Marilla's touch in fright—it didn't belong to her. It did not belong to her at all.*

Zaire kept slowly walking until they stopped hesitantly, looking towards something that had Althea wanting to look away from. Their orange eyes held a strange tone to them, strange emotions washing over their face as they shook their head with a sigh exhaling into the icy air.

There was a large memorial sight *for Althea* in the centre of Lorundio, Althea realised, and the 'lost Queen' watched as Zaire slowly dropped blue flowers at the bottom of her plaque. *There wasn't any mockery there?* Just suffocating silence that had Althea swallowing her breath as she shook her head in ignorance.

Had Kylen done this? Had he mourned her death—but that felt so outlandish, he had no reason to mourn her...

The next memory had Althea wishing she didn't have to drown in this torture as she watched the last moments of Eloise's life play out before her very frail eyes. Althea shook her head again against it, and as if Willix could sense her misery, he helped her ground herself slowly. *"Breathe, Althea. Take a deep breath, feel the ground, hear my voice,"* Willix stabilised her as she beckoned every inch of the memories within her burning mind to calm.

To breathe.

Althea saw her father last. Except he was in the position of Willix, who stood before her.

Her father was watching her with those same shadowed eyes that had her soul feeling so belittled and her actions so appalling. He looked as though he could see right through her, like he had the mission to demean her on his mind, and the silent words already leaving his tongue that were out to slice her skin apart. He made her feel like she was worthless, nothing but a walking burden, because she could never be anything more than that in his eyes—no matter how hard she tried.

Willix was quick to speak her name, and Althea forced herself to realise that her father wasn't there. Willix was. And he seemed kinder.

"Let's take her back *home*. It isn't safe to stay out in the open like this." Marilla ushered the young, frozen children forward, leaving Althea to stand there before Willix *alone* as she took a deep breath for the first time in a long time. Marilla didn't wait for a reaction from Althea of any kind; she just merely allowed her to catch herself as she had already been doing for so long now.

Her eyes slid to the male at her side; however, she realised that he was holding her arm. His hands were on her elbows, holding her up with a touch that *should be poisonous*. It was like Willix could sense Althea's sudden panic, as his hands moved away from her flesh no more than a second later, watching as her body went rigid because of him.

Breathe. Breathe. Breathe.

"I'm not going to hurt you," Willix said quickly, his face dropping of any colour. Althea clenched her jaw; she felt so overwhelmingly embarrassed to feel threatened by this male. She could kill him if she felt like it—*why is she afraid of a man?* A scrawny old man—well, he wasn't that scrawny or old... But still, he was a man that, in the strangest of ways, reminded her of her father, *and that entirely said enough.* "I would never."

She nodded, forcing her voice to even as she whispered, "I know that."

But did she?

Half of her mind willed it to be said out of spite, and the other half was saying anything at all in order so that she could remove the uneasiness from her palms.

Willix looked at her as if he didn't believe a word she was saying. As if she was speaking blatant lies—*and perhaps she was*—but Althea wasn't going to admit that to him, nor herself. "Walk with me?" Willix prompted, and Althea dipped her head down as she stepped forward automatically. Her breaths felt uneven and heavy, as if there was a ball of cursed magick trapped in her lungs that was becoming quite difficult to avoid. She had done this all before, walking through a closed-in paddock with an older male at her side—she just needed to breathe and remember that her father wasn't here.

"I don't have much of a choice, do I?" Althea mused in a gentle voice, still forcing it to stay even. It wasn't meant to sound bitter, but it still came out that way.

Her eyes were captured by her surroundings no more than a second later. Althea noted how everything was breath-taking. The trees, the leaves, the grass, the flowers, all of it. At least that allowed her a snippet of a distraction as she walked through a place that didn't look real.

Because it wasn't, this was death.

"Of course, you have a choice. You could either walk that way and see what you can find throughout the depths of the afterlife, or you could go and sit somewhere and see what magick you can access here since you did seemingly *show off* before," he said with a wink. A deep chuckle left his lungs that was so unking-like that it had her shoulders relaxing *a touch*. "But Althea, you will always have a choice with us. All we want to do is help *you* get home. We want to make sure that you live to see another day, to feel the warmth of the sun lining your skin as it had when you were a child. You deserve that much."

"When I was a child, the only thing I felt warming my skin was the blood of my victims." Althea looked hastily back to him, ignoring how the memories of her last few moments in the true Realms had her heart burning with a pain so fierce. She had been so much stronger than this once upon a time ago; it made her want to cackle at how far she had fallen. Now the silence was her greatest friend. "You are going to help me get back?" Althea questioned.

"Of course," Willix said, lifting his chin towards that same wind that had her fingers flinching at her sides. His eyes met hers, and almost instantly, she looked the other way. When she was just a child, Althea had learned that she wasn't one to willingly hold eye contact with her father—his gaze felt as if it could see through every one of her securities. And that was a feeling she wished no soul would ever have to experience. "You are too young to be here, Althea. You have so much more of a life to live."

"If I recall correctly, your children were younger than me—you and your wife still had so much more of a life to live... not to mention I gave up my life for *your* son," Althea said, feeling as those memories circled within her aching mind. "Wait—*is that why?* Do you feel like you owe this to me because I saved your son? If anything, you should try and get your own children back to the physical Realms; this is no place for a child who isn't even ten years old." Willix stopped walking, looking to her with an expression that had her wanting to run the other way as she furrowed her brows. "Did I say something wrong—"

"Can I tell you a secret, Althea?" Willix questioned, cutting her words off.

What a curious thing to ask.

Althea parted her lips, her brows dropping in uncertainty. "*Sure...*" she murmured, although that answer wasn't clear whether it was the right one or not. But she wouldn't deny her once daring curiosity.

"Marilla and I have looked over you since the day we died," he mused with a glimmer radiating from his features. He looked to her, and there was something so pure about the way he crossed his arms across his chest. He inhaled so much air that she was sure he would burst—and yet when he exhaled, even more delicacy laced his features. "In our minds, you were always our second daughter. Here in the afterlife, if you try hard enough, *that is*—which is quite difficult every now and then, you can sense what the future holds, what the Gods have spun in your web. So, since the moment we died, we learnt how to do exactly that; we already knew that you and our sons' lives would cross paths at one point or another." Willix's eyes confidently held hers, and Althea hoped with everything in her that he couldn't read minds because if he could, then he was about to see all that whispered within the harsh demeanour she threw at him. "I always wished that there had been a way for us to live so that we could've taken you back to Lorundio when you both were children. I wished that we could've been the parents you deserve... because Gods know you deserve better than what you had."

Deserve.

They speak of her as if she isn't standing on the brink of death.

Althea looked down to her feet as she followed the cobblestone pathway that led her to a cliff that overlooked the afterlife. Marilla, Elara, and Huntio were also approaching, but they all remained silent. Althea felt the agony behind her eyes, the exhaust; it caressed her cheeks as if the curse was still tempting her with death. But Althea couldn't risk it, not when she was in the presence of those she had once wondered about.

So, she bit down on her bottom lip, suppressing the ache that laid there.

"I'm sorry for everything you went through, Althea—"

She knew that he was trying on her behalf. She knew that he was trying to separate the idea of her father and his whole being —but she didn't know how to act under circumstances like this one. How was she to possibly know how to act when the man in her mind was so different and yet so similar to the man before her? The difference was uncanny if she thought back to the early days. "I don't like talking about it," Althea said before realising the words had left her lips. She only knew that she had said something daunting when he gave her that specific look that parents shed on their children when they were trying not to react in an unkind manner. Althea shivered in her flesh, loathing the way she sounded like such a horrible being for feeling this way —for reacting this way. It was as if she was a wild animal left to be protective of herself. "It just—*it makes me uncomfortable.*" Althea chuckled, except her laugh was anything but pure. It was torturous, reminding her of the first time the spirits had visited her in that old cell and how she'd laughed in their faces.

Althea looked to him, and she whole-heartedly expected to see the mirror image of her father glaring down at her with mean eyes. She expected that Kylen Noxwell's *father* would be annoyed or frustrated at her because she dared to interrupt him —*not to mention for having anything but a sweet tone.* Except... he didn't. Willix didn't look at her in a harsh, menacing manner; he looked at her with an emotion that she had been dreadfully deprived of growing up. Such a simple sentiment and gesture that in front of any normal soul, it would be hidden amongst the stars. But for her, it was different.

The stars had never been that good at hiding the confronting truth from her hands.

Willix looked at her with understanding, nodding his head as he offered her a gentle smile. "Okay, thank you for letting me know—*and thank you for allowing me to get some of my large speech out* before cutting me off. I really do hope that you know that I would never lay a single hand on you. Us lone royals have to stick together, you know? I know something of what it's like growing up to the type of father you had, so never feel as if you cannot come to me."

If she'd had this type of father growing up, then perhaps she wouldn't be standing in the midst of the afterlife, her eyes connected with the ones reflecting the soul of a dead man.

This was all happening extremely quickly, Althea noted as she nodded in response, finding her tongue impeccably dry as she at last released her grip on his eyes. Just five hours ago, she was hidden within a cell of the abyss, clinging to the scratched flesh of her knees as she stared at the white wall before her with not a single thought in her mind.

Now, however, she was standing before a man who looked like an older version of the man she *loved*. A man who genuinely held a shade of kindness in his dead eyes—even though Althea had grown up only knowing brutality in the eyes of death.

She didn't know what to do to slice the tension out of the air and discard the body so that no one would find it, so Althea just offered him a frail smile in reply, nodding only once more since words failed her. She wanted to leave it at that, except he said one last thing that had her truly wondering if he had watched over her all these years. His words made her judge her own mind, sending one of those psychological questions through the bruised mind hidden behind her ears. "I know it is difficult for you to trust people, but I would like to hope that one day I will earn your trust... *perhaps if I show you my library?* I have a few books I know you will like."

With that, Willix turned away, and Althea was left biting her bottom lip, attempting to suppress her revolting thoughts from taking capture of her. She didn't want to fall for his manipulative ways—because she was sure that that was exactly what he was doing.

This man doesn't care for you. The spirits hissed as they heard the uproar in her mind. *He wants your power just as we do. Succumb to us, and we will keep you safe from fathers like him.*

Willix didn't expect a response from her as he continued walking, and that much was evident from the way he dismissed it altogether. It was good. Refreshing. It had her nodding in gratitude as she willed herself to breathe. *Just breathe.* But it wasn't that he was making her uncomfortable...

It was more so that she had grown up in this world *by herself.*

She had been the one who'd taught herself how to do the simplest things (such as make breakfast and birthday cakes to celebrate surviving) and so-called 'life lessons' that had her wishing to be decaying beneath the soil's corpse. She had taught herself everything there was to know—never once needing the help or support from a man that could be a father to her.

Althea was her own *father.*

And *mother.*

And *brother.*

And *sister.*

And *friend.*

And *foe.*

She was the only *soul* that she would ever need.

With a gentle breath, Althea approached the far cliffsides that had a glistening waterfall weeping down it. One that seemed to welcome her with a gentle cry, a gentle hello. She tried to hold her head high, to have that same personality and stamina that she... *'died'* with... but Althea felt lost.

That girl was one that she did not remember and did not miss. In her mind, Althea Evangeline was still a stranger. Because while she remembered everything that had happened before death swept her away with a melody of a kiss, those memories felt as if they belonged to another.

To another soul that was meant to be happy now and living their best life.

Althea felt so inevitably lost that she didn't know what to

think or what to do next. So, she followed Willix and the Noxwell family through the parting water *that didn't dare to rain on them,* and she entered into a large cave that had doors and a house moulded into the very mountain.

A home for those that life did not care for.

EIGHT
KYLEN

Insane. Insane. Insane. Insane. Insane. Insane. Insane.
Insane. Insane. Insane. Insane. Insane. Insane. Insane.
Insane. Insane. Insane. Insane. Insane. Insane. Insane.
Insane. Insane. Insane. Insane. Insane. Insane. Insane.
Insane. Insane. Insane. Insane. Insane. Insane. Insane.
Insane. Insane. Insane. Insane. Insane. Insane. Insane.
Insane. Insane. Insane. Insane. Insane. Insane. Insane.
Insane. Insane. Insane. Insane. Insane. Insane. Insane.
Insane. Insane. Insane. Insane. Insane. Insane. Insane.
Insane. Insane. Insane. Insane. Insane. Insane. Insane.
Insane. Insane. Insane. Insane. Insane. Insane. Insane.
Insane. Insane. Insane. Insane. Insane. Insane. Insane.
Insane. Insane. Insane. Insane. Insane. Insane. Insane.
Insane. Insane. Insane. Insane. Insane. Insane. Insane.
Insane. Insane. Insane. Insane. Insane. Insane. Insane.
Insane. Insane. Insane. Insane. Insane. Insane. Insane.
Insane. Insane. Insane. Insane. Insane. Insane. Insane.
Insane. Insane. Insane. Insane. Insane. Insane. Insane.

Insane. Insane. Insane. Insane. Insane. Insane. Insane. Insane. Insane. Insane. Insane. Insane. Insane. Insane. Insane. *Insane.*

Everyone thought that *he,* the mad king, was insane. That he was allowing the screams and torturous screeches of everything he had ever let loose from his decaying grip to drive him to insanity and whatever was beyond. They whispered that he was standing in the wind at the edge of the cliffsides that were already giving way to the agony his manacled soul held.

But Kylen wasn't insane.

No—*he wasn't.*

And it made his fists curl at his sides to hear his brother say such shameful things. How could he? How could the boy who he had once built bloody cubbyhouses with inside the halls of the castle that was their home… *say that he was insane?* No. He was a survivor—Kylen had survived, had he not? How did that make him weak?

His steps were quick as he followed behind Atticus, staring into the back of his head as if he could physically burn the judgments from his mind. *He wanted to.* He wanted to rid his brother of the thoughts that had Kylen's splinter of security melting away.

He wasn't insane.

He wasn't.

Kylen felt Atticus stop walking, his lips forming into a smile as he greeted a stranger whom Kylen had no will to talk to. To so much as interact with. He wanted the world to leave him be. To soothe his worries and tell him that he was a good person.

That he wasn't insane.

Atticus cleared his throat, a line of something more appearing there as he began to ask the male such *ridiculous* questions—questions that had his eyes engraving graves into the stoned road ahead, not daring to make eye contact with anyone in case they saw the trembling pain and weakness that lingered there. *His true fatal flaw.*

Kylen had no will at all to respond or interrupt any of the questions and answers coming his way—but then he heard a few disastrous words that had his eyes dragging up, his lips parting in a threat of a scowl, and a wave of shadowed darkness consuming Kylen's soul as he willed time to reverse so that he could remember what it felt like to wake up on those blissful and peaceful summer mornings in *Lorundio*.

"No, we could never blame the king," the Aeonian stranger mused with a shrug of his shoulders before crossing his arms across his chest; his body vibrated in a laugh as he grinned broadly at Atticus as if they were going on a stroll through the park. "He had been possessed for so long—*sheesh, I mean*, the man deserves peace. A break to actually breathe!" he sniggered, and Kylen already found himself fantasising about how his death would taste.

"Possessed?" Kylen echoed in a tone that was quiet except audible enough, although despite the question in his tone, *Kylen knew exactly what he was talking about*. He had heard of all the preposterous rumours—all the *little sayings* that had a thirst for blood forming in the back of his throat.

The stranger nodded as Atticus turned a look of warning towards Kylen, an unspoken plea in the look he sent him. "Yep. Haven't you heard, mate?"

Kylen shook his head as a punishing laugh erupted from his lungs. "No, I mustn't have... *mate*." Kylen began picking at his sleeves, unbuttoning the two black buttons, and rolling the white material up so that his dark, riveting skin was shown. Atticus shook his head, most evidently beckoning for him not to do any of what he was *dreadfully* intending.

But then again, Kylen was the King, and Atticus was not.

His brother cleared his throat, swiftly going to say something that was most likely going to interrupt the two... but *nevertheless*, the stranger seemed to yearn for death. "Yep," he replied with a pop of his lips. "It turns out this whole time that the King was probably somewhat of a decent man. I mean—it will still take a while for his name and reputation to be cleared. But his daughter did the deed of wiping the curse from his bruised mind. Pretty little thing, wasn't she? Too bad she's dead."

"*His daughter?*" Kylen sneered, yet the male went on, oblivious to the way Kylen's hands balled at his sides. He was going to make him pay... and perhaps he would use his new and unused magick that was beginning to stir beneath his trembling touch.

"*Mhm,*" he hummed, once again agreeing with every little thing that left Kylen's quizzical lips. "She willingly sacrificed her life for that man, killing herself to wipe the curse away and free him. Some say she was the curse itself—*and I must agree with them.* I mean, never once did she come and visit us despite all of the horrors. What kind of future leader is that? A *fucking* selfish one that is—"

Kylen couldn't control it.

He didn't want to control it.

He could only welcome this splattering blood and beg for it to cool this agonising burn.

Kylen pushed the man back with such force, his hands curling around the fabric of his blazer as he threw him back into the murky alleyway. His body landed on the ground with a thud, a shocked cry bleeding from his lungs. "*Hey—hey—hey—!*" he went to rasp, but Kylen cut him off by smashing his head into the crumbling walls behind him, watching and feeling as such magnificent blood began to trail over the clenched fingers holding him up.

Althea would be proud.

"You watch what you say about her~" Kylen rasped, taking on this merciless tone despite the rapid beat and stumble of his own fatal heart. "She did not willingly sacrifice herself *for him* —nor did she choose to become one of the curses fucking victims!"

Victims, victims, victims, victims, it had killed her—he had failed.

"Kylen," Atticus warned from behind, earning a cruel laugh to leave Kylen's lungs as he refused to send his brother a second glance. He had called him insane. He believed that he was insane —Atticus did not matter. *He* should not care for him.

"What is your problem, mate?" the male he held against the wall screeched, his eyes flickering swiftly across his as if he held the mythical abilities to calm him down. *Mate. Mate. Mate.* What were they? Two old friends having a fucking picnic in the royal parks...

There was nothing that was going to calm him now.

Kylen snickered again, shaking his head as he asked, "My problem? I have none—if anything, your people are the problem for speaking such utter bullshit," he seethed. "She did not deserve to die—your cruel King did, *and I swear on the Gods' name that I will make him pay.* I will!" The male in his arms tried to squirm to his escape, but Kylen shoved him back once again, not paying notice to the way the rotted wall began to crumble behind him. Causing a pile of ash, debris, and rot to pile just below the male's dangling feet.

If the roles were reversed, Kylen would've been sure to kick him in the groin by now.

He would already be free.

The stranger sent a helpless side-eyed look to Atticus, his eyes pleading that it was honestly amusing—earning Kylen to laugh once again... *as if he had genuinely lost his sanity.* If they wanted him to be mad, he wasn't going to deny them their offer. The male looked from Kylen to Atticus with pleads in his eyes, *evidently* shaking his head as he whispered in panic, "*Are you going to help me or not?*"

Shrugging blankly, Atticus released a sigh of defeat. He appeared on the right of Kylen, crossing his arms as he sent him a tiresome look. Kylen wanted him to react—he craved a reaction of some type. They needed to realise that if they were calling him insane, then he was going to *be* insane. "There's nothing I can do, *mate*," Atticus retorted, spitting the last word as if it was the very curse they had been running from for so long now. "It's not my fault your people are acting ungrateful for all the Queen did for you."

So now Atticus decided to play nice: when he'd come to realise that he had truly crossed the line. Kylen slightly offered his eyes to his brother, looking him over before looking back at the stranger. He didn't need his pity, his sympathy. He would've been perfectly fine if he had been here by himself. He would've been perfect. "Queen?" the man chortled, earning Kylen's gaze to darken and sharpen on him. "She was barely a child. Barely a woman grown. We never wanted a child queen—"

Kylen didn't wait to hear another word. He simply punched him, watching with a blank and missing satisfaction as he fell to his feet, kneeling before him as he desperately tried to flee.

Except Kylen was not done with him.

He punched him again.

And again—

And again—

Muttering the same words repeatedly as if they were the only cries he'd ever been able to murmur. *"Don't touch her—don't touch her—don't touch her—"*

His tears began to burn his vision, silently fleeing down his cheeks as he felt the blood continuously splatter across his skin as if he were a King crowned in the most glorious rubies known to mankind. Atticus stepped forward without a single word leaving his pursed lips, his hand silently reaching for his shoulder. "You are going to kill him," he whispered, and Kylen could only cackle in response. *No fucking shit.* He wanted him to die. He wanted them *all* to die.

"Let him die," Kylen said gravely—*and instantly, he wished his tone had been sturdier*. Except the tremors had been there, and Atticus slowly tilted his head to the side as he shook it. He was feeling bad for him and mourning for the brotherly king he once knew. Kylen kept his eyes ahead, ignoring how his tears were mourning for a life he now wondered whether was truly lost or not. Against his will, the tears wordlessly trailed down his cheeks, picking up the reflection that the stars *too* had left behind before they'd fled to Realms beyond. Kylen closed his eyes. Breathe. *You won't be able to find Althea if you end up going insane.* He took a short breath, forcing himself to ignore how the tears burned his bruises. The wind sniggered beyond, earning Kylen to turn his crumbing face away, ignoring how his whole body *ached beyond measure* as Atticus slowly knelt at his side.

Kylen hadn't realised yet, but he had also fallen to his knees —his body aligning with the unconscious stranger laying several feet away. His face was unrecognisable to the man Kylen had met several minutes earlier. His skin was swelling, his bruises presumably forming under the clotted blood that Kylen partially had flickered across himself.

Kylen already knew how this would end; the stranger would wake up and assume he had gotten into some sort of drunken brawl... Little did he know that the King of the Kingdom, once all praised, had beaten him bloody. *What had he done?* He was once the King people looked at with a wide smile. Bowing to his name before Kylen laughed and merely accepted a handshake because he was rather eager to get to know and understand every single being that passed through *his* Kingdom.

Now he had beaten one bloody.

Even if it wasn't his own—he still thought of all as *his* people to care for.

Kylen's lips shuddered as he shook his head in ignorance, running a hand through his hair as Atticus slowly reached for him. "Leave me be," he begged—except Atticus didn't listen. *He never listened.* Kylen shoved his hand away; he hadn't forgotten what the boy had suggested earlier. *Insane. Insane. Insane. They all thought of him as insane.*

"Kylen," Atticus ushered—this time again in a tone that had him feeling like a child being scolded by a parent who was alive and *well*. "It's okay—"

"No," Kylen exhaled as he turned to him with narrowed eyes. "*None of this*—none of it's okay," he persisted, shaking his head before scoffing on the blood that ran off of his tongue. "*She shouldn't be alive—but then I want her to be alive more than anything—but if she is, then I have to figure out if she is truly the one who killed Sayah—*" Kylen shook his head, feeling as the stars began to weep too, rain pooling over his shoulder and running down his spine with tears of regret. "I don't know what to do."

Atticus nodded. "I know. Neither do I," his tone was so soft, so gentle; he was being cautious around Kylen, and *Kylen didn't want that—*

The air swirled throughout his hair, and Kylen shook it back as he turned to him, trying with the weakest of attempts to push him away as he rose to his feet slowly. "It isn't the same for you. You called me *insane*." Atticus' gaze furrowed. "I may have just lost the woman who practically raised me because the woman I loved murdered her... and that leaves me standing here like a fucking fool."

Several seconds of silence passed, and two drunk men wandered by the alleyway without noticing the King drowning in his own self-pity. Kylen went to turn the other way when Atticus scoffed. "It isn't the same for me?" he echoed in an awfully sour manner, and from the look rocketing off of his soft features, Kylen knew that he was about to hear of a time he had no will to drown in. "Kylen, I grew up with no one. I didn't have a single consistent person in my life until I met Uzziah and Zaire; even then, their mother treated me as if I was their family's *slave*—" he paused, swallowing away the agony that coated his expression as he kept his stare fixated on Kylen. "Did Sayah ever tell you how I met her? You know that I knew her before I knew you, but do you actually know how or why?"

Kylen hesitated for a moment: knowing that no words would possibly make it off of his tongue. "I had just murdered my *first* victim. My magick got loose and I-*I was seven*—not knowing how I could possibly control such Elemental *cruelty*," Atticus said, his voice surprisingly strong despite the words he was saying.

Cruelty.

Because that was all magick was in the debt of time.

Kylen felt his heart strain, already moving to shake his head when Atticus continued on. His brother had never been the type of person to be straightforward about anything, yet of course, he still had his moments. "Sayah found me covered in *their blood*, running through the dark streets of a village far north—while I was a literal boy, a child that hadn't even yet hit double digits. Sayah found me, and she didn't have to use her magick on me to calm me down. No, she held me, telling me to practice my breathing pattern until I felt everything silence. *Breathe in, breathe out. Tell me what five things you can see~* I didn't know it yet, but I had a mental disability that caused me to feel and consume things differently. So that night, whilst it had been my outburst to murder those morals, it was still my fault no matter how many times Sayah begged to differ. And yet... even when Sayah and I did learn of it, she still treated me *just the same*; she still held my hand. I don't know why I half expected her to look at me differently; I just assumed the worst because that was all I'd ever known. She brought me back to the palace, and the next day, I met you."

Kylen remembered that day as if it was yesterday, the day he walked into his throne room only to find Atticus standing tall with an awkward toothy smile on his lips. If only he'd known that the next week Kylen would again walk in, only to find

Atticus and his two other siblings, that were now also *his*. "She claimed despite not even knowing me, that I was one of the finest fighters she had ever seen—*just because she knew that I needed a home*. Since then, she had been the one I relied on—*we all relied on*." Atticus shook his head, yet as if he had grown taller than Kylen ever could, he kept his vision straight. "So, you cannot say that this doesn't affect me. It affects me entirely—but you just haven't realised that yet. Because you have locked yourself in your room for the past several lifetimes, drowning your sorrows in liquor and the sea while you left your family—*us*—to all burn."

Burn? Was that seriously what he thought Kylen had done? Atticus, the boy who was always one to please people, was beginning to wither, and his animal-like snarls set Kylen's bones chilling. *Kylen hadn't left him to burn; he hadn't left him to suffer at all.*

"We needed you—*I needed you!*" Atticus remarked, and Kylen saw the pain covering his face like a tidal wave. Atticus' nose was scrunched, his eyes bloodshot... when was the last time that he had slept? "You didn't come to her funeral, her memorial service—you didn't do shit! And I tried—I really —*really* tried to give you time for mourning, except Kylen, you didn't just mourn Sayah's life; you mourned all of ours. Because one by one, we all disappeared. We all fell in the graves *you* dug."

The wind grew older at that, and the hair on Kylen's arms and legs rose on end as his eyes stayed laced on Atticus'. Kylen stared at him, watching and feeling as the silence that echoed throughout the air began to suffocate them *both*. "That's not fair. I'm sorry—but I just couldn't cope with it anymore—with anything anymore. Everyone I have ever known, *loved*, cared for... has died on me."

"I'm still here," Atticus said as if that was even close to the truth.

Kylen laughed, and he knew that it was ignorant of him to be so loud, especially when people were beginning to flee from the night markets. Still, too many thoughts circled his mind, and he was desperate to spill all of the ones holding his tongue hostage. "But you aren't. And you haven't been for a long time now. I went to your memorial service every year. I went to your graves and left fresh flowers every moonfall in hopes that the Gods would reward me for my kindness... It took a fucking God to bring you back, and then I couldn't even keep her heart beating."

"Kylen—*we came back.*"

Didn't he realise? That in the dead of night, when Kylen dared to step further than his doorway, he was searching to make sure that the last of his family were still breathing? Some nights Kylen even found himself staring over to the large concreated memorial plaque that he could just see in the east window through the parting of the trees. He watched it, staring at it as if he was waiting for the moment his brothers would truly come back from the dead. He knew they were physically and mentally with him now, but he wasn't there—Kylen hadn't felt truly alive for a long time now.

"Yeah, well, you were still dead for a great portion of my life, and one can't just rid themselves of something that quick. So, excuse me if I am mourning too much for you—I am just tired, Atticus, and I don't think I can survive this great war any longer."

It was a silent plea for help—a silent inevitable plea that begged the Gods to slice his throat and push him to the ground only to never get up again. However, there was an echoing sound that brought both of their faces to the left of them, and as if they were still in the lost mythical lands of Harlia, Kylen could suddenly sense the nostalgic magick of *Adonis*. The magick that haunted him every time he closed his eyes, as the memories of finding Althea in that overgrown palace floated about through his head. Why could he feel him? Why could he sense that inevitable rage that had Kylen's heart thrumming several beats far too quickly?

"We've been out in the open for too long," Atticus noted, dismissing him and the subject entirely, earning Kylen's eyes to look back to him in pure utter disbelief. Had he not just served his heart to him on a silver platter? Did none of that mean anything to him?

As if he was a mere dog being pulled by his lead, he followed Atticus silently. Ghosting down the streets and hiding within the shadows as they arrived at a place that was a little, quivering memory in his mind. A place that he both wanted to burn and cherish.

The old broken down and yet glorious Theatre of Whyntiou stood tall despite the harsh storms before the very two of them. It was a large brown building; however, it was rather worse to wear. The darkness that fell from the skies had spread over the once lively, lettered signs, leaving Kylen to stand there dumbfounded for a second too long before realising that this was the hideout he used to hide in as a child.

A child who was visiting a Kingdom to meet the girl his parents had once jokingly told him to marry—if only they realised that he would have to do the impossible after walking in on their rotting corpses.

Atticus moved first. Acting as if he was a wild spider with the longest of legs as he climbed up the wall to the entry only they knew about. Atticus used the cracks in the bricks to slip his feet in, hoisting himself up towards the little gap that was covered and hidden by the breath of night. He moved the large sign aside, and Atticus pushed himself through the rusty hole that had been an outcome of one of Kylen's own cursed outbursts, leaving him now to stand there like a fucking fool. *A fool he was.*

Kylen looked around with a noiseless heave of his chest. He ran his hands over his face, feeling the weathered and aged skin beneath his touch that ached for any kiss of blissful warmth. A second passed, then two, and Kylen inhaled again, feeling and breathing in how *silent* this Kingdom concerningly was. It was always quiet, he wouldn't lie, but back in the time when one could smell death as it withered across their hearts, *you could always hear the ungodly screams of the lost bleeding out in the midst of the air.*

Now, it was just silence, a strange, eery *silence.* The air was as dead as anything, and the ghosts passed through the wind without a second thought, echoing through their once-cursed minds. It was plain old silence, keeping the heads from turning or rolling.

Ultimately, Kylen knew his options. He could flee and search the castle for the King they, *the people of this retched kingdom,* still believed to live there—*when really, he was searching for a royal who was a mere black hole in his heart.* Or, if he chose to be the *kind* brother he once was, he could turn around and stitch the opening of a wound shut. No matter how cruel and out of line he was *acting.*

And that's, unfortunately, what he did without a second arrogant thought.

Kylen climbed up after Atticus, squinting his eyes against the harsh weather as he moved the sign aside. He could feel the wind and rain nip at his scarred skin; the spiders were as dark as the several seas running across his fingertips. But the magick he had refused to notice burnt them to a crisp, leaving Kylen to watch as the wind carried their corpses away without so much as a crackle of thunder.

When he was only an inch away from climbing through the small, withered hole, the sound of a daring old crow brought his eyes to the long-time abandoned building to his right. It was an old factory; they were all appearing to be old factories. But that made sense, as if Kylen recalled correctly, this part of the kingdom housed the larger yet older structures rather than the newer parts. However, all of which didn't lack the one consistent theme that floated throughout the Kingdom like a ghost.

They had all been abandoned in the pandemic of the first Great War. The same war where dragons as beastly and merciless as the Gods' rivals were rumoured to burn down the world that once was. The same war that left ash in its wake as the old Kingdom of Lorundio was left to succumb to darkness as the court watched from beyond. That war had murdered his great grandfather, King Aleorien the third, forcing his firstborn, Queen Rivernia, to claim the crown that later passed onto Kylen's father.

When armies raided through the kingdom in the first war, the dead of the cursed rose from their graves with swords in hand, ready to unknowingly take down whatever crossed their paths. And after that, when the owners returned, the king had chopped off their heads and sent their souls burning.

The crow with beady yellow eyes stared at Kylen like it wanted him to understand something beyond comprehension. He waited silently as the wind threatened both of them to falter in their movements, but nothing ever came. Nothing ever happened. Kylen shook his head and turned back to the fractured structure, hearing in the back of his mind as the bird flew away and into the eye of the storm.

Pesky old creature.

Atticus had sat against one of the many old, poster-covered walls, his hands hovering around the small candle that burned with a pang of hunger so intense. He didn't lift his eyes as Kylen sat next to him; he didn't even look to notice Kylen as he fiddled with the buttons of his white shirt. A small habit he had developed from his anxiety.

Filtering through the air now was a barrier that Sayah had taught Atticus how to make years ago. During one of her many lessons in the old castle where she would spend hours at a time teaching them different ways to defend their honour. Kylen loathed how the child that he was back then didn't listen... didn't pay any notice as he figured that *he would be dead soon enough, so what was the point?*

Kylen had been merely too fixated on the reoccurring question of when Sayah would let him travel out on the seas next; or when the next fighting and training lessons were.

Of course, Kylen ended up having to have special one-on-one lessons with the siren, as he had problems that they did not. But he had enjoyed those lessons immensely, and it was in the midst of the mornings when he found himself remembering those times. Kylen had always had a disadvantage that the others were blindsided to, but Sayah had always been so patient with him, so kind. While he could boastfully say that he was gloriously marvellous at fighting nowadays—*he knew that that wasn't always the way*. Kylen used to be unable to summon a simple blade, except no matter how many long days it had taken, Sayah had sat by his side through it all. *Even the darkest of nights.*

Even while Khatri was older than Kylen, he still saw him as an older brother since he was always there to joke around with him and always guide him into making the right choices. He was someone who was *always* there for him—always willing to understand—until now, as it seemed. Khatri used to join in on the lessons Kylen spent loathing, offering the young boy a little bit of entertainment as Sayah strained for him to listen... although he knew that she enjoyed watching the two of them get along. It helped fuel the idea of a family that she had craved so profoundly.

That time felt like a mere fragment of his cursed dreams. One, he would be willing to bleed all of his now healed blood to live again.

Atticus kept his callous stare fixated on the candle, watching how the flickering fire reflected patterns upon patterns across the chipped wooden floorboards Kylen didn't trust one bit. He heard the wind outside—the way it mourned for the depths of Kylen's soul that was still being tortured by the curse that no longer resided within him. He didn't trust anything.

Anything or anyone.

"I didn't know what to do," Kylen admitted in a low tone as he moved his gaze back towards the candle. Perhaps if it was to explode into large flames, then he would finally be able to think again. "I don't know how to live after Sayah—and Althea—and all." He felt Atticus' attention slowly move towards him, and yet he ignored it. He forced himself to ignore it. If only he could get him to understand, *that was all he really needed*. "It felt like everything I had ever known and believed in was all crumbling down and just... leaving me to stand there and watch. First, it was Althea, and while I didn't think I could possibly live without her presence, I was trying to survive. Sayah was one of the reasons for that; she was the one who watched over me as I finally slept, the one who *h*-held me as I finally broke over everything that had happened..." Kylen allowed his words to flow through the air, his eyes darkening as he closed them. Forcing the darkness that begged to corrupt everything good about him into oblivion. "Then I walked into her chambers— going to finally ask if she could come with me to visit the memorial our people had made. Yet I found death and only death there. And what seemed to be the worst part of it all was that I sensed *her* magick there, and I knew Zaire did straight away too—I could see it on their face." Kylen turned his gaze towards Atticus; his eyes were bloodthirsty for the force behind this evil. "I could practically feel Althea kill Sayah, and that left me with questions that I wanted nothing more than to *murder*." He shook his head, a withering laugh escaping from his lips as he spoke, "I didn't know what to do then, and I don't know what to do now. It seems as if life truly wants to leave me breathless because I feel —I feel as if I have just been released from the cruelty of time."

Atticus hummed a sound that Kylen could not figure out. Whether it was one of mockery or not: Kylen still leant into it, scrambling for any touch of the old times. "That's how I felt when I came back," he replied, the rest of his words going unspoken… *'when I came back from death itself'*. "I didn't know what to do, and yet… Kylen, I am still *here* trying."

Kylen turned his gaze away, sensing the way Atticus was silently pleading for the conversation to change no matter how much they both needed it. "Do you think, Althea—*if it truly is Althea,* that she would bring Sayah back from the other side as she did with you?"

Atticus shrugged, and Kylen knew that it was an impossible question to answer. "I think we'll have to learn whether she was the one to murder her or not first." Kylen didn't want to know the answer to that dreadful question. He didn't want to know about any of that. "I just want you to realise something, Kye. You aren't the only one in this war. You never have been, and you most definitely are not now," Atticus spoke, and his tone was so different to the one before, almost as if he wanted to make up for all the scarred daggers he'd thrown his way. "I want you to talk to me, and I want to know what you are planning—"

"*Do you believe that I saw her?*" Kylen interrupted him, an urgency to his words that had even the lost Gods cackling down at him.

Something changed in Atticus' eyes, but nonetheless, he still said, "Yes."

It was a lie.

His brother had never been good at lying.

But Kylen was tired.

He was exhausted, and there seemed to be no worth in fighting anymore. He cleared his throat in response, nodding his head subtly as he moved his eyes back onto the candle that had gone blue. In response to the pleas he had sent him just seconds ago, Kylen whispered, "Okay."

NINE
ALTHEA

Her mind still felt to hold many loose screws, and her bones still felt to be a little too withered for any of her liking. With every breath she inhaled, she could physically feel the cruel and merciless emotions gliding towards the lungs that were incapable of going back to what they had once been. She could feel the spirits trying to reach her; their presence was like a drug to her mind. Every time they got too close, she felt herself doing possibly everything in her power to force them back.

Althea Evangeline, the girl who was deemed dead by the world and was now truly lingering in the actual unimaginable afterlife, watched the *family* before her with sceptical eyes, noting how their bodies slithered around the room as if they were alive and this was any ordinary day for them—when really *it was not any ordinary day*, and they were all dead.

Because really everyone who ever potentially cared for Althea was dead. Dead. Dead. Dead. Her mind ever so mockingly noted with a tease, but Althea didn't react to it in the slightest. She never reacted to it. If anything, she had grown rather talented at avoiding the obvious. Rather awfully skilled at ignoring the palpable.

Elara, the girl who had been the one to save her, stood tall by her father's side. She held the same identical wisdom and adventure in her eyes as a boy she'd once known held. It was a gleam, a glimmer, one that caught in her iris' when she got something right or purposely wrong; h*ow Althea craved that happiness. That freedom. How was it that they were alright? Used to the idea that their bodies were no more...* Willix had one hand resting on Elara's shoulder, a gesture so familiar to Althea as it reminded her of a time she had always unknowingly cradled within her chest.

When she was young and *mindless,* if Althea recalled correctly, there was once a time when her father had treated her in the same delicate manner. *With genuine kindness that didn't strive to bruise her flesh.*

But nevertheless, that was a lifetime ago, and now Althea couldn't strip her eyes away from the lively child that was laughing with a shimmer in her eyes.

Elara had long, thick, brown hair that complimented her dark green eyes. Her skin tone leant more towards Willix's than Marilla's, as while she still had a rather dark olive complexion, her skin was slightly paler than her brother Huntio's. "Oh, I was right! I was right!" Elara mused with a clap of her hands, and her widened young *yet aged* eyes appeared to be looking towards the cluttered, messy table that was covered from one end to the other in random pieces of paper and scattered leather maps.

How did they have either? How did anything exist in the afterlife? It was beyond Althea's knowledge when it came to anything in regard to death. It was a topic that always spooked her. *Ask, ask, ask away,* her soul was evidently pushing, but considering she yearned to taste the sun on her tongue once again, she knew that it was better not to ask but rather blend into the darkness.

Kylen would have loved being here; it was obvious. While he wasn't one to jump onto the topic of his dead family, Althea was aware that he missed them dearly... and seeing this... would have healed that eternal ache in his soul.

"No—I don't think that's it. Try the other way," Willix muttered, and Elara nodded as she tried doing whatever it was that the two of them were working on. Elara replied to whatever it was that her father said as they moved in sync; however, Althea noticed how nearly everything they did was near identical. *Their mannerisms and all.* It took away from the fact completely that she was literally in the afterlife, watching dead people do real things.

Althea moved her eyes to Marilla next, watching as she leaned against a chest of drawers, sipping at her lavender tea. Could Althea even refer to it as tea? Wasn't it all just really a manipulation and lie *of reality?*

Huntio stood in the doorway silently, picking at his skin as he observed all who stood before and near him. Every now and then, he joined in the conversation, saying something that earned everyone's attention every single time.

The Noxwell family were different to what she had grown up knowing, Althea realised with a twist of her heart. They never made anyone feel as if their voice wasn't heard, no matter how random it was they had to say. *It was always worth it.*

How amusing it was that she had been here for ten minutes, and already she could see the difference between their home and hers. In another life, one where she grew up with a true mother and father, maybe she wouldn't be *'dead'* right now. Perhaps she would be a happy little girl in an overgrown cottage with stained windows, piles of books, cats, and a reflection that was glad to see her.

Not to mention that this family was trying to help *her* reach her so-called Realm. A place so far from her reach and yet shimmering at the end of her fingertips. She wouldn't deny the fact that she could feel the sensations that the curse was sending her —she could feel it caressing her fingertips, murmuring against her spine.

So far, what Elara and Willix had discussed (quite quickly, if she may add) was that they needed to channel the outer world on the anniversary that Althea got her *Markings*. And because time supposedly worked a little different here, *as Marilla had quipped on Althea's behalf,* that would be in a little under *eleven* days.

So really, they had eleven days to figure out what to do, how to do it, and what the consequences would be. Leaving Althea to feel as if she had chains as heavy and daunting as the four lost Gods draped over every inch of her flesh... *Holding her down as tens of thousands of blades pierced through the delusional soil beneath her.*

If Althea had learnt anything from the life forced into the oblivion of her soul, it was that there were always consequences. Always. Which meant that she had to be careful—which wasn't exactly Althea's speciality, unfortunately. She excelled in doing anything that wasn't careful; if anything, it meant that it was definitely something she had to keep in mind as she gathered closer to the end of the eleven days.

That seemed like a dream that was unreachable.

Like a breath of fresh air—the type you only long for when you have been deprived of it for so long.

Althea heaved a breath, but the air here (whatever it was) was nothing like the air she had dreamt of. It was heavier, cloudier—as if she was physically standing in the centre of a cloud. Beckoning the missing air to cleanse her lungs. Althea looked from one face to the next, observing their every little movement...

Except that was awfully short-lived, as within moments, her eyes were captured by the doorway, feeling how the room before her crackled with a darkness that had her stumbling back.

~Althea, Althea, Althea, ALTHEA~ The curse cried, and

Althea was quick to dig her nails into her sides. She needed everything to silence. She needed to hear herself think. She needed to have the single second to just simply breathe. *We just want to play—play, play, play—we won't hurt you; we would never hurt you. We can bring you peace... an eternal, comfortable peace.*

She didn't think the Noxwell's could hear the foul-sounding screeches. She didn't think that they could hear what had such forced control over her mind. But then Huntio squirmed to his mother's side, a panicked fear seeping over his features as he looked through the air for the source of such venom. His face rippled with agony, tears pricking the corners of his eyes. "Mother—"

Willix beckoned Althea forward without a single word. His arms opened for hers as if her touch didn't frighten him. Did he truly think that he could possibly protect her from all that she feared? It was a nice thought, a humorous one. But it was also so unlikely.

ALTHEA, ALTHEA, ALTHEA, ALTHEA, YOU CAN RUN, BUT YOU CANNOT HIDE. WE WILL FIND YOU LIKE WE FOUND YOUR MOTHER... YOUR FATHER... The voices began to screech again, this time their words sending Althea's hands rising to her ears. *Watch your back, little-little thing; we know of every bone in your body—we control every bone in your body. Try anything—and we mean anything—and they will all snap. SNAP! SNAP! SNAP!*

Good thing Althea was never afraid to get herself bloody.

She lifted her eyes off the frozen floor gradually, removing her hands from her ears. Willix slowly exhaled as he moved his extended hands away from her. Giving her the space she both longed for and loathed. "It's okay; we are safe," Marilla uttered quietly, and Althea looked towards the family that was planning something so meaningful to help her... yet to her utter dismay, she found all of their eyes on *her.* Staring through hers as if they were waiting for her to crack, for her to show the true pain she felt riveting in her blood.

She pleaded for them to look away. To not look at her the way Kylen, Sayah, Atticus... et cetera all looked at her. She couldn't bear it.

It wasn't that Althea wasn't grateful for what they were doing. For how Marilla was squeezing her shoulder gently in reassurance as she passed. For how Willix smiled at her with a nod of his head as if this wasn't all her fault—she was grateful... if anything, she was *beyond* grateful.

But her heart had been ripped out so long ago.

So really... her soul had simply been lost to the craft of brutality.

Which meant that she didn't know how to act.

How to *react*.

The memories of everything and anything were still haunting her, running down her spine and across her fingertips like a mouse running from its predator. Her memories were following her every step, curling around them as she approached the table with a large diagram that caught her eyes instantly. Already she was acting like the spirit's words held no effect on her, acting like she didn't care but was instead used to this entertaining game.

When really, they had more of an effect on her than anything. But now her mind reminded her of a face she wanted to look to, a face that was a lighthouse to guide her home on even the stormiest days.

It was Kylen's face, Kylen's laugh, that called to her.

Except that laugh was short-lived as another replaced it, and her father's face, her father's laugh appeared before her. *They were all out for her.*

"Stop it," Althea hissed to herself, forcing the cruel thoughts from her overbearing mind to for once listen to her. She looked to the map with a chilling sigh, doing all that was in her physical power to try and blink away the throbbing agony that held her by the throat. *Just look at the map.* There were many lines and colours on the papers before her, many drawings that made little to no sense to Althea. Confusion washed against the bridge of her nose as she observed all of the many realities Willix had drawn onto one of the specific larger papers that had captured her eye—*how many worlds were they wanting her to jump through? Sure, in some sense, she was a God, but she hadn't been a God for very long now… and she didn't consider herself very good at it since she rather disliked the idea entirely… why waste energy on trying to perfect something so ridiculous when for so long it was deemed as a hatred in her mind?*

Althea swallowed the nonsense away, feeling the intensity of the eyes that were burning into the side of her head as if she was the one to personally slaughter every soul in this room. *Did they blame me?* She partially blamed herself, so she wouldn't blame them if they did. She was a curse holder—*even if she didn't exactly hold ownership of the curse anymore.* Her magick had still murdered families and filled mass graves as if there weren't enough corpses rotting beneath the surface.

As if there was some type of magnetic force shared between the biological Noxwell brothers, Althea looked to the young boy, who was posed with a quizzical look on the creased edges of his eyes

He looked so similar to Kylen that it was honestly bewildering and startling both simultaneously. "May I ask you a question?" Huntio abruptly whispered like he didn't want the spirits beyond to hear. Althea narrowed her eyes on him as she nodded, ignoring how her cheeks burned due to the sudden silence centring around her. She didn't like this attention and the way each dagger of the eye sliced her burning flesh. It reminded her of all those long hours spent in the old dining hall, staring down at her food because Althea knew that if she was to look up, she would find her father's grotesque gaze.

"Go ahead," Althea replied *easily*, and her voice was both awfully soft and tragically frail. Hopefully, they couldn't see through her as her father had once been able to.

Smiling at the fact that she hadn't denied his offer, Huntio nodded. "Is it true that you are a God?"

There were little questions in the world that Althea didn't know the answer to—but this, *to her alarm,* was one of them. Althea parted her lips as she went to reply, except it was then that she genuinely realised that she didn't know what she could possibly say.

Was she a God? That wasn't a question she had ever been asked before. Her bloodline and experiences/trauma argue yes. But her abilities and stamina argue no. Shouldn't a God want to be a God? The God's her father had taught her about were all said to be rather... *"full of themselves"* as he had described them... and while Althea *wasn't* full of herself... she instead merely knew of her greatness... *that didn't involve her Godly new abilities.* Plus, a God shouldn't be someone captive within their own body. They shouldn't be drowning within their own mind.

And yet here she was, staring into the eyes of a child who had been killed by *her* very curse, and she felt to be anything but a God. Gods were meant to be generous people. She'd always in her heart believed that the Gods were meant to save people from death; they were meant to lead the lost children into the afterlife with care and hold their hands as they crossed the white bridge.

Except, the Gods the world had grown to know were awfully cruel. They denied their presence. Watching from afar as children screamed over their mothers' corpses, clinging to their fathers' arms while they tried to ignore the fact that they were covered in their mother's blood. The Gods were mean, and they deserved to die...

So perhaps she was one, after all.

Althea cleared the bitterness of her memories away as she

shrugged her shoulders lightly. Digging her nails into the flesh of her hands, she forced a laugh of uncertainty from her tongue. Causing tiny little crescent moons left to scar her heavy skin once again, although the question still remained, was the skin even real? "Something of the sort," she eventually answered.

Huntio nodded almost instantly, with his satisfaction *clear as day*. He stretched out his arms before him, and for whatever apparent reason, that seemed to be *enough* of a weak answer for him. "That's cool; I've always loved learning about the Gods, even if you are *something of the sort* of them," Huntio quipped with immense amusement. He picked up the book to his right, and his eyes glistened as he grinned at her.

A sight so sweet.

A sight so lost.

Althea didn't mean to, *Hel, she wasn't even aware that she still had this ability*, but slyly, as she dipped her head away, a smile edged against her own lips. It was strange for someone to speak of the Gods in such a gentle manner. In a way that didn't make her feel cruel for holding such abilities. Sure, Sayah, Zaire, and Kylen all spoke in a way that was still positive and motivating; but she meant the overall general public. Those in Aeonia loathed the Gods; they loathed them for abandoning their people in a time of need... even Althea *had* loathed them.

A single echo of a sweetened laugh had Althea's attention magnetically dragged towards Marilla, who watched from afar as the two of them spoke. Althea didn't have to be a God to know that she was remembering a time that felt to be so long ago. A time of dreams. A time when children could still see their hope dancing across their fingertips.

Marilla smiled, taking a deep breath before the words slowly pieced themselves together. "Hunt has always been a very religious child. He and Willix used to go down to the temples every Sunday morning to lay an offering out for the Gods. I'm not so religious myself—which does, in fact, feel quite awfully strange admitting to a God right now." She laughed. "But it was a sweet tradition of Elara and mine to bake in the wonderful kitchens as we awaited their return. The high ceilings, the patterned wallpaper... oh, I still remember that scent of the sweet treats when we took them out of the oven. –Do tell me that the kitchens are still the same; they were always my favourite part of the castle, even if Willix was the one to use them the most. I liked sitting on the bench, or on the floor... or the chairs; watching and speaking to him as he created the most wonderful meals..." There was a bittersweet reminiscence waltzing across Marilla's mind, a memory that had Willix squeezing her shoulders before pressing a kiss to her cheek, a look in his eyes that Althea couldn't help but long to experience one day. "Oh, those times were wonderful, weren't they?"

As much as Althea would love to spend her mindless time telling Marilla of all the beautiful rooms she'd found herself wandering through back in Lorundio, Althea's attention was captivated elsewhere.

"*Yes, they are quite beautiful*. Much better than the kitchens I ever knew. But what do you mean... by *temples*?" Althea questioned. She had never known of any temples. Especially in Lorundio—they were never mentioned in any of the books, and she definitely did not see anything of what Huntio supposably adored so gleefully. Althea would've known of any temples... surely.

"Yep, temples," Marilla replied with a pop of her lips. It was strange, hypnotising; she had replied in a tone that didn't make Althea feel ashamed for never knowing about such things. She sat down the papers and mug she was holding on Willix's behalf, and Althea noticed how the mug had a small, elusive handprint on the front of it, and underneath the golden hand were the initials, '*K.N*'.

Kylen Noxwell. *Did he even have an idea of how dearly missed he was by his family?* Althea wanted to choke on a sob.

The small, bruised child that she once knew would've done anything at all for parents like these. A family like this.

"We have a few of them across the Realms of Lorundio, but they are more hidden away—we even have one at the bottom of the ocean," Marilla continued. Althea knew from the way her face had tensed that she knew what Althea had caught onto. "There used to be a couple in Aeonia, if I recall correctly. Except *knowing* your father, he probably had them blown up long ago— which is presumably why you don't know about them."

She had to have misheard Marilla just then—

"You *know* my father?" Althea barked with widening, astonished eyes.

This time Willix was the one to answer her as he leaned back against the wooden table with enchanted markings engraved into the dark oak wood. It was circular shaped with what looked to be markings of the moon cycle and several more elements engraved into the surface of it. But then again, even on the singular middle leg of the table, the wood had to have been crafted with a prestigious eye. One that belonged to the bewitching eyes of the Gods —because no man, no woman, no mortal or immortal would have been able to craft something that astonishing.

"Althea, dear, your father and us two used to be great friends. There wasn't anything that we wouldn't do together. We even, *that is if I recall correctly*," Willix said as he turned his eyes to Marilla, who was already looking at him, "used to claim the world as our own." His words had been captured by a tone of mourning, Althea realised as she crossed her arms, and he let out a horrible ache in his lungs that he tried to disguise with a trembling laugh. Willix coughed once, and his eyes were brought back down to the paperwork before him, pretending to look fascinated at the papers he had already gone through multiple times. "Your mother too. We were all quite the friends; I'll have you know. The greatest."

The greatest friends.

Why hadn't Althea known any of this?

Was that why the Gods had supposedly told Kylen to marry her? Because it was really Althea's mother trying to reunite the next generation of a so-called 'great friendship'?

Did Kylen know? —No. She didn't want to think about him. She didn't need to think about him. He had hurt her again, she mustn't forget. Even after she had been prepared to follow him into death—he had shaken hands with her father. *Kylen had made a bargain of some type with your father. With the man who abused you both physically and mentally—you do not need to think of him right now.*

"You were friends with both of my parents?" Althea questioned, but before she could ask anything more or even react in any way, Marilla shared a glance with her husband and began to usher her children away and out of the room. Althea listened to them both groan as they turned to her with eyes that asked, 'are you serious?'.

Although a part of Althea knew that Marilla wanted to hold onto the idea of them as sweet children, to not corrupt their already dead souls despite all that they have been through and *suffered*.

With curious eyes to the childlike nature of two souls that were no longer mentally children, Althea watched as Marilla, at last, ushered her children out of the room and into another stone room of the outlandish house that they were currently hiding from the curse in.

Just before, when they'd approached the miraculous waterfall, Althea had watched with such wide eyes as Marilla had the water physically part for them. From a single touch, the water had split into two. It opened as if it was a door, welcoming them personally to a place that would *try* to protect them against all the evil that lingered in the children's dreams—*as Willix so kindly noted on Althea's behalf with a wink*. He looked overly ecstatic to be able to tell someone of all he knows while knowing that they don't know a thing—*about anything*. The girl with white hair felt as if she had forgotten all that she had ever known.

Ever learnt.

Her mind was a wondrous pit. An empty land that had long ago been burdened by the Gods entertainment—*that* she hadn't forgotten.

"Friends is an understatement; we were as close as anything," Marilla sighed with disappointment as the door began to shut behind her children. Right as the door was a second away from fully closing, Althea watched as Elara sent her a 'thumbs up' for *luck*, presumably.

The child thought that she needed luck when there was once a time when the Princess of Aeonia never needed luck; she was the only luck she ever needed.

Except now, she felt as if she needed anything she could possibly clasp her wilted fingers around without fearing that it may run loose. "I apologise for those two; they don't like when we keep things from their prying ears—but there are just some things out there that aren't for the ears of children, you must understand, don't you? I expect that when—*if you have children, you most definitely do not have to if you don't want to, it is completely your choice*—but say you do, I expect that you would want to keep all harm, all pain, all agony from their innocent ears."

Althea shifted uncomfortably in her own feet as the strange idea caressed her mind. She couldn't possibly imagine herself as a mother; if anything, she would be a horrible one. How was a girl who was raised with a lack of any kind of parenting meant to know how to parent?

She knew the classic saying, *the abused becomes the abuser.* It was something that was carved into the hearts of those that were left forcibly vulnerable for a second too long. The saying made it sound that all those who'd had a life similar to Althea's were left to play those merciless roles of the villain in the next chapter of their lives. However, it was ignorant, arrogant, and not true in any which way. Sure, some may fall victim to the vicious world, but that saying shouldn't define every soul that was wronged; every soul that fought to survive while not knowing what they would find when they made it to the surface.

If Althea were ever to have children, she would not be her father.

She would not yell at them for spilling their water.

She would not drag them from under their beds while trying to escape the tests.

She would not curse their existence entirely.

Althea would be the parent she'd always needed, the parent she sought in her dreams.

Perhaps if she were ever given the strange opportunity to raise a soul, she would prove the problematic words wrong. She was awfully petty, so why not be especially petty when it comes to idiotic myths that mortals make up in fits of rage?

Yet, she wouldn't deny the fact that the question was one that Althea knew she could be dwelling on for days if she gave it the dreadful time—but she also knew that it was best to ignore such cruel thoughts, or else she would be led into the conflict of the past; where Althea would be left to remember the girl who wanted to adopt as many children as she possibly could. The girl who wanted to be different to all the brutality she ever knew. It was humorous, although, as her father even knew of these 'dreams' of hers, and he'd always been the one person to believe that she would be a wonderful mother.

Even if he was the reason behind these doubts.

Willix cleared his throat uncomfortably, shifting the papers in his hands before slowly casting his eyes towards Marilla. He lifted his chin into the air as the cold breeze caressed his withered skin, urging the words to leave his tongue. "My love, they are not children anymore," he acknowledged hesitantly.

And they weren't.

Because if they were alive and in bodies capable of aging, both Elara and Huntio would most definitely not be children anymore. Althea wasn't aware of their ages, but she knew enough about the spell-binding abilities of time to know that it would not deliver them justice.

Whether Marilla had heard Willix's comment was oblivious to Althea, as Marilla didn't utter a single word in response or react. She simply allowed time to take its toll, blinking away her silenced agony.

Willix squirmed in his broad shoulders as an eerie silence stretched through the deceptive air. However, Marilla continued to stare at the frozen hands she had perched neatly over the purple fabric of her stomach. Did she remember the time when her children were one and all alive? Was she reminiscing on the nights when she would lean over Kylen's childhood bed while singing her lullabies in her mother's tongue as she awaited the birth of the twins? Althea didn't know how or why these ideas were grazing her mind, but they were warm as she welcomed them; they were kind to her aching skin.

Althea wanted to feel pity for this woman; she wanted to feel sorry for her, except Althea felt detached from the emotions that stirred within her soul.

She felt completely and utterly emotionless.

"What happened between my parents and the two of you?" Althea questioned after another second of insufferable silence; she couldn't take it anymore, not when it reminded her so much of a time she had only just escaped from. Not to mention that it was a question that she both wanted to know the answer to and yet was terrified beyond measure to even acknowledge in the slightest. "—If you don't mind me asking, of course."

Althea Evangeline does not ask for permission, her mind coldly noted. But all Althea could inevitably do was ignore.

Ignore. Ignore. Ignore. Just as she ignored the curses clammy hands every day and every night.

Willix shared a glance with his wife before reaching a hand up to the back of his neck, rubbing it slowly as if the words were physically making him uncomfortable. "Your father murdered your mother, *our friend…* that's what happened. An unkind memory, if anything."

He was so abrupt with it that Althea no longer found the will to control how distraught her features drastically turned. Instead, she merely began to hold her breath, digging her nails into her palms before nodding twice.

"Right," Althea whispered, averting her eyes, releasing the breath that had her lungs suffocating. She didn't want to relive those memories. The treacherous time periods that came to her mind every time that ordeal was mentioned in the slightest, "That makes sense… *At least your morals are in check,*" Althea said, and as her voice began to fail her, she uttered the last few words in the hope that they would dance off her lips.

Despite all the months she had been so graciously gifted with wandering through the infinite, Althea had never truly accepted the fate that had found and slaughtered her mother in her very presence. It wasn't one that made sense to her—if anything, it left her with more questions than she began with. All these long years, Althea had preferred to blame her mother for *choosing* to leave her—she found it easier to blame her for abandoning her to the man who abused his power as if he was gambling his very life away.

Except now… now that she, unfortunately, knew all that she'd done and that she had chosen for whatever reason to leave her behind… it left her with conflicting emotions. Sensations that had her confused about how to go on with that knowledge.

Studying the table before her, Althea's eyes beckoned every little thought that had been missing from her heart for so long to leave her be once again. It had been so much easier to breathe when her heart had been free of that cage. It had been so much easier to think when her mind wasn't already clouded. *Except her soul wasn't listening to her.* It was doing anything but fulfilling her darkest wishes. Althea tucked her curled white hair behind her ears, placing both of her hands onto the table before her as she tried to do possibly anything in her grasp to distract herself from the overwhelming thoughts that had her swallowing the quivering judgements.

Her father had been a murderer.

Her father had been the one to murder her mother.

She knew this—she did. *So why did it feel so much more painful every time her mind was to make her understand the lengths of it?*

It just seemed so bewildering to understand that she had been living with a murderer for so long. That the man who used to check for monsters in her wardrobe and under her bed, had turned out to be the very monster she feared. Had he known that Althea would be the one to come across *her* cut-up body? Had he known that Althea would slip in her mother's blood and find her eyes connecting with the ones that were forever frozen in the delicacy of time?

How was she honestly surprised or hurt when he had come to murder her at last?

Althea should've known better. She knew not to be so ignorant.

Marilla must've noticed her absence of mind as she stepped forward before saying, "Althea." The word wasn't too loud nor too quiet, yet it still had Althea's hands jolting on the table before her. She looked up at once, meeting with a face that had a hint of concern laced across it. Althea shook her head, dismissing her thoughts entirely as she focussed on the task of looking at the Queen with a smile that *didn't falter*. Her smile was one that an assassin who was marvellous at her job sent her prisoner seconds before decapitating the head off *his* shoulders.

"What?"

"Are you okay?"

Those three words inevitably had to be the three words she loathed most. They had to be the ones that had her begging for a way out of this miserable excuse of a life. Althea smiled again— and again, her lie of a smile didn't meet her eyes that had been murdered so long ago. "I'm fine," she mumbled, although all three of the other souls seemed to already silently know that it was a *lie*. She was a lie.

As if life didn't feel as if Althea had bled enough, it dawned on her then that she had basically died for nothing—*even if she hadn't physically died*—she had died in some sense, and what was a heart without a soul? Her death had been for absolutely *nothing*. Her father was still alive. He was still breathing and living the life he wanted to live while Althea was suffocating in the Forgotten Realms. The curse was still alive. Controlling her skin whilst wiping out the souls she had sacrificed herself to protect.

Kylen was still alive, too—

But again, she didn't necessarily want him dead anymore— nor did she want to think about *him*. She didn't need to think about him. It caused her heart an agony that should've been sewed shut long ago.

For so long, his death had been one breath away. In the sense that she was going to kill him and, in another sense, where he was already dying. But had she known that? No. Did it still dangle a noose before her eyes? Yes. It felt like one ridiculously cruel game written by the Gods for them to wither in. —The same Gods that decided to have a daughter who they didn't care in the slightest for. But she was always a daughter who wanted to murder and punish them all for creating such a bloody sin; a daughter who wanted to watch their souls bleed and their minds scream as she watched from afar; a daughter who just wanted to live.

It didn't make sense to Althea why her mother had willingly walked to her deathbed. Tiptoeing towards it as if there wasn't a child waiting for her mother to come read her favourite book to her, as they did *every other night*. Sure, she had said goodbye to Althea in some impeccably cruel sense—even if the three-year-old she had left didn't remember it. *She had still said something of a goodbye*.

The tension before her was a crucible, and Althea looked between the eyes studying her, shrugging her shoulders once again before crossing her arms across her quickly beating chest. "I'm fine," she repeated in a sterner voice, despite the over-whelming number of questions staring through her mind... all of which were aiming for the throat she blindly picked at with her fingers, causing red blotchy spots to appear since she was still technically alive in the strangest of senses.

Willix nodded cautiously. It was as if he was afraid of her fire as he slowly reached forward, picking up the small notebook that had his initials engraved into the brown of it. "Very well," he hummed in an attempt to force the agony away. "Why don't we rest for the remainder of the 'day', and when it gets bright out, we can test what abilities you can still access?" The smile on his face wasn't transparent. For what felt like the first time ever, Althea couldn't *exactly* dictate whether he was being smart with her or genuinely... kind towards her.

She nodded for what felt like the hundredth time since she had broken free of that stale prison, and as she did so, she caught the unbearable sight of her masked smile faltering through the reflection of the cracked mirror on the wall to the left of her. "Sure. That sounds good." *But did it sound good?* No. The days and nights, the light and dark... none of it made any sense to her. Everyone here was dead, was it not? How was time even able to move? How was her magick accessible? It was honestly beyond Althea's understanding—all of it.

And that, in *itself*, said a lot.

Althea fidgeted with the skin around her fingers. A nervous habit her father used to growl at her for whenever he noticed that her fingers were bleeding. Yet it was a strange feeling that overcame her as she felt the skin rip under her very *own* touch.

While she knew that she was currently not in her physical body, everything she did seemed so… real, so truthful. The only thing that had her truly understanding that she was nothing more than just a soul, was that the heartbeat she could feel stretching through the distant air was her own, *but despite that,* it was not in her control. And it was not the heart that she now bore in the afterlife.

The heartbeat that had been captured by the curse.

The curse she failed to slaughter.

Althea tensed her jaw as she looked down with a heave of her lungs. The smallest part of her wished that Sayah was here to guide her through whatever this was—*but that was if she was able to be here and keep the life she so rightfully deserved to live.* It hurt Althea's heart to think about all the ways in which Sayah had been wronged. It hurt her to think that she had acted as if Althea was her friend when she most definitely was a bitch to her—*but there was just something about the siren's delicate memory that she wished Sayah would be the one to lead her into the eternal abyss.*

To welcome her home.

But no, she *knew* better, and despite never admitting it, Althea was beyond grateful that Sayah wasn't in the afterlife alongside her. She didn't think she could deal with losing her too, not after she had been so kind to her, so sweet. Her touch, her hold, her love had been all she had dreamt of growing up, and then, at last, she was gifted it.

The platonic love that is said to heal the soul.

Althea sceptically glanced at Willix as he cleared his throat for the hundredth time in the last second. How was Marilla not growing mad at that irritating sound? His face had many marks on it, and from what she could see, his body looked to have many freckles, also. Willix offered her a small grin, and Althea nodded in exchange as she averted her eyes once again.

This time, however, as she moved the tip of her nose through the air before her, Althea swore that she could feel the harmony of Sayah's words wrap around her bony shoulders, a tingle to them that had her eyes moving to the doorway that remained shut. *You've got this, sweet girl. Don't falter on my existence; worry about reclaiming yours.*

What would happen if she was to open that door and find the siren standing on the other side? She would be happy, yes. But Althea would also be horribly pained. She didn't think she would be able to go on, knowing that the siren was suffering after everything.

Yet, what made her different to the Noxwells? They deserved to live, too, did they not?

"Glorious!" Willix praised with a clap of his hands. His voice alone made Althea jump, although she believed that she played it off quite well by turning towards the many sheets of paper. "If you don't mind following me, then I will show you to the room you can stay in, *dear child*," he announced as he stalked over to the very door that unsettled Althea. She watched carefully as he opened it, watching as his hand curled around the handle, anticipating something horrible to jump out at them and slaughter their souls.

However, she released a subtle sigh as nothing, but withered air stood tall on the other side of it. Not a sight of the siren her heart both longed and yearned for.

Marilla muttered something under her breath, but it was inaudible. She looked to be still curiously watching her husband, except that didn't last very long as she was quick to turn away and disappear through one of the other many doorways. This still felt like a mysterious, horrible dream, one that Althea was trapped in. How long would it take for her to be able to breathe

the cold air once again? How long would it be until she could feel the rain caress her fingertips?

Althea closed her eyes as she forced a quick breath into her lungs before any new overwhelming idea swarmed her mind. She needed to instead push herself to focus on silently following the tolerable male to wherever it was that he looked quite eager to guide her towards.

This would be okay. It would be fun…

But why did it feel as if she was tiptoeing to her death? Waltzing towards the blade that was already beginning to fall?

TEN
KYLEN

Atticus' easy breaths scattered across the dust-covered floorboards as Kylen mesmerizingly watched with an exhaust lining his own narrowed features. He was going to do this—he was actually going to do this. *Think with your head, Kylen,* ignore your rotting heart... except that frail old *heart* of his seemed to have so much more of a cursed hold over him as a whole.

He was purely a mindless puppet. One ready to claim the delicacy of his rival's blood.

Atticus exhaled slowly as he turned to his right. This sleep of his had been rather restless, full of monsters crawling down the corners of his dreams. His breaths were heavy, Kylen observed; it stirred an unwelcoming feeling in the depths of his stomach to watch his brother like this, to look at the man who seemed so vulnerable in the eye of war when really, he was anything but *vulnerable.* Atticus probably assumed Kylen was the vulnerable one, the weak one; after all, he practically called him what everyone else had been for years now. *Insane.* Atticus stirred again, his breaths becoming heavier by the second as if he was too feeling the everlasting aching pain that filled the absence of his heart. He was asleep and safe, Kylen had to remember. *No harm could reach him here*—not with *Sayah's* barrier protecting him. She would always protect him, even in death, and that allowed Kylen to figure out what to do next without risking the boy's health.

It would be okay.

With one last fatal glimpse towards the boy he wanted— *against all*—nothing more than to *protect*, Kylen fled into the dead of the night silently. He needed to figure out what to do and how to act with the delusion of a *sane* mind. He needed to figure out where he could possibly go next, *with a sane mind.*

He knew he had made a promise to his brother; *Kylen was well aware that he had made a promise to his brother*—except he had this irresistible urge within him to prove that what Kylen had seen was true. That he wasn't losing his sanity as *every* soul in *every* one of the Realms before and under him was preaching so profoundly. *He wasn't insane.*

The streets were murky as Kylen crept through them, the sound of rain splattering against the cobblestone path he paced down sounding so familiar to the sound of blood hitting the cement walls every time he took his burdens out on the old King. It had only been around two hours or so since the two *brothers* had stumbled into the old theatre, which meant that it was another three until sunrise—*if the sun even still dared to shine in a mourning kingdom of darkness*. Kylen doubted that the sky would even change shades in the slightest when day crept up on them. This wasn't Lorundio anymore—Hel, nothing was anything anymore.

Althea's '*death*' had been sure to swipe the last of the eternal purity away from these Realms. *From the existence of all.* Everything remained in the time capsule of grief, remembering what the world had taken advantage of every chance they got.

Kylen was fearfully quiet, not daring to breathe unless he had to. He could see the bloodcurdling castle in the distance, and he saw the way the darkness curled around it as if it was claiming it as another one of their victims. It looked like a haze from the cruellest of his dreams, a blink of illusions as if he was dosed on the deadliest drugs known to mankind. The curse seemed to be truly flourishing here. That assured him of one thing or another... the curse remained—so, *did she?*

Did he want Althea to be alive? *Yes*, with everything in him, he did. Did he want her to be the one that had murdered Sayah? *No*, of course not. Not in any lifetime would he want that to be true.

However, with whatever was left in his clammy palms, he willed there to be some reason—*some factor*—some sort of explanation that he had not yet stumbled upon if that was to be in any way partially the truth.

Because Kylen refused to accept that she had been the one to kill Sayah.

Kylen refused to.

Althea had adored Sayah, had she not?

They had been friends. *Family even.*

Kylen's body and soul had been set on marching right into the palace and demanding the truth from whoever he may find, but something that was far more worrisome than the ghosts of the past crossed his features like a breath of all that he feared. Something so horrific that it had him flinching back in both shock and anxiety as mortals upon mortals began to slip and run past him with laughter waltzing through the air.

It was the middle of the night... why were people smiling ecstatically as they walked alongside each other, arm in arm, hand in hand? A herd of the Aeonian citizens passed him, a herd made up of oblivious morons who appeared to be making their way down the single brick road that led straight towards the palace *itself.* For a second, Kylen figured that he might've been hallucinating, but then one citizen ran right into him, and his doubts were short-lived. It wasn't that they were willingly walking towards such homicide that had Kylen frozen in his steps; it was that they all looked to be laughing and smiling. Holding onto their *posters* and *masks* as if they were on their way to a cheerful ball in a kingdom that was located in the breath-taking Sommsia Realms. Was someone throwing a party?

"What—" The word didn't get the chance to leave Kylen's bruised lips as an eery, ice-cold hand clasped onto his arm and tugged him forward into the horrific parade. Kylen's head whipped to the left, his eyes widening and his inexperienced magick awakening as a laugh beyond sanity echoed through the thunderous air. *"Get—"*

"Haven't you heard?" The stranger with a wispy brown beard asked with a great cackle. He turned to Kylen with astounded eyes, something deadly creeping within. He wore layered murky-coloured clothing, all of which were several sizes too big for him. His voice was high in octaves, a laugh rumbling through his chest still as he clapped his hands in glee before him. "The King has decided to throw a ball! And all are invited! Truly a new era, I tell you, a new time at last." Kylen didn't have time to register what the stranger was saying before the man disappeared into the semi-well-dressed crowd that Kylen reluctantly stood within. Such confusion laced over his features as he avoided each curdling body.

Someone was claiming to be the King…

And they were throwing a ball…

Was it Althea? Was she even good at throwing a ball?

Kylen certainly did not have a good feeling about this. In fact, he felt the opposite of optimistic as he twisted his way through the crowds, wielding himself as one of these ignorant *fools* while slowly hiding away from any prying eyes of the birds above.

There was no doubt about it that the old wall that stretched around the palace of Aeonia was beginning to fall after centuries of war. Still, as Kylen passed through the tall and rustic gates, it was clear just how drastically fast the wall, the castle, and all of Aeonia were beginning to collapse.

Now that the curse was supposedly 'gone' or redirected elsewhere (which was a lie, he believed), the wall had nothing supporting it, ultimately meaning that now the effects of time were finally bringing it down.

So perhaps Althea and the curse weren't within the Aeonian walls? Perhaps it was the King of the East... Was he truly going mad? Were these mere phantom hallucinations of the one thing that had made his blood heavy all these months?

Silently and very hesitantly, Kylen followed the crowd through the second pair of tall, black, wired gates, approaching the great golden castle without a murmur of a song. The castle was lit with several floating candles that breezed through the air, a rhythm echoing across the grounds that caused the stones and cockroaches to flee in dread as something as foul as death began to stretch its way through his nose. This scent was so *familiar*; it was filling the depths of the wounds in his soul that had been left bare from the curse what felt like lifetimes ago.

He didn't have a good feeling about this.

No.

But when did Kylen ever have a good feeling about anything?

The people of Aeonia were dressed in various colours and tones that were all rather muted, dull, and yet elegant in their own *twisted* ways. Was it the layered fake gold? Or the jewellery Kylen knew to be fake also? Their ballgowns and suits appeared to be from trillions of years before, back when nobody knew what true fashion was, *how Sayah and his father would growl at that.* Then again, Kylen couldn't really judge their appearances since he looked worse to wear himself. He was quite literally wearing a leather jacket and pants that were covered in *mud*. Well, at least he hoped it was mud. Kylen was quick to shed a look over his shoulders as he pulled out his sack full of gold, picking out a single astra that had his charming face stamped onto it. Kylen rolled his eyes before turning on his heel, offering it to the first man at his left in exchange for his luxurious *old* blazer.

An offer no man can deny.

An offer no man would dare to deny.

Kylen shrugged the new tatty blazer on, ignoring the stench of liquor that drowned his senses. With several steps, he began to ascend the steps that he remembered almost tripping up the day he had arrived in Aeonia for the very first time, back when he was *just a boy*. He still remembered that feeling that had rocked his stomach as if he was new to the ways of the sea. He had heard so much about the Princess who had never been seen... but to meet her gave him some purpose. Of course, everything had been quick to turn to shit since he did end up torturing them both.

However, now Kylen had to bite down on the insides of his cheeks in order to physically restrain himself from acting the way his heart begged him to. He wanted to scream. To laugh. To unleash the wrath he knew could burn the world if he so dared. Instead, he remained quiet, looking around as if he was a bloody tourist.

"Here goes nothing," he mumbled under his breath, and as he looked one last time towards the babbling crowd that was heading towards the same castle that held a blade to his heart, he prayed that he wasn't walking into a death trap.

Because then all these people would be too.

And while he did want to murder them all himself...

There were children.

Families.

Souls that hadn't wronged him, no matter that *Kylen still blamed them.*

It was quite comedic how the Gods always wrote for him to end up in situations like this one, but then again, perhaps it was his own unrighteous doing. Perhaps the Gods had given up on Kylen long ago, merely residing to watch as he got himself trapped beneath the surface as always. *Yet what was a dying man meant to do?* Sit home and wait for death to consume his withered bones like an old man watching the storm rain in? He wouldn't dare. He would sooner chop off his own head than do nothing.

"*William, come back here!* We must make ourselves look *wealthy* and *proper* to approach the King! Get back—HENRY!" Kylen turned his head as a woman with two children rushed past him. The smallest of the sons bumped into his leg, and the same fate would've met the woman chasing him if Kylen hadn't been quick to jump back. The three of them appeared to be chasing after a small boy who held a mysterious haze in his eyes, one that he could remember seeing in another boy's gaze long-long ago. *His own? His brother's?*

Kylen turned away.

He couldn't bare it.

The entryway to the grand ballroom had always been such a disappointment to Kylen. *Expected,* he reminded himself. He still remembered what it was like when he had first stalked towards it, expecting and imagining such glorious architecture to meet his gaze, considering that the *further these halls went on, the fancier it got.* Yet it had been nothing more than a bore, a manipulation as everything else in this kingdom was. By either side of the elevated entryway to the *'grand'* ballroom (that looked to have been untouched since he had last been here, considering the large cobwebs and dust covered corners), stood two males partially hidden by a shadow Kylen recalled all too well. It wrapped around their bones as if it was feasting off of their corpses, hiding their features away from prying eyes, making it look as if they were utterly standing in the wrong spot at the wrong time. A murder of the finest arts.

The two men were handing out masquerade masks that were

as extravagant and ornamented as something he would typically see in one of the northern kingdoms. *The dazzling kingdom's where the sun was rumoured to no longer shine.* They were golden, silver, metallic, and bejewelled. Kylen reluctantly took one of the masks they handed, reaching his hand for it as the shadows threw it at him with a laugh. They knew he would come; *was this all a trap?*

Kylen didn't have the time to worry. He tied it around his head slowly and was instantly bewitched to find that it wielded to his features like a nice fitting blade. Slithers of darkness stretched across his skin from the mask itself, melting into his flesh with an icy sensation that left him shivering. *How he would do anything for his trusty blade right now*—that old thing was sure to be relaxing at the bottom of the sea after he threw it in there with such blinding anger. A snicker sounded out from over his shoulder, earning Kylen to keep his gaze steady and concentrated on the men who didn't look to even be mortal. *Alive.* No, they just continuously passed the different masks out without a word.

This wasn't the time to do anything reckless, he reminded himself. Although, he was never one to listen to his brain when his heart was always one step ahead.

"Welcome, welcome, gather around, dear friends," a deep voice from somewhere within the halls chanted repeatedly. It wasn't the voice of the King of Aeonia, nor the one of the Princess he yearned with every part of his soul for. It was a voice that was arcane; however, an irony to it that Kylen couldn't quite pinpoint as to why. The King of Lorundio slowly came to a stop at the top of the stairs as he looked out to the ballroom that reminded him of a time long ago.

At a time when he knew of the anguish that was slowly creeping in on *them both*, he had chosen to ignore it in the hope that he would be able to spend some more fragile time with the girl who he knew deserved more than he could ever possibly offer.

"No! We are going to get caught, Kye!" Althea, who was running rhythmically at his side, practically screeched in a low whisper. Kylen chuckled with a roll of his eyes as he came to an abrupt stop of realisation. He turned to her with his head cocked to the left, a beam of his own toying at the end of his lips. Hadn't she realised what she had just done? What she'd just called him?

"Kye?" he challenged with a raise of his brow, and the look seeping across Althea's face truly was priceless. She looked beyond distraught. Caught in the fire of her own actions. Kylen barked a laugh again before she slammed her hand over his mouth, and he could inevitably say that he wished he could pull a mirror out of the air itself and show her just what she looked like.

It was a sight he wanted Sayah to capture in one of her many paintings.

"I—I just thought that it suits you, you know? I mean, you call me Thea without anyone asking you to, so I thought that I'd play into your own game?" It was clear that she didn't know what she was saying, that Althea was trying to think of anything as an excuse.

But he didn't care.

He thought it was sweet.

"I like it. I think I'm going to get my brothers to call me that too."

Althea's eyes glistened at that, and he didn't miss the way her lips curled into a smile as she lowered her head to hide her glee. Her hands dropped from the sides of his mouth, clasping together before her stomach as she skipped in her step. "You have brothers?" she asked, and whilst he knew full well that she was trying to redirect the conversation, he also knew that someone who was deprived of any genuine relationships for so long was bound to want to wander into the unknown. It was a human tragedy, a bound of a mortal's heart.

"I do," Kylen chuckled as he raised four fingers. "Four—and I also have another sibling and a Sayah."

"What's a Sayah?"

"Oh, wouldn't you like to know?"

Kylen would give anything to be that young and unaware boy again, to be the boy that still had a fragment of light left in his heart despite all that he had *suffered*. He wished on every hidden star out there that he was that sweet child that had spent his trip to Aeonia running down these heartless hallways with a girl at his side who smiled like she was the brightest star of them all. *The daughter of the moon. The saviour of Realms.* He would give anything at all to be hiding away from the monsters of the night as his chest heaved with bodily laughs.

Was it ignorant that his eyes automatically sought the white hair and diamond-blue eyes that he had known and *loved?* Was it foolish of him to still believe that perhaps the Gods may give him one blessing to hold onto, despite all the wrongs they had stuffed down his throat? Kylen needed to remind himself that *that girl was gone.* He was now looking for the girl with black hair and deadly eyes that had managed to capture the tone of the sea just seconds before a lethal storm.

A girl who he had apparently hallucinated just a few hours ago and yet begged for that to not be true.

But what was he honestly going to do if she was alive?

How was his heart possibly going to react?

A push at his backside had Kylen stumbling down a couple of steps that seconds ago had felt to be holding him back. And it was factual that if Kylen was anywhere without prying eyes right now, he would've reacted differently to the woman who pushed past him. *"Hurry up,"* she snarled, and Kylen could already imagine how glorious her death would be. In fact, any one of these souls would feed the hunger he had consuming his blood.

It would fill the need he had sweltering his every thought.

No, don't be ridiculous. Focus on finding the answers, even if that means escaping the ballroom—

The moment his feet met with the cracked, black, marbled tiles of the large, empty floor, music that was loud and booming shrieked through the air as if there was no tomorrow. Kylen recoiled back as the people *of a literal graveyard* began to wield themselves into a dance he had once seen rivet through his own kingdom.

The waltz of the eleven kingdoms.

Despite the fact that the majority of them were now burnt to a crisp.

Their arms connected, their feet syncing into the same movements that were easy and light. All of their souls looked as if they had been carefully crafted by the same Godly hands, and while the scars of the curse were evident, these people were laughing and smiling like none of their past held any effect over him.

How he was jealous.

Couldn't the Gods see that he wished to be free?

His hands tightened at his sides, hardly realising until a second too late that there felt to be something rather icy breathing down the spine Kylen willed to keep straight. *Kylen Noxwell, Kylen Noxwell~ Kkkkkyyyyyyllllllllleeeeeeennnnn~* His eyes widened as he heard his name echo throughout the space of his mind with a shadowed darkness trailing after it. He knew that it was the lungs of the darkness speaking to him because now he had a pounding headache forming that felt unbeatable. His heart threatened to fall into the deepest and darkest bits of oblivion as he looked through the room for any answers of the sort. *Kylen Noxwell~* Someone grabbed at his arms in his fatal moment of distraction, and before Kylen had any chance of fending them away, he was brought into the deceptive dance he had once performed alongside his parents in the ball the week before their deaths. He could still recall the moments he'd looked up at his mother as they twirled alongside one another, closing his eyes briefly as she pressed a kiss to the centre of his forehead.

Several hands grabbed at him, all of which were laced and scarred with the past that had in no way been very kind to him. Kylen grimaced as he danced the waltz that was once rumoured to open the very gates of Hel. *Wouldn't that be nice? More death to dance alongside his very heart.* His eyes searched through the room that was beginning to reek of death, holding onto that strange sensation that had his lungs suffocating and his heart leaping several beats faster.

Only masks met his eyes.

Several hundred golden masks that never seemed to hold the darling eyes he wanted to drown in—*to get drunk on.*

The *lost* king—the *lost* boy—the *mad* mind—the girl at the end of his arms gazed up at him with sheepish eyes, but she did not hold the face that he craved with every bone in his body for. Her delicate features weren't the ones of his mind's desires. *No.*

The ones he longed for were the ones that belonged to the face he briefly met with of the girl who *now* stood several feet away. The girl who caused him to stumble swiftly back and straighten in his steps as he beckoned for this malicious hallucination to give way.

Because Althea Evangeline couldn't be standing just several feet away, allowing the people of her Kingdom to dance around her as if she was *invisible.*

It just wasn't possible.

But that beloved hallucination didn't give way, and Althea's unwavering eyes held his as if she knew the very effect she had creeping under his skin.

And while *she* didn't dance, *she* didn't smile, *she didn't so much as blink...* he knew that no hallucination could perfectly capture the way Althea's Evangeline's lips pursed when she saw a challenge alight before her. She most definitely was the creation of all of his deepest desires in their beloved malicious form.

The mask that she wore only covered the skin around her eyes and was duskier than all the others that floated about through this suddenly very trivial feeling room. It had a shadowed glisten stuck to its curves, its edges, truly highlighting the corpse-like skin that hugged her godly bones. She was beautiful. Breath-taking. Just as how he had only ever seen her—despite how different she looked.

She was still, and always will be, the most beautiful woman he had ever laid eyes on. There was nothing that she could do—that *they* could do—to make him perceive her as anything less. It was her soul that was beautiful. Her mind. Her wit. Her stamina. The way she constantly looked down at him despite physically being shorter than he was. All of it—that was what made her beautiful to him. The way she held features that sent the Gods fleeing was merely an added bonus.

Kylen laughed, sighing as if a light caressed his tongue; but, his heart felt cold, unsure. *He looked unsure*, and it was deathly clear that he did not know what to do as the people danced around them both.

It felt as if they were the only two in the room. The only two actually alive.

Kylen knew he'd felt this same way when he'd been fighting the harsh, quick-witted currents to reach Althea despite the war that had been going on above the surface. He remembered looking into her eyes with such emotions in his, and yet the one that was the most prominent was *telling* him to only focus on *her*.

Because she was all that mattered.

And he would give up his chance at survival in every lifetime if it meant giving her a chance to truly live. She deserved that much.

Althea's mask covered the majority of the top of her face.

Still, Kylen could tell from the purse of her lips, the glisten of her eyes and the sharpness of her jaw that she was the girl he would flourish in the ashes for. The girl he yearned with every inch of his soul for.

Kylen studied her in his moment of starstruck. He didn't miss the way her eyes held no emotion as she observed him—he didn't miss the way the few areas of skin visible to him were as gloomy and muted as the castle of Aeonia itself.

She genuinely looked like a corpse.

He had to be hallucinating, was he not? Althea was alive... *Was she not?*

Althea's head dipped slightly to the left, her senses looking away as if she was listening to something that he could not hear, *and yet he felt a tremor slip across the floorboards beneath him.* Kylen tensed his brows, looking around the room as he felt the air electrify in his very palms; he flexed his hand before balling it into the fist, feeling as his magick reacted to the same strange cackle that fluttered against his skin. Kylen could not locate what it was that had Althea's eyes fluttering shut as she squirmed under the wrath of her own flesh; he could only quizzically stare as she again shrugged her shoulders with a grimace on her lips as if she was struggling to even breathe. *So, she was alive?*

Kylen didn't wait another second. He physically could not restrain himself any longer. There was a desire on the ends of his fingertips, and he needed to touch her, to feel her, to know that she was here and that she was alive. This was a day he had been dreaming of for so many long sleepless nights now; he needed to reach for her, *to touch her*—to know that she was real. Kylen began to run towards her, his steps dreadfully quick as he dodged every other soul as if they were the curse itself.

This was it.

This was what every moment of the last few months had led to. This was what he had spent every moment *killing* himself for. This was the type of moment that seemed to be in reach when really it was moonfalls away, a moment that had been crafted by the delicacy of time and only experienced once in an immortal's lifetime.

Kylen quickened his steps as he slid past several bodies that waltzed around his; they tried to pull him into the dance, to lure him into the depths of the seas with their siren-like melodies… But Kylen was no longer a fool. Not anymore.

Althea didn't try to flee from his *wrath* as he had expected, but she also didn't fight back against the way the crowd beckoned her into their dance once again.

Which, to his dismay, led Kylen to fall victim as they beckoned him also.

As if this was another one of his merciless dreams, Kylen found himself waltzing across from the girl who looked to hold the authority of death in her eyes. *Knives in her heart.* He repeatedly blinked, willing for this vision to give up and reveal the truth to the desperation on his tongue, but every time he opened his eyes, he found the same astounding queen before him. The same girl that stared at him with a look that he didn't recognise —a look that made him feel as if he was playing dress up and wearing the skin of a stranger.

Kylen thought he knew all of Althea's looks; he had so stupidly assumed that over the course of their few weeks together, he had begun to know every little thing that there was —*yet apparently not.* As this ghastly look had him feeling like a guest in a palace that he'd helped build. It had him feeling as if he had travelled through Realms after Realms to reach this deception of a girl who didn't recognise him.

"Althea—" Kylen's heart strained at that… except nevertheless, he found himself unable to move a single muscle. He felt enchanted; her presence appeared to always do that to him. In the eyes of the world, he had all the power, but in the eyes of Althea, he gave it all to her.

Kylen was under whatever spellbinding, merciless spell she

had ever so carefully roped over his throat, her long black nails trailing across his every breath as he closed his eyes and gave into her addictive touch.

Althea tilted her head to the side as she was turned out into a swirl, her right hand and arm raising into the air as the man she waltzed with tipped her back.

As he watched, a spike of jealousy bloomed in Kylen's heart; though, a quiver of a smile found her magnificent lips, and she mouthed two words that had his mind finally falling silent.

Two words that defied every beat of his heart.

"Hello, Kylen."

Kylen didn't know what he was meant to do.

If he was meant to smile, cry, scream, or *run*.

All he could do was allow his eyes to wander into the what if: the very what if's that were waltzing in a mythical dance right before him.

All it took was another beat of his heart for the girl he swore he was hallucinating to appear a step away. Once again, the sound of her sweet laughter formed a noose around his throat as he looked down to her. It didn't seem real, how he now found the body he craved, the body he prayed on, standing directly before him, matching his every step as her hands crept over his neck. *Her sweet—sweet hands.*

Kylen closed his eyes as he felt her fingertips caress the skin of his throat, her nails slightly pressing into the scarred wounds to remind him that he was alive. *It was her.* He could tell from the curve of her fingers, from the pattern of her flesh—the pattern of her scars. *"Althea,"* Kylen breathed as he leaned his head forwards, his forehead meeting with hers... he felt as if he was dreaming.

Because there was no way that this was truly happening.

It felt too good to be true.

He was in shock—he knew that.

Had she always had such powerful control over him?

Althea tilted her head to the side with darling temptation coating her leering lips. The candles above caught the flicker of darkness that shimmered throughout her eyes, the beautiful eyes that took him in now. She breathed once, and leaned into him, her black dress hugging her skin sensationally, her lips stopping an inch before his jaw. Kylen tensed, her very breath sending his blood chilling as his eyes shut in an agony that was of a different type. "I see that you have come for my feast," she noted, and Kylen felt as if her every word had his heart faltering and leaping through Realms. This was really her—and she sounded exactly the same to how she sounded several months ago. *That voice, that voice, that voice.* Kylen felt his lungs begin to suffocate him as he heard her elegant voice fill his ears once again, his eyes opening as he beckoned for her to say anything more at all. "Kylen Noxwell, King of *Lorund*—"

Within a glimpse of a moment that had the world threatening to spill from beneath his feet, the words she concocted began to choke her, and Althea's eyes forcibly fell shut as her hands on his body froze in despair.

The people around him began to act the way she did, too— their steps halting and their movements... almost... *glitching?* Their bodies were seizing mid-air, and their eyes were wide and... *bloody*—looking as if they were some robotic experiments of Atticus'.

"No—" Kylen felt something familiar creep across the fingertips that were tightening on Althea in fear. *He couldn't lose her again—not after he had just found her again.*

KYLEN NOXWELL~ His gaze dropped to her waist, his blood beginning to spill from an invisible wound. His hands suddenly fell very still, and to his great confusion, he found little slithers of the curse creeping across his bones, his flesh.

It appeared as if there were trillions of tiny black spiders submerging beneath his flesh, festering on his blood before scrambling on top of one another to consume every little inch of him. It was almost like they were racing to seize his soul and make him *again* fall victim to the brutality of the curse. Kylen could feel their touch; he knew that they were inserting the curse slowly back into his blood... but for whatever reason that there was, he could not bring himself to shrug them off him.

"*Lorundio*," Althea finished saying, except her tone sounded awfully different this time. It added to the same realisation that there was something distracting her. This was as clear as the days Kylen mourned for, the days that were so far, and yet he remembered as if they were yesterday. Her eyes were no longer on his but instead peering through the mystic air in search of whatever rhythm it was that caused her breaths to still and her eyes to widen. Was he a fool for saying that he wanted to murder whatever it was on her behalf? Still, even when he felt the daunting presence of the curse wielding around his spine, there was an urge to do whatever it was to make sure that the girl before him would get the chance to live. "*Lorundio*," Althea repeated, acting as if she hadn't already said that word just several seconds ago.

Kylen furrowed his brows, his hand subconsciously tightening on her waist. It wasn't until the ice bled through her clothing that it stood out to him just how cold her flesh felt, and when he moved his hand up to the base of her throat, Kylen realised that there was no warmth beneath her skin whatsoever.

Although he couldn't exactly hear whatever it was that had the air crackling against his touch, he figured that Althea must be able to hear something of it *and that it wasn't a very nice...* As there was a deep, eternal pain flashing across her sharp features. A pain that caused her brows to furrow and her lips to purse, flinching against Kylen's touch—*it was ever so subtle that one's soul may not have even noticed if he hadn't been holding her and watching her so intently.* Kylen's fingertips halted on her skin, his eyes grazing down her body as she slowly returned her luxurious eyes to him. He felt the cold quivers of her blood rivet against his touch, and her eyes again appeared to darken on him as he met them once again. A challenge appeared in her irises, one that he knew had caressed his breaths every time the curse grew bored.

Oh.

Kylen's heart began to flee, his lungs feeling extraordinarily small as he shook his head with a scattered breath. Now he knew to what extent the curse had consumed her body and soul, and it appeared as if this was the moment Althea had been waiting so long for.

Kylen Noxwell~ Oh, Kylen, Kylen, Kylen Noxwell...

The power in the air turned on Kylen, earning the hair to raise on his arms and for his own skin to feel extraordinarily cold. "You're cursed," Kylen seethed under his breath, and Althea merely raised a brow in response, an action so uncanny to the girl he remembered. Her face lost any remaining colour, her brows furrowing as she began to slowly shake her head with a cackle. "Sweetheart—*I can help you*—"

"Help *us*?" Althea questioned as she tucked the loose strand of hair over her shoulder.

It was now Kylen's face that was drained of any colour. *'Us?'* He didn't understand what she meant—*he didn't understand who it was that he was staring at*—it was his Althea, was it not? The girl he was betrothed to? The girl he would give anything in the world to marry?

"Oh, diminutive *Kingling*, we don't need your help. The only help we need is to have a glorious feast..." The words echoed through the air, a screeching sound that sounded identical to a blade being scraped against cement floors. Kylen took a step back, and against his own will, he forced himself to let Althea go. "And if you look outside right now, you will find that the gates are finally *shut*." A cackle that was deep and rustic trembled across Althea's lips as she wielded herself a blade. Her head cocked to the left, and the blade noticeably nicked her skin as she twirled it across her fingertips. *But she didn't flinch? She didn't cry? She didn't react?* Not even as a single droplet of black blood ran across her flesh. Althea's pursed lips turned into a grin as she studied Kylen's fearful gaze, and her smile was beyond his utter understanding. "Which means my dinner has finally been served."

A firm push at his backside had Kylen stumbling several steps forward; however, a deafening scream that echoed from the shadows before him had his feet coming to an abrupt halt. No matter how they almost slid to his death. "Feast?" he echoed, and the word must've done something to him as he felt his breath slowly became heavier by the second. Althea reached her hand for his, embracing his calloused palms as she ran her thumb over the scars that lay bare. Could she see what she was doing to him?

Her grip tightened, and she nodded as her smile turned into one of teeth: challenging him to keep rambling whilst her nails plundered into his flesh. Kylen's eyes were beginning to feel heavy, exhausted, on the brink of consuming all that had survived within his life as he tried to spit the words at her. "What do you mean—what? *Althea?*" Kylen asked, cutting himself off entirely as his grip tightened on her. His legs were beginning to sway, his eyes doing everything they could to fight whatever it was that was beckoning him to fall victim again.

Kylen Noxwell, Kylen Noxwell, Kylen Noxwell, Kylen Noxwell~

Althea took two small steps back, her absent touch earning his own touch to quiver at his sides. "Althea—" The whole room was beginning to fall silent, no noise stretching throughout his mind as the girl he had prayed every second on watched him stumble to his knees with a cackling thud.

Tricked, tricked, tricked; you still knew that it was a trick, and yet you quipped~

Slithers of darkness formed around Kylen's face, prying his mouth open as Althea slowly turned on the back of her heel. He could feel and hear as his jaw cracked, his teeth threatening to splinter, as his mouth widened beyond compare. The masquerade mask he wore was releasing something lethal, shadowy death consuming every inch of his body that it possibly could.

In the near distance, Kylen watched as Althea disappeared around the corner. Still, before he had a second to interpret everything that had just happened, and what his eyes had witnessed, he fell into a coma of darkness as every other soul in this castle did. Were they even real?

This wasn't Althea—it *couldn't* be.

But who the Hel was it?

ELEVEN
ALTHEA

Growing up, the young girl who felt nameless had always been rather curious when it came to wondering what life would've inevitably been like if she had been allowed to grow up in a palace that bloomed with warmth and light. A place where all angels came to rest and no wrong could ever possibly end with one bleeding out on the cold tiles of the place you once praised. Except, of course, the Gods had other plans for young Althea, as she had been confined to grow up in a room that was awfully eery and withered, the only source of warmth coming from the candles that were seconds away from exceeding since they had been used regularly since that fatal day of her birth.

It was on the lonely nights when she would close her eyes and wonder what her room, her home, and her life would all look like if she was just another character in her favourite books. She liked to imagine that her father and mother would take her out and show her off. *Not be afraid but instead proud*. And now that she was old enough, they would allow her to choose just what it was that she wanted her room to look like.

There were so many questions that she would dwell on

through those glorious nights. She would have to pick between the maroon wallpaper and the ivy cream dresser or the black one, and occasionally, depending on how she was feeling, she liked to imagine that her *chosen* father would help her paint those large walls without the fear of spilling paint.

Althea imagined that he would address her by her name and smile at her presence *instead* of cowering from it.

Would this be the type of room that she would've been given if she had been raised by the Noxwells? A room that was colourful, a room that had warmth, and a room that had books? That all said an awful lot since this was quite literally the *afterlife*.

So how was any of this even here? Even physical?

Althea listened as the door shut behind Willix with a creak, a small echoing click of the lock telling her that she was alone at last, and with that, she was finally able to breathe again. Willix hadn't said anything, really. Other than showing her the room and saying that she could do whatever it was that she wanted with it, he had succumbed to the gratitude of silence.

Nonetheless, it was a sweet gesture in Althea's eyes, a *strange* one.

Perhaps this was some artistically menacing form of manipulation? That they would ignorantly believe that the moment she got comfortable enough to start changing things about this beautiful room, they would strike her from behind and take the last of whatever abilities were hidden within her soul and leave her for true death to claim.

But that seemed like a problem for *tomorrow*.

For now, she wanted to look around.

To try and breathe after having been separated from her own lungs for so many months now.

It didn't take many steps for Althea to reach the bed, and she was awfully surprised to find just how comfortable the mattress was when she sat down and dragged her knees up to her chest. It was so drastically different to the bed in Aeonia but so similar to the one in Lorundio that it brought back even more memories of a time she almost wanted to keep hidden.

The room was small, but it was a comfortable size. It had one built-in wardrobe, a large bookshelf that stretched to the ceiling, and a window that changed its view/scenery every few minutes. It appeared to be a rotation of some type, capturing glimpses of the different Elemental Realms from their physical world. Of course, the room had many other small bits and bobs that scraped throughout the interior with a homey feel. Still, these were the main eye-catching aspects... overall, it was one of the nicest rooms that Althea had ever been in.

In comparison to the last bedroom she'd had *(the one in Aeonia),* the room was much brighter and far more colourful, with small tweaks of personalisation that had her dreaming of all the endless what-ifs. Her curiosity was sure to be the one thing that would tie death across her bones. On the walls that were slowly beginning to feel as if they were caving in on her was a patterned wallpaper of the marvellous stars she yearned to touch, reminding her so much of the Kingdom that, too, resided safely within her heart.

Althea had always adored the idea of the stars despite the fact that before she had ventured to Lorundio, she had only seen them once or twice. She liked the idea of them as they reminded her that she wasn't actually alone and that there had to be someone out there who was experiencing something of the pain that she felt to be murdering her.

This room was nice. It seemed to be on the brink of a memory suffocated in nostalgia. Except Althea didn't want to stay in here—she couldn't stay in here.

For one thing, it was starting to feel too small—reminding her of the cell she had only just escaped from. And for a second thing—this emptiness was allowing her to think.

And she really did *not* want to think.

Because if she allowed herself to think of one thing, then that would lead to another, and then another, and then another after that, it would lead her mind to wander and her chest to heave in such a panicked pain as she would come to realise that she had fallen down the eternal rabbit hole of *doom*.

"Stop it," Althea silently hissed at herself as she tucked her hair behind her ears. It was quite comedic that she already knew that if the Althea from eleven months ago were to lay eyes on this dreadful mess of a girl... she would laugh at her in pity. She was a disgrace to her own name—but soon, she vowed to herself, she would figure out just what it was that she needed to rebirth the girl who was hiding behind the stars.

The girl that she once was—she will find her again.

Despite having only been underwater once in her life (a time that she both wanted to remember and forget for many gracious reasons), Althea felt as if now, her hair was floating beneath the several currents, all trying to make her their victim. There was a frequency to how her hair stirred in the afterlife's air that seemed so angelic and ethereal. It was almost as if the Gods were trying to earn her forgiveness by making her seem like an angel in their scarred palms.

That was if there were even any Gods left.

Althea was pretty sure she had butchered them all.

Right down to the bone.

The wood of the bookshelf was smooth as she ran her fingers over the delicate engravings and markings. Her eyes grazed over each individual book title, and her heart practically leapt (that was if it was in her possession) when she saw the familiar title of a story she had grown up dreaming of.

'The Tree of the Lost Ones'

It was a book Althea had found when she was four. Her father had been out of the kingdom for a meeting somewhere far, and there was only so much to do and so much time until a soul grew bored of the mindless cursed guards... *so she had gone exploring.* The only reasonable response.

There were many rooms amongst the cold corridors that Althea had been forbidden to enter, but she had quickly learnt when the best time to take risks were.

And that moment then was one of them.

It was in between guard rotations when Althea had used her own portion of the curse to force the enchantment on the door to burst. She hadn't realised it then, but now looking back on that frail memory, it wasn't the cursed magick that had opened the door but rather her Elemental magick, as she now knew just how horrifyingly different both the magick's felt—nevertheless, she could still remember how uneasy it had made her feel; if only that girl had known how she would feel the month later when she was forced to take her first victim. How amusing, indeed.

That nausea had been even worst.

A type of pain that could drive one to insanity.

Althea could still remember how loud her heart had sounded as she opened that frail door. Within, there looked to be an old study of some type, which appeared to have been untouched for quite some time. All the furniture had large white, dusty sheets scraping over them, keeping them from her view or any other prying eyes. It was like her father was forever trying to preserve whatever it was that she had just stumbled upon.

She remembered approaching the large wall before her first with silent steps. There laid the largest white cloth of them all, and her curiosity had always been a burdened thing—especially when she pulled the sheet away, and that revealed to her the face of someone she missed more than anything.

Her mother.

Despite her mother already being gone for a year in that moment, the wound was still gaping.

Althea recalled how she had started crying then; fresh agonised tears spilled over her youthful cheeks that were yet to be scarred. Althea couldn't bear to look at her—to memorise her eyes, cheeks, and beautiful face one last time… it was all far too painful. So, she had turned away on the back of her small heel and ran out of the room when she tripped and fell on the floor with a great thud. Her muscles hurt, her bones hurt, and her soul hurt, yet it wasn't clear whether it was the exhaust of it all holding her to the ground or not. Either way, Althea had stayed lying there, sobbing for the life she should've had, as everything that had possibly gone wrong caught up to her. She remembered so clearly how it felt as if there was an actual weight holding her down—as if there were chains bounding her wrists and ankles together, leaving her for dead. It was only when her tears had finally begun to clear when she spotted the small book that appeared under one of the sheet-covered couches—but it was strange because before, when she had looked there, nothing remotely physical had stood out to her.

Nonetheless, Althea was still quick to take the book and flee the room, at last, closing the door behind her and praying to whatever evil was out there that her father wouldn't realise.

He had, of course.

But that was a story for another time.

Now, Althea looked down at the book she had picked up and off the shelf; she ran her fingers over the golden letters and willed herself to breathe. This was a book about children escaping their abusive homes and finding families that loved them for who they were as a person, not just their names.

It was peaceful for a moment, a second where Althea had the ability to close her eyes and not feel her own blood drip down her cheeks. However, the godsforsaken sound of the creaking door behind her had her turning, and to her dismay, Elara Noxwell had snuck in.

"I hope I'm not interrupting on anything; I wouldn't want to impose," she was quick to say as she fixed her posture. Her hair was awfully messy, and there were smears of something choco-late-wise on the front of her blouse. If Althea had had it in her, she would've laughed and given into the happiness she longed for herself to find... as it was so strange to hear a child speak in such a proper way—especially when they genuinely looked like a *lively* child.

Althea shook her head with a wave of her hand. "You aren't imposing," she replied, and as always, her voice felt so small, as if she was still that four-year-old that deserved eternal happiness. "Don't worry about it." The number of times she recalled feeling as if she was never more than a burden to the air itself was honestly amusing; she would stand before her father, and he would act like she wasn't truly there at all.

Several seconds of silence passed, and Elara awkwardly shuffled in her steps. She nodded her head towards the book in Althea's hand, gesturing towards the infamous idea that she wasn't too pleased with the silence of others. "Is that a good book?"

"It's a grand book. It got me through... *a lot of tough times*," Althea said as she went to put it back; however, Elara was quick to leap forward and snatch it from her hands in a friendly manner that wasn't at all rough as she had initially expected. "Oh, I—"

"The Tree of the Lost Ones," Elara read aloud before nodding once more in approval. "Sounds like something Huntio would've liked." The girl put the book back on the shelf, walking over to the small sofa against one of the empty walls.

"Would have? He can borrow it if he likes; after all, none of these things belong to me."

Elara smiled softly, almost as if there was pity in her heart. "These things belong to no one. They are the objects that the mortals, immortals, and creatures of all the Realms lose and never find again. And if we, the souls of the afterlife, were to wish hard enough, we can find those lost objects and give them a new home. For instance, this wallpaper," Elara uttered as she ran her fingers across the cold walls, "was lost to a forest fire. But no, I don't think Huntio would want to borrow the book, as he cannot read. He was a lot slower at learning than I was, and because time got cut short for the two of us, he hasn't been able to learn since."

"Can he not learn to read in the afterlife? That makes no sense; you can practically do everything else," Althea beckoned as if it wasn't obvious enough. It seemed like a bewildering thought, a horrible one.

"No. One's mind cannot process any new information or learning of that extent. But well, *hey*, when you become the true one and only God, that can be your first... *job*?" Elara offered with a hint of a giggle. The light in her eyes was so familiar to the dying light she had seen in Kylen's that it was somewhat discomforting. "Whilst we can still mentally grow and age in our minds, we are not capable of fully learning new things. In case I wasn't that clear, while Hunt may get to know a couple of words here and there, his brain will never fully allow him to understand every word out there since it's basically dead."

She was so abrupt with it that Althea hadn't had a single second to compose herself before the door Elara had previously shut sprang open as if the words that had left her lips had put a mere enchantment on it. "Your brain is dead too, you know," Huntio quickly replied as he strolled in with a raise of his brows.

"Wow, what a great observation you have made, *dear brother*," Elara chimed as she scrunched her nose and leaned back into the warmth of the chair. It held her like a warm hug, a fortune in a time like this. The girl crossed her arms across her chest whilst Huntio decided to walk over to the couch and sit next to her. The boy rolled his eyes at Elara, and Althea dared to almost smile as she watched the two exchange words.

Truly, she would've given the sun and the moon to have someone to go through life with; but at the same time, she thanked whatever was out there every day that she didn't have to watch her sibling suffer the way Eloise had.

That had been treacherous.

"What does it feel like to have a proper, working brain?"

Huntio queried after another second of silence; it seemed to be that the children were just as bad as suffering in silence as she was, an observation that had evidently been made minutes ago. "Does it feel any different to having a working brain?"

Elara turned to him with a cock of her left brow, a knowing look on her face as she shook her head. "How would she know the difference? Her brain was never—*you haven't ever been braindead, have you?*" Elara paused mid-sentence, and she was quick to turn back towards Althea, who was already shaking her head. "That's what I thought. Hunt, she wouldn't know the difference."

"Well, how was I meant to know that?" Huntio said, shrugging his shoulders.

Elara clapped her hands on her thighs as she again leaned back in her chair, crossing her arms across her chest as she furrowed her brows with an evident question in her eyes. "What are you doing here? I thought you were helping mother make dinner?"

"—You can eat?" Althea interrupted the two with a bark of confusion.

Elara barely sent her a nod before Huntio answered her with a small, "Yes." He cleared his throat, and the tension seeping off his quivering movements made the room stiffen. Elara's face dropped of emotion, and Althea knew that she had caught onto whatever it was that her brother had been implying. "They're fighting... again."

It was subtle, but Elara looked down at her feet for a moment as she gathered herself together. "It's okay. Everything's okay, okay?" She turned her eyes towards Althea as she fiddled with the end of her curls. "They fought once last week, and that was really the first time in a long time... but still, it's strange to see the two of them not getting along—*but it's okay,* okay, Hunt?"

Huntio nodded, and although he smiled at her, it was trivial. "I know. I just wanted to find you." His features looked drained, exhaust creeping into his heartless mind as he shifted in the chair that looked to just about consume him.

The way the two interacted was poetic. They looked to be two characters from a story where the world was ending, but all that truly mattered was keeping the other safe. It was evident that they leaned on each other for comfort and reassurance. Despite having died as children, they looked to have old minds. Kindred spirits. Elara held hope in her eyes—even if it was purely deceptive, and Huntio sought that strength—even if he was beginning to realise just how untruthful it was.

Althea cleared her throat as she rose, flattening out the front of her clothes as she gathered whatever strength left in her weak bones to say, "Well, I don't know about you two, but I would love to stretch my legs out and have a good look around; care to give me a tour of your humble abode?"

That was the last thing Althea wanted to do in any world.

She wanted to rest her mind and try to figure out what to do next because she honestly had no idea. But she could tell that Elara and Huntio needed a distraction of some type, and she knew how troubling it was for one's mind to comprehend the pain that comes from a parental figure. Plus, didn't she owe them this, at least?

Althea was a God. And what good was a God if she didn't sacrifice herself over and over again for her people?

Elara and Huntio both nodded in sync, and as Althea went to take a small step towards the door, her movements completely froze as she felt pain of another type slither across and down her bones. Her chest heaved, and she stumbled back into the wall behind her. Books fell, objects fell. Elara jumped to her feet, rushing towards Althea as her mind fell victim to the one voice that was louder than all of the rest.

"*ALTHEA~*"

The very word had Althea's lungs feeling extremely tight as her eyes flew over her shoulders, searching for the man she felt to be breathing down her wounded spine. "No—" Althea rasped as she dug her nails into her throat, pinching at her skin as she willed everything to silence. She didn't have to be the smartest in the world to know whose voice that belonged to... although it was impossible...

Because Kylen wasn't dead?

TWELVE
KYLEN

T his was a dream. *It had to be.* Kylen may be deemed insane by all he has ever known—but he hadn't lost the last of his mind not to realise that this haze around him wasn't real life. Everything was shadowed and blurred; nothing was clear or fully before him as he stretched his hand out towards it. Kylen could feel the way his skin ached, the way his bones begged to crumble as he rolled over, feeling the hard stones of the ground beneath him dig into his flesh as something warm and sticky dripped down his forehead.

"Kylen, Kylen, Kylen, when will you ever learn, my love?"

His body stiffened, but even that seemed to hurt his throbbing bones. Kylen shook his head with a muffled whimper as he leant into the delicate voice that had him wishing against all odds that he was back on that *old ship of his,* just days before that merciless bomb went off and ruined absolutely everything that there was.

His head ached beyond compare, a constant throbbing that had the blood on his cheeks feeling like nothing of a worry. Kylen raised a trembling hand, one that he wanted to cut off if it meant that it would no longer ache the way it did now. He narrowed his eyes against the thrashing air, squinting them against the darkness that waltzed across his forming skin... *forming skin?* Why was his skin forming?

Kylen didn't have to be *mad* to realise that whatever reality he was staring into wasn't real in any obscure way, no matter how he longed for it to be true because the voice that swirled throughout the mist of the air was so angelic... Althea's voice.

Was he hallucinating? *Or was he trapped inside of his mind and had actually gone mad?*

The last thing he remembered before all fell into the clammy hands of darkness was that *Althea* had been standing before him —but no, it wasn't genuinely *Althea*, it was someone else —*something* else... that just had to have taken over her Godly body. He knew his wife. He knew his girl... and that was not her.

But that didn't answer the question... where was he right now?

A dream? A hallucination? A vision?

He presumed that he was still unconscious, but how was he looking into a world that was a figment of his own?

Kylen closed his eyes again, clutching them shut as he willed anything at all to come to his mind instead of this abused power. *"Kkkyyyllllleeeennnn Nnnoooxxwweeellll~"* A sharp pain struck either side of Kylen's temples. It was so fierce and firm that Kylen was sure someone had sliced his head into two before pushing him to the ground and trampling all over his weak corpse. His body flinched at the throb that spread across his flesh like a tidal wave: convulsing as another cry that sent his bones rattling urgently left his lungs.

Fuck, Kylen wasn't one to famously swear, but he truly did feel like swearing at whoever the next person to cross his path would be. *Pull your head up; just pull your bloody head up.* With a painful grimace leaving his lips, Kylen slowly lifted the head he hadn't realised to have dropped, but as he opened his eyes yet again, this time he found that he seemed to have opened *his* true and physical eyes that were in the Realm he was imprisoned in.

So, was he trapped in a hallucination, or was he not?

The boy King looked around, except while he knew that this was the reality where his skin and bones physically lay, he seemed to have realised that his soul and mind were trapped elsewhere. Kylen appeared to be entombed to a callous iron chair in the dungeons of Aeonia—the very dungeons that had Kylen shivering at the bare memory of Althea's *dear* old father walking him through these deep and cold tunnels once upon a time ago.

Kylen looked down to his arms, finding them trapped at his backside with slithers of darkness holding him to the steel that burnt wounds into his skin. Something far before his *physical* skin stepped out of that same demeaning darkness, but before Kylen could go to whisper another word, his head flew back, and his *physical* mouth flew open *yet again*. Why must he be the victim of the curse's distaste? Why couldn't the hallucination that he was half in consume his physical body soon—saving him from the unrelenting torture that whispered against his flesh?

"Don't be afraid, pretty little King, you will be reunited with your sweetheart in Hel, soon, soon, soon... enough."

Kylen felt as his jaw was forced open beyond repair, a crack filtering through the air that he knew had been an outcome of the crushing of *his* bones. The curse forced its way down his open throat, earning visions of every Realm out there—*that they had touched and slaughtered,* to flash across Kylen's mind speedily. They went past his eyes too quickly for him to catch a true sight of anything bewildering, but he heard many voices all calling out for him as if someone actually cared.

But Kylen wasn't strong enough to fight against it anymore.

After all, he only felt to hold the mind of a young, mindless boy... a boy who had been an adult, a king, a ruler, a leader, *a man* since he was twelve.

Kylen fell back into his trance, hallucination, dream, *what-*

ever it was and the strange, new source of eeriness that had spread over his limbs in this darling hallucination of his... suddenly took control of his soul as well as his mind.

It began showing him what would've happened if he had just shown up at the castle instead of sneaking into the ball... but why? *Why, why, why?* His head, that had never truly stopped throbbing, began to ache beyond compare, and his hands as scratched and malicious as the eleven seas tugged his mind into oblivion.

A flash of colour before his very eyes had Kylen watching as a breath-taking young Althea ran towards him from the top of a small hill with a fire of wildflowers running down it. A cry escaped her lungs as he ran with all his might to catch her, but then the vision changed, and he saw Althea appearing out of the shadows of the streets, looking to him with eyes full of mysterious emotions. The flashes kept turning, his thoughts running.

Why did he need to see any of this?

The next vision, *however*, had his blood curdling. Because it wasn't just another flash of one of his many *'what ifs'*. It was a physically *complete* story... One with an ending that would leave the reader mourning for days on end. Then, when they had *at last* idiotically thought that they had caught a break from all of that burdened grief, they would hear of another reader's journey with the dearest novel, and all of that punishing pain would resurface and consume their constellation of grief.

The wind nipped at his ears, and Kylen's eyes were quick to come face to face with the large wall that had obscurities clinging onto it as if it was a safe haven for all evil to hide. He already knew where he was, where the curse had specifically placed him in this hallucination.

It was the awfully daunting fence that kept the castle of Aeonia and the Kingdom of Aeonia separated. The one thing that prevented the curse from escaping the clasps of the palace and spilling into the streets where the corpses were already rotting.

Kylen held his breath, not daring to do a single thing wrong as his eyes stirred to the withered gap in the structure that he was just able to ascend through—but he had to ignore the way the different pieces of old metal that had presumably once helped with keeping this wall up, ripped at his cloak and shirt as if it too wanted to toy with his withered soul. There was no time for pain in a time like this, no time at all. Crimson blood trailed down the flesh that Kylen had once cherished, and once again, the harsh brutality of this world was reminding him, in all of his agonies, that he truly was freed from the deadly curse that seemed to still be haunting his every breath.

Following his every step.

A crow echoed from above, warning Kylen of the war he would be walking through if he was to take another step forward. But that wasn't the reason as to why Kylen halted his steps abruptly. No, it was because he was now actually taking the fatal second to look up at the castle that had burdened his soul for what felt like lifetimes now. He looked up at the palace with walls that looked to reach the storms that were hiding in the dark clouds above, his mind remembering the small, blameless boy he had been so long ago when he had first been amongst these deceiving walls, how he wished that he could call that boy inno-cent, how he wished that he could say that that child had not yet seen the cruelty the world loved to torture its victims with.

Except that boy knew all about it.

In fact, he was an expert on it.

And he knew that boy had already begun to reek like death.

Kylen wondered if the authors of all of those old histories of the Kingdoms had ever actually taken a look at the castle of Aeonia. If they had even spotted the peeling paint of the castle's walls, the cracked slithers of the castle's tiles, the rotten gardens of the castle's exterior, or the dark shadowed corners where the wildlife that there once had been, too, faced the eyes of death. The words of literature made this cemetery seem fresh and deli-

cate, golden, and elegant. Kylen had spent so many of these past long months nose deep in those words of literature, in the hope that it would explain something of the stained-glass storyboard that he'd unfortunately found in the warzone of Harlia. However, to his dismay, he had learnt about a lot more than what he intended—and none of it was of any use to him.

Kylen had learnt about the story of Astaria, the curse's origin, the origin of Erwin, and every fucking castle and its maker in all of the Realms.

As if he cared for the girl who had died before she was even born.

As if he cared for the hatred, the Gods spat at their people.

He cared for none of it.

The grass beneath his feet was dead—in fact, he wasn't even sure if he could genuinely refer to it as grass. It was more like ash, already lost to the cruelty that lingered in the casualties and silhouettes that tiptoed upon these lands. Kylen forced his head and eyes to look away, glancing towards the fortress that he swore was laughing at the fear he refused to so much as acknowledge. His emotions were so estranged from him nowadays—he needed to tie them down and throw them to the bottom of the seas, never to be seen again. Or, if he felt like getting his hands dirty, he wouldn't mind strangling them until his brain went pop. That would be nice. Perhaps then he would finally be able to think clearly again.

Kylen was steady to beckon his feet to move once again. It was almost a subconscious order that went unspoken as he held his breath and felt the force of his own magick pull him forwards. He moved towards the same faulty window he had snuck through all those times he had to return to the castle after a night away, trying with everything in him to figure out whether there was anything he could do to stop the outcome he already knew was coming for his throat.

The betrayal of Althea Evangeline.

One of the greatest mistakes of his life.

If there had been any way at all that was possible, Kylen would've preferred to be the one to come out of that cruel day with his blood coating his hands. Not the other way around.

Why were the Gods so stern on the fact that he had to be the helpless murderer of his very own heart?

Kylen could still hear the words echoed throughout his head all those years ago. His mind had been beyond his reach, and yet he'd already come to the realisation of just what it was that he had to do. "Sayah, I don't think I can do it," he'd whispered to nothing but the air. But sure enough, no longer than a second later, Sayah had responded through her sirenix abilities; and her words weren't the ones that either one of them wanted to hear. "I know, my love, I know. But we do not have a choice. Trust me, if there were any other way, I would tell you to do that instead—but Kylen, we need to act on that information. We need to act—" The signal of her magick had gotten lost to the malice of the air, but that hadn't wiped the pain from ceasing Kylen's heart as he heard Althea enter into the room behind him. He knew what he had to do—and if he didn't do it, his people would die.

But how was he to choose his Kingdom over the young girl who was smiling at him? The girl who had a thousand stars in her eyes and the moon in her heart.

That time may have been a lifetime ago, but it felt like just yesterday.

Now, Kylen's fingers slipped under the gap in the loose flaky white paint of the windowsill—and for a moment, he was reminded that none of this was real. It was a hallucination, and yet Kylen still wanted to figure out whatever it was that they—the curse—the spirits—wanted to show him.

A mocking laugh crept over his shoulder blades, and no more than a second later, several words followed behind. "Go on, Kylen~ go, go, go, go!"

Kylen stilled his breaths, but he forced himself to keep going.

He wasn't going to let his ignorant fear of the curse's power hold him back this time. He began to move again, feeling for the one certain button that would allow the window before him to open without so much as a crinkle of a sound. But really, what did that matter? This was a hallucination, a dream; it really was nothing but a flicker of a star in the heavens above.

The window rose silently, earning Kylen to freeze as he inhaled the icy air that escaped from within the castle's manacled walls. It was as if the air outside wasn't as ridiculously cold as it was because the air he breathed now—was beyond death.

The lost King was cautious not to allow his shoes to creak against the floorboards; instead, he focussed on making sure that there were no unwanted souls targeting his. He hesitantly glanced around, marking every exit, every hallway, and every window that he could flee through if the curse decided to allow things to get a little bloody... but it wasn't like he feared blood, not anymore.

Kylen's hand nipped at the fabric at his waist, and as if he hadn't noticed this before—or perhaps he didn't physically have it before, Kylen now suddenly found a long, sharp, hand-crafted dagger sitting vigorously at his side.

It was soft against his aching flesh, smooth to the hallucination of the hand that gripped it firmly as it twirled between his fingertips. Whilst Kylen may be deemed as an insane adult by all he'd ever known or come across in his years; he wouldn't ignore that childlike joy that sparked a small flame within the midst of his heavy heart every time someone gifted him with a new spectacular blade. It was one of the few things that had his heart thumping in his palms, washing against his bones with an unfamiliar sensation that, in some sense, calmed him.

Why didn't whatever Gods that were out there realise that the exact reason Kylen had fled these lands was because he didn't want to feel the way he did now? Trapped within the shadowed burdens of his memories and forced to replay the last events that occurred within these burdened walls. Kylen tried to focus and purely look for any potential sound or sight that would reveal Althea Evangeline—

Still, his mind was now throwing the sound of her laughter at him: the scent of her intoxicating, addictive, favourite perfume...

Kylen was enclosed within his own mind, and that took him away from the girl of his dreams and nightmares despite the fact that he was willing to get on his hands and knees and beg.

Kylen was the man who didn't know what to fear more.

The curse... or Althea.

His Althea.

Slowly, he exited the room that he presumed to be some sort of 'living' area... although he wouldn't deny how comedic that name inevitably was for a dull place like this. Kylen's hand tightly wrapped around the wooden delicacy of his new blade, his feet stretched down the hallways that were overspilling with the lost souls of those who now sought vengeance. Silence met him with a mocking laugh, and Kylen pushed his steps to keep going, to not turn back and lock eyes with those that only wanted to feel his pain. He kept his spine straight—no matter how withered it felt. The wind howled beyond, catching the screams of the dead and forcing them to haunt Kylen without any choice. He watched as the shadows left by a strange light source beyond reflected all of his misery onto the floorboards before him. He knew it was a phantom sound, but something about feeling and hearing the childlike version of Althea running by his side sent his heart thrumming with such intensity.

The shadows must've caught onto the emotions that washed against Kylen's feet as they began to curl around every corner and rummaged for his blood as he took each hesitant step.

Practically waiting for him to falter.

"Kylen, Kylen, Kylen, do you really want to look into the beyond when you could turn away without a second glance?" A voice inside of his mind asked as he gazed around. "If you

choose to turn away now, then I will set your true self free, and you will wake up with the ability to return to your kingdom without a wound tracing your charming skin. However, if you do not, you will have your soul consumed by the many starving mouths that have been deprived for far too long. We are giving you this chance because we know your history with the curse, boy, we know it all."

Kylen shook his head, his own laugh leaving his lips. This was ridiculous. Insane. Did they really think that he had come all this way just to turn around now? He would sooner murder himself than forfeit a battle like this one.

As he grew deeper inside the castle, certain sounds and voices became more apparent to him. He could hear children's laughter, children screaming, children being the common fuel of all he ever feared. Kylen could hear noises that had his blood chilling. Noises that dared to have him turn around and never look back.

It wasn't until Kylen felt his chest jolt in confrontational panic and his feet stumble back in catastrophic fear before he realised where the daring halls had led him to. The walls suddenly felt all too daringly small, the floors feeling as if they were seconds away from collapsing and butchering him whole— he'd already known that nothing of what the curse was showing him could be kind, but this—this was utterly merciless.

Except, no matter the number of daunting memories that were quickly tying a noose around his throat, the only thing Kylen could do in that vulnerable moment of shock was widen his eyes as he watched the door before him slowly creak open at his very presence.

It was a horrifying sight, if any.

One that turned the blood in his veins black—despite time having healed only that.

Kylen looked across the room he knew and remembered with the complexities of his heart. He saw the bed he had sat on multiple times, the grounds he had laid on just so that he could get a better look at the stars whilst he told the stories of all of his many adventures to the girl who'd never been allowed to wander further than her palace's walls. Everything about the room was the same, nearly identical. Had her father not allowed her to change the way her room looked? Or did she simply not have the energy to waste such precious time?

For a single moment that felt beyond consuming, Kylen took in how frozen everything appeared. Yet, he didn't miss how there was a fair and even layer of dust spread across it all.

An evident token of time, the one thing to remind Kylen that he was no longer just a boy.

The sight before him was like the faintest memory of his mind had decided to try and form itself together. Everything had been left in place as Althea herself had left it in... like the curses that hung around every corner of this haunted manor expected the girl that had been kept prisoner by the man who was meant to protect and help her grow was to return.

There was once upon a time when Kylen would strongly argue that there was no way in utter Hel that she would dare to return to these lands—yet because of all the misfortunes that had occurred in his life, now he didn't know what to think, what to believe... Hel, perhaps she had.

Or perhaps it was that he had actually gone insane and that she truly was dead, and the girl at the ball had been a hallucination, and now he was dead too because he was just an idiotic king who thought he knew everything.

"Dare to turn around, my love?"

Was this what he would remember if he chose to walk away? Would he remember finding the palace empty without a soul in sight? That he'd found the halls of this whimsical memory frozen in place because it was true that Althea was forever gone?

The curse seemed to be acting kindly towards him, offering him a chance to forget the past if it meant moving on.

No.

Kylen was never someone to leave a war without winning and claiming every life on the battlefield.

Something delicate and fragile began to echo through the wind that gently caressed Kylen's mind. Easing all of the many whispers that willed him to open his true eyes and forget everything that he'd seen and come here for.

It appeared to be a broken melody of a music box that he remembered. One that held a little white-haired ballerina that had been left to face the consequences of this world with her bare hands.

Kylen held his breath as he approached the now waltzing box of harmonies, his gaze drifting across the turning scarred ballerina that he reached towards with a trembling hand. The melody churned as he touched it. A stray in the music had his hand flinching back as if it was going to burn his bones.

It felt to be in the moments of yesterday when Kylen had seen the little music box for the first time. He could still recall how proud it had looked in the shop's moonfall themed window. Standing tall on its own as the ballerina continued to spin throughout the deep winters. Kylen had gifted it to Althea when the two of them were finally alone for the first time and away from the prying eyes of death. He wanted her to have it to remember him by—so that his memory wouldn't be as burdened as he knew it would soon become.

Something as transcendent as a breath of warm air ran over his shoulders, and Kylen didn't waste a second to turn around and embrace it. His overgrown hair caught in the cold wind as he stared through the empty abyss that was thick with the darkness of blood. It was obvious to him that the curse was near, yet nothing stood out to him in the open grave he stood in. Nothing at all was different as he released the breath that sent chills scattering across his skin.

But then Kylen heard another sound—one that had him

moving down the halls far quicker than he had initially entered them. "Althea," he whispered. His voice was a plea to whatever God would send him a second look. "Althea," he pleaded again, scattering down the second corner that almost had him crashing into the walls.

Except, again and again, no figure of a memory came before his quivering eyes. Nothing at all came to light, no matter how loud his mind screamed.

He needed to see her—he longed to see her.

He yearned to know what came next because this could not be the end of their story, he refused to accept it.

What had truly happened the night of Sayah's death? He prayed that Althea—the true Althea, would tell him that she had no part whatsoever in it: and that would cause his heart so much ease. So much dreadful ease. Of course, it wouldn't heal it in any which way, but he would be closer to the chance of almost being able to breathe again if that was even still a thing.

Kylen could feel the shadows running across his skin, skimming up his arms and escaping within his lungs as if the curse was searching for a familiar home that had recently been freed. Piss off, he sneered at the whispers of his mind, but Kylen truly doubted that they were even listening. "Althea—"

Insanity was on the brink of consuming every little breath that came from Kylen's aching, dry throat when he heard a laugh that felt blood-chilling and had the hair on his arms standing on ends. He turned to the left before pressing his hands against the cold wooden door, pushing it open with a single breath as the shadows began to dance. They took the shapes of children running, children laughing. A family like no other replacing the ones that had been burdened with time. What was with the curse choosing to torture him with children?

Kylen couldn't will himself to move an utter step as a small girl with brown hair, bright, vibrant blue eyes, and olive skin ran by. It was the first sighting of a child that might've been the reason behind these generous sounds. A boy ran after her, and he had the same olive skin—a mix between Althea's and Kylen's. Not to mention, he had Althea's radiating white hair covering his own small head. Kylen felt the air still in his lungs and around him, his blood running cold as he stared at the children before him. They had his face shape, the turn of his eyes and the bump of Althea's nose.

They were his and Althea's.

Oh.

"Do you like what you see, King of the Madness?" a voice asked through the crackling air of the room. "How it truly would be kind if life gifted you with this." Several seconds passed, and Kylen could only stare. There were no words echoing throughout his mind. Everything was utterly silent. "You could have something similar if you were to only turn away now. No one and nothing at all will blame you."

Out of the shadows that clung to the walls before him walked a girl who was one he remembered and spent every day mourning for. One that had his heart racing as if he was seeing her for the very first time just now.

Her beauty was like that, and as always, it had the ability to send an army to their knees with Kylen beating them to it.

"Althea—" he went to murmur, except his plea was inaudible as he realised the woman was translucent and not actually standing there before him. She held one hand on her stomach as she walked, the glow of pregnancy eating away at her already ethereal skin. She was saying something that wasn't lavish enough for Kylen's ears to hear, yet he could still figure out just what those words were through the way her delicate mouth moved.

"Hunter, be nice to your sister."

Kylen—except not the Kylen who stood in the doorway barely breathing; another Kylen who was a mere image of him, approached the girl with her white hair perched on the top of her head in one famous and elegant bun. "Hi," he looked to have murmured, and was it ridiculous that Kylen was jealous of the variant of him who could touch her, hold her? The other Kylen rested his head on her shoulders, leaning down with his arms wrapping around her as he smiled and laughed at something one of the children had chirped so proudly. He murmured some luscious words to Althea before leaning over and pressing a kiss to her throat, making Kylen physically turn himself away before gagging.

Althea—except not his Althea—smiled up at the other Kylen as she turned towards him. She reached her hands up and to his cheeks before pressing a kiss of her own to his lips.

How he would give anything to be in that Kylen's position.

To have Althea alive and well in his presence.

To be his—No. Whilst he did want her to be his, he didn't know what she wanted. And if she wanted nothing to do with him, then so be it. He would prefer to be alone in every lifetime if it meant knowing that Althea Evangeline was happy for the first time ever.

Althea rose on her tippy toes to reach him, and Kylen—the ghost of Kylen, leant down to reach her. He smiled into the kiss as if he was mocking the Kylen who watched with a rigid soul. It was truly a prospect like no other. A torturous method that the curse knew would have Kylen's soul wanting to burn.

Yet... as he blinked, it all took a turn for the worst—causing his heart to stagger and his vision to diminish away as he faltered back into the wall behind him.

Because now...

Now he was left staring into the eyes of children who were overcome by the spirits.

The curses.

He was left looking towards a King who was on his knees as he held onto his wife and children whilst screaming and pleading for the lives that were already lost. Gone.

Because that's what Kylen's life had been cursed with from the beginning of time...

A war that was never to be won.

A war that had already been lost in every Realm out there.

"What a pity that this is a consequence for your sins, boy," a voice that flowed from somewhere beyond spoke, travelling through the electricity of the air and towards his nauseous heart. "This is your final warning, King of the seven seas. Stay away from us and turn away now, or this will be the future you will be the cause of."

Kylen took a step back, feeling as something warm and ever so cruel slowly seeped through his shoes. He felt as if he was going to be sick as he looked down: finding blood staining the old, emaciated wood he walked across. Kylen went to run, yet chains formed across his skin, and his feet slipped no more than a second later.

His heart began to race as he scrambled back and into the door that would not open, no matter how hard he tried. Kylen's fingers warped around the handle until his grip turned white, yet despite the strength bleeding from his soul as he tugged and thrashed against the rotten wood, the door would not open: it would not budge.

"Don't go looking into the memories of the past, the visions of the future—unless you are willing to sacrifice all." It was locked. Shut. He was trapped yet again by the curse that felt to be the consequence of his very existence.

Kylen shook his head, curses of his own fleeing from his tongue as he spat such insanity towards the shadowed darkness spreading around him. Why couldn't they just give up? Kylen wasn't going to let them win, nor was he going to abandon this war—even if it meant forcing himself to drown in the blood that flowed through the air as he looked back over his shoulder and towards the children that stared at him with eyes dripping of the curse.

He wasn't an idiot.

He wasn't stupid or insane as the rumours said of him.

No.

He knew that those children were supposedly his and Althea's and that this was meant to make him drown in his depression rather than flourish in his anger. The spirits teased him with the idea that in some mythical Realm out there, he was given the purpose of being a father instead of a murderer—and yet still, nevertheless, he would only ever bring death to the people he loved.

With a stifling breath that had Kylen's hands tightening at his sides, he looked from the children to the man who watched him. Every little emotion struck for his throat as he took a deep breath, daring to try and stop the wrath from bleeding from his soul. But Kylen was furious. He was so fucking furious. Why was it his life that was cursed? Why was it that he was the one the Gods constantly liked to spit on? The wind and many wicked voices at his spine brought Kylen's eyes to the soaring brick wall at his side—however, now it appeared as if he was outside... and that he was currently looking towards the many posters that were all featuring the same bloody message.

The same words that were actively proclaiming the same death.

'The Ball of Aeonia—the REBIRTH OF AEONIA.' The posters were announced in big and bold letters. A sign that no eyes could possibly miss because of the many enchantments that oozed off of them. 'Allow the curse to claim all that we are owed —to claim the mightiest of all mighty magick and finally save thou from the torture thou are left to scramble through.'

They were going to try and claim the magick...

The magick of Althea's soul—it truly was not her...

Kylen's entire body jolted awake as his eyes widened in such fear and understanding, except his vision was blurred, and his skull was still severely aching. A wave of exhaustion had Kylen whimpering as he thrashed against the chains that held him to the chair as if it was glue. His head felt so heavy, a thousand words feeling to hold him beneath the surface.

His head dropped within a second, falling to the left as he forced his eyes to stay open, to remain awake and alert.

Yet he wished he hadn't opened them again the next second and that he'd not allowed the exhaust of his lungs to wash him away to the delicacy of unconsciousness yet again.

Because now he was staring at the pile of bodies that were layered upon one another.

Kylen pushed himself up slightly, realising that these were the bodies of those who had attended the ball. *They had all been real people*—not hallucinations as Kylen had initially expected… And now they were all dead, their eyes dripping with a dark black blood that Kylen could still remember the taste of.

THIRTEEN
ALTHEA

"How long did it take your father to craft this?" It was a question that, for the first time in what felt like months, had an actual depth to it. Her tone wasn't frozen, imprisoned; there was curiosity there, earning a warm breeze to spread across Althea's bones as she shed the question towards Elara.

Her fingers trailed across the stone wall that apparently had been engraved from the very cave that the beloved Noxwell family hid within. The markings were marvellous. Every little detail looked to have taken a trillion centuries, at least, to create.

They looked to have been made from the ends of a God's fingertips—perhaps if Althea had been leisured in another life, she too would have this same ability. She would be able to also create something so magnificent. So mesmerising.

Elara shrugged as she dragged her eyes up from the bottom of the wall to the top of it—all of which was covered in astounding art. "I'm not sure, maybe a century or two?" she pondered. "Mother helped him every now and then. It was some-thing that helped them both fully comprehend just where we were now." A second of silence filtered through the two. "It took them a while to realise that we were dead." Elara laughed, although there was a hint of sadness lingering behind as her fingers dropped from the wall before her. Althea looked to Elara, who offered her a sheepish smile; there were dimples carved into her cheeks as well as scattered freckles. What would she have looked like if she had been allowed to grow physically? *A wondrous and intelligent beauty,* Althea was sure. "Since you have been asking all of the questions, may I ask you something now?"

That very question had Althea shivering in her shoulders. A sensation so uncomfortable as it captured her perished breath. "Go ahead." Despite her words, she wished to turn away now and never look back. *No. These are Kylen's siblings—they deserve your full attention and to make them know that they are cared for. Get your bloody act together.* Althea offered her another smile, but truthfully it had been so much easier when Althea didn't particularly care for the feelings of others. *So, so, so much easier.*

"Do you miss my brother?"

Althea barked a laugh before she had a second to compose herself.

Of course, Elara had to choose that glorious question of all questions. It was one of the few questions that left her tongue running dry as she tried with all of her stamina to think of an answer that would make any possible sense. Except how was she to form such a thing when her tongue was as wordless as an imprisoned frog? *That was a childhood story that she rather adored*—perhaps she could bring that story up and change the conversation altogether.

"That is an awfully difficult thing to answer," Althea whispered as she cleared her throat. Huntio must've returned from wherever he had wandered off to, as now he stood in the doorway watching from afar. Did they want her to suffer? This, of all questions, had her rubbing the back of her throat, trying to piece together anything at all. "I mean… of course, I miss *a version* of him…"

Elara nodded deceptively: like she truly knew something of what she was feeling. But how could she? Althea didn't even know herself. "And what version is that?" she prompted. "Kylen the king? Kylen the fiancé? Kylen the privateer? Or the Kylen who *was upon a time ago… your friend?*"

She truly did have the Noxwell wisdom, the one trait that had gotten Althea stuck within her soul in the first place.

Nevertheless, as Althea crossed her arms across her chest, she knew that she didn't have to answer the godsforsaken question, as both children who watched her steadily already seemed to be aware of the dreadful answer.

They had known it before she had—*Hel, she still didn't know if the answer sweeping her heart away was one that was truthful to herself.*

A rhythmic and lifesaving knock at the door had Althea turning towards it with her hands perched inches before her stomach, fiddling with her fingers as if that would solve all of her many problems.

It was like Marilla could sense the tension that had Althea by the throat because the expression she wore as she peeked her head inside was both apologetic and yet laughable. Althea looked to Marilla with an appreciative smile—although it was still one that did not meet the eyes.

"You two, stop torturing Althea; your father wants you."

"We weren't doing anything," Huntio was quick to reply as he raised a brow. Despite the situation being one that had Althea wanting to kick children, she would admit that it was nice seeing *these two* have some fun—considering all.

For them, she would allow it.

Elara folded her arms across her chest, casting a look to her mother, that was both adventurous and smart. *She was most definitely Kylen's sister*, and that, if anything, was beyond terrifying.

Althea didn't think she would've survived if, when she had met Kylen for the first time, there was a smaller, female version of him at his side. It was far too daunting for her liking. "I was just getting to know her. Is that truly such a crime, Mother?" Elara questioned in a confronting tone, earning Marilla to roll her eyes as she beckoned the two out of the room with a quick wave of her hands.

"Dinner is almost ready; go help your father set up, please."

"And what will you be doing?" Huntio retorted as he copied his sister's movements and crossed his arms across his chest. *Gods, they were all like Kylen, every last one of them.* "Why aren't you helping?"

"My boy, who do you think made dinner? Your father and I have done it all, and now he is merely adding the final toppings, that's all. Now run along; I want to have a word with Miss Althea."

Miss Althea.

Was that meant to sound kind or inevitably cruel?

She really did not want to be confronted by the woman who was praised by all—that was torture she didn't think that she could survive.

Althea watched with yearning eyes as the two children scattered out of the door frame like blind mice. They both cast her one last look with toothy grins and childlike humour to their laughs as they waved her goodbye. *They weren't too bad.* Althea exhaled deeply, turning her eyes up to the old Queen, who watched the two with the faintest of smiles on her cheeks. Her skin looked aged and weathered, except Althea wouldn't deny that she could see the heavenly glow that illuminated her corpse. "I apologise for them. They are good kids; they just sometimes don't understand when it isn't a good time to let your curiosity win this fatal battle."

It was as if Althea was once again bewitched by the curse because as she turned back towards the wall with many murals engraved into it, all she could do was nod. Her voice was not apparent to her; it was silent. Forcing her to be the child her father always dreamt of.

Instead of the loudmouth one that got scarred every other week.

Marilla also kept quiet as she reached Althea's side. Out of the corner of her daring blue eyes, she watched the Queen trace her fingers over the delicate lines of this *'memorial room'...* as Elara had described it.

"How are you, sweetheart?" Marilla questioned, and it took everything in the young girl not to react the way her heart beckoned her to.

To not cry and weep and sob for the eternal ache left in the crevices of her heart.

"I'm fine," Althea merely stated instead, and truly she wished that her voice had sounded kinder than it was. Gods know that was what this woman deserved for caring about such inevitable things. *"Fine,"* Althea repeated, despite only echoing the last word.

It felt like that was the one word she needed to engrave into her mind—the one word that was causing her immense trouble believing because of the problematic stance behind it.

Marilla nodded as she intertwined her hands. A sigh escaped her pursed lips as she offered Althea a hint of a second glance before turning on her heel. "While I didn't fully get a degree in psychology in my schooling days, I was halfway through my course before dying; nonetheless, it doesn't take a psych major to know when someone is lying," Marilla noted, and it sounded as if her words could be straight out of a poem. *How poetic.*

The lie of wind howled beyond the cave walls, and another breath of a phantom pain caressed Althea's spine as she glanced over her shoulder and towards the woman who was looking at the large book that sat on the wooden table. "I've been locked up for several months now, Mrs Noxwell; I apologise if my 'fine' isn't to your expectations."

Marilla was quick to turn around at that, and her expression was damning. She shook her head, stepping forward towards Althea, and before the girl got the chance to pull away, Marilla had already clasped onto her. "Oh, don't be ridiculous. Nothing you could do or say could ever... *not meet my expectations*. You are beyond perfect—Hel, I'm impressed just how far you have come from the small girl I held in my arms."

"Pardon?" Althea gasped as she raised her brows and pulled back slightly, although Marilla still had quite the clasp on her arms, and for whatever reason, Althea didn't seem to care that much. "What do you mean by held me—I thought that I had never met you or your husband... till now?"

"I was friends with your parents, Althea; of course, I met you when you were young." Her tone wasn't undermining or foul; it was soft and knowing. A smile toyed at her lips as she physically restrained herself from tucking the loose curl behind her ear. "I only ever held you once, though. Oh, I can still remember how tiny you were and how proud your mother was of creating such a beautiful thing."

Althea nodded as if she understood.

But she didn't know what to understand.

She didn't know what to think.

Everything felt beyond her capability.

Althea forced a smile to her lips, and *boy did she hope that it looked real*... because it looked as if the woman standing before her needed it more than she did. It wasn't clear whether it was her magick or not, but Althea could feel the nervous energies that radiated through the Queen's body like the tidal wave of the curse that had killed her. "That's nice," Althea uttered, *but Gods, was her smile laughable*. She could feel the pain wash amongst her soul, that strange ache that sent the skies riveting. But she held herself back from giving in to it; she needed to merely focus on whatever it was that this family had planned, and then she would be alive again.

Oh, but these mortals deserve so much better.

I know—trust me, I know.

As if Willix was another soul who was apparently meant to be her lord and saviour, his deep yet muffled voice echoed throughout the air. Marilla practically tugged her towards the door in search of it, *galaxies shining in her eyes.*

"Come on! Maybe since you are still technically alive, you will be able to taste Willix's cooking. There's nothing like it, I tell you. *Oh, please do tell me if you can taste it*—and be sure to be *extra* critical about it. Elara and I love watching him squirm in his shoes while awaiting approval." Did the stars take pity on her too? What about the moon? Surely, they saw just how hard she was trying not to be entirely numb. Yet with every step she took, every swallow of her lungs, every quivering little blink, she couldn't help but feel the tears begin to swell in the eyes of storms.

Althea held them back, of course.

She wouldn't allow herself to look so weak in front of a family that had suffered so much worse.

FOURTEEN
KYLEN

K ylen wasn't aware when the stars had fallen, and the sun somewhere far had dared to attempt to partially rise. He wasn't aware when the many entangled curses had thickened as they crept down the streets, devouring the ghosts of those whose bodies were now piled on top of one another in the cell next to his.

Except Kylen was, *however*, not oblivious to the smell of rotting corpses that haunted his mind as he took every heavy breath. As they smelt exactly how his parents and siblings had when he first stumbled upon their darling rotting corpses in a place that seemed so far from here.

A memory one's mind would never allow them to forget.

Though now, as Kylen's mind burned with hunger and pain that seemed everlasting, he found that he ultimately didn't know anything—other than the fact that he was *exhausted. Beyond exhausted.* It felt as if every little bone in his body had been snapped and put back together again in the wrong place, only for then, his bones to be burned and tortured after everything, as if the Gods found joy in his agony.

It was like a game—

And his body was so tired.

His muscles were *so* sore.

With a slow roll of his head, and a whimper leaving his bloody lips, Kylen tried to move, feeling as the unforgiving and harsh ground beneath him scattered in the purest form of fear. Kylen grimaced at that pain, but his attention was soon fixated elsewhere when a firm rock rebounded from his cheek and scrambled across the cobblestone floor. His body flinched *as again, only a second later,* another small and yet sharp stone collided with his flesh from somewhere in the air above, landing on the ground before being devoured entirely by the darkness that Kylen watched with tired eyes.

What?

Was he on drugs?

Nothing was clear to him—and the thoughts in his mind were beyond foggy.

Of course, he had some recollection of what had just happened; however, it left him with so many questions that were just unanswerable.

Kylen held up a weak hand, attempting to shelter away the light that was aiming for his throat. Still, nothing was clear; it felt as if he was actually imprisoned in a haze. A haze of a memory that made him feel like he was intruding into someone's mind—no, he had already apparently done that: which meant that this was purely his own lovely mind. Kylen squinted against the ice of the air, feeling as the crisp winds sent an uncomfortable shiver down his back *when to his utter dismay*, another stone came flying right at him. *And it was clear that he had definitely not imagined that.* "What—"

"*Open your damn eyes*," a voice snarled—one that brought his eyes to the left of him. Kylen's vision was still appallingly blurred, except with a Hel of a lot of effort, he managed to make out the shape of a small rectangular window that was positioned at the top of the cell wall. Perhaps, in another mystical world,

Kylen would be able to reach it if he was to run and jump with such stamina, but his body felt far too heavy to even think about that, and this had never been a mystical or forgiving world. So, he truly doubted he could even lift an utter finger under these conditions. "Kylen, it's me—*don't look at me like that.*"

Atticus.

That was Atticus—*his* brother.

The brother he wanted to punch.

With another several rushed blinks, Kylen's vision began to clear, and slowly he saw *far more clearly* the outline of Atticus' face on the other side of the metal bars that separated the two of them. He looked awfully pissed off and confused as he assessed him with a scowl. *Good, he wanted him to feel something mean. Something cruel.* "What—"

"*Look at you.* Are you seriously that pathetic that you decided to walk into a castle that reeks of the curse? Are you that much of an idiot, brother? I ask you that." Kylen swore he could see the spit flying from his brothers' clenched teeth. Atticus looked at him with a shadow of disbelief to his features, shaking his head as if that could bring Sayah back from the dead—or Althea back from wherever she was. He ran a hand through the brown curls hanging over his eyes, growling several foul words under his breath as if he had been in a drunken brawl. "My Gods —wait, I'm going to find another way in. Just wait there—*oh,* and also, I sent word to the other *three,* but I doubt it will reach them in time… or that they will even bother to help conquer whatever the fuck this threat fucking is."

The other three? That sounded so awfully damning when it used to be *four.*

Uzziah, Khatri, Zaire, and Sayah. *Sweet, darling Sayah.*

"*No*—Atticus—*Althea*—" No matter the number of pleas he would scream into the electrifying air that was waiting for the storm to erupt, he was too late. The boy was already gone, walking to his death. "Inconsiderate ass," Kylen seethed under his tremoring breath, although he knew that he was probably the one in the wrong this time.

A low rumbling groan slipped from Kylen's lips as he pushed himself to his knees, a sneer slipping from his lungs as he tried to shake away the pain coaxing his bones. He felt as if he had been hit by another curse. He felt as if every possible evil magick out there had collided with his soul and ripped it apart until there was nothing left.

What had *she* done to him?

Was it even Althea?

The wind howled from above, warping around his spine and pushing him to sit up with a cruel laugh. His still quivering gaze dropped to his bruised and bloody hands as the memories of what had happened earlier dawned on him. *Althea* —she had been alive? She had been real—she had been right there. Yet... *why didn't she look to recognise him?* Why didn't she have that same agonised look in her eyes as the one haunting his?

Wasn't she at all as affected by their past as he was?

This couldn't be her.

It wasn't her, and he had already realised that.

Althea was good.

She had a heart—no matter how she claimed differently.

He loved her heart. He would have, and he still would dare to go to war for her heart; suit, armour, and all.

That heart had been the one thing he had researched about for all these long months now. Kylen had done everything in his physical power to find out anything about the girl who was supposedly lost, the girl who had supposedly drowned in this darkness...

Yet where had it led him?

Nowhere.

Absolutely nowhere.

Except now he had somewhat of a lead in his research—if

you were to look past the fact that he could potentially die at any given moment, *that was.*

Kylen tried to move again when the air seemed to electrify around him, a deep harmonising melody skimming the edge of his skin that had the wounded heart within him panicking.

A heavy and fragile force warped through his fingertips, practically holding the boy to the ground as the sound of footsteps echoed through the dungeons of Aeonia.

"So many thoughts running through that little head of yours —" an ethereal voice noted with a quiver of a laugh bleeding into the heavy air. The electricity was a sensation that he unfortunately remembered with every inch of his soul. It spread through the darkness like a drug, soothing the eternal burn that withered his face as the *girl* stepped out of the shadows that hugged her flesh and bones as if *she* had given it everything it could possibly ever ask for. "Hello again, *boy.*" Her features were narrowed, tight. Kylen could see Althea more clearly now, and she had the same haze on her face that had been on his *sisters, brothers, parents...* when death, at last, had met them after a manacled tidal wave of the curse washed through the Kingdom of Lorundio.

Except, the lady before him didn't wear it with pride—she hid from it, something Althea would never physically allow herself to do in front of *anyone.*

"You aren't Althea," Kylen retorted with a shake of his head, and the mask of confidence that he wore with such pride was fuelled by pure rage. A rage that was burning because of all the curse had taken from him. "You *can't* be her," his words came out like a slur, his head hanging forward as he looked at her with a brutal emotion wielding around his heart. Whatever the *spirits and the lost souls of the curse* had done to drug him had managed to create a lingering effect that made the world feel unbelievably uneasy under his feet.

The spirits laughed out of Althea's astonishing lungs, their corpse-like fingers twirling a strand of her *obsidian black hair* around and around. "Oh, he's gorgeous and smart; we like a boy who can be both." She tilted her head with a narrow of *her* eyes. "But is that so?" They challenged with a raise of a single brow. "You know, I must give it to you that you are a lot more intelligent than your dear old pops. He was in so much denial when I possessed your mother's soul—your siblings. Oh, I can still hear their screams! Such melodies, I tell you."

There it was.

The crack in who it truly was that managed to confirm that Kylen was right in who he had been expecting. But despite him having had something of an idea, the idea was raw and could've been potentially made up of all that he feared.

Except now he knew that it was true.

And it was the *spirits of the curse.*

Amongst all of his research over the course of the last few months, the few things Kylen had actually managed to learn was about the curse and how to bring back *one from the dead*—and while he had always found himself stumbling upon the *rumours* of the curse's *origin,* for the most part, everything else went unspoken or was briefly mentioned.

It was rumoured amongst those who dared to speak in such scarred places that after the events of Harlia and the last time the two had crossed paths, Erwin had gone off the grid of all of the Realms once again. The lot of Kylen's *family* had figured that it was because the curse had been butchered, that the curse was suddenly gone; therefore, he was too... but the moment Kylen had felt that same descant of the curse's aura twist across his skin in Sayah's untouched, bloody bedroom, he'd known with every inch of his mind, that *Erwin was still alive*, and so was the curse.

It was mean; it was punishing because while the King was spared of the curse's wrath, that didn't take away from the fact that he was always the first to sense it.

Always the first to *scent* it.

Yet knowing that the curse was still alive had confirmed Kylen's horrible fear that Althea had utterly '*died*' for nothing.

Absolutely nothing at all.

Back in the early mornings when the sun had just begun its fatal strike, Kylen had found himself learning from all the many old history books that the curse, *once upon a time ago*, had had its own soul. *Own mind*. It was said to eagerly collect all of the screams and souls that had become lost to those it was murdering, creating a voice that had driven those like Erwin and his lost, *nameless* brother to insanity. Atticus had claimed that Kylen was purely reading into it and that he was going to drive himself to insanity if he kept going on about this—but Kylen had been adamant about learning the truth.

Had Althea inherited that soul?

Was that what the darkness was that hid within her body now?

...Or was he just in complete denial of it all?

Althea—*or the spirits in control of her body* raised a brow, her chest heaving with a laugh as the door to his cell opened, and against Kylen's will, the curse tightened its hold on his skin and raised him into the air; forcing the boy into the cold metal chair that was covered in someone else's decaying *blood*.

"What did you do to her?" Kylen demanded through a snarl. He held his chin high as he stared them down, such disgust and disgrace in his eyes as he watched 'Altheas' every little flicker of a movement. If a gaze could burn—his would be sure to leave the world in flames. "If you—"

"*Relax*, boy. We *weren't* the ones to *kill her*, no matter how hard we had tried. A strong one, that is. She was our prisoner for several months, *yes*, and then with the help of a *deathling...* she escaped," the spirits explained as they—in Althea's body, leant back against the long thick bars of the cell directly before him; they looked over him as if they were stripping him of every little security he possibly held. A stare so intimate: so cruel when it was through *her* eyes.

Except he *couldn't* care less about what happened to him.

He *wouldn't* care less about what was happening to him.

Not when the truth was skimming his heart with a blade that had just been sharpened.

Several months.

Several months.

Althea had been alive... *for the past several months?*

Kylen felt as if he was going to be sick. He looked away with a shake of his head—she was probably waiting for him to show up*: to prove to her that she was all that mattered.* And then, when they were both finally free—they would work on getting Sayah back.

Because *surely,* she was not truly gone either.

Why couldn't he have tried to figure out what had killed Sayah and gone after *it* sooner rather than later? Perhaps then he would've saved her *too—*

"Oh, relax, pretty-witty boy. She is still alive, just not currently in... *reach*—which is why we are referring to her as... *dead,*" they cackled, and a strand of dark hair wrapped around her bone-like finger. Her features looked utterly lifeless. No colour, no humanity, no nothing. The hem of her sleeve fell as she let the curl go, and Kylen caught a horrid glimpse of one of the many terrifying scars that appeared to be lacing her arms. There were fresh scars and bruises that all of which cruelly pinpointed how the curse had been torturing her flesh all this time. Did they take their anger out on her? Did they want her to feel the pain that they had suffered?

Kylen was going to murder every last one of their souls.

And Kylen wasn't dumb; he was more than aware that they would try and slaughter her to consume every little speckle of magick within her blood, as that would give the curse the immortal ability to conquer the world and everyone and every-thing within it.

All would burn.

All would die.

Homes would falter.

Walls would crumble.

Nothing at all would survive the complications of the curse.

But that was going to be the last thing he would let happen. Kylen may be heartless, but he was also considered insane, and slaughtering the curse seemed like a rather *mad* thing to do.

"Where is she?"

The body of Althea shrugged with a merciless laugh, she leaned forward with temptation, and it took everything in Kylen's soul to keep his breathing even. Her chin was an inch away from Kylen's nose, her eyes staring down at his so that he could get a good look at the curse that swirled within. *That was not Althea.* "She's a God; she could be anywhere right now… I sense her lingering in the afterworld, though, but past there, we no longer have the ability to track her every movement, *every breath*, so she could be long gone by now if she so dared. She—*if she chooses, could truly be dead, and we wouldn't even know, *would we?*"

Kylen's brows furrowed as his lips pursed to control his anger. He needed to be strategic and think of what to do next that would, one: not damage or leave any marks on Althea's body. And two: actually save his arse before he got himself murdered (Gods know that wouldn't be easy to do). "Why is she in the afterworld—"

"Boy, does it look like I—*we* know all the answers? She's probably visiting a dead loved one or something. Leave it to her to make peace with the dead while taking advantage… *of the dead*," the curse sneered with a roll of Althea's eyes.

Kylen pulled his chin back, his brows narrowing tightly together. He shook his head—nothing was making sense in the slightest. Eloise and her mother wouldn't be in the afterlife… their souls had been demolished by the curse.

So, had his families—*who was it that she was possibly going after?*

"Why are you in Althea's body?" Kylen questioned, looking back to the mockery of the girl who he had mourned for. While he knew that the answer was as clear as what once was day, Kylen was also trying to buy his *dearest* brother a scrap of time. *Whilst he was a pain in his ass,* he was also his brother—and someone needed to keep that boy alive. Gods know he was practically incapable of doing just that. "Why are you trying to murder her? Go after the King instead, I will personally bring him to you, and I'm sure his soul will be far more pleasant to devour."

The quiver of the air around the two tightened, and Kylen watched slyly out of the corner of his eye as a twine of dark magick began to flow out of Althea's chest and through the sky. It attached itself to the piles of bodies that were lying amidst a puddle of dark black blood. Kylen could practically taste that foulness; he had grown up on it, after all.

They were feeding.

The curse was feeding off of their souls.

Unfortunately, Kylen was not exactly oblivious to what the curse was presumably trying to do. He'd had the disastrous pleasure of learning long ago that those whose bodies became infested with the curse were left to rot while the curse slowly took over their every last heartbeat. It may only take a couple of days, a week, a month, or it could happen over the course of several years. Either way, it *always* took over. Kylen tensed as he beckoned his stare to straighten; somehow, for Althea, it had taken something similar to *death* to occur.

That brought his eyes to fall back to the ground as his soul swayed with memories of the past. He would never forget how it felt to look over and see Althea's limp body… he would never forget the way she felt in his arms—both in the moments when she was content and alive—and in the moment when she was dead, just another victim of the curse that they'd both run from for so long.

But those memories were what he often found his mind falling asleep to in the dead of night when all else failed to captivate his mind and silence the thoughts.

"You forget she's a God," the spirits stated as a matter of fact as they pushed themselves off the bars at her back. "She has the ability to control every aspect of every Realm out there. She can do whatever she likes whenever she likes—she just never got the chance to drown in that idea." Althea's body stepped forward, and the spirits raised a hand towards his stern face. *They knew that they were torturing him* and that this sight before him was all that he had ever longed for. "We want our bodies back, our souls back. When we get this ability... we will be able to have *whoever* we want *whenever* we want."

Kylen clenched his jaw as he inched his throat back and away from their touch as they stepped forward again. However, if it were the true Althea, his throat would've already been hers. He would've succumbed to her power and given her whatever she pleased. Althea had that power over him, and Kylen adored it. Except as he stared at the curse, his gaze was cold, his eyes cruel, reflecting on all of the wrongdoing that Althea had suffered through.

And Kylen knew that he needed to separate Althea from the soul before his.

He needed to realise that this may be Althea's breath-taking body—but his Althea was long gone from *within* it.

He remembered some of the first steps of Homicidium; after all, he'd spent so many sleepless nights rereading that same page. Yet had he ever fully taken in the knowledge? Maybe. Maybe not. Kylen remembered parts of it, but the rest was drowned with the whiskey and the rum.

'Homicidium':

The darkness that consumes

It is said by those who managed just to escape before the darkness fell, that the only way they made it out of the shadowed realms was through the ability of an <u>anchor</u>.

An anchor is a soul who is persistent with bringing another soul back through the realms—furthermost pinpointing how their souls in every world are one.

How on earth was Kylen meant to act as an anchor?

Sure, Sayah had always said that Althea and Kylen were one of the same; but he doubted that this was what she meant.

"Althea is still connected to you, is she not?" Kylen asked, and he watched the moment confusion flashed subtly onto her features. They went to speak—Althea's lips slightly parted, but Kylen was quick-witted to interrupt her despite having no idea what it was that he was rambling about. "What will it take for me to reach her? A single word? A single laugh? What will it take? While you were wasting your days in this castle, I was learning of all there was regarding that darling murderer of yours." *The curse.* "I know that there is the rare chance one of the lost souls can respond to those calling to them—yet I also know that if I choose to be her anchor, I *will* get her back."

"Give it up, boy. Althea is as good as dead," the spirits growled, and Kylen cocked a brow. Did they truly learn nothing from being inside the mind of a mastermind? "She has nothing to live for—her soul is bruised and a mere burden. What good is life in this world?"

"If there is one thing that I have learnt… it's that people love to underestimate her. She is a lot stronger than you all assume. *She is a Queen, a God.* So really, all I have to say is, *'Althea, fight'*… and she will probably have your head within a moment —I honestly wouldn't put it past her; that woman is beyond magnificent."

The spirits began to stumble back, walking into several sets of bars as Kylen watched with a steady gaze. They were afraid and confused. Kylen had done that—*he had actually talked himself into a battle that he seemed to be winning?* That would prove to all his brothers that talking was a skill and that he was indeed marvellous at it.

Such noise erupted into the air—causing Kylen to flinch only once before his soul became used to it. *He was going to get her back. He was.* Althea's hands rose to her ears, and Kylen watched in horror as dark black blood began to drip down the sides of her face from where her nails dug into her flesh. He didn't want to hurt her—he didn't want to cause her pain. *This wasn't Althea.* They were trying with all of their cursed will to suppress the many howling voices that were beginning to rise, their hands flying out in every direction as the curse began to shoot into the air and flood it with darkness.

Kylen looked away in panic, attempting to fight off the restraints, except it became no use when the darkness already managed to pry his jaw open and squirm its way against his bellowing lungs again.

But he didn't care. He couldn't bring himself to care in the slightest.

As that confirmed all that Kylen ever needed to know.

And if he had to endure this torture in order to get his queen back, then so be it.

FIFTEEN
ALTHEA

I t was a strange concept that the current time of the afterlife was deemed as night. Yet, the night that shone heavenly upon the lands of death was all a mere deception—and that there was no actual element of time here.

The stars that were briefly spotted just a couple of hours ago when Althea had glanced beyond the cave walls were all a mere delusion; because while they partially looked to be real and true, if one were to focus their eyes on them a little too hard, they would notice all of the tiny little flaws that reinforced how none of this was real. And that Althea was truly not in the physical Realms anymore.

Hel, she was beginning to forget what those lands even looked like.

How was Althea to know she wasn't trapped in one big hallucination? And that when she was to wake up, she would find that she was still trapped within the cell of her soul, a prisoner to an evil she had worked for so long now to escape.

Although it wasn't truly night, that didn't stop the nightmares from erupting. It didn't stop Althea from clinging to the flesh of

186

her arms and legs as if her weak bones would protect her from all that seemed to want her head.

Except the damning nightmares didn't haunt her unconscious mind: they didn't haunt her at her weakest and most vulnerable state. No, they haunted her very conscious mind. Pricking at it with a freshly sharpened blade as she stared ahead with lifeless eyes, memorising the shadowed wall before her because, *really*, that was all that she could bring herself to do.

Althea was merely waiting for time to show her kindness.

The dinner Willix had prepared had been wonderful; however, Marilla was wrong when she thought that Althea would be able to taste anything at all because she couldn't. It almost felt as if she was eating the air she breathed. That tasteless sensation wasn't fulfilling her mortal cravings.

It was intriguing to watch the Noxwell family interact. To hear them chatting away about their days as if the day they had lived had been one of living and breathing.

Without anyone telling her, Althea had learnt that the stories they shared at the table had been ones that were all completely made up. It was almost as if she was in a play where the cast could perform whatever role they wanted at that moment when the spotlights began to shine.

Elara had been the first to speak, and she'd apparently decided to go into the 'Kingdom' *today*. Sir Elliorndio was said to accompany her as well, and he'd taken her to the finest markets of them all on the east edge of the kingdom's square.

When it was Huntio's turn, he'd replied by saying that he had *brutally* trained through the day and nights with Sayah, perfecting his stance and flips so that when the darkness threatened to fall next time, he would be prepared to tackle it.

It was a sweet idea.

A heart-warming one.

One that Althea supposed she should now be smiling over rather than feeling nothing at all about. Except her mind felt so loose. As if it was caught in the storms and the quick racing clouds were dragging it through several Realms at once.

Marilla and Willix had added onto each other's sentences, and eventually, they made out the story that they had taken their *darling boy* Kylen shoe shopping. *Bloody shoe shopping, of all things.* And while Althea somewhat expected the air to tense and for the room to shrink at the mention of the son who'd lived, the lot of them kept talking with grins on their lips. Reminiscing on how Kylen always preferred the brown shoes over the black shoes his father wore—but if Althea recalled correctly, which she did because while she had only recently just gotten her memories back, they were never wrong, her *once* fiancé had only ever been seen wearing black shoes.

The black shoes with 'W.N' engraved into the back of them.

It felt as if Althea would give into the curses pleads at the very moment if it meant that she would be turning over in her bed sheets and locking eyes with the boy she didn't know if she missed. It felt as if she would give anything to know that she wasn't completely alone in the darkness and that he would hold her hand as they walked through it together.

Sure, a part of her did miss the boy Althea remembered. But then the other parts of her remembered all too well how, in her final moments of breathing true and pure air, the man she had grown to care for again had shaken hands with the man who had been the cause of almost every physical scar on her body.

But not all of the mental ones.

Althea couldn't bear this; she felt like she was staring into oblivion, and her bones were about to melt. She pushed herself up and off the mattress to the point where the dip in the bed under her threatened for her to collapse back into its warm arms. Her eyes grazed slowly through the darkness that wasn't like the darkness she feared—yet it was far too similar for any of her liking.

It was unbelievably suffocating, causing her face to tense and her eyes to shut in a whimper.

The stone flooring of this sincere cave was cold beneath Althea's feet. The ice was slithering into her flesh that wasn't her true flesh in any way, shape, or form. It was a *lie*.

Just like everything else she'd ever known and believed in.

Whilst Althea knew that it was almost impossible for the cave beneath her to physically make *her feel* cold, Althea still reached for the earnest maroon robe Marilla had left out for her on the back of the small wooden chair by her bedside table.

It strangely appealed to her.

Not because she was afraid of the monsters that lurked for her flesh—it was more so because she sought that comfort, that kindness.

Any true warmth that wouldn't deceive her.

Only unbreakable silence greeted the girl who tiptoed out of her room after taking another deep breath of confidence. Only pure silence had her spine straightening and her breaths quivering. Her magick was actively dancing beneath her touch as she trailed her long fingers across the stone walls; she could feel it as tiny little vibrations that had the hair on her arms and legs rising, except there was something that went subconsciously unsaid that held Althea from using it.

An unspoken law against all she ever knew.

She was suppressing it because not only was she afraid of allowing the spirits to consume it, but she was also afraid that it would make her feel more than what she was already feeling. She was afraid that if she were to succumb to it, it would make her weaker than how she already felt.

And really, she didn't need to be any more vulnerable than she currently was.

It was disgusting.

As if the house she was cautiously treading through was tracking her every movement, the candles on the left of her were beginning to burn every time her body aligned with them. Then once she had passed them, a gust of wind from somewhere unknown had them darkening once again. Leaving for the girl who once rejoiced in the nights, wishing to have a blade to defend herself against whatever evil lingered in the abyss behind her.

Althea could be walking into a trap for all she knew, but it felt nice to be *finally able to walk again.* To know that she was no longer confined to a single miniature room that had her lungs daring to smother her every time she began to so much as think of that dreadful *moment.*

Yet, despite Althea now being free of that cell, she wasn't mentally free.

She still felt trapped.

Confined.

Lost.

Althea's trivial steps had come to an abrupt stop as her eyes fell on the glimmer of light that radiated from beneath an *almost closed* door. She shouldn't pry—not on a family that had taken her in and so far, appeared to be trustworthy… but there was just something about the way that she had been deprived of mortal interaction for so long now that had her craving it more than anything.

With a tiny breath that made the decision for her, Althea slowly stalked towards it, stopping just outside the entrance before realising that the door was just resting shut and was not fully closed.

Which meant that she could peek inside if she was cautious enough.

They did once call her the assassin of the night, *did they not?* This was easy.

It was a risky gamble; Althea knew that, but again, as if her reasoning wasn't enough, she had been trapped for so inevitably long... so was it really such a crime for her to want to watch real people act in real ways?

Even if they were dead.

With the softest touch, Althea pushed the door slightly open ajar, peaking inside before her eyes landed on the target of a woman who was softly humming to herself. She must've had a charm of some type on the door to conceal the sound, as Althea had not heard a hint of her presence before. *How was her magick even working here?* Althea had originally figured that because she was the only soul that was partially alive, that was the reasoning as to why she had magick?

So, why did Marilla?

It was confusing... all of it. Yet, Althea had already decided that she would bother with learning the complications of this world tomorrow.

Althea's eyes fell upon Marilla Noxwell, who sat with a paintbrush in her hands. Her lips were slightly pursed, and her back was arched. She was focussing on the canvas before her, biting onto her bottom lip as if she was trying to figure out just what it was that she was missing.

It was at that moment then when Althea decided to look around the homey room that Marilla sat in, and it was also at that moment then when her heart threatened to falter... because her eyes landed sight on the boy she had almost truly forgotten.

The boy she *did* miss.

Althea didn't care about her cover being blown as she pushed the door further open; she didn't care that she could feel Marilla's eyes fall on her as she entered the room; she only cared about walking over to the wall that was covered in portraits of Kylen Noxwell, the boy who was stirring damning emotions in the pits of her soul.

From left to right were portraits of the current King of Lorundio that varied in age as the wall went on. On the left, Kylen was young. He was only a boy, yet he still held the weight of a kingdom in the palms of his hands. On the right, there was the Kylen Noxwell that Althea had known and had grown to *love*. The boy who had danced with her and slept alongside her. The boy who had washed the blood from her flesh with such sincerity in his eyes that it threatened for her mind to weep.

Marilla had captured his smile so flawlessly. The way his cheeks became fluttered with dimples, and his eyes disappeared to the point where only joy was visible on his face—all of it. No one would ever know of all the pain Kylen had suffered; they wouldn't know of the eternal wounds that marked his own soul —*as he was the charming king that brought grace to all...* The charming king that had kissed her days before her soul was lost.

Althea's hand slowly dropped to hold the pit of her stomach as she willed herself not to let any emotions show. "Gods," she whispered under her breath. However, it came out as more of a weep than anything.

She did miss him.

She missed him more than she ever knew to be able to.

And it hurt like Hel.

"I'm afraid that if I stop painting him, I will forget what he looks like. I mean, sure, we have the ability to take a glance every now and then into the physical Realms, but who is to say that we don't have a number of opportunities to do that and that ours will run out soon? Who is to argue that we are able to do this forever—because if I forget my boy...? I don't know how I will survive."

"He hasn't forgotten you, you know," Althea admitted as she turned her eyes over her shoulder, looking towards the woman who had gotten up and was now standing only a metre away. Her eyes were too on Althea, looking at her with a small smile as she nodded, but her eyes revealed everything. And she looked to not believe a word that Althea was preaching. "He still remembers you all, and all he wants is to make you proud —even if it is going against me." Althea looked back towards the painting, beckoning away the anxiety that clawed at her tongue. Her features must've looked somewhat distressed because as she turned, she had caught a glance of Marilla's face —and there were no words to describe how empathetic they looked. How could a boy with such good intentions do something like making a deal with the literal devil after he murdered his fiancé?

Was this all a gamble of time?

Was that what this was?

Marilla parted her lips as she went to say something; however, they abruptly shut as she furrowed her brows together in thought. "Kylen didn't betray you, sweetheart. Not again."

Althea shook her head without shedding her another glance. "I don't need you protecting him or me, Mrs Noxwell. I'm a big girl now; I can protect myself." *But can you?* Her mind asked, daring to put the troubling question into her already wounded thoughts.

And Althea honestly didn't have an answer that was the truth.

"Again, call me Marilla. But Althea, he has your father chained in the dungeons of Lorundio, and that boy has held off from killing him because he is waiting for you to do it," Marilla admitted with such ease, acting as if it was nothing at all. Althea turned around as if her flesh was being physically pried from her grasp, her features crumbling as she shook her head. "He loves you, and I know that because he looks at you the way Willix looks at me. I don't care—*well, I do partially care on Kylen's behalf*—but I don't care if you don't love him back, not after all you have suffered, but I do not want you thinking that that boy wouldn't go insane for you if you asked him to. The last thing Kylen would want to do is hurt you again, okay?"

There was something about her tone that was daunting— something about her tone that made Althea feel as if she was a child being scolded by her mother.

Because she sounded *to not be lying*, she realised, almost as if she was laying the truth out before her and gifting her the rare opportunity to do whatever she pleased with it.

As if the paintings before her were physically the embodiment of Kylen Noxwell, her eyes flew back towards the wall that still managed to have her heart-stopping. *That can't be true.* It couldn't be true.

For so long now, even if she hadn't always held full control of her memories, her soul had decided to link that agony and pain with him. Her mind had decided that he was why her heart wept in the depths of the night and why it was holding on.

It had been easier.

It *had* been.

Now… Althea wasn't so sure. And that made her feel uneasy and beyond horrible.

Marilla shook her head slyly as if she felt for the girl, and she moved closer to her without uttering a single word. Her touch was warm and comforting as her hand met with her shoulders, and Althea knew that it was dumb, but she couldn't will herself to move out of it.

Marilla looked to be seconds away from whispering something when the ground began to tremor beneath the two. However, the tremors didn't last very long, as they were quickly replaced with judders that were so much more consuming: causing both of their thoughts and sudden actions to still, as panic arose within the cage of her chest.

"*What—*" Marilla seethed. Her voice was awfully loud over the ruckus, although it was quick to be cut off. The shaking became so ruinous that it caused Marilla to stumble several feet forward. Yet, Althea was ready and quick to reach for her. Attempting to hold her back from collapsing onto the floors that looked active with slithering dark, shadowed evil.

Had the curse finally reached her?

Every instinct within Althea's soul told her to run and hide. Her mind screamed at her to smash one of the frames on the walls and to use a sharp shard of glass to defend herself against whatever force of evil that was seconds away from coming for them—except before Althea could so much as take another quivering step in any direction, an indescribable pain pierced through the centre of her chest, causing her to cry out in agony as her legs gave way. She collapsed to the ground, and Althea knew that somehow, against whatever odds, she was bleeding. She could feel it pool through her hands, glide through her fingers. She didn't know *how*, but she also didn't find it in her to exactly care at this very moment.

She just wanted the pain to stop.

Marilla dove for her squirming body within a splinter of a second. She tugged her into her arms, and Althea clasped onto her skin with blood-covered hands as if she was the only light to guide her out of this darkness. The throbbing that took over her mind felt to consume her every breath. It didn't help that the room was beginning to fill with dust from the cracks and splinters spreading across the walls and ceilings like wildfire. She tried to breathe—except every time she tried to gulp down the air of the afterlife, she felt as if she was underwater. "*What happened?* What is it, Althea? W*hat is it?* Is it the curse?" Marilla's words spat out like quick pleas, and when she didn't receive an answer, her head flew up with a panic that was honourable. "WILLIX!"

If Althea was quite literally not beginning to seize in this women's arms, and she had the glorious time of day to watch this happen to someone else... she would almost laugh. A stranger—a stranger who was *dead* and had supposedly been watching over her for so long... was now holding onto her with an expression of distress on her lips.

Almost looking to genuinely care for her. The most wicked lie of them all.

"Willix—" Marilla didn't get the chance to finish her cry as the door quickly flooded with three other souls that reeked of *fear, terror, and distress.* Except, that throbbing notion of their presence didn't last long, as Althea found that she could no longer see anything.

Or sense anything.

Or hear anything.

They felt to be worlds away—*she* felt to again be worlds away.

Panic struck the bottom of Althea's stomach, her mind out of her reach. "*Marilla?*" Her vision had gone dark, and she felt as if someone or something was physically holding her underwater —*like there were two clammy hands with rotten flesh and dark nails that held her back from escaping the water's surface.* Althea looked around through the midst of the ash, a cry burning her lungs as she felt the curse trace intimate Markings across her arms and legs. She had gotten so used to ignoring the Elemental Markings on her arm that on some days, half of her mind had already forgotten that they were actually there, and yet now they burned.

They burned so badly.

And that burn had her eyes and her mouth flying open in an attempt to flee.

The curse forced its way down her lungs no matter how hard Althea tried to struggle against it; the whites of her eyes disappeared as she slowly morphed into *just another victim.* It was quick, but for half a second, she thought she heard the cries of a man she knew. A man she missed. Althea thought that she'd heard the cries of Kylen Noxwell—but that didn't make any sense because why would he be struggling too?

Who was *she* anymore? She was a survivor, was she not? So why was she not surviving this? *Give into us, Althea. We can make your dreams seem more peaceful; we can take away the brutality from your scars. You will no longer grieve; you will no longer cry. You will look upon your lifetime and smile because you will be at utter peace—*

Burn in Hel.

Althea hadn't physically been the one to snarl the words at the spirits, but she had heard the rage that fulfilled every one of them.

This was it.

She was going to die, and the only people that would've known that she had survived for this long would be the family that was also dead.

Murdered.

Forgotten.

'What was life without pain? What was pain without life?' Althea remembered her father asking her those very questions when she was only young. He had told her that in several years from now, she wouldn't remember all that she had 'suffered'. No, he had said that she would only recall all of the power and wealth that she had gained. He had forcefully told her that *'it didn't matter how you managed to make your way to the top of the food chain, it only mattered that you would stay there and protect your honour.'*

But he was wrong.

Because Althea did remember her pain.

And she did remember all that she had suffered.

The curse forced her jaw to widen, slithering down and conquering every inch of Althea's humanity as she began to feel her darling magick quiver within her bones. Except, this time, it wasn't cracks of what had once been, it was all of it, and it finally decided to come out from hibernation. It didn't present itself as much as a decision before her; no, she just decided to act in self-defence, grabbing onto the makeshift blade before her and dragging it across her own throat with no mercy in her mind.

And before she even truly knew it, that same glistening ethereal light that she had watched save Kylen countless times erupted from within. Blinding her immensely.

Althea's body jolted with such stamina, almost like there

were two hands banging on her chest in an attempt to revive the body that was never meant to be. Her body thrashed, and her eyes fell back with a lost will; she felt herself hit the floor despite having been on the floor this whole time, the ache of the cobblestone tiles meeting with her flesh that caused a mumble of a cry to slip from her own chapped lips. Althea lifted her head up slightly, finding her own scarred hands digging into the ground beneath her. "No—*NO!* Leave me alone—*leave me alone, please* —" Althea screamed as she scrambled back, already throwing another arrow of a heavenly lethal glow towards the shadowed darkness. She didn't where she was, who she was—if she was even herself... it was maddening. The spirits took the form of a tidal wave, except that dreadful wave was coming for her from every direction she turned. This was it. This was it. *This. Was. It.* The air felt heavy on her tongue as she leant on her knees, and yet it seemed to taste different. *What a coward she was*; she couldn't even stare death in the eyes as he consumed the last of the life from her soul: her father was sure to be ashamed—

"*Althea?*"

The spirits looked to have soothed because of that single spoken word, freezing just inches away from her face as something wonderful brought Althea to her feet. Except she had not been the one to say that fatal word—and it wasn't from the lungs of Marilla, Willix, Elara, or Huntio. *She now knew their voices...*

Slowly and without an utter of a single breath, Althea turned around on the back of her heel, feeling as the sharpness of the ground dug into her bare flesh. She looked towards the darkness that was slowly disappearing into the wind, flying out of the barred windows that looked all too familiar.

She was dead.

That hadn't been that... bad.

And she was wise enough to know that there was something about the air that she breathed now that told her this wasn't the afterlife.

A familiar face took shape on the other side of the clearing darkness, a face that the curse had tried to mock her with one too many times now. A snarl left the edge of Althea's shimmering lips as she shook her head, and in the palms of her hands, the godly light began to mix with something far more deadly.

She was going to burn it all in flames.

And that was a promise.

But the boy she held eye contact with shook his head, an ignorant laugh leaving his lips almost as if he was the one who should be in disbelief. "Is it really you?" he whispered, and that simmering light in Althea's palms was quick to burst into *nothing*. Why did his voice, face, and soul have to be her ultimate downfall? "Oh, Gods, it is—*my love...*"

"Kylen?"

That word felt like a prayer on the tip of her tongue. A prayer to the Gods whom she always wanted to rely on and yet knew better against it. They had let her down one too many times, but it seemed since she had taken up their position that time decided to change their ways and bless her with something more. A glisten of a boy who looked to see her for her, not the power she held, not the death in her palms.

But that didn't answer the question of why he was tied to a chair with the darkness acting as restraints?

Why he was covered in blood—

The boy before hers' face was inescapably consumed by many mixed emotions. While he looked distraught and staring into the eye of a blade, he also looked as if he had just witnessed a miracle in a world where miracles didn't exist.

She remembered those eyes.

Those kind brown eyes.

And she remembered that skin.

That glorious dark skin that looked so much healthier than the last time she had seen it—she could see freckles too? That almost earnt a laugh. Darling freckles lined his cheeks with constellations of stars that had her heart thumping. She always knew the stars to be kind, and now it looked as if they had sent her, her very own gift.

Kylen nodded, beckoning her to realise that this was, in fact, all real, and while his features looked aged and withered, he still put on a smile as he whispered, "Hello, my darling."

His hair was also longer, delicate curls almost hanging over his eyes.

"...*Kylen?*"

Althea slowly stepped towards him, but she wasn't fully convinced that this wasn't a mean joke played on her by the cruel spirits.

She leaned down and picked up a small stone, tossing it his way before watching with astonishment as it hit his cheek and fell into his lap without him disappearing in the process. Kylen, however, rolled his eyes and cocked his head to the left as he raised a singular brow. "Seriously?" he quizzically muttered. "Must everyone throw stones at me?"

She didn't know whether she should laugh or *cry*.

But either way, she quickened her steps as she dove towards him, reaching her hands out for his cheeks before halting them an inch before his face. She wanted to hold him; she wanted him *to hold her*. She had burned alone for so long that she'd begun to forget how it felt to have someone rejoicing in her flames. To feel her power and not cower from it, but to instead admire the eternal warmth. Althea had never needed someone to care for her. Still, there was something about Kylen being the one on the other side of the blade that had her reconsidering. "Kylen—" Althea mourned, but she couldn't seem to wrap her head around understanding that it was him.

Kylen's eyes flickered across her face, a smile on his cheeks as a droplet of crimson blood began to trail down the left side of his face. Althea reached for it without thinking, her simple action speaking louder than any word possibly could. She gently wiped away the blood, her thumb feeling the strange realistic warmth that kissed her palm as Althea shuddered a scattered breath. This couldn't be real—*how was it?* She was trapped within her soul a second ago, but now she was here, standing in the dungeons of Aeonia, where she had once slaughtered people to earn her father's applause. "Breathe," Kylen beckoned in a forgiving voice, and her eyes unhurriedly trailed back down to his. "I'm so sorry," he exhaled quickly, although Althea no longer knew what to think, how to react. "I'm so, so, *so* sorry for failing you, Althea."

She could only stare, her thumb subconsciously drawing circles on the side of his face as Kylen leant into her touch. No one had ever done that. All had been feared from the damage that she could do—none dared to get to know her grace.

A whisper of a smile lined Kylen's cheeks, and his eyes slowly trailed over every feature on her face. "You are as beautiful as the moment I lost you," he whispered in a low tone, almost as if he was afraid that his words would scare her.

Althea noticed it then, the dark hair that fell over her own shoulders, the deathly pale skin that coated the hand she had pressed against Kylen's cheek. *She was a monster.* They had turned her into her true being. Althea's ghastly heart skipped several beats, her head shaking as it tried to wrap itself around whatever it was she was looking at. "What happened?" Althea whispered, but it was a useless question since she knew the answer—she simply refused to accept it. "What happened—"

"*You are okay—*"

"Are you hurt? Did I do something to you?"

Kylen was the one to shake his head this time as he tilted it back and let out an effortless laugh that was sweet and caring. She wanted to melt into that laugh; because she knew that it would save her. "My love, you didn't do anything. The spirits are the ones who did it." Another droplet of blood began to trail down the other side of Kylen's face, and this time she reached for it with her other hand, and that very droplet challenged all that Kylen had said. "I may be a little injured, but it's okay. I'm okay."

I'm okay, I'm okay, I'm okay, I'm okay.

Althea furrowed her brows, her hand reaching up for one of the curls that she wrapped her finger around. "You look different," she noted abruptly, and that earnt Kylen to let out a deep chuckle as he again leant into her touch.

"And you look beautiful... a little different... but still beautiful; I guess we're back to normal already, hey?" A small smile of her own slipped against the edge of Althea's cheeks, and that certainly didn't go unnoticed by Kylen. "But eleven months of grief does that to a man."

"You grieved?" Althea echoed with a scoff, her brows becoming lost to the creases of her forehead. "—*For me?*"

"Gods, *don't sound so surprised*. Of course, I did, Althea," Kylen admitted, and the use of her name *again* had her breaths stilling—her fingers halting. "You are my Queen, are you not? Even without a Kingdom, you would still be the one that I'd want standing by my side. You would be the one that I—" Kylen's eyes widened, his words running loose as he suddenly began to jolt against his restraints. "LOOK OUT!" he shouted, but it was useless because the sculpture of a girl who looked solely made of shadows had already clasped her hands into the sides of Althea's head, and the darkness had already taken over her last true breath.

Althea opened the eyes that she hadn't known to shut with a gasp that was treacherous. Warm hands instantly leapt for her own cheeks as she scrambled back and into a body that was already trying to soothe her; however, this time, as she looked around, she found that she was no longer in the dungeons of Aeonia... *no.*

She had returned to the afterlife.

...With Kylen's parents looking down at her in such distress.

"Oh, *sweet girl*," Marilla cried as she held her to her chest, but the only thing that seemed to register in Althea's mind was the fact that she had just been in Kylen's presence.

And now he was gone.

She was gone.

"Kylen—"

SIXTEEN
KYLEN

"What did you do to her?" Kylen demanded as his magick began to burn. Simmers of ash began to tread lightly through the air, warping around the two physical bodies as if the mental ones didn't count. Still, ultimately, he didn't quite care to learn whether that was his doing or theirs. Kylen shook his head, not allowing the spirits to answer him before he hissed again, *What the fuck did you do to her?*" His words held no sorrow in them, no grief, just pure *ruthless* anger, and that anger was prepared to wound the mockery of the cursed 'girl' who was slowly rising to her feet, staring at him as if he was the one who was the fool. When really, the girl was, in no way, shape, or form *his* girl.

Making them the biggest fool known to man.

"What did *we* do to her?" the spirits crooned in challenge. With a single and abrupt movement, they brushed their hands off on Althea's clothes, the fabric immediately staining with fresh black blood. However, it was clear that they had been injured in one way or another, as Althea's body was quick to flinch as they picked a rock out of her mutilated skin—earning Kylen's heartstrings to darken with a rage that was known to send even the

204

Gods fleeing. "We taught her a lesson—*because apparently,* her father didn't do a very good job; therefore, we were left to pick at... the crumbs of it all." For the second time within ten seconds, they went to cleanse their hands on Althea's stomach, wiping Kylen's blood into the fabric that hid Althea's scars from view. Their eyes sharpened on Kylen's. A hint of pleasure to them as they widened in mockery. An array of laughter began to filter through the air, and the hair on his body stood on end as he felt the wave surround him. "But we will thank you, *Kylen Noxwell,* because now you have made the girl far more accessible. You have reattached the string to Althea's soul, keeping her in palms reach—"

It was almost as if Kylen was sitting in the first row of the audience at one of his beloved shows. Watching as the scene plays over and over again until the actors dare to get it right—*if they were even capable of doing so,* that was. Because as Kylen still sat there in his own blood, he watched as Atticus now used an ungodly amount of magick to force unconsciousness around the throats of the spirits.

While Althea's eyes were the ones to roll back, the dark blood of the curse was quick to consume them as Atticus hit the handle of the sword into their head.

Kylen didn't want to think about how that may affect Althea.

Surely a God couldn't get brain damage—or maybe she could?

Was now really the smartest moment to dwell on all of the what-ifs? No.

"What the actual fuck, what the actual fuck—" Atticus quickly sneered as he wiped the splattered black blood off his face. He shuddered in his shoulders, his fingers digging into the oblivion of his blade, making it look just about ready to shatter beneath his very touch. His eyes were quick to fly around as he spotted the pile of bodies, and the bile looked just about ready to

erupt from his throat as he stumbled several steps back. "*Kylen—Kylen—Kylen—what the actual—*"

"I'm the one who just saw my *bloody* fiancé *quite literally* come back to life—why the fuck are you freaking out?" Kylen replied as he beckoned the boy to untie him with a wave of his hands. Nodding, Atticus quickly realised that Kylen was quite literally trapped, and as he went to walk around him, he began to flip his sword through the air in preparation to let the darkness mellow. Whilst Kylen could no longer see Atticus' *charming* face, he could still, fortunately, hear the disgust seeping off of his tongue in a groan as the sword came into contact with the darkness.

And Kylen could feel trillions of tiny black spiders fleeing across his skin.

"Is Althea really alive?"

"Is the moon playing hide and seek with the sun?" Kylen retorted as he rose to his feet, although he was quick to fall forward in pure agony. His hand stretched out for the brick wall before him, digging his fingers instantly into it as he felt the wounds on his body leek with pure crimson blood. "I told you she was alive. But instead, you chose to be ignorant and not listen. Claiming that I, your *fucking* brother, was mad," Kylen hissed as he turned towards Atticus, shrugging his brother's hand off his shoulder as he fully braced himself to take a second step.

"Kylen—" Atticus whined, except Kylen merely shook his head with an unspoken dismissal flowing through the air. He pushed past his brother and practically stumbled towards the unconscious girl who laid on the floor. She looked dead. Kylen could see the scars and wounds lining her arms, and he could also see the harsh words the spirits had carved into the skin of her Markings.

'God Moordenaar'

God killer.

If Kylen hadn't already lost any sense of his appetite, he had definitely lost it now. His fingers curled around Althea's arm, his eyes falling shut as he swore death upon those who had done this. "Help clear the path for me," he instructed as he picked Althea up bridal style, watching as Atticus' concern evidently washed his expression away. His brother saw the blood trail down Althea's arm, approaching it as if it was a magnetic force of some delusional type. Kylen felt as if he was about to pass out, as if his consciousness was slipping from his grasp, and now he was left to watch himself wither.

Yet, Atticus was quick to dive for her other side. It was almost sweet to watch the brother who had just knocked 'her' out cold now reach for her arm so carefully: like he had a chance to think about his actions... Because he now didn't have to act defensively, he didn't want to leave any more scars on Althea than there were already.

"Where do we put her?"

"Not here; I can't be down here anymore." It was a pathetic excuse of a sob, but what was it other than the truth? He could feel his sister's laughter echo through the air, his brother's inappropriate jokes despite quite literally being a child. He could feel and see it all—almost as if what his non-biological brother had been preaching this whole time was true.

And he truly was going mad.

Atticus nodded instantly, and Kylen couldn't will himself to shed him a second glance. He followed him down the small pathway covered in ash and up the severed shadowed steps. Kylen's hands tightened on Althea with every step he took; however, it was never to the point where it would hurt her, *Gods know that he would never hurt her—he would rather have himself tortured in every single utter lifetime,* but more so to the point where if she were to wake up, she would know that she was safe.

And that he would protect her against all.

If Althea had heard the way his mind was speaking, she

would probably have been disgusted, loathing the way his thoughts praised every inch of her. He praised her because she was the only God he would sacrifice himself for. The only God he would live for. Yet, if she could hear his skyrocketing thoughts, she would bluntly claim that she didn't need any knight in shining armour to save her, that she was fine on her own.

And Kylen knew that.

But he would still show up for her, even if it was simply to watch the blood spill.

He would still show up and stand from the sidelines with a smug grin on his lips if it meant showcasing to her that he would always be there to support her.

No matter what.

The castle looked to again be picked from the mind of his memory. Everything was like a haze, a glisten of perspective that left Kylen succumbing to the nausea in his every step. He knew that it was now day—well, he figured that it was since night felt to have gone on for centuries. Either way, the only light that shed its soul to the walls of Aeonia was from the slight tone in the clouds in the far distance.

It was assumed by most that the curse was one for the simple game of hide and seek, and now that Kylen was stalking the halls of the literal *soul of the curse* with an *unconscious Queen* in his arms, he, unfortunately, realised exactly what they meant. The curse was scattering away and hiding behind anything it possibly could, like little fearful mice on a stormy night. Fearing Kylen's very presence as if he was the one that had done *any wrongdoing*. It didn't sit right with him, the way the curses melted around his bones like they were welcoming him back. It threatened his spine to snap, his soul to drain. *"Let's go to the throne room,"* Kylen murmured in a voice that was almost inaudible, but considering how quiet the palace itself was, Atticus had heard it loud and clear.

With a great thud, his brother pushed open the two wooden

doors that led to the throne room. Kylen followed behind, slithering through the crack of the doorway with his mind racing beyond reach. He shed a glance down to the girl in his arms, watching as her small breaths sounded so *hollow*, so *ill*. He would do anything to reverse the positions that once was. He would sacrifice his own being if it meant her never experiencing this agony.

He might've not been trapped within his own soul, but he sure as Hel had been trapped *nonetheless*, growing up in a time where he never once genuinely got to live.

Only survive.

A trial of health.

So really, he only knew of imprisonment.

"Here, let me help," Atticus murmured as he helped Kylen place Althea gently down and against the throne, but before he could even go to turn to his brother to say anything at all, Atticus had already begun searching for anything to tie her down with. Being the one to avoid him now, how utterly ironic. "Have you begun to experiment with your magick yet?"

That earnt a laugh from the mad king. Out of all of the questions, he just had to go with that one. "I'm not sure if you've noticed, brother," Kylen began as he watched Atticus stalk throughout the large room, and within a splinter of a moment, he too had himself looking around, reminiscing on a time that felt to be both seconds and centuries ago, "but I've hardly had the time."

Time was never on my side, after all.

Atticus sent him another look from across the room, a look that purely said it all. Except Kylen wasn't bothered by hearing any of what he had to say, he wanted to focus on the girl that he finally had a lead on. "Surely, you've at least... *experimented with it?*" His tone sounded both condescending and belittling, causing Kylen to turn back to Althea as he dug his nails into his palms. He wanted her to awaken and be as good as new. He wanted her to open her eyes and beckon both men to hush as she healed all that had been damaged.

"No, I have not, and I don't plan to. If my magick was of any use, it would've helped me prevent... *all of this*."

The *death* of his siblings.

The *death* of his parents.

The *death* of his Sayah.

The *death* of his Althea.

And the *death* of his *kingdom*.

Lorundio, the Kingdom that Was.

"Kylen, you've been sick since you were born. Your magick is hardly to blame for any of this," Atticus argued with a scoff, leaving him to wonder when that small and kind variation of his brother had been lost. "Who knows, imagine you test it, and then suddenly you have the ability to be... a necromancer."

The ability to raise one from the dead... again, *how utterly ironic.*

Kylen winced at that; he didn't need to go wandering into the thorn garden of his past. "Oh, Hel, perhaps I could be a fucking elf while I'm at it. Plus, if I go down into the bloody rabbit hole of my magick, then who else am I meant to blame? I already blame myself, my *magick*, my abilities—Hel, Althea has been alive this whole time, and I wasn't smart enough to figure that out on my own."

I should've. I should've. I should've. I should've.

Atticus stopped walking and crossed his arms. He turned towards Kylen with a hint of defeat on his features, as if he was the one in the slightest affected by all of this bullshit. "*You were mourning, brother.* No one can blame you for that," he whispered in a tone that sounded to be a plea. A plea on the lips of the one who once believed in the Gods the most out of them all. Kylen still remembered the early mornings when he would accompany his brother to travel to the overgrown temples. It was a place that was sore in his mind, and yet the place where he felt closest to his *family*. "Again, you can hardly blame yourself for that." Kylen didn't respond. He physically could not bring himself to. It was making him nauseous just thinking about it. "I will go and start looking for anything that may be powerful enough to tie her down. My magick is more so useful in battle than it is... trapping a girl—well, the body of a girl to a seat."

No. The castle was quite literally a bomb full of the curse— Kylen's heart skipped several beats. He shook his head, feeling as his stomach dropped with something like *fear*. "You can't explore the castle; you will end up dead before you even get the chance to leave the room," he stated firmly. Atticus could tell that he was distraught at the very idea, and if he didn't know better, he thought that Atticus' gaze had turned pitiful. *Pitiful of all things.*

Except Kylen couldn't bring himself to care about the reckless pity his brother sent his way. Death lingered around every corner in this place, and he was rather content with keeping the last of his family alive. *He had to.*

Atticus offered his brother a minor smile, but it was nothing like the ones he used to receive when he was just a harmless boy. Those smiles were ones that threatened him to laugh when he was meant to be quiet. Those smiles were the ones that drove the teachers and professors insane because they knew that it would take Kylen a while to recover. "Kye, if I recall correctly, then the power source is within your arms reach—"

"—*I'm afraid* that His Majesty is right," a voice spoke through the midst of the haze, and Kylen's blood was quick to drop in temperature as his lungs gave out. *He had been right—he hadn't been insane to think that that presence had been nearby.* "The spirits have an army of curses lingering throughout these castle halls, all of which are starving and quite ready to feast upon your bones." The air thickened, and the presence came about so quickly that Kylen hadn't had time to realise just who it was that camouflaged within the quivering magick that covered the corners of this damned room. He had just assumed that it was the curse itself—not an entirely different source altogether.

Except Kylen wasn't ignorant of the voice that fluttered through the air with a delicacy of a lost king, and he recognised that voice instantly—*after all,* it was the one that lingered in the background of his nightmares as he watched Althea repeatedly fall lifeless to the ground. The hatred, anger, pain, agony, love, betrayal, joy, smiles, laughs… all lost from her soul.

In every dream, it was the same story.

And in every dream, he was left scrambling for her bones as he begged the Gods to let him end it all. He couldn't do this—he couldn't live when he only succeeded in death.

Yet the Gods only took their mockery out on him; as just several weeks later, the story repeated, except with Sayah's time-less body.

He had willed himself to wake up.

But it hadn't been a dream.

As Sayah had been truly gone—too far from reach.

As well as Althea.

Kylen struggled forward as the agony of his mind blinded him. Atticus wielded a blade from the air itself and tossed it his way, already seeming to know his plans without uttering them in the slightest. Kylen didn't take any notice of the blood that leaked out of the wounds on his legs like a wave of the curse; he ignored it all as the only thing on his mind seemed to be murdering the man who had made Althea's last moments *awful.*

"What are you doing here?" Kylen seethed through clenched teeth. "I would demand that you leave now, but unfortunately for you, I have better plans in mind." *I don't want to have to remind you about what happened last time you were around.*

Adonis raised a brow, seeming as if he did not care that Kylen was prepared to rip his eyes from their sockets. "Oh, please, we both know that—"

"I have mourned for two lives that you practically took

from me. Trust me when I say that I am prepared to rip your heart from within its cage and crush it with my bare hands— and that isn't a threat; it is a promise, Adonis. A fucking promise."

A scoff echoed from Adonis' lungs as he raised his hands like he was taking the joy out of mocking the two. "*Hey—*" Adonis went to laugh; however, Atticus cut him off with an icy scowl that lingered beneath his breath. His fingers flexed at his side, and magick filled the air. Kylen could see as the small enchantments Sayah had taught him set in place, and the air concealed Adonis within—confiding him to meet Kylen's hands that were already quite eager to puncture his heart. "Oh, come on, I don't mean no harm."

"You don't mean no harm?" Atticus retorted with a menacing laugh, and for the first time in seconds, Adonis' face dropped its amusement. "Then why are you here? You haven't been present at all throughout these last months that Althea was believed and deemed to be dead... but now that she is rumoured to be alive, you suddenly show up? I thought you fucking knew where her body was—after all, you were the one to insist on keeping it in bloody Harlia."

Adonis didn't get a second to shed his reasons before Kylen had allowed his anger to consume his body and soul. He pushed him against the decaying walls, holding his skin and bones in place as he vowed death onto his name. Adonis struggled beneath his touch, yet his eyes stayed locked on Kylen's as if he was trying to identify who this man was. Gods know *he* didn't recognise him. Gods know Kylen couldn't even recognise himself. He was gone. Lost. The brutality of this world had swallowed him whole and spat out a skeleton of a man that once was. "Let me kill him," Kylen breathed, and even the words mourned for the kindness his soul had once held. Atticus didn't have to hear him twice before he had already captured that merciless gleam in his eyes and began to wave his sword through the air, preparing to stab it through his skull like this was what they did on a daily.

Murder those who had wronged him—

When really to achieve that beautiful goal, he would have to murder every soul that wandered these treacherous Realms.

"NO! No!" Adonis quickly replied, and his eyes were wide as he shed his bargaining. "Please, please—*why won't anybody hear me out?*" His hands shot out with a magick that appeared similar to the curse; however, since Kylen was awfully familiar with the dreadful ways of the curse, he knew that it was mere deception. A decoy. "I can help you reach Althea. I can help you speak to her and work out a plan with her to get her back, *please* —" Kylen shook his head as Atticus snickered from behind him. His magick, which seemed to be a mixture of everything nowadays, helped holster Adonis up and onto the wall, weaving its way through the crackling air with such force, such godsforsaken stamina. The dagger he held in one hand pressed against Adonis' throat, and in a cowardly, weak attempt to fight back, he pushed his head all the way back against the wall.

"I don't believe a fucking filthy word that you are preaching," Kylen sneered, and Adonis shook his head against the blade, a risky game as blood began to trail. Kylen didn't avert the blade as Adonis had hoped, and evident shock seeped throughout the brown of his eyes. "Why are you here? Why didn't you tell us that Althea had left the supposed 'tomb'?"

"Why would I worry you with any news that may have led absolutely nowhere? I am not a monster, you know. I wouldn't want to get your hopes up before I know of anything with actual potential," he reasoned, but this time Kylen was the one to shake his head.

Kylen screwed his brows together. "She is my fiancé."

"And she is my Queen," Atticus scowled, finishing his sentence for him.

"The two of you don't need to get married anymore, if I

recall correctly. You aren't dying; therefore, you don't need a Queen. Her father is your prisoner. Therefore, she is already free. I doubt she will still want to get married now that there is nothing holding the two of you together. That girl hasn't even seen the world; she has never but once been past her own castle gates. My lady will want to explore and live life; who are you to hold her back from doing that? It was only ever a game of chance, after all."

Kylen's hands tightened on the boy that he wanted to murder. Did he truly think so low of him? That he would force Althea to marry him after all of this? If things finally come to peace, she decides that she has no intention of being his Queen, then Kylen would learn to live with that. He owed her that. *He owed her that much.* Hel, he would gift her his new ship and allow her to travel the world on her own if she so pleases... although he doubted that she was at all fond of the sea after all that happened the last time they sailed upon it.

Nonetheless, Adonis squirmed, and Kylen wanted to be the one to slit Adonis' throat and watch the blood drip off of his hands before pooling at his feet. He wanted to rip the boy's eyes from their sockets and watch as he scrambled for any strings of life to clasp onto. *He just wanted him to feel the agony that Kylen had felt since he could remember.*

"You aren't doing yourself any favours, mate," Atticus warned in a simple mutter, and Adonis' eyes slid from his brother to him. "Tell us, *insight us,* why are you really here?"

"I've told you. Because I want to end the curse once and for all. Sure, I may have different reasonings than you two, but we can cross that bridge when we get to it—after we get *our God* back."

Gods.

Oh, how he prayed gloriously on his death.

"—*Althea* back," Kylen corrected, although his hands didn't loosen but instead tightened. He gripped at his black shirt as if it was the curse itself—and he begged to feel the spirits scream across his fingertips as he stared the man of dragons down, willing him to fall victim to the murder that promised. Where was that beast anyway? He supposed it would be a good 'welcome back from death' gift if he was to gift Althea with a literal dragon when she arose from the dead.

Atticus was watching him intently, awaiting the final decision that was to leave Kylen's tongue whenever he so chose. It could either be that he wanted Adonis' head, or it could be that he wanted to hear the male out; nevertheless, it was *his* choice. Whilst his brother may not deem him as his favourite friend at the moment, there was one thing that he couldn't ignore no matter if he begged himself to: and that was that Kylen was *his king*. His lord. His ruler. Atticus had sworn a blood oath to protect him the day Sayah decided to initiate him as one of his faithful guards. Since then, he had vowed to do all that Kylen so chose for him to do. "How exactly do you plan to… contact Althea?" Atticus asked warily over his shoulder, and for once in this retched *day/night,* he was thankful that his brother had been the one to ask the damning question.

Adonis nodded eagerly, evidently pleased at the very question being asked. "A little thing called nightshade… your kingdom's speciality, *My Lord.*"

Kylen scoffed at his very words before releasing him. Was he a fool? Had he truly lost the last of his wits? *Not that he'd ever had them in the first place.* "Yeah, my kingdom's speciality… *seventy hundred years ago.* I'm not an idiot, Adonis. My kingdom ruled out the poison of Nightshade when my grandfather still ruled."

"So, tell me why all the equipment for growing the deadly berry is deep within the palace of Lorundio? Tell me why that if you dared to venture left instead of right, you would find yourself a laboratory that had kept the dazzling purple plant pristine in time?"

Atticus narrowed his eyes as he turned to Kylen with a hint of confusion on the end of his nose. "Am I missing something here, Kye? What is nightshade?" he asked in a hushed voice. Kylen wished that everyone in this room would just give him the eternal silence he craved.

Whilst the question was directed towards the king, who was currently trying to run through his thoughts speedily, Kylen found that he could not bring himself to answer, so, of course, Adonis took the courtesy of doing it for him. *How kind of him.* "Nightshade was the plant that the descendants of the Noxwells decided to invest in centuries ago. It was discovered one moonfall, and since then, the plant has been religiously respected by all who come across it. However, due to how lethal it is, each plant was relocated beneath the palace of Lorundio to hide and has been hiding there ever since. It is a purple... *flower-like plant* that produces berries that could kill a child if they consumed two or more. And while it would take a few more berries to kill a grown adult, there are effects such as hallucination, confusion, and seizures that could allow us to gain an advantage on the spirits of the curse."

Kylen shook his head; his confusion was still quite evident. Did he really think that he was going to poison Althea willingly? "Let's say that you are being truthful, and there is actually some reminisce of the plant beneath the palace... how do you suppose we will get it to affect the spirits and not Althea? It's her body, is it not? If we murder the body... we are bound to murder her too. And I will not let that happen. I won't."

"Because of how powerful the spirits are and because of the fact that Althea currently resides in the afterlife amongst the dead, the poison will affect the sole owner of her body. Therefore, it will capture the spirits, and with them being on the verge of death and quite weak—you will be able to contact Althea then."

And I can be her anchor.

The line to bring her back.

Several seconds of silence slid through and out of Kylen's grasp as he held his breath. He didn't know what possible decision would be the right one to make or what possible decision would be the one to make sure that no harm came to any surviving member of his family.

He didn't know the answer, and that was awfully daunting.

"Kylen?" Atticus questioned, and he knew that he was waiting for any order at all.

Any direction of some type.

However, Kylen's compass had been crushed, and now he was left to wander the endless abyss in search of a girl that he yearned to touch again.

"How do you plan to get the nightshade from Lorundio?" Kylen asked, and Adonis cocked his head slightly to the left, a gleam of something more on his lips as he raised his brows.

"I don't need to. I already have it here."

As if his very words were a spell of some type, all it took was a mere wave of his hands for the purple-flowered plant to appear. Kylen observed it silently as Atticus sounded like he was choking on the very air in his lungs; his magick truly was of the dragon's ability.

The plant's roots sprangled through the air as if it was trying to flee, every leaf and every petal wilting in every which direction. He had only ever seen the deadly flower drawn in old books.

The ones that reminisced on a time that had been forgotten long ago.

"Okay," Kylen murmured. He didn't know if this choice was the right one to make or not, but it gave him a chance that appeared to be a light in the darkness. "But if you so much as do one thing out of line, I won't hold myself back from—"

"Yes, yes, I know. *You will kill me*," Adonis breathed as he walked past Kylen. Even the way he walked and held himself up annoyed him.

Adonis looked over his shoulder at him, watching him like a lion watching his prey. Did he have it wrong? He must know that the moment Kylen decides that he wanted him dead, *he would be dead*. He wouldn't last an excuse of a second. Whatever decision Adonis was dwelling on seemed to have been made as a look of disgust washed over his features as he turned yet again away. Atticus rolled his eyes as he threw his head back in a sigh. Kylen could tell that his brother wanted to start something, to confront the tension in the air with one of his darling swords. Yet it appeared that he decided to go with words instead. "I will have you know that it's a crime to interrupt your king."

"My whole existence is a crime. Get in line, mate."

Kylen was already regretting his choices as he looked over to Atticus in distaste, that simple look didn't last long as he realised just where Adonis was heading, and before Atticus could snarl another word, his brother was running for Althea.

Adonis didn't care; he allowed Atticus and Kylen to run past him as he clapped his hands before his very chest. "Now, I will need your help Kylen Noxwell, as it is an aspect of your magick that makes this drug affect the soul and not just the outer exterior of your victims."

THE
SEARCHING

SEVENTEEN
ALTHEA

The air felt so severely tight as it warped across her frozen flesh, and the burns to her lungs had Althea struggling to think straight as she intently watched Marilla and Willix dwell on all that she had learned. *All that she had seen.* "But I don't understand—" Marilla whispered as she shook her head. That was all that they seemed to be able to form after hearing of such things—Hel, their faces felt to be forever engraved into Althea's mind because of how distraught they had reacted after they'd heard about how their son was currently doing. "Why would Kylen be confined to a chair? Why would the curse want to consume his soul when it's already severely damaged? *Why*—" She knew that it didn't make sense. That there were so many unanswered wavering factors that she wanted to know all the answers to since she had 'died'.

Died.

The world believed for her to be dead, and yet time looked to still be spinning.

Except Kylen had mourned for her—and his face had lit up the moment he realised that it was truly her.

Althea leaned back against the wall, which felt extraordinarily cold at this very moment. Everything about the afterlife felt cold—she didn't think she could ever get used to it. At first, it hadn't seemed so terrible; she had sought some warmth through the fact that she didn't exactly remember what the true physical Realms felt like. But now that she did, she felt as if she was in the endless loops of time, again, confined to that tiny little room that had her heart plummeting to the bottom of the ocean.

With a heartfelt silent sigh, Althea brought her ice-cold hands up to cup her own cheeks before she rubbed them over her eyes. The exhaust was eating at her—consuming her body and soul as if she was nothing at all. *Kylen had grieved for her.* He had mourned her name—remembering the life that she had *held* as if it was worth anything—as if she had made a name for herself after all.

When really, who was she but her parent's daughter?

Who was she but the one who deserved to actually die?

Maybe, just maybe, if she were to believe hard enough, to think hard enough, she would believe that he partially did care for her. That there was a part of him that *loved* her. He deserved more than her, and she knew that. Yet, how could she deny the small child who had prayed on love every second of every day? How could she deny the younger *and far more vulnerable* Althea, who thought about the soul who was going to dare to rescue her as she did her hourly ballet class each day?

But really, in the scheme of the universe, what worth did love hold?

It was all a misused gamble of time. A fabric of time marvelled together to deceive those with wide eyes and open hearts of all the pain and suffering the Gods had written for them.

It was cruel.

Merciless.

It felt like everything and everyone was merciless nowadays —that no one actually cared for the other unless they had something in return for them to take. *For them to greedily hold.*

And it seemed those who never truly got to hold anything in return were the ones who yearned for the least. It seemed as if those who had never felt the warmth of a candle were the ones to get burnt by the flickering flames.

Except now, now, as Althea stood small in the afterlife clinging to her own skin, it appeared that she no longer had anything to offer Kylen in return. Hel, even her body was soulless, merely just a walking corpse that was no use to a king. Not to mention, Kylen didn't need her as his Queen anymore... so inevitably, it didn't make sense. None of it made any tragic sense.

Why had that idiot mourned for her?

Why had he been tortured by *her* body in exchange for answers?

Not to mention, all of Marilla and Willix's sudden catastrophic questions had Althea wondering about the past —*which was an awfully dangerous game for her to play.*

It had her wanting to know how Kylen was even cursed in the first place. She knew that he had *'been born cursed'*, but she never actually caught onto whether he was being factual or just dramatic. *And she found that he was usually dramatic.*

"*No.* No... It's good that he is there and seems to have some idea of what's happening. Hopefully, he will figure something out and... well, he may just be able to bring you back, kid," Willix mused out loud as he clapped his hands before him. He passed his eyes from Marilla to Althea with a smile on his lips that was surprisingly *unconvincing.* He looked just as fearful as Althea felt—*yet she would rather die than admit that aloud.* One was never to know just who was listening.

Kylen had been so bloody.

So *bruised*.

He looked far older too.

So different and yet so similar to *her* Kylen.

"He's strong," Marilla whispered more so to herself than to anyone else, except Althea partially knew that it was intended for her to also hear. "*Our boy*, he is strong. A fighter. Whatever this is, I am sure he will find a way to get out of it."

Did she even want to return to the true physical Realms? That made Althea feel as if she was betraying these people that needed *a Godly type of blessing*... It had her stomach burning with a guilt that was so physical she was sure that she was bleeding out.

"There is no good in dwelling on it any longer," Willix abruptly announced as he ran a hand through his hair. "Say, Althea, if you aren't going to go and try to have a little more rest, why don't we test out your magick and see what you can do with your abilities *here?* We know something of the sort—but it would be good to know just what we are dealing with."

Althea nodded before she really thought it through, but she felt like she just needed to *escape* this confinement. The walls felt to be tumbling in on her, and the ground beneath felt to give way any second now. She didn't want to be trapped within these brutal walls any longer—she physically could not bring herself to *stay still* any longer.

She yearned to see the world, to taste the breath of life on her tongue. "*Sounds like a plan.*"

Marilla offered Althea a trivial smile before Willix walked over to the dark brown door and opened it. The tension that was sizzling within the air was deafening. It had Marilla stumbling over to a small wooden seat where she was quick to sit with her head folding into her hands. A pain shot through Althea as she watched her, a grief like no other.

Was it ridiculous that this pained her to see the woman in

such discomfort? Althea couldn't begin to imagine what it would feel like to quite literally be trapped on the other side of a glass wall from those you love.

It would be agonising.

The cruellest form of torture out of them all.

Althea pushed herself off of the wall slowly, walking over to Willix, who was looking away as if he couldn't see the waves of death that had Marilla suffering so intently. *Or so Althea ridiculously thought.* "You go on, kiddo. I will meet you out there in a couple of minutes." The look he shed her was kind, but there was mourning behind it. Grief. Althea hesitated, and Willix nodded to her, beckoning her through the simplest of ways to accept that all would be alright.

She had barely made it out of the small door frame when Willix had glided hurriedly past her, walking over and towards Marilla in such a hassled yet tender manner. His face was covered in despair, clinging to the woman he loved for any type of comfort. Althea shook her head as she looked away; she truly couldn't begin to imagine what this was like for them. She would never *want* to.

To have someone you love with your whole soul being trapped worlds away—that sounded like actual Hel. *It was Hel.* Althea clung to the shadows as if they were her kindest friends whilst she observed, her own grief taking over her heart as she watched Willix pull Marilla into his arms that were already ready for her. *They were made for her. Like they had done this all before*, he pressed a kiss to her forehead as his eyes fluttered painfully shut, murmuring something in her ear that had her nodding before hiding away in the crook of his throat as her tears ran loose; forming a lump to lob in Althea's own throat.

He'd probably told her that this was all going to be okay, that all's well would end well; except Althea had a feeling that things wouldn't end that way this time—except there was a small star burning far too brightly in Althea's soul to ignore how it was yearning to make everything right. *To make it up to them.*

Why couldn't her parents share that same undeniable love that was undoubtedly catastrophic? Why couldn't her father look at her mother as if she was the moon and more?

Yet, of course, her father had been a mere curse holder and her mother, a literal God. Opposing *blood-thirsty* enemies in every way, shape, and form.

It was in these moments now, where all was lost to the exhaust of the world and this cave peculiarly felt like the forbidding castle of Aeonia. It had been a demoralising realisation to make, but nonetheless, Althea had realised it whilst she slowly tiptoed down the long hallways with silent steps, cautious not to awaken the sleeping children that at least deserved to *live* through their beloved dreams. Everything was so awfully dusty and gloomy, a taciturn wind swallowing her hole as the sound of running water washed soothingly across her soul.

In the strangest way, it felt like the childhood she partially remembered, but at the same time, she knew hardly anything about it. It was as if her grief, mourning, anguish for herself and the life she was left to bore was holding her mind captive. Similarly, to the curse's cruel ability, where her mind had taken away parts of her memories.

Was it to protect her?

Cause her ease?

Soothe that eternal ache?

Althea shuddered in her steps as the blissful waterfall parted gracefully for her, and with a droplet of hope in her heart, she reached her fingers out to feel the *running* water. Praying to whatever was out there that the genuine and physical sensation would remind her that she was alive. *That she* had a *life* to *live.* *That she was owed time where she could actually breathe…*

—Except this was death.

And nothing was physical in death, earning Althea to turn away with a scowl.

To admire the stillness of the air entirely, Althea found herself hiking up to the top of the small mountain, meeting the top of the waterfall before it spilled over and dared to claim the land as its own. Althea wondered how far the afterlife actually stretched or whether there was no end at all, but instead, was infinite.

The deceptive moonlight in the hazy sky above reflected on the running water Althea intently studied as she sat down, reminding her of a time when she had danced on a ship with the strangest of hopes in her heart.

A small smile—*against all odds*—crept onto Althea's cheeks as she felt the manipulative grass beneath her make room for her body. A grimace left her bruised lips, and despite the fact that she tried with all of her will to ignore the way her bones and muscles cramped as if she had just walked out of the other end of a battle: it didn't help her shake off the darker thoughts that began to crackle across her shoulders.

It didn't make sense to her, no matter how hard she tried to wrap her head around it. Why, oh why, had that boy risked his life to reach her? Why had Kylen come for Althea?

He was risking his life to save hers.

That boy truly was a fool. The greatest fool of them all, and that had Althea burying her head in her hands as she fought back the strange, sly smile.

Was it silly to admit that she couldn't wait to see them again?

Kylen, Atticus, Khatri, Uzziah, Zaire, and sweet darling Sayah?

Althea found herself even missing the hassle of dealing with Zaire and Uzziah—sure, they hadn't been too keen on her in the beginning, but they had somewhat defended her name, her honour, her soul, at the end of it all. That had to count for something, did it not?

The sound of footsteps coming up the same track behind her had Althea lifting her head out of her hands. Her shoulders lifted and spine straightened, forcing herself to take a much-needed breath that felt like such a hassle to perform. It was pure silence echoing throughout the depths of the 'air' until Willix, who was now somehow standing by her, asked in a small and quiet voice, "How are you feeling?"

That was a question Althea didn't think she knew the answer to; a question that had her eyes dropping to her folded hands as she fiddled with the skin around her nails—despite the skin or nails, *or her body entirely,* not being real in any way.

On the one hand, she felt horrible to have seen Kylen again. He was bruised, bloody, and in agony over what *her* body had done to him. Not to mention that he had supposedly grieved for her when she had only ever been a nuisance—*time truly had not been kind to him.*

But then, on the other hand, *he had mourned for her.* And the act of mourning is usually performed by *those* who love or care for another's soul so undeniably that when it's being ripped away from theirs, it feels as if their own has been burned alive.

Kylen had grieved for the loss of Althea's presence, and that had to count for something. She had missed him more than she would admit—it had felt as if the heart she had never known to be taken had been restored again. Now she was watching Kylen take his damn time as he slowly sewed all the gaping wounds closed.

"Fine," Althea replied as she looked over to him with a nod. "I'm fine, thank you. How are you?"

Willix gave her an awfully condescending stare as he raised a single brow. A stare that had Althea sharpening her gaze on him. "It doesn't matter how I am. You are the one who went through the torture of—"

"Please, that is not torture. I've been through far worse things that are most definitely deemed as torture, and while that… that was painful, to say the least, it was not torture."

I had seen Kylen—and he had cared for me?

"Fine." Willix nodded, seeming to arrogantly understand just where she was coming from. But did he? Althea didn't even truly understand. "Very well. I don't want to push you on the matter," he breathed before crossing his arms. "So, why don't we start with the basics? What magick can you feel riveting beneath your skin? Can you feel electricity beneath your touch? A vibrancy to your bones?"

Althea's eyes dropped to her hands once again, a sigh departing her lungs as she pursed her lips. It had been so long since she had willingly contacted her magick and willed it to be of any use, that she felt to have forgotten every single aspect of it. When she had used it to save the Noxwell family, Hel, even Althea hadn't realised to have called out to it.

It had just appeared.

Boom.

And then reality had tragically dawned on her.

"Nothing, really," Althea admitted through a fatal breath, and she turned back towards Willix with uncertainty. "Sorry."

Willix raised his brows with a face that had her expecting mocking laughter to run from his lips; however, no laughter came as he relaxed his stance and shook his head. "Please, don't apologise. You have nothing to apologise for—especially not for that."

Althea was the one to laugh now as a chuckle ran from her own lips, and her head dipped forward as she tucked several strands of hair back and behind her ears. Did he really take her as a fool? "Oh, I have plenty to apologise for. I fear that I have not been the kindest in my life."

"This doesn't sound like the Althea I know at all."

"You don't know *Althea*, and you wouldn't want to. I hear she is a bitch."

Willix chuckled as he rolled his eyes. "I may not *know*-know you, but I watched you grow up. I watched you grow into the person you are now—huh, you should think of me as your guardian angel."

"I thought guardian angels are meant to save people from suffering. If I must note, you, Mr Noxwell, didn't do a very good job of it." Althea counterpointed with a click of her tongue and a tilt of her head, almost acting identical to her old self.

A sigh scrambled from Willix's lips as he looked at her with a hint of anguish and amusement on his lips. A conflicted look indeed. "I know, and trust me when I say it is one of my deepest regrets. Oh... if I had hold of your father now, I would love to see him suffer—"

"—*You and me both*," Althea interjected, although it was both partly the truth and partly a lie. Because while she wanted to watch her father bleed out for his crimes at her feet, she wouldn't deny that the small four-year-old girl who loved her father against anything couldn't bear to watch such a thing.

"But truly, you don't need to apologise for anything. You have done what you have in your life to survive, and people should never undermine that. Marilla and I... words cannot express how proud we are of how far you have made it. You have survived; you are a survivor—Hel, that is more than I did. I didn't survive."

That took an awfully dark turn. Althea furrowed her brows as a shocked laugh left her lungs. Never in a million years would she imagine such a thing to leave the lungs of a soul who'd been wronged in such a grotesque way. Hel, never in a million years would she have ever imagined being in the position she was in now. "That got dark very quickly," she noted, and again Willix returned her laugh with a laugh of his own.

"I know. I thought I should lighten the mood."

Although Althea hadn't realised it yet, she was smiling. And it wasn't one of those smiles that *didn't* meet the eyes—this smile *did* meet the eyes, and it warmed Willix's heart as he smiled in return.

"So," he said after several seconds scrambled from their palms. "Let's see what magick we can do—and please feel free to set some things alight. I miss the chaotic...*ness* of magick—it always caused Mary to panic, but me a damn thrill."

EIGHTEEN
KYLEN

There was only one thing that his *dearest* brother's stare was translating to... and that was that he didn't trust the myth of dragons one *little* bit. Atticus didn't trust his intentions, morals, loyalty—anything at all. *In fact,* he looked to want to scorch his name to pieces, to erase the fact that Adonis was even here, standing in *their* dreadful presence and trying to get Kylen to contact his magick that he was sure had been buried long ago. Atticus' brows were furrowed, his gaze penetrating. He looked at him as if he was the bringer of all his pain, the haze of everything that had happened *yesterday* shining heavily in his dark eyes.

Kylen hadn't forgotten either.

He hadn't forgotten how Adonis had caused Althea such haunting distress in her last moments. And while Adonis wasn't exactly the one to wound her heart into two, he had done enough to earn his beloved spot in Kylen's dungeons, awaiting the blades that were thirsty for the wine of dragons. *He could already imagine how his blood would taste.*

"Get a move on with it," Atticus scowled under his breath, and Kylen didn't have to shed him a second glance to know that his face matched his distasteful tone. "You have been at this for half an hour already, and while the little trance you've put on our Queen has kept her down for this long: I doubt it will hold up any longer."

Adonis turned his eyes to his brother as he shook his head, many words on his quivering, pursed lips, yet only a few were actually able to form. "You should be saying that to your almighty King instead."

That had a bubble of hatred turning in Kylen's stomach. Didn't he understand that Kylen wasn't one who was familiar with the magick of his blood? He was never one who had the privilege of being a small boy who got to experiment with the flames he could throw, the ice he could brew... Hel... Kylen didn't even know the extent to his magick nor the little bits and tricks that any king was meant to know. Sure, he had a few random ideas that were formed off of his parent's and sibling's abilities; but he rarely saw their magick in full shine, and before he got the actual chance, they had died.

Murdered.

Not to mention, he wasn't in any way at all keen on his magick.

If it was worthy, it would have saved his heart.

But it had not, and when he glanced across the room to the mirror that showed him a scarred man, he could confidently say that he was nothing more than a stranger.

The air around them seemed to darken—*if that was at all possible*, and Atticus turned his blade across his fingertips, a move Kylen had taught him when they were only boys. "Watch what you say about my King, neither of us are too keen on you, nor do we exactly need your help. Be grateful that we are giving you the time of day at all," Atticus warned in a low voice, except Adonis merely rolled his eyes without a care in the world before turning back towards Kylen.

"Focus—"

"Focus?" Kylen retorted with a snort, was he at all sane? "Perhaps I would be able to focus if you weren't breathing so bloody loudly—*and if you two stopped bloody bickering.*"

"You cannot blame me for the immaturity of your guard," Adonis was quick to reply with a 'matter of fact' raise of his brows. He knelt opposite where Kylen sat cross-legged on the floor, his hands resting on his knees as he stared at the nightshade before him. The plant looked familiar; he would give him that; however, it looked so different than it did in the pictures, and it had a bluish-purple aura that reeked of the dead. "Close your eyes and feel the blood of your palms. Try and contact whatever it is that is lingering there. Often, when magick goes unused for so long, one is left to scramble at the loose threads to find the actual soul of it all."

Although it was against his morals to do what Adonis was saying, Kylen did it, nonetheless. *This was for Althea—you would be able to save Althea.*

He felt the moment the male, who wasn't as unknown to him as he willed him to be, piled several berries into the palms of his hands. Kylen curled his fingers around them, begging something to appear sooner than later. *He felt ridiculous sitting here, looking like a bloody fool.*

Yet, as always, the Gods above didn't care for him in the slightest, and nothing was responding to his calls; *nothing was responding to the pleas he sent the murdered heavens above.*

It had his blood turning and his mind boiling.

Kylen grew restless in his stance: and apparently, that was all Adonis needed before he began to speak the *glorious* speech he looked to be born to perform. *Cruel, merciless boy.* "I want you to remember all the moments that have led up to this *very* moment. The many storms, *wars*, and losses that your soul has mourned over and yet been forced to survive through. Try to bring your soul back to the ruinous day where you peered down the fracture in the earth and found *Althea Evangeline* standing there in all of her once-lived glory. I saw your face then, Your Majesty, and I know you loved her against all. You may try to deny it to yourself or to the last of your family: but you care for her more than a king should care for his queen." Adonis paused, and Kylen beckoned his face not to show the true despair of his restless features. He felt as if the walls were crumbling down on him—as if the last of the surviving Aeonian palace was daring to claim their bodies. "Then, I want you to remember how you were left to crawl over to her limp body after almost dying yourself, the lifeless memories of the life she was destined to live forever stained on the features that you felt to be made by the holiest of them all. I heard your despair, your anguish. It was as if all you had ever known and prayed on had been a dear lie, and now you were left to scramble for yourself through the darkness of this world. *Althea Evangeline* was dead, and a few months later, so was *Sayah Linix*."

No. *No*.

How dare he speak of them—how dare he whisper a trembling word of their names.

A hurricane of the emotions *the Gods had once tried to erase* crashed across Kylen's face with an iciness that had the hair on his body standing on end. *No. No.* Kylen dipped his chin with a shake of his head—he felt like a child. A child who longed for the one object they'd had taken away from them.

In the back of his mind, he heard Atticus step forward and grumble something into Adonis' ear; but whatever it was, was unknown to him.

The only thing Kylen could focus on was both of *their* deaths.

The only thing he could see was *their* corpses.

The only thing he could feel was *their* blood—their cold, cold blood.

The only thing he could smell was the agony of leaving them

both behind as the scent of their rotting corpses followed him down the darkest hallways.

This was it.

The feeling Adonis had wanted him to grab hold of now had complete and utter control *of him*. Kylen was tired of this endless cycle. The exhaust of waking up and reality setting in on him as he stared at the same wall every day for twenty-two or so years.

He didn't know the exact depths of time anymore.

Hel, he could be thirty-five for all he knew, or perhaps he was still twenty-one, awaiting the queen of his nightmares to journey into his kingdom and plan for his head.

With everything in him, he could say that he didn't know— nor did he exactly have the time of day to care.

Kylen clung to his bruised skin as he remembered looking down at both women's bodies. Frozen in time as the inevitable fate that was waiting for him consumed him whole. *Let it go. Let it go. Just fucking let it all go.* But he didn't want to let it go; he didn't want to release the emotions that had hibernated within his blood for so-so dreadfully long.

Because he knew the moment that he lost his hold on it, all would end in his inevitable downfall.

A hand, as delicate as the wondrous and endless what-ifs, clasped onto Kylen's shoulder with a gentle, *reassuring* squeeze. He expected the pain to strike his soul into two now that he was vulnerable—except nothing treacherous ever came, and he opened his eyes only to realise that *again,* he was trapped within a trance that he wanted to consume the last of his name.

Kylen's eyes dropped, and he looked to the hand holding his shoulder before his blood dared to freeze. He recognised that hand, that skin, those fingers. He recognised the rings that even her corpse wore to protect her against the evil spirits. Kylen held back the cruel sob that stretched at the back of his throat, and slowly, he glided his eyes towards the mother who had always treated him as her own blood.

"Hi, sweet boy," Sayah whispered through a small smile. "How are you doing?"

This wasn't real. It wasn't real. It wasn't—

Kylen got up before he gave himself a second to sanely reconsider. His heart leapt several beats as he quickly pulled her into his arms: the many thoughts and endless worries keeping his mind utterly frozen as he stared blankly ahead. A laugh left Sayah's lungs as she, too, held him to her body, her head resting against his shoulders as if all was well.

"How are you here—how are you..." Kylen shook his head. There were no words to sum up all that he was left to wonder. He pulled away, looking at her with eyes that vowed to murder any of those who took him away from her again. "How are you here?"

Sayah reached forward, tucking a strand of hair behind his ear. "I'm not really here," she admitted in a soft whisper. "You are attempting to contact the soul of your magick, and it seems as if you correlate your magick with me." Kylen furrowed his brows, except Sayah didn't give him the second to say anything before she kept going. "It's rare, but it seems as if your magick can sense your distress as if your mind knows how bruised your soul is... so it has decided to gift you a certain someone to try and calm you."

"You aren't real?" Kylen asked whilst his voice threatened to tremor, and Sayah shook her head with a look of grief on her lips. It hurt him because of how badly he wanted her to be here, standing before him with life blossoming across her flesh. "Still..." he uttered as he swallowed his grief, "you have no idea how good it is to see you right now."

"I believe that it would be as good as if I were to lay my eyes upon you after death, *dear boy.*"

Even her words felt true. Even her words fell to leave the lips of the woman who helped him attend his family's funeral and then his coronation all in one day.

One, two, three; there were three knocks that echoed off of the door he had kept shut for the past forty-eight hours. It was strange to hear the sudden noises when the kingdom had felt so deathly quiet since they'd learned of the sudden news.

The sudden deaths.

When Kylen didn't go to answer it, he heard the creak of the door opening before shutting again several seconds later. He didn't have to turn to know that it was the siren. Hel, he didn't have to shed her a glance because the warmth of her magick had said it all for her.

Sayah didn't say anything as he entered his wardrobe, gathering out a black layered suit before laying it down on the edge of the bed. Kylen could feel her eyes on her, the pitiful look that had shed more tears than she had been able to all this time. "It's time, Kye."

Gods, even her voice was dripping in grief.

Even her voice was mourning for all that he had stumbled upon.

Kylen shook his head, his eyes falling shut as several silent tears slid down the side of his young face. "I can't do it."

With small steps, Sayah crept over to the side of Kylen's bed, sitting down wordlessly before she reached out to tuck a strand of his hair back and behind his ear. She was trying to keep her voice strong, unwavering. But Sayah had always been a terrible liar. "That's okay. I'll be there to help you take every step."

Kylen's eyes glided to hers, and the grief that consumed them was overwhelming. "No—no, I don't think so," Kylen whispered, choking on the words that he was sure were out to get them. "I don't think I can move; I don't think I can go on—I'm just a boy."

He wouldn't admit it aloud, but he had heard the violent conversation that occurred just an hour ago. He had heard Sayah scream at one of the many men that had entered and left these halls over the past two days. The male had told her that the funeral and coronation were set to go ahead today—but she'd argued that that was awfully cruel of them. He was a child. Barely double digits. How was he to run a kingdom?

"You aren't alone, sweetheart. Everything will be okay."

Kylen couldn't get another word out; he merely shook his head before another wave hit him and dared to send him beneath the surface. Grief was like this, he'd realised. It came in waves, and right when one was on the brink of believing that their tears had alas dried out, another wave hit them, and Gods, he didn't think he was able to keep afloat any longer.

Sayah pulled him into her arms as he sobbed. The tears came so quickly, yet Sayah didn't pull away as the tears stained her black dress—the first time he'd ever seen her wear such a shade. "It's okay, let it out—let it all out, baby. Let it all out." Sayah only held him tighter, pressing kisses to the top of his head and trying to soothe his burning soul with delicate words.

The rest of that day had been a blur.

He remembered standing at the end of the church, watching as his people said their farewells to the four caskets, two large and two small, that had to remain closed. Then, before Kylen even knew it, he was watching his family, his blood, his heart, get lowered into the ground, hearing in the back of his mind as the kingdom wept for the royals that were kind to them.

Yet none of it had ever felt real.

And Kylen had begged for this all to be a mean dream.

After all of that, in the cruellest attempt to keep the air light, everyone was heading towards the church again. Kylen was left to be crowned the same crown they had pried off of his father's corpse.

While everything seemed like such a burdened mystic haze, he remembered one thing.

Kylen remembered looking over the left of his shoulders, looking towards the woman who held her head high as she returned his gaze. Words of wisdom in her eyes and her heart in her hands. "I love you," she said through the simple action of tapping the top of her hand twice, and Kylen subtly nodded before turning back towards the man he wanted to stab.

How dare they force a crown upon a boy who was wallowing in his family's blood?

How dare they force him to suddenly grow up and act as his father when his heart had been ripped from his flesh?

"I miss you so much," Kylen mourned as he turned back to Sayah. Her eyes were sad on his, her touch tightening on him as if she wanted to protect him from the death that had already claimed *her.* "I miss you so—*dreadfully much.*"

Sayah nodded as she pressed a kiss to his forehead, reminding him of that fatal time that went in a fortunate blur. "I know, baby. I miss you too." Her touch was so warm and firm. It was all that he needed—the thing that helped him survive and almost live for so long now. "We will meet again... but for now, I need you to help contact your magick so you can get our girl back."

With a gust of wind that was drastically cold, Sayah pulled away. When Kylen went to look at her, he realised that she was fading—and the most terrible feeling of pure guilt washed over his stomach as he shook his head. He couldn't lose her yet—he had only just gotten her back. "I don't know how."

"Yes, well, we can fix that, can we not? I am the—"

"—*finest magick teacher in all of the lands...* yeah, I know, I remember," Kylen said as he finished her phrase for her. His voice was bitter, yet the sadness was the most evident melody of it.

Sayah nodded as an airy laugh left her lungs, and she tilted her head to the side, cupping his cheek. "You need to hurry and return to your world now; you are giving poor Atty a dear heart attack."

"I'm afraid Atticus isn't my biggest fan at the moment," Kylen admitted, and again, that made Sayah laugh such a sweet sound. It reminded him of his childhood days that were swept away by the memories of pain.

Amusement showed heavily in Sayah's warm eyes, and she nodded with a raise of her brows as if she was truly standing there before him. "Yeah, well… you two are brothers. You will get over this; you always do."

He doubted that; Kylen felt like holding onto this grudge. He cocked a brow of his own this time, noting the exact words Atticus had called him over the past couple of days. Just thinking about that had his heart faltering, his lungs suffocating. "He basically called me insane," Kylen murmured, and he wondered where that once charming brave king had gone?

"And if I recall correctly, you get him back with equally as harsh words, Kye," Sayah pinpointed, and it felt like such a surreal moment. It was as if time had truly swallowed him whole and spat out the bones that were of no use anymore. "Close your eyes, and you will feel the soft quivers of your fingertips. Reach for them, fold your hands around the physical presence, and mould it into something that will be of more use."

Kylen did as she said, although he couldn't will himself to close his eyes. The thought of losing her again—*despite her not even being real*—had his mind silencing. "I don't want to lose you again."

"You can't lose me again; I'm not truly here, remember?"

And that was the worst part of it all.

It pained him to accept, but Kylen knew that he needed to know that it was true. "You will see me again, sweet boy. It may be one day soon, or perhaps it will be lifetimes from now. Either way, you will be okay. Don't push those who mean the most to you away from you."

Kylen closed his eyes to her words, feeling as the twines of glistening magick wielded around his very fingertips. He reached for it with a heave of his chest, and as if Atticus was trapped on the other side of a glass wall, he heard a hint of Atticus' voice echo through the air. He didn't know what he wanted or where he wanted to go. He knew that he wanted to try and get Althea back, but it felt hopeless, and he had no other hope to cling to.

As he reached for one of the tremoring twines, Kylen rose rhythmically to his feet. He clasped at the magick, and a rush of several unnameable sensations radiated through the depths of his bones. He felt the berries physically mould to his fingers, feeling as they began to quiver against his skin, blending with the poison that could pain anyone of his choosing.

Open up your soul to its full potential.

Kylen heaved a heavy sigh. It was one that sent a physical throb throughout his soul, and within a scattered moment, the berries were no more. Instead, they melted into his blood, his magick. Kylen reached for the limp girl several feet away, inaudibly pushing that very spell-binding magick into *her* veins.

Please don't hurt her. Please don't hurt her.

A storm was brewing beyond the castle walls, earning a coldness to leak into the air Kylen breathed as his head jolted back and his eyes rolled to the front. "Kye—" Atticus exclaimed as he appeared at his side. His hands reached for his arms, holding him up as Kylen gasped down the air into his heavy lungs. He watched as the bluish-purple magick flooded beneath Althea's pale skin, seeping into her veins before causing a slight glimmer to flash across her skin. It was like a pure cursed wave washing upon the shores of Lorundio, claiming all within its reach to fall victim.

"Did I do it right?" Kylen asked quickly, yet he was ignorant not to notice the sudden strange thickness in the air as he turned his head. "I didn't hurt her, did I?" He reached out towards the throne to hold himself up, each exhale causing the throbbing of his body to intensify. *"Tell me—"*

Atticus' brows furrowed as he looked from his king and towards Althea; there was an abnormal hint to his gaze as he blinked, one that looked to be assessing something that was unknown to him. "Mhm," Adonis hummed, was that seriously all that he would give him? "Now, we take a seat and wait."

"That's it?" Atticus scoffed on Kylen's behalf, and again Adonis merely nodded.

"That's it," Adonis sang.

A gust of wind that felt consuming had Kylen slowly turning around, stalking his way towards the closest wall before pressing his back against it. His head swayed with every movement, every breath, his features feeling the exhaust before he did. Kylen dropped his head to the side as he slowly melted to the ground, and Atticus was quick to join him as Adonis observed from afar.

"Now we wait," Atticus whispered, and Kylen nodded, shedding him a glance that was awfully heavy.

"It will be a couple of minutes until the poison fully floods into her bloodstream. And another couple of minutes after that until we are able to reach out to Althea and beckon her to return," as the words shuddered from Adonis' lips, Kylen slyly dipped his eyes to Adonis' hands, watching as something *familiar* wrapped around his fingertips.

It was dark.

Shadowed.

Slithering across his flesh before disappearing under his skin.

"You're cursed," Kylen mumbled under his breath, and his brows were quick to furrow as confusion had his eyes wandering. He had seen it before—but he had been so sure that it was a joke—a deception. "*You're cursed.*"

Adonis flexed out his fingers before shedding him an apologetic look. "I don't mean to be," he whispered as if it was a joke. "If anything, I wish that I wasn't... but of course, all sins must go punished, and it seems as if my greatest sin of all was wanting the world to heal. Peace to be restored."

"Why do you want access to Althea?" Atticus asked again, and this time it was quite evident that he no longer found that he was able to push himself to his feet. His hand slipped to his blades instead, clasping them to the point where his fingers turned white.

"I want my family back. I want the king to return my husband and child back to me—is that so bad? I ask you, is that so dreadfully bad?" Adonis queried with a shake of his head. He was walking in circles, his fingers lopped throughout his hair as if he was doing everything in his power to hold himself back. Kylen needed this wave of nausea to clear—he needed full power to jump to his feet before claiming Adonis' blood as his own. "So, I must return the *God with magick beyond reason* to the King who can give my family back to me. You have to understand. If you got the chance to bring your family back—I am sure that you would do everything in your power—"

It was then that Kylen found that he could no longer open his eyes.

It was then that Kylen found that he was falling into the darkness as his hand slipped to the dagger taped to his hip. Except, it was no use because he was already unconscious, and Adonis' face was the vision to follow him.

NINETEEN
ALTHEA

I f one were to ask the small girl who spent endless hours secretly reading about all of the different types of Elemental magick that there was, if she would ever dare to feel comfortable with allowing her own *cursed* magick to shine... she would've most certainly said no.

She would've screamed it for all she *endlessly* cared.

And for what it's worth, that still stands.

But her Elemental magick, on the other hand... That magick made her feel as if she was inhaling the warm air on what she imagined to be on the celebrated Sommsia mornings. That magick made her feel as if she was floating on the water's surface, knowing with such certainty that she wouldn't have to fear drowning.

It felt like all she has ever longed for.

All her mind has yearned for.

And that's awfully strange to accept, especially when she has been in denial about it for so horribly long—perhaps death changed her, *or whatever this Hel was.*

Althea kept her eyes steady on Willix as he watched the spirals of magick waltz upon her palms. His brows were furrowed, and his lips slightly parted, almost like he was memorised. Her magick was performing a dance that she had never seen before, but it was one that she felt to know every ethereal move to.

A glimmering awe twinkled in his eyes; *pure, relentless... awe.* It was a troubling feeling to watch someone at *the same age as her father* study her magick with not a single little hint of disgust on his lips. Althea was practically almost waiting for *it*, expecting *it.* She could already feel how that same dreaded emotion would captivate her eyes as he spat loathsome words at her for something *she didn't want to hold—and yet was left to conquer.*

Except instead... *Willix laughed a sound of veneration.* His eyes were heavy with both admiration and glee as he glanced up at her with a clap of his hands.

Was he trying to deceive her into believing that he was... good? Kind? Nice? Surely, he didn't think of her as a blindsided fool?

"Very good," Willix praised, and Althea almost instantly averted her eyes as she suppressed those peculiar sensations that confused her.

While she wanted to hold her chin high and gaze down at him from the tip of her nose, it didn't at all feel right for someone to be praising *her abilities. Especially the abilities of her Elemental magick.* It felt like she was being deceived or manipulated—either way, *tricked beyond measure.* "How about you *try...* turning your hand around and thinking of something that causes you pure rage, and perhaps your magick will... *change?*" Willix suggested, and it was quite comedic watching as his thoughts all came together second by second.

He was encouraging her magick.

Encouraging her to do more with it.

Kylen's father was... rather nice.

"Change?" Althea echoed as she observed Willix—how on

the Realms name did he expect her to change what she was doing when she had spent the last hour or so trying to do *this?* Was he out of his mind? "What do you mean... *change?* Shall I try to do something else?" *What if there was nothing else that she could do?* What if this aura-looking ball was it?

That was awfully *fucking* disappointing.

The Noxwells would most definitely give up on her then.

This was the catch—the bloody catch that was about to get her head caught on the end of the blade Willix was sure to be hiding at the end of his sleeve. "I don't know what I mean," Willix admitted through a steady grin. His smile was identical to Kylen's, the dimples and all. It was nauseating. "Perhaps try and channel your magick into something specific... *for say...* think of the moment Kylen told you about the curse."

Willix's words were cautious and carefully articulated. However, she knew that he wanted to somehow summon a reaction from her, no matter how it would greatly cost her soul.

Althea's eyes widened as she caught onto exactly what he was suggesting, and she watched as the colour of her magick instantly changed into a shade that was severely darker.

So that had somehow worked.

Amusing.

The magick that folded into itself in the midst of the air was pitch-black with a twinge of gold running through it, and instead of slow and delicate movements, it was moving fiercely and rather quickly, becoming larger as each second went on.

"You know, Althea," Willix cooed as he raised his brows. He dusted his hands off before him, flexing them into the air as if they were covered in his physical skin that had the ability to be pained. "That boy has never had good time management skills. Once, he told Elara *on a rather important morning* that he had lost the cat she had recently adopted and... *well, safe to say the rest of that day was ruined.*"

An ordinary life.

One where a brother and a sister were safe to interact as if all was well and the evil of the night wasn't watching their every step.

"Another time, Kylen showed up half an hour late to his own birthday party because he was apparently busy going for a wander in the woods."

Althea smiled. That did sound like the Kylen she knew.

"And then, of course, he got lost, so that just made him even more late..."

Within a second and a blink of her eyes, Althea's gaze just so happened to catch sight of the *ghost of something more* that floated in the distance, just past Willix's head. Shivers ran down her spine as Althea straightened her stance, narrowing her eyes. What was it that she was sensing? Could they sense it too? *"Little miss, little miss, we've found you! Little miss, little miss~"* They sang, and Althea's breath hitched in her throat. *"We found you! We found you! We-we-we-we-we-we-found-found-youuuuu~"* Althea leapt to her feet, her hands flying out before her as her chest heaved with a sudden pain that had her falling immediately back to her knees.

"Stay back!" Willix yelled. The darkness was beginning to drip from the heavens above, forming puddles of lost souls to quiver across the ground as it shook with such power. The hair on her arms and legs rose even though it wasn't real.

The curse.

It had found her.

Just days ago, she had been held hostage by the agonising foul spirits. Then, by a rare miracle that just so happened to be performed by another member of the *Noxwell throne,* she was saved. But really, could she call it being saved if she was literally sitting in the afterlife, locking eyes with the darkness that was out for her head?

Althea stopped breathing as she looked towards the spirits. She'd seen what the darkness could do to one's soul if they were to get too close—and despite all of the previous pain she had managed to survive through, Althea was almost adamant that she could not survive this.

Willix's hand found hers as he pulled her behind him, and she looked up to him to find that his face was awfully stern. "Stay there," he whispered, already gliding both hands back to the front as he steadied his lungs. He was preparing for war, to fight… but didn't he see that there was no use? That they were stranded in the middle of the flames in a field of ash? It seemed that even those captivated by death lifetimes ago couldn't rid themselves of old habits. *The mortal's way:* that was something Althea remembered reading from one of her father's many boring textbooks. "We have got to go below," Willix was quick to mumble, and Althea could already tell from his tone that she was right to fear the night. *She was more than right—perhaps she shouldn't have pointed it out but instead enjoyed the soft moment for once in her grotesque life.* "They cannot reach us if we are in the cave; there are set enchantments there—they should work, *they should.*"

It felt like he was genuinely afraid of learning what the spirits could do to a soul that mocked theirs because of the way Willix was treading carefully around Althea. If she were in his position, she would like to think that she would've already handed the pathetic excuse of a *girl* off to the spirits to feed upon —so why hadn't he done that? Althea couldn't see how she was anything but a burden to him…

And it wasn't that he was a beast.

A monster from the depths below… that haunted her every breath.

But instead, it was because he was reminding her more and less of her father as each second passed. And it was honestly exhausting having her depictions change. She didn't know what to think or when to think. She felt like that idiotic child who still cried out for her mother in the midst of the nights.

There were some speckled moments in time when her father was a kind man. He had managed to blend himself into the idea of what a father was supposed to be, gazing down at her with eyes that held all of the answers to her many questions. He was a man of wonders, a man of laughter. *He only ever wanted to give her his all*—but that was until his all became her burden. Althea found it impeccably difficult to forget and erase the man her father was meant to be from her soon-to-be hopeless mind.

So ultimately... that man appeared in glimpses through Willix's smiles, his laughs. Reminding her of a time when she wasn't grateful because the rain managed to silence her cries but instead because it was a melody that she could waltz to.

The wind began to howl around them, nipping at the edge of Althea's skin that felt to be crawling with the many hands of varied sizes that belonged to the dreadful curse. It was hardly the sound of a normal... everyday storm... but instead, it perfectly captured the way the skies wept and bled minutes before a hurricane. Althea looked back and towards the great distance, staring towards the brewing storm that looked to be approaching *ever so slowly* and yet far too dreadfully quickly.

However, if one were to be a *Kylen Noxwell* in a situation like this and focus solely on the positives that come out from being put in danger, they would note how her mind had been so focussed on ignoring the cold slithers that was beginning to seep uncomfortably across her bones, that she hadn't noticed the fact that she had wielded herself a blade in a... *eccentric act of defence*.

Humorous.

"Practical," Willix hummed with a nod of his head, and again as if it was Kylen Noxwell who actually stood before her, she could practically see the sarcasm dripping off the edge of his nose. Althea would've replied something unintentionally snarky had she'd had the unforgiving chance; however, he'd already tugged her forwards.

Away from impending doom.

As the two souls departed underground to the cave that Althea was starting to notice the security to, she found Marilla and her two dead children standing tall. They were already waiting for them. Could they sense it too? The way the air was electrified with the screams of those Althea had learnt to mute long ago...

Willix shared a glance with his wife, one that wanted to save her from the impending doom that ceased to always destroy every moment. Marilla's eyes fluttered shut in a pained wince of *acceptance* before she gave both of her children's shoulders a squeeze, nodding once and then twice as she clenched her jaw.

"We can feel it coming," Huntio murmured aloud, and the glance he shed Elara had Althea noticing how deathly pale that small child *now* looked. They *both* looked—Something had evidently changed since the last time Althea had seen them... was this her doing?

There were now evident dark bags under their eyes, and they weren't the type of dark eyebags that were natural to mortals. No, they had black veins running through them, almost as if the 'Gods' were sharing with Althea what both children had looked like when death had claimed them at last.

As well as that, their cheeks looked dreadfully hollow, and their jaws drastically sharp to the point where Althea could sharpen her blades on them.

If anything, they were truly living up to the fact that they were utterly dead. Rotting corpses buried in the 'ROYAL GRAVEYARD OF LORUNDIO'... why they hadn't called it a cemetery on the sign, *Althea didn't know*. But she really didn't think now was the time to dwell on it. Marilla sighed as she ran her other hand through her hair before dragging it across her face: attempting to wipe away the exhaust lingering there.

"They have found us, *Will*," Marilla quietly noted, her voice nothing more than a hiccup of her agony.

Silence, as if it was the greatest poison of them all, settled on every soul that stood bare in the room, allowing Althea to actually understand the extent of what her beloved curse was doing to these people. *Her people.*

No more than an eery moment passed before Althea dared to glance up at Willix and face his judgement. However, the sight that found her was awfully... intimidating, as his features now also no longer held that Lorundio shine. *They were hollow too.*

What were they waiting for? For her to do something? To say something? To bless them all since she was a *fucking* God? Hadn't they realised yet that Althea was hardly the God the people expected? Hel, she was hardly the God she expected—*she couldn't save them;* she hadn't even been able to save herself.

Althea's hands began to shake at her sides as she took a faltering step back. This was *her* fault. The curse was after *her.*

"Let's think," Willix suggested as he stepped forward, and Althea took that quick opportunity to take another step back. She needed to leave; that would do the job, wouldn't it? Then at least, she wouldn't have to burden herself with harming the Noxwell family anymore. Her existence had already done enough damage as it was. "Let's... try to channel Kylen again—*let's try to...* reach out to him, and that will give us a chance to actually... *breathe...!*"

His fake enthusiasm said both nothing and everything that there was to it.

Marilla nodded, guiding her children forward with a smile that was all too awfully fake. How many times had they done this? Was it a reoccurring thing, or was this the first time they'd been reminded of that fatal day? Elara glanced up at Althea, presumably going to make a comment of some type when she froze. *Could she see the panic that rippled across Althea's heart?* Could she tell how desperate she was to make sure that she didn't lose anybody else? What would the curse do if it reached them? What would the curse do—*would it erase them completely?*

No. No. No. NO—

Althea took another step back. She needed to go. She needed to run. They would be safe if she were to disappear—they would be okay and survive. So, what if she allowed the spirits to consume her body and soul entirely? Either way, she would lose something or another. Either way, *somebody would die.* Althea took another step back, and she felt as Willix's burning gaze turned to her. Sympathy would only make it worse; she didn't need him trying to stop her or be the problem solver Kylen desired himself to be.

There were no other thoughts to it; Althea turned on her heel before she could get a single word out, except a hand, *to Althea's panicking dismay,* was quick to grab hold of her arm in a firm clasp.

"Don't. Even. Think. About. It."

"*What?*" Althea practically gaped as she looked to Marilla, who had been the one to surprisingly speak. Her eyes were narrowed, and her lips pursed. Althea knew that she had been a Queen—but this was the first time she truly looked like a ruler.

"I know what you are thinking—Hel, you and I think the same thing; and I know that if I was in your position, I would most certainly go ahead and walk right into the eye of danger without an utter care in the world. But I'm not going to let you. I always needed and partially relied on the people who dared to hold me back, even if I didn't exactly agree with them in those fatal moments. So now, just to your luck, I am going to be that irritating person *that you are probably going to loathe,* and I am going to hold you back." Marilla took a breath, but Althea could tell that there was more coming. "I don't care if you want to now spit at me and kick my grave because of this, but I am not going to be another one of your parents who watch as you walk to your death. You deserve to live. To grow old—and you deserve to actually experience something of life. We care for you, Althea. We love you—and if you think for one moment that we are going to let you go... you are sorely mistaken."

Althea's jaw dropped with a laugh that was more confused than anything else. She shrugged her shoulders, fixing her posture as she tried to avoid her harsh expression. Althea had never been one for confrontation. It made her terribly uneasy most of the time. But was this *real* confrontation—it confused her, and that made her even more uneasy. "If you haven't realised yet, you will... completely and utterly die if I stay here. Your souls will be erased and again consumed by the curse. You won't be able to care for your children; you won't be able to reflect on your past life—all of that will become a mere memory."

"So be it," Willix huffed on behalf of his wife this time, and Althea was almost certain that they were setting her up for pure relentless failure.

Elara and Huntio both sent her a small smile as they watched her, their expressions nearly identical. "It's best not to argue, Althea," Huntio warned as he picked at the fabric of his clothes. "When they have their mind on something, they never... *ever...* budge."

Marilla cocked a brow as if she was challenging her. Did she really want to start bickering with her when the curse was inches away from murdering them all? At least Althea could now understand where Kylen got his wit and stamina from. "We haven't waited and planned for this long *for it to all go to shit!* If you think that we are going to go give yourself up to those bloody monsters... *willingly...* then you are wrongly mistaken. Althea, you don't seem to understand, but if you give your soul up to them: there is no coming back from it. The world will burn. Everyone will die. You are a God, may I remind you; therefore, your abilities, your magick, your power has the chance to either destroy or save us all... even the dead." Althea's expression faulted, and yet Marilla went on. "We love you, okay? And the last thing we want is to pressure you into saving the world because of the faults of your parents... but if it means giving you a chance to live, then we are going to push."

They loved her?

So far, the idea of what would happen if the curse was to claim her soul had been a mere small whisper in the back of her mind. She'd already realised what would happen if they were to steal the last of her magick, and considering what was at stake now, she had, for the most part... accepted it.

Who was she to be the one in charge of saving the world?

Who was she to be the one to restore the purities of the land that had only ever scarred her?

This wasn't some cruel mythical story where at last, the hero is found after being hidden in plain sight. No, this was a cruel game, a wicked gamble. If anything, it was sourly ironic: everything seemed to be bloody ironic nowadays, and it was exhausting to keep up with.

"I—"

"Again, I wouldn't try to go against her, Althea," Elara warned this time as she raised her brows. "As Hunt said, once either of them, but mostly *she*, has their mind set on something... let's just say it's not good to cross their paths or to fight against it."

Would this have been what life would've been like if I had grown up with them? Althea wondered: and she would admit that she probably could've gotten used to it. Having someone actually care about such things, that was. It was nice.

Something in the air caught Althea's attention. A thickness that had her hearing memories of her past caress her spine. "They're approaching," Althea wearily said, and both Willix and Marilla again shared a glance that was challenging.

"Follow us."

A year ago, Althea had been the girl who constantly stalked

the halls of Aeonia. Searching for any potential secret holes or cracks in the walls that could lead her to escape the tall Aeonian walls. But, of course, nothing had led anywhere. And she had still been trapped... but that was until her father presented her with a chance. A gamble.

If she were to kill Kylen Noxwell after giving him her hand, then she would be free.

Now, after *not* marrying Kylen Noxwell and going *against* her father, she was trapped again. Except this time, in the gods-forsaken *afterlife*.

And she was walking down the stairs to a 'secret' bunker that apparently even Elara and Huntio hadn't known about... considering their expressions.

"This has been there this whole time?" Huntio gawked, his tone drastically snarky. "Why didn't you tell us about this? We could've helped with... building it or something."

Marilla peered over her shoulders at Althea and her son, a laugh quivering against her lungs as she shook her head. "There are important things down here, Huntio. Even I have only been down here once or twice in my days of death."

That didn't resonate with Huntio whatsoever. He merely grumbled something under his breath before rolling his eyes, earning an amused smile to nudge the edge of Althea's lips.

The room below was filled to the brim with a candlelight glow that was from no physical or visible candles. It simply had a haze that spread shadows across the floors and walls that Althea ran her fingers across. Also, on the walls were many sheets of cream and grey paper that were covered in different pieces of writing (in many different languages) as well as Markings and drawings that had her curiosity brimming.

It didn't take many steps for Althea's eyes to meet with the Markings that she knew to be her own. Althea would notice them anywhere; after all, she had spent so many long months loathing them. Ignoring them.

Now, they didn't seem like such an issue in the scheme of things. They still didn't seem like a blessing, but Althea didn't have to worry about them consuming the last of her name and soul whilst plotting to take over... every Realm known to man.

The stones scattered from under her feet as she turned towards Willix and Marilla with many questions in mind. They were murmuring something to each other whilst their eyes stayed locked, yet it was far too quiet for Althea to hear anything. "Have you learnt of anything regarding... my Markings?" Althea asked the moment Willix turned away from his wife, and he appeared rather grateful for the sudden change in conversation.

"Yes and no," he replied. That was definitely *not* the answer she wanted, but what was the answer she wanted? That seemed to, again, be another question that was unanswerable. "We already know the basics, of course... that your Markings indicate that you hold the Elemental magick. However, due to how... *impressive they are,* it is also hinted within them that you are of the Godly ranking." *I've already figured that,* Althea went to say, except she held herself back from doing so. "But I've also been thinking, and I am wondering whether your Markings hint at exactly what you can and can't do. It's a working theory, *but I am still working on it.*"

"But we have figured out some other things," Marilla added in an attempt to keep the conversation light. "And while we do have some ideas on how to reach the other-other side, it is still... *also a working theory.* However, one's that are far more reliable than the Markings situation."

"What are some of your working theories?" Althea asked, and because of the expression that bloomed heavenly on Willix's healing face, she assumed that that was the right question to ask in an impossibly dark time like this.

TWENTY

KYLEN

K ylen could feel the jagged rocks beneath him piercing into the flesh of his backside. They were sharp and *rough*, making his head throb as he slowly rolled it to either side of him. His attempts were weak, but he was merely attempting to look through the air that felt awfully tight in the lungs that ached.

Why must this keep happening to him? If this was what insanity was, then perhaps he truly was insane, just as the rumours said.

"Kylen. *Fucking*. Noxwell."

With a weak attempt to rise to his feet, Kylen rose a hand just above his eyes, peering past it towards the *faces* that were staring down at him. Oh, Gods, he *was* dead. And so, were they? He knew death was sure to catch up to him at one point or another—he just assumed that the kingdom would be able to see his charming face one last time before death was to at last kill him. Or perhaps he figured he would die in a blaze of glory in a battle prompted and started *by him*—then that way, he would at least make it to the holy lands.

"Answer me," the voice of Zaire seethed, and Kylen coughed

multiple curses under his breath as he took in the redhead for all of their glory.

Kylen fell back down with a great thud, earning many particles of dust to rise in his honour. "How did you die? –*How did I die?*"

"Oh, my absolute Gods," Zaire whispered as they shook their head with a cackle that had Kylen's blood-chilling. "*How did I die?* Do you really think that low of me?" Kylen knew that was a trap—he was *not that* ignorant. "My Gods, my Gods, *my Gods.* Tell me why, Kylen, I ended up running into Uzziah in the literal Kingdom of Death—only for the *bloody* darkness of the hallways to swallow us whole and send us into *bloody unconsciousness!*"

"You returned my letter?" Atticus whispered in near disbelief from somewhere Kylen could not see.

Kylen pushed himself up as the scene played out before him. He looked towards Atticus, who stood quizzically behind both Uzziah and Zaire, his arms crossed and eyebrows raised. It was the same performance every time Kylen pissed someone off or miraculously did something wrong. Zaire and Uzziah were confronting him, Atticus watching from behind... And Sayah and Khatri were off doing Gods know what. Except, this time, Sayah was dead, and Khatri basically was too.

From what Kylen was noticing from his rather uncomfortable position on the ground, was that out of both Zaire and Uzziah, Uzziah's hair was the most overgrown. However, he'd shaved the back of his head, Kylen also observed as Uzziah turned to Zaire with a raise of his brow. On the other hand, Zaire had their hair in braids, so he didn't quite know how long or short it was, but he presumed it had to be quite long if it was in multiple braids.

"Of course, we did," Uzziah sneered as if it wasn't obvious enough, "we weren't going to sit by, village to village hopping after knowing that Kylen was quite literally walking to his death." *Walking to 'his' death?* Kylen was not walking to his death. He was walking to save the girl he owed his very life to—they all owed their lives too. "Plus, I'd had enough of our so-called camping trip, and I wanted to come home. Yet, of course, when we got there, we received the letter."

"To my dismay, that is," said a voice he wasn't expecting to hear. A voice that had Kylen's head cocking to the left before peering past the three mortals before him. "Don't worry. The moment I kill her, I will leave you *all* to be, and we can go back to ignoring one another," Khatri said with a hiccup in his voice. He looked almost identical to how he'd looked the last time Kylen had seen him. Drunk. High. And off his head.

Zaire turned to him with a narrow of their brows. "What's up your ass?"

Oh, he couldn't bear to have this conversation again. Khatri would growl a reply of nothing, but they all knew that it was so far from the truth, which would end up pissing him off even more.

Kylen shook his head, his eyes locked on Khatri as he rolled them and waved his hand in the air. Pleading with the Gods themselves for everything just to quieten a little. "I've already told you it's not Althea."

Khatri clenched his jaw as he shoved his hands into his pockets. He went to turn on his heel, although Atticus was quick to grab hold of his shoulder and force him to face the undeniable truth.

The two held each other's gaze as Zaire and Uzziah shared an equally as distasteful, questioning glance before looking towards Atticus, who sighed. "He's right. It isn't her."

"But we thought you said—"

The sound was almost identical to the one of a carriage scattering across the loose pebble pathways leading to the Kingdom of Lorundio, which had the air thickening with heavy smoke, the dust beginning to rise, forming into a tidal wave that threatened

Kylen to rise to his feet awfully quickly. "Yeah, turns out I was wrong. Very, *very* wrong," Atticus wearily replied as he reached for Kylen, pulling him back and away from the dust cloud that was bigger than them all combined. "And now I think we are all trapped in the curses unconsciousness... if that's even a thing? *Is it a thing?*"

Kylen tensed his jaw as he looked around. He appeared to be in an arena of some type. One that looked as if all had been carved out of pure stone. The walls were high and stone. The ceiling was also high and stone. The air was dark—yet there was some type of enchantment set on it that allowed everyone to be clearly visible—was this the mind of the curse? "What is happening—"

"*We gave you a chance, Kylen Noxwell, King of Lorundio.* We gave you a remarkable chance to live in peace, to forget all of what has happened and turn a blind eye to the war that you know is approaching." There was no answer as to where this voice was coming from, but Kylen had managed to understand that it was coming from somewhere in the air as it grazed the tip of his nose with many pondering thoughts. "Yet you repeatedly have tried to make a fool out of us. How pathetic do you take us to be?"

Kylen took a step forward, standing before the darkness that hid the spirits he knew were speaking to him. He could hear their words spit at his skin, and his spine straightened as he felt their many breaths scatter down his bones. "We know that your soul is damaged, that you will unfortunately not taste as great as your dearest friends here; however, we yearn for entertainment. And what better way than to have you perform the famous acts that were around when the majority of us still dared to breathe?"

"Kylen," Atticus urged, but he couldn't dare to answer him: he needed to figure out a way to break out of this trance. By now, he should be an expert at freeing himself of such evil; but the curse had perfected this craft many lifetimes ago. *And they did say that every now and then, the curse would choose a few lucky ones to entertain them through the despairing nights.*

"We have paired you into two; however, due to there now being an uneven number of you... we have had to make some *adjustments*."

Confusion bloomed heavily on Kylen's features as he tried to understand just what it was that they were preaching. He furrowed his brows; what entertainment were they searching for? Kylen tried to take another step forward, but Zaire's hand was quick to hold him back as they tugged at his shirt. That startled him the most—Kylen was almost certain that Zaire would be rather eager to watch him succumb to the darkness that had always been one step ahead of them. Yet, as he looked towards them, it was clear that against all odds, they still, for whatever reason, cared for Kylen.

From out of the dusty air before them walked a girl who was evidently *not* the girl he was expecting to lay witness to.

Kylen had figured that because the spirits were talking to him, therefore that meant that they were in Althea's mind and Adonis' peculiar plan had worked. That also had him presuming that the cursed Althea would be the one to descend from the shadows before them all...

Except, the girl before him was not Althea's cursed body or even Althea herself.

And yet his heart still bled for this Godly woman.

"*Sayah*," Khatri uttered, and his voice was no longer fuelled by pure, inevitable rage; it was instead quiet, full of all the grief he had suppressed for so long.

Sayah took a small step before her feet came to an abrupt halt. There was a thick twine of dark slithering magick wrapped around her head and throat; it was preventing her from uttering a single word as she looked to Kylen, Khatri, Atticus, Uzziah, and Zaire.

Her eyes were noticeably filled with such sorrow: tears

threatening to spill every time she blinked. However, Sayah had always been awfully stubborn, which was one of Kylen's favourite traits of hers.

She held her head high, gazing at the spirits of the air, her eyes narrowed.

Sayah's head was quick to shoot left as she sensed the spirits form several seconds before Kylen did; her eyes sharpened on the darkness that clung to a ruinous body, a lethal glow to them that vowed revenge.

Althea—except the version of her that looked like the curse, stepped out from the shadowed haze of the arena with a clap of her hands. Now that 'she' was standing before them, Kylen could hear the several trillion screaming souls that echoed from 'her' every breath.

"Kylen, what the fuck is this?" Khatri muttered under his breath as if he expected Kylen to know the answer. And perhaps he would've if he had been able to tear his eyes away from the woman he had hallucinated several minutes ago. She had been in the curse's possession—*all this time?* She had been their little toy, *their little plaything.* Of course, he knew that she wouldn't have been able to reach the afterlife simply because of *how* she died—but there was some hope in his heart that, as the mythical rumours said, she would've eventually found it with great determination striving her every step.

Kylen felt sick; he felt the bile crawl against his throat and puncture his heart.

"Let the games begin."

Before the spirits had even finished their sentence, Kylen felt something sharp waltz across his flesh before grabbing hold of his legs. The magick pushed him back and into alignment with the others. However, that didn't last long, as one by one the curse began to push each one of them back and forth, forming a crisscross type of line, but it appeared as if Kylen was pushed further forwards than the rest of them, as he was the only one not in a line of some type.

Zaire was *standing* next to Uzziah.

Atticus was *standing* next to Khatri.

And Kylen... Kylen was now *standing alone* before Sayah was pushed in line next to him. So many words filled her eyes, saying everything that there utterly was to say in a time as horrible as this. Yet her mouth remained closed, and the air again darkened in anticipation for what the spirits were to say next.

TWENTY-ONE
ALTHEA

I feel like a fool, Althea wanted to snarl as she kept her eyes steadily closed. Instead, she heaved a small sigh before balling her fists on either one of her knees. She was restraining herself, careful not to upset the family that deserved so much more than Althea could ever possibly offer. "Nothing is happening," she noted as if it wasn't obvious enough; and her voice was rather even and steady despite the lump that fumbled in her throat.

"You have to focus," Marilla assured as she reached a hand for her shoulder.

If there was one thing about this family that Althea had noticed, was that the Noxwell's awfully loved *physical touch...* something that she couldn't stand no matter the situation.

Althea narrowed her brows. *Remain calm,* she seethed to herself, *but that was a lot easier said than done.* "My mind is too distracted by the curse—I fear that the moment I become immersed by my magick, the curse will find us and—"

Willix sat down on the chair in front of her. His expression was calm and understanding. He nodded as he sighed, evidently carefully collecting his thoughts before preaching them aloud.

That was another thing Althea had noticed; they were always so careful not to say the wrong thing, to not react in an immoral way. "You have done this before, Althea. When you were on the ship with Sayah, and she got you to... *reach your inner soul.*"

"But now I am my inner soul," Althea replied with a sarcastic smile flashing against her bruised lips. She was trying, truly, except it was awfully difficult. How was one to know how to act like they've reached the shore when they are trapped beneath the surface? "I don't understand how I am meant to reach my inner soul if *I am my inner soul.* Shouldn't I just look in the mirror and be done with it?"

Marilla chuckled under her breath as she offered Althea's shoulder another squeeze. However, Althea was focussed on the moulding expression of the man before her. She was practically waiting for him to spit such filth at her. He would be certain to tell her off for her smart mouth and say, *'that's not how future queens are supposed to talk'.* Except, again, as if Willix was all that she had deserved in another life, he did anything but that.

He laughed of all things, a grin appearing on his lips as he dipped his head back, and Althea was sure that she had just opened her eyes to the curse consuming the last of his soul —*because why else would he be smiling?* Gods, Marilla was smiling too. She was too late—they were gone.

Dead.

"What is going on in that head of yours?" Marilla asked as Althea's stare became one that was awfully panicked. "It's okay; we are right here," she assured, and the hand perched on her shoulder slipped down to Althea's hand.

She was going to do everything in her power to make sure that the Noxwells saw the light of day again. Althea was going to do anything.

Willix clapped his hands together before placing them in his lap; he leaned back against the wooden chair, looking from his children towards Althea as he tried to decipher what he could say. "Well, I would like for you to have to be in the position where you have to reach your inner soul... *right now*... but unfortunately for us, that's not the case. So, I basically need you to reach your outer body. The one that is being controlled by the curse."

Althea grimaced. "Again, that sounds a lot easier said than done."

Elara reached up and placed a hand on top of her other hand. Such a gentle touch that she could've almost mistaken it to be a touch of the Gods. "You've got this," she murmured, and Althea was left to look at her as if she had just taken every burden off her shoulders. Did it make her an ignorant fool to find such meaning in those small words? Did Elara even realise how much that meant to her? Did she even realise that those very words had her wanting to embrace her? *And that said a lot since Althea was definitely not a hugger.*

She was a stabber.

It caused her great ease to stab people.

With *a very heavy breath*, Althea closed her eyes and willed her consciousness to melt into her 'bones'. She had this. She just had to merely focus on the aura around her and reach into it without a single care at all.

What was Kylen doing right now? Imagine how laughable it would be if he were trying to reach out to her.

Did she want him to be reaching out to her?

Althea rose her hand forward, and it seemed that she now had great experience doing this, as she already knew that she had not lifted her physical hand up and into the air. The 'air' in her mind felt like the soft waves crashing into one another before meeting with the sand. The water wasn't cold nor warm; it was just right, allowing her to drown within it if she so wished. *Show me, Kylen,* Althea willed, not knowing for certain whether that was the right next step to take or not.

It seemed to lead her somewhere; however, as the air before

her began to form into colours, and those colours began to form into shades that led her to see the image of Kylen lying unconscious against one of the walls in the *Aeonian palace.* Dark black blood was dripping from his eyes, and his veins were throbbing with the exhaust of the shadowed darkness.

Oh, Gods—

The spirits had killed him. The spirits had murdered him—she had been too late—

Althea's true hands (well, whatever was true in the eyes of death) began to tremble as they rested on her knees, her nails digging into the illusion of her flesh as she felt the panic take over her every thought. Elara tightened her hold on her hand, Marilla sounding to be whispering something to her that Althea didn't listen to whatsoever.

She knew that they were trying to calm her—to ease her breaths.

But there was inevitable rage blinding Althea, and she wasn't going to let the curse win. She couldn't. She *wouldn't.*

Her brows furrowed, and Althea felt an almighty burn begin to scatter through the depths of her chest. It rattled her bones, forcing her breaths to quicken. She was going to reach her physical body one way or another, and this time she was going to make sure that the curse didn't have a chance of getting back up again.

TWENTY-TWO
KYLEN

He didn't know what to do. He didn't know what to do. He didn't know what to do—Kylen felt as if his heart was about to plummet into the depths of whatever Hel was down below. He felt as if his skin and bones were about to pierce his soul into two and butcher the rest of it in flames *purely so that he would suffer*. Kylen didn't know what to do, how to stop it, or even how to prevent the deaths *that were about to happen,* from happening.

But he needed to do something—*anything*.

"Don't," Sayah pleaded as she tried to step forward, except the 'girl' that was before them merely tipped Althea's cursed head back and scoffed a laugh as if this was the entertainment they so desperately yearned for. "It doesn't have to be this way."

Oh, but it does; the air seemed to crackle in response. And Kylen wanted nothing more than to burn everything involving the curse.

To butcher it all and be done with this miserable excuse of a mess.

Instead of answering Sayah's pleas with a snicker of their own, the spirits merely began a speech on something entirely

270

different. A speech that had Kylen's eyes widening and his heart withering as his mind tried to calculate how they could possibly escape. *Except his magick and their magick all seemed to be blocked by a force of some type—*

"The first game is a game that I rather like," the spirits began, and slowly they tiptoed around the six frozen souls with *Althea's eyes throwing daggers at them all.* Zaire held their chin high, trying to stand before Uzziah in a hopeless act to protect him. Still, it was useless because they were frozen in place with the curse breathing over their shoulders and down their spines. "*And~* by the end of all of this *gleeful* fun, there will only be three... remaining... souls..." Kylen's stomach twisted as he looked to either side of him, glancing towards the family that had been there for him through it all. They were going to die, *and it was because of* him. Althea's head twisted slightly to the left, her eyes picking up on something that wasn't visible to him and yet apparently angered the arrogant minds. The air darkened then, the mist slowly rising off the ground whilst Althea's hands balled at her sides. Something truly was pissing them off, and it had nothing to do with Kylen —perhaps Adonis; Kylen would pay good money to watch Adonis be ripped to shreds. "*However,*" they whispered as they turned around with a furrow of their brows, presumably searching for something hidden from view, "I will return in a couple of minutes, as there seems to be something I must attend to first—"

Kylen was right; there was something more than what met the eye.

Althea's body vanished within a snickering second as the words filtered uneasily through the air, leaving only a shadowed substance in their wake as Kylen heard Atticus release a quick-witted breath. "Where did *it* go?"

Kylen wanted to answer that question with an answer that was certain to be right. But he didn't know. He was a weak excuse of a King, a ruler, a friend, and a brother. He was hope-less at even keeping himself alive.

A hand that was warm and free from any calloused scars nudged Kylen's arm, and it dawned on him then just who it was standing tall at his side. Kylen was quick to turn towards Sayah, finding that her arms were already open for his. "*Hi, Kylen*," she whispered as Kylen melted away under her touch—the childlike pity claiming the last of his bones. Sayah laughed gently into his embrace, and his eyes fluttered shut as he willed this to both be a darling dream and wretched real life. *He didn't want to let her go;* he didn't want to open his eyes and find that again she was nowhere to be seen—and yet he was conflicted because he wished that Sayah had at least found something of peace.

She deserved that much.

She deserved more than he could ever offer.

Sayah pulled back, her hands rising up to clasp his cheeks. "Hello to you all."

Her touch was so warm, so sincere. It made him feel as if he was a small boy again, holding onto the memories of what was because he knew that both the future and the past would not dare to be kind *to him*.

Zaire inhaled slowly like they couldn't believe what they were seeing, and if Kylen didn't know better, he would note how there were evident tears in their eyes. *Tears that had been long overdue.*

Zaire had never cried, had never shed a single tear. They had merely said how something bad was bound to happen, that no one ever got lucky in a world like this.

It had been on one of the darker nights in the early months when Kylen had walked past Sayah's chambers and noticed how her door was open a crack. For most of it, he tried to avoid that part of the castle entirely; however, that day, he *needed* silence, and he knew that no one dared to wander down there anymore.

Or so he thought.

Kylen had found Zaire sitting on the edge of Sayah's bed, staring into the abyss before them with mindless words floating about through their mind. They didn't say a word as they noted Kylen's presence; they didn't even look at him. Zaire simply stared.

"Is it really you?" they whispered in both shock and horror as their eyes danced over Sayah's soft features. The very question earned all of their hearts to still and their breaths to halt. Zaire's voice cracked ever so slightly, and it was then that Kylen noticed how Atticus had silent tears staining his dust-covered cheeks.

Khatri was the one who worried Kylen the most, however. He hadn't uttered a single thing. He looked like a reference to one of Sayah's famous portraits; a soul who was frozen in time as the Realms left dust to wither on the frames. Khatri looked mortified, petrified: staring ahead with eyes of many whispers and lips that were mourning the life that, in the end, he never got to actually hold.

Kylen would admit Khatri had had quite the detrimental life.

The first thing was that he had woken up one morning without realising that time had turned without him. Then, he had learnt that his family had moved on and that the woman that was once his absolute everything *and had been pregnant with his child* was now, at last, moving on *after losing him* and mourning him.

Then, she had died, also. *So, he'd lost basically everything... again.*

Kylen couldn't bear to see his brother in such a state—none of them deserved this. None of them deserved to suffer this way.

Sayah fidgeted in her steps as if she could feel Khatri's atrocious emotions, and she offered Zaire a saddened smile as their chest heaved with a shake of their head. It was evident on both of their features that they wanted to run to each other. To hold each other after spending what felt like eternities apart. However, *they could not.* Because they were quite literally frozen with darkness wrapped around their legs like chains, and the curse was still lingering about without actually being present at all. This was their state of mind, after all. "*Fortunately*, yes, it is really me. I wouldn't want to leave you alone with all of this… *fun*."

"It's good to see you." Atticus smiled, *and if they were in any other circumstance but this,* perhaps it would've been a sweet and memorable moment. "It's really *bloody* good to see you." Atticus wiped at his silent tears and nodded once and then twice, trying to gather himself up before them all. Kylen knew that it was paining him to be vulnerable in front of everyone; it always had been. But what could he possibly do? He had always been this way. It's what made him… *him*.

The smile Sayah shed Atticus was both sombre and kind. Mourning for the life that was evidently lost whilst she nodded slowly. Her skin didn't look aged or time driven; it looked exactly the same. As if no time has passed at all, and it felt like that hurt the most. "It's good to see you too, *monstrum parvum*."

Atticus' nickname

His beloved childhood nickname.

Little monster.

Although the question hadn't been spoken aloud, Kylen knew that practically all wanted to ask the dreadful thing. They wanted to know what being dead was like. If it was as kind as some said, or if it was a brutal trial of life—almost like what they were trapped within right now. Except, Kylen doubted that it was like actually being dead since she had basically been held prisoner for the past several months.

Uzziah lowered his head before Sayah, and his face softened instantly when he glanced back up at her. "The Kingdom mourns for you, S. As do we." It was evident in the splinters of the past several months that he had tried not to mourn too loudly. He had known and still knew how much Sayah meant to Zaire and didn't want to be the one to remind them that she was *gone*.

Sayah waved a hand in his direction, playfully rolling her

eyes as she snickered. It really did feel as if no time had been lost. "Enough with the formal mannerisms. It's just me. Dead or alive, it is just me." A pause. "*But...* we seem to have greater issues at hand right now, and we need to figure out just what we need to do to get out of here—"

The dust began to rise from the ground once again, the ground beginning to rumble. Althea's manacled body stepped out of the darkness before them, except her face looked very different this time, as there was a large, jagged wound stretching from her cheek down, and the shadowed darkness was spilling from within. It always looked like string—twine... legs of a spider attempting to flee from the spirit's wrath.

The spirits assessed them all before clapping their hands before them. "Now, let's begin," they whispered, and a smile that was monstrous hugged their lips. "The first game is one that one of our fathers created. It is a game where one from each group must... die, and if they do not... *well, then you will all die a very slow and torturous death.*"

The spirits were so abrupt with it that Kylen almost wanted to scoff out a laugh. It seemed beyond unbelievable—insanity in its purest form.

"What the sick Hel is this?" Atticus sneered on behalf of them all. "You are making us fight... *to the death*?" The very concept of it reminded Kylen of the many arenas all kingdoms held many lifetimes ago. However, his grandfather had genuinely been the first one to rid his kingdom of the cruel games, leaving a sort of change to filter through the air for the first time in centuries.

"Oh, don't sound so surprised, *boy*. This is a... *trial*. A game. These are the type of things we had to endure when we were alive, so it's only fair that you are to suffer the same fate."

The bile in Kylen's throat stirred uncomfortably, and he felt the physical yet invisible force at his back turn him around to face Sayah. Her eyes were wide, falling down to the blade that dropped with a loud clatter onto the floor before them.

Instead of keeping the two frozen in place, small bubbles of their own formed around each pair, trapping them into their own miniature arena that strived to taste death.

So... he was to kill her or be killed?

Kylen already knew who was to die.

And that decision was a rather easy one to make.

"Kylen," Sayah whispered, and the fear in her tone had Kylen shaking his head. If she thought that he would kill her, she was insane. Beyond insane. He didn't want to do this, to stand here and watch the others suffer—*there had to be some way for them all to make it out alive.* "It's okay, stab me and then save *them*. I'm already dead. Where's the harm in dying twice? Perhaps I will actually make it to the afterlife this time." Sayah tried to keep her voice easy, but the fact that she had already accepted her so-called fate made him uneasy. Bile scratched against the edge of Kylen's throat, succumbing to the snickers of the spirits from somewhere beyond.

They approached cautiously with a tilt of Althea's head, a shine of death twinkling brightly in the black blood that dripped from *his beloved's* eyes. "Oh, it seems as if I have forgotten to mention a little something, little kingling. If the old Captain of your Guards is to... stab you, murder you, kill you, then she will, fortunately, earn herself a physical spot on the true Realms. She will get to live her life—the same life that your gamble took away."

"I will do no such thing," Sayah replied with a raise of her chin. Her hand shot out from her side, holding Kylen back from stepping in between the spirits and her. Despite there being an enchanted barrier of some type surrounding them, he doubted that it would work in their favour and save them from the treacherous torture.

"Oh?" the spirits prompted through Althea's lips, another

snicker scattering into the air as the dust that covered the ground began to form into pictures. At first, Kylen spotted silhouettes of mortals running—no, fleeing. All of their expressions were panicked, silent sobs seeping into the air from the lungs that burned. Then he watched as their lifeless, transparent bodies fell to the ground before the dust, again, moved onto something new.

"So, then," the spirits murmured as they caught Kylen's gaze once again, "are you willing to allow Kylen to *murder* you instead? Taking away your last chance of having the life that you have always dreamt of? We have heard your thoughts, *Sayah of Sommsia*; we have heard your dreams—the longing of your nightmares. Since you were only a child born, you've dreamt of having a family of your own. One that won't leave you but instead will fight by your side until the very end."

"And in the end, I got just that," Sayah answered coldly without a single waver of her tone. Kylen didn't have to look towards the others to know that they were just as mesmerized as he was, looking towards the artist who had transformed into the very art all were left to get on their hands and knees to praise.

"Yet, you will let them kill you... interesting."

Kylen shook his head as he pushed past Sayah's hand, his own fingers dropping down to hold her frail wrist. He just needed to know that she was actually here. "*There is no way in Hel that that is—*"

"Of course," Sayah said, interrupting him. "If that is what it takes to guarantee his and the other's safety, then I would happily rip the muscles from my bones in every lifetime."

Kylen scoffed a manic laugh. Was she delusional? *He would do no such thing.*

The spirits raised a brow. Slowly tiptoeing around the specific two whilst they assessed their every little action, their every little breath—except this time, their eyes and words were directed to Kylen. He could tell that Zaire, Uzziah, Atticus, and Khatri were trying to plot something grand. He could tell from their shared sceptical glances and their quick gestures that an unspoken plan was being moulded as their lives became threatened. "*So…* you would allow the others to suffer because you can't put your loyalty aside? Because you can't bring yourself to slaughter the siren that has shown you something of loyalty…" they pondered, and Sayah and Kylen stilled in their steps. "Very well, *very, very well.*"

Before neither Sayah nor Kylen could utter anything more, the spirits raised Althea's hand into the thickening air. A dark twine wrapped around her fingertips, piercing into Althea's skin and puncturing wounds that bled black. With a swift flick of her fingers, a gut-wrenching scream erupted from Zaire's lungs as the arena flickered with a sinister pain.

Kylen looked over in the nick of time to find Zaire falling to their knees, crimson blood spurting across their flesh as Uzziah dove for them with widening eyes. "*My arm—my arm—*" Zaire sobbed, their voice breaking over every word, every syllable. The bone of their arm had pierced neatly through their pale flesh, capturing the entertainment the curse appeared to crave so profoundly as the pride flickered across Althea's face. Zaire twitched against Uzziah's hold like a rabbit when the arrow missed its heart by an inch. Their chest heaved, the blood splattering onto their face. "My arm—my arm—"

Sayah rushed over to the edge of the barrier before she began to hit her fists against the unwavering magick with such lethal force. The enchanted curse didn't react nicely to that, *however,* as her own crimson blood began to splatter against her own skin every time she so dared to make contact with the barrier. "NO! *NO!*" Kylen knew that she didn't exactly care what was happening to her and that her flesh was now raw and bloody… she never cared about anything to do with herself when the lives of those she loved were being threatened.

"Don't hurt them! *Don't hurt them—*" she attempted to scream, but it appeared that her pleas didn't matter and that the curse had silenced their miniature arena, as no one could hear a thing.

"Three will die. One from each pair," the spirits said to Sayah as they looked from Zaire towards her. The artic tone within Althea's eyes swirled as if Kylen was staring into the eye of a hurricane. It was so physical, so real, and so unsettling, earning his own blood to curdle as Zaire thrashed in Uzziah's arms. "Some may deem it as unfair; some may scream forever, and yet their pleas will never be heard. Tell me, why would I let you go without a second thought when we never got that luxury? We were forced to murder our partners, lovers, and children. We were forced to murder the ones we once cared about so that when the curse came along... they knew we no longer had it in us to try and survive."

We didn't have it fair, and neither will you, the wind whispered breathlessly.

Zaire lifted their head, looking towards the cursed girl with venom dripping from their eyes. Their jaw clenched, evidently swallowing away the pain that had their eyes faltering shut as their throat bobbed. Without uttering a single word, they pushed their bone back beneath their skin. Zaire's face crumbled in agony, and yet they refused to cry a single word, not as the curse watched them, waiting for it.

"I'm going to kill you," Uzziah bellowed as he glanced up. Although he had been cursing in their native language seconds ago, these were the first words he seethed that were audible enough to shake the delusional soil. *"And I'm going to make it hurt."*

The spirits chortled a wicked sound before stretching their fingers through the air once again—mocking the mortal fear that had everyone tensing. Sayah's hand reached for Kylen's, waiting for anything to come... except nothing ever did, and that scared Kylen the most. "Hurry on with it. We find that we are growing rather bored. Three must die; *three will live.*"

Kylen didn't look at Sayah before he turned around. The decision of his fate had already been made, and he was adamant the sensation of the dagger splicing his heart into two would be the release he had been yearning for. At least, that was what he was telling himself to ease the dread.

"*Firstly arms, then legs, then fingers, then toes, then throats, then skulls~*" the spirits sang, and Althea's cursed eyes were on Kylen as if they knew that he would be the first to break.

It didn't take another step *or another bruised thought* to reach the blade that threatened everything Kylen had ever known. As he wrapped his fingers around the handle, he allowed his eyes to falter shut with a tremble of his heart.

Growing up, his mother had always praised his sensitive heart. She'd said that it was a good thing to hold emotions, as that was what gave a mortal their soul: *and without a soul, a King was nothing more than a joke.* His mother had said that it was good to feel things, to understand both the brutality of the world and the beauty of it. How would she feel now if she knew that Kylen was about to slaughter it? That he was giving it to the very source that had piled the sins on top of his castle walls. "You can kill me, *Kye*; it's okay," Sayah whispered—but didn't she understand? Kylen would rather kill himself in every lifetime if it meant keeping the ones he cared for safe. "It's okay."

The curse grew closer, except Kylen shook his head, turning to Sayah as his fingers firmly clasped hold of the obsidian blade that was seconds away from splintering his flesh. "I'm not going to kill you," Kylen admitted as Sayah's brows furrowed. "You deserve to live; you deserve to actually experience life. I cannot—"

Sayah's eyes softened as she shook her head. "And you don't? Kylen, you're only a boy; you're a *child*..."

"I haven't been a child for a long time now, S, and you know that." It was harsh, but it was the truth, which seemed to be exactly what life was like for a king who was a child only yesterday. Sayah's hand reached out for his whilst her golden eyes stayed holding his, but Kylen was quick to take a step back. "I can't kill you," Kylen declared, except he was aware that Sayah was not listening nor caring for what he had to say. "I order you to let me do this."

"*Every couple of minutes lost—another bone is broken.*"

The sharp intake of Atticus' breath, as well as an uncomfortable *crunch* that echoed through the air, earned Kylen and Sayah's eyes to fly towards the boy who was clasping his left wrist as he rocked back and forwards. Atticus turned, and Kylen caught sight of the finger that appeared to have been snapped in half like one of the wooden pencils Kylen would throw at the roof as a boy. And due to the uneasy, horrified look that masked Atticus' face as he swore under his breath, Kylen figured that he had come to the same realisation. "*Mother fucker,*" Atticus vowed as he clutched his with a muffled cry. "Fuck."

Khatri glanced from Sayah to Atticus with his own fate waltzing across the tip of his tongue. There had always been aged stories filtering through the history of Khatri's eyes, but now that he was in a cage where death was the only thing to bloom, they had grown awfully withered. With a small rise of his chest, Khatri picked up the blade that defied his every breath, his fingertips clutching it to the point where they turned white.

Almost as if he was afraid of Atticus snatching it away and inflicting crimson pain onto himself.

"Kill me," Khatri murmured wearily, earning a look of surprise from Atticus. His eyes widened with the realisation of what Khatri meant as it dawned on him, and he slowly shook his head with a frail whimper that rocked his chest.

Just yesterday, they were small boys playing hide and seek in the palace that had become their playground; *now…* now they were staring at each other in awe as Khatri offered him a genuine smile for the first time in months. "It's okay, brother. *It's okay.*"

Kylen wanted to stop this.

He *needed* to stop this.

He needed to do something—*anything* at all to save them from this ruthless game.

It was cruel.

Wicked.

It was the consequence of Kylen's heart.

He moved his gaze to the next pair of his court, his *family*—did he even have the right to call them that anymore? Family wasn't about blood. It wasn't about biology. *It was about those who you wanted to care for and protect.* Those you were meant to guard with your life because you couldn't bear to go on without them.

But he was failing them now. As their blood was spilling and devouring the memories of their past, making them nothing more than just figments of a time where blood was the proudest jewel any ruler could wear.

Kylen examined Uzziah and Zaire, and he, unfortunately, realised how while Uzziah was watching the situation of Khatri and Atticus with dumbfounded eyes... Zaire was holding the blade.

And it didn't look as if they were going to use it on their brother—nor would they ever dare to.

"Three will die, three will live; a game that your ancestors forced us to suffer through. *It is only fair.*"

Silently, Kylen's hands began to tremor at his sides, and his head fell as he looked at the quivering blade in his hand. *He could do this.* Use it on himself; therefore, he would save everyone else because Sayah was sure to think of a plan by then. *It was easy.*

"It's okay," Kylen heard Zaire whisper in the near distance. When he looked over again, he found Uzziah shaking his head, demanding that Zaire gives him the blade, but they kept moving it out of his reach. "*It's okay, Uzziah.*"

"None of this is okay," Kylen cried under his breath.

"Please," he begged as he walked over to where the body of Althea stood, observing them all. He knew that he was a desperate fool in their eyes, but he needed them to live. He needed them to be okay. "Please don't do this. Kill me, or I will do whatever you like if only you let them live. *Please—*"

"We don't care for your pleas, boy. We gave you a chance, a miraculous and generous chance. So perhaps next time, you might learn to behave and be grateful," the spirits cooed. They raised their head as they spoke, their fingers silently twirling at their side.

Another blood-curdling scream erupted from Khatri's lungs as he fell to the ground with an echoing crunch. His bone was emerging from the skin and material of his leg, his jaw and body tensing as blood spurted across the rest of his flesh.

Gods.

Oh, unrighteous Gods

"Stop! *STOP!*" Kylen screamed as he looked towards the body of the girl who was once his saving grace. "Please. I beg of you—I will do anything; *I will do anything at all.*"

The spirits rolled *Althea's* eyes as *Althea's* head fell to either side with every step. Such humour coated Althea's shadowed hands as they fiddled with her fingers, and the new scars that lined her flesh certainly didn't go unnoticed. "You should be ashamed," they sang, "you're just as weak as your pathetic excuse of a father."

Kylen shook his head as his hand tightened on the dagger. "My father was an honourable man." He scowled, although he knew that now was not exactly the best of times to fight over the reputation of his father... even if he was the bravest man he'd ever known.

The spirits looked at him before looking away. They turned on their heel and approached the shadowed corners of the arena that accepted them within seconds, leaving Kylen to stand there like the fool he was. Why hadn't they hurt him yet? Did they honestly know that he would choose his own pain over anyone else's?

When the curse didn't go to answer his cries, Sayah gently pressed a hand to the bone of his shoulder, beckoning for him to turn around and fully look at her. But he couldn't. He had failed her... he had failed them all. Her other hand dropped to the blade he was holding, her fingers curling around his whilst she awaited him to fall victim to her sirenix power.

But he had learnt to ignore it long ago.

"I don't want you to be the one to have to do this—I don't want you to have this burdened memory of me in your mind, and I especially don't want this to be our last memory together," Sayah whispered. Kylen mournfully felt as Sayah wiped away the single tear that dripped from his eyes, her own gaze soft and kind, as she beckoned him to let the blade go. "When you think of me, I want you to remember the girl that would enter your chambers on the warm Lorundio mornings. I want you to remember the girl that would open your curtains and windows to embrace the glorious summer days as she sang her... *darling melodies as you all love to call them*." Another tear slid from Kylen's eyes, and again she wiped it away, a rhythmic dance they both learnt to master. "I want you to remember the girl who loved you as her own, who will *always* love you as her own."

Kylen shook his head. "I can't let you go again—*I won't*."

A saddened smile left Sayah's lips as she flickered her eyes over him. "All will be okay, my little prince. But I cannot let you be the one who dies. I'm hoping that if I die, this bubble will burst, and you will be able to take the spirits down once and for all. Remember, we may be in their power, but we are in all of your minds. Therefore, *you have the power*."

Before Kylen could take another breath, Sayah had moved the blade before her very heart, hesitating slightly whilst she turned around so that he would not have to watch. Kylen's hand, however, caught onto her arm, holding her back from sheltering him any longer. "Please—*please, don't leave me*. Not again."

"I don't have a choice."

Fresh crimson blood began to seep out of the material of Sayah's chest as the blade pierced the first few layers of her skin. She inhaled slightly, the pain radiating across her features no matter how hard she tried to hide it. *Deceive him. Shelter him.* "Sayah, please—" Kylen urged as he stepped forward; however, she was quick to step back with a tremor of her lips. "Please."

If there'd been another gracious, fatal second, perhaps Kylen would be staring at the same scene he vividly remembered from the last time he had laid his eyes upon the true Sayah. Surrounded by her own blood as the curse rotted her corpse. However, as the blade punctured deeper into Sayah's luxurious flesh, a bizarre force of nature that was swift and rough had the blade flying from her clasp; and no more than a second later, they were, too, flying back and into the enchantment of the barrier. Hitting it with such thunderous force. *"What—"*

"Oh, please, you call this entertainment? I figured that you would've *at least* gained the intelligence of how to throw a bloody good blood bath when you consumed the exterior of my body," a voice from the beloved shadows whispered. "This —*Gods,* this is pathetic."

As dumbfounded as the spirits looked, they didn't get a shudder of a chance to react or defend themselves as a blade slit the cursed Althea's throat. The darkness of their eternal soul spilled out of them as screams of the dead erupted into the air. Nevertheless, their presence was erased by the wind, revealing a white-haired girl who appeared in their wake, a sword in her hand that reeked of that *same* blood.

A white-haired girl that had the appearance of a Godly Queen.

The only God Kylen would ever get on his hands and knees to pray to.

Althea Evangeline—the true and glorious Althea Evangeline stood tall, her eyes skimming through the arena before narrowing on Kylen and Sayah alone. Her jaw was sharp, her skin clear from the curse. Althea's eyes were as blue as the ocean on the days that reminded Kylen of the nostalgia of his childhood. Her hair was white, too, reminding him of the dainty little cat who'd claimed Sayah's bed as her own.

Althea was the embodiment of his dreams, every constellation and every star that he would go to war for. *She was perfect.*

Althea caught hold of Kylen's eyes, and despite the current conditions, a sly smile edged against her lips. "I take it that I've missed quite a lot in the past few months," she murmured through a shocked laugh, although nothing was quite audible enough to hear as she took the rest of the arena in. Her eyes widened slightly as she returned her whimsical gaze to Kylen, and the same light curl of a smile stayed on her cheeks as her chest tremored with another strange laugh. She was breathtakingly beautiful. Like a breath of fresh air that had healed the lungs the world had left so severely burnt. In the back of Kylen's mind, he heard Uzziah, Zaire, and Khatri all quizzically gasp as Sayah smiled over to the girl that *she didn't look to loathe.* "What did I... *miss?*" Althea quipped, and Kylen was left to stare at her as if he was looking into the eyes of an angel. What did she miss? There was awfully a lot to catch up on.

Sayah narrowed her eyes on her whilst her hand slowly reached over to Kylen's shoulder, "Is it really you?" she asked warily as she rose to her feet, although it appeared as if she already knew the answer but was merely asking it for the sake of the others in this dreadful trance. "The real Althea, I mean."

Althea grinned unsurely with a shrug of her shoulders, but the smile on her lips was one that defied every rumour, myth, and whisper about her. It was *his* Althea. "In the flesh—*well, not in the flesh,* but practically in the flesh," she said with a wave of her hand, and Kylen was hanging for the moment that the barrier holding him back burst.

"That wasn't you? Before?" Zaire questioned, and Althea shook her head as she horrifyingly noticed their arm. A hint of a grimace skimmed her lips as she looked at each soul that floated about, and when her gaze landed on Kylen's once again, it almost looked to completely soften. Almost like he still had that splinter of a touch to him that reminded him of the old ruler that had once been. The charming, kind one.

"Did it look like me? That was anything but me," Althea sniggered as she took several steps forward. She mumbled something inaudible under her breath before assessing the air around her; whether that haze in her gaze was horror or amusement was severely unknown—but Kylen figured it wasn't good in any way. It was the same type of look the spirits had held in the depths of the other Althea's eyes when they had sensed a problem from within—but now Kylen was figuring that the actual Althea Evangeline had been the problem all along. What an astounding problem to have. He would have that problem every day if it were his choice.

"Can you do something for Z's arm?" Atticus questioned, and Althea nodded without actually knowing the answer. "—*Oh*, and it's also *really* fucking good to see you. I just don't want anyone to bleed out and die when we are this close, *I think*, to outrunning that son of a bitch."

Althea smiled as she looked back towards Atticus, a hum of a laugh leaving her lungs. This smile met her eyes and he saw how her eyes truly had the ability to either set the world on fire or restore peace as the prophecies dared to profess. "You too, Atticus. In fact, *whether or not it is the high of this whole situation,* it is really, really, good to see you all… not to mention communicating to those that aren't dead—" Before the last of her words left her lips, Althea's eyes shot towards one of the darker, shadowed areas of the arena. Her body tensed as she assessed the lingering fear; however, she was quick to glance back towards the others and shoot them a half-hearted smile before walking forwards.

There were so many questions, answers, and *words* that Kylen wanted to say to her—so many whispers that his heart was reciting. Except he found that he, *too,* shared her fear of what was forming in the shadows of the corners. "Okay, *wait,*" Althea muttered before anyone else got the chance to say something more. She took a deep breath before shaking her hands out before her, stretching her fingers out as if she was preparing for a race. "Let me try something."

TWENTY-THREE

ALTHEA

You are a God, you are a God, you are a God, you are a God—this should all be terribly easy. *An utter breeze...* So why was it taking a ton of bloody mindless strength to gather the idea into her palms?

Althea opened her eyes after having them squeezed shut for the past several seconds, feeling as the power she had suppressed for so long shone heavily through the whites of them. *Easy enough.*

Was it strange to admit that she had partially missed this feeling?

The specific *freeing* sensation, the feeling that had her skin and bones on display, and yet they were not made vulnerable in any way. For once, every time she used *her* magick, she felt like the world saw the beauty of her soul and admired it immensely without trying to scar or harm it. Had her mother felt this way about her magick? Had she adored the sensation that had her bones riveting—the Realms dancing? It would've been nice if, in another lifetime, Althea had gotten the chance to accept and explore these abilities with her mother's help; it would've been quite *exceptionally* nice if she had been raised to see the glorious nature of it instead of the brutality that had followed her down the narrow halls of Aeonia.

Despite having no idea of what it was she was to do, Althea glided her hand out towards Zaire first, the mindless words, '*heal their arm*', echoing throughout her mind as she kept her hand raised and steady. Except there was one… *main* factor that had Althea's attention drifted elsewhere, and that was Kylen Noxwell himself, the boy who was wordlessly staring at her.

She wanted to give into it so badly, to turn to him and melt under his embrace, because for whatever reason, she knew that she did not have to hold fear in her heart for him anymore. She didn't have to look at him and expect to see a blade covered in her blood in his hand…

Ignore Kylen. Ignore him. Let's deal with that… situation in a fatal second. For now, focus.

Those few words must've been enough, *surprisingly*, as, within a squirming second that had Althea's knees threatening to break, the echo of Zaire's bone actually fitting back into place made Atticus gag at her side. Althea lowered her hands as she assessed the wound. From what she could see, all was well, and there was surprisingly no trace of a scar left. Their skin was fine, and Althea had been the one to *actually* do that.

She took a step forward, turning towards Khatri with a raise of her brows.

There was something off about his look, Althea observed. Something strange about his gaze.

He looked at her as if she were her father instead of… *herself*. Hel, he looked at her as if he were her father, and she was nothing more than a burden to humiliate his life. "Your turn," Althea mumbled as she looked away, and it took every thought within her mind to keep her breaths and words even.

One by one, she healed the few broken bones of those wounded by the spirits. Her magick slithered through the air and summoned a light that had Kylen studying in pure, blissful awe —something she tried not to fixate too much on.

Althea released a heavy sigh the second she'd finished on Atticus' finger, hearing in the back of her mind as it, too, snapped back into place with a gut-wrenching crunch. It was exhausting doing all of this, leaving a constant war to be fought behind her eyes. It didn't help either that she could feel the curse *and its victims* squirming against her every breath. Their presence was going very much noticed, and it had her blood boiling because of the multiple barriers that were keeping her from doing anything to quicken the godsforsaken process of escaping this mess. *She was a God, for God's sake. Why wasn't she able to burst the barriers with a mere thought? Why wasn't she able to flick her wrist and wish everything was fixed?*

With a shake of her head, Althea clenched her jaw in a weak attempt to ignore her thoughts. She took half a step forward when again she felt as if her gaze was being swept away by the boy on her left, *as if there was an invisible string tying her to him.*

Kylen was watching her with kind eyes, a glisten to them that looked ill—and yet appeared to be fighting. Althea had once seen that similar haze in the galaxies above Aeonia. The stars there were all on the verge of slipping into the wrath of death, and yet for whatever reason, they were fighting to remain alight. Had they known that one day Althea would be relying on their hands to guide her home? Had they known of the girl trapped behind her castle walls, also slowly falling victim to the blood she spilled each and every fatal day?

"What happened?" Althea carefully asked, keeping the tremors from the voice that begged to break. "It appears that a lot has since our last… encounter."

"Kylen decided that he was adamant about saving you from the curse," Atticus mused aloud, and despite the evident coldness spilling over her shoulders, Althea found herself looking towards Kylen's barrier with a wondrous gaze.

So, he did want to save her from the curse... that was a strangely nice thought.

For a splinter of a moment, the air around her tensed. An evident coldness to the air caused her body's hair to rise on end as if she were about to be slaughtered. Although Althea didn't exactly give herself a fortunate second to dwell on whatever was coming, as she had the consuming desire to reach Kylen Noxwell with her small steps.

Her hands felt restless as she relaxed one of them against the roundish surface of the small, buzzing barrier. It wasn't electric or painful as she had originally thought; it was easy, cold, and grounding. Althea wanted to do more. She wanted to try and channel her magick to save them all from the darkness she could feel and yet not see. This was her fault, was it not? She had dropped her guard all those months ago, and now she was left to scramble after the mess she had made. "You were trying to save me?" Althea questioned with a shake of her head. There was something so unlikely about that very question that made it rather questionable.

"I already told you this; of course, I did," Kylen admitted with a soft smile. He slowly raised his hand to meet hers on the other side of the fatal barrier. His eyes dropped to it before looking back to her, a warmness to his features that Althea wanted to drown in. "I will always try to save you, even if you don't specifically need it or want it, I will always be there."

A smile that was unlikely crept upon the corners of Althea's cheeks as she kept her gaze on him steady. Was it weak of her for falling for his kindness? For realising that just what Marilla and Willix had spoken about had all been the truth? "Well, that is awfully charismatic of you," Althea mused, and the shine in Kylen's eyes had Althea wanting to melt into his embrace. It dawned on her then about just who she had been working with to get here—just *whose* helping hand was holding hers in the abyss of the afterlife. Althea's eyes widened, and the smile on her lips shook as she gasped. *"Oh, you will never guess who I met—"*

The last of her words hadn't been able to leave Althea's lips as something horribly strong and manically sharp threw her back and against the wall of the arena itself. She felt as if her body had made contact with a stone wall of some type, and a horrible agony rippled through her as she began to fall down the varying levels of the arena.

"NO!" Kylen roared, except his words were quick to fall victim to the blade of silence—or perhaps Althea had hit her head a little too hard.

This time, as the spirits stepped out and into the mystical light that shone from above, they no longer held a 'physical body' of any type. They didn't wear the skin of another variation of Althea that had been massively affected by the death from within. *It was pure cold-blooded shadows.* The shadows had clumped together and formed a beast with no physical body parts. It looked like the rain as it fled from the storms, the waves in the midst of the darkness when they were left to fold over one another.

Slithering twines of obsidian that looked to be from the mindless threats her father had spat at her as a child.

Althea stood tall, her back straight. Her hair had been tied back into several braids that sat perfectly on the top of her head, making her look like perfection in front of the new King she was left to greet. She could hear the carriage approaching, the sound of the wheels crashing against the gravel echoing throughout her head alongside her heartbeat. She stood by her father and several cursed guards, awaiting the presence of the King her father had supposably 'gifted her with'.

Yet Althea knew that whilst her father was partially taking the piss out of this whole situation, he also wanted to make allies in which he could steal from.

Her father's presence at her side didn't go unnoticed. His breath skimmed the edge of her ear as she stared ahead with fear in her eyes; fear that had been irreplaceable since the night her mother died. "Althea," her father beckoned, and she turned her body around to face his whilst she held her breath. Don't breathe before him, Althea had taught herself. That way, he won't be able to sense your terror through your stifling breaths. "I don't want to have to remind you twice, but I expect you to be on your best behaviour once they arrive. If you aren't accommodating to their every need, their every want: the darkness will come." Her father paused. "You've heard of the rumours, have you not, dear? The children who go against their parent's wishes have been vanishing in the midst of the night. Only soulless corpses are left in their presence, leaving their parents to mourn for those manacled souls. Do you understand?"

Althea nodded, continuing to look away, except the quick, harsh grip that clasped at her arm had her turning to face her father with panic on her quivering lips. "I understand."

If only Althea had realised, then, that her father had been the one murdering those children. Butchering their souls.

Pain erupted through Althea's body as she tried to scramble up to her feet. Her hands pushed out from beneath her, a wave of shock washing through her mind as she noticed the blood that appeared speckled on her hands. Crimson, *unaffected*, blood. *Was this real for her?* Was it because it had both her physical and mental body involved? *Could that mean that she may actually die?*

Another wave of brutality hit her harshly, and Althea's head flew up to face it, a mocking cry escaping from her lungs as she felt her mind flash back and forth between the afterlife and wherever this was. Nausea climbed up her throat, burning her lungs raw. Althea had to do everything in her power to swallow it away, everything in her power to not let the weakness show. For a splinter of a moment, she saw Elara staring at her with fear bleeding in her eyes. She saw Willix and Marilla talking with terror and distress lined over their features as they presumably tried to figure out what they should do.

How they could possibly help her.

Because even the good saw the bad as worth saving.

"Channel her! Channel her!" she heard Willix screech in a faint voice in the distance.

"I don't know how!" she heard Marilla reply as something tight warped over her skin, threatening for her vision to waver.

Slithering tentacles of the shadowed darkness wrapped across her arms and legs, holstering her up into the air before scattering across her throat in order to choke her. It burned. It burned. It burned. Althea squirmed under their hold, growling deep beneath her breath as she channelled the fire that she could feel burning in the pits of her own stomach.

If they wanted her to react, then she was going to fucking react. And she was going to make it rain hellfire onto all.

The shadowed monster took a callous step towards her, assessing her struggle as the light burst *again* from the pits of her chest. It was a tingling sensation, one that had her alert of the magick that was swirling within the power of her Markings. That quick moment of pure, unrelenting Elemental magick allowed her to rip the tentacles that had a tight hold of her body into two, and Althea was left to fall to the ground with a Realm-shattering thud.

She rolled forwards, forming two long blades from the midst of the air before charging towards the beast that she wanted nothing more than to eliminate. Would it kill Althea if she was to take it out? Would it send her back to the afterlife after all of this wasted time?

Althea didn't find enough in her to care.

She was solely focussed on saving the ones that were vulnerable and trapped within their own cages. *Growth*, Althea sourly mused within her head. *How spectacular.*

She was only a step away from her own sword nipping at the physical shadows when a force of another type had Althea propelled back once again. *Except, this time, it felt different;* she could feel the army of the curse's victims trying to bring her down. She could feel each and every one of the hands that were trying *to make her bleed.* Their screams threatened to make her ears weep. Their screams had Althea experiencing *their deaths.*

And it was traumatising; leaving Althea's hands to shake at her sides as she tried to do all that she possibly could to avert her eyes.

However, it wasn't until then, when Althea was being dragged across the ground, that she'd realised that the curse must have put a *noise-cancelling enchantment* on each mini barrier: as they all appeared to be yelling out to her—and yet not a single utter word was heard except for her own thoughts.

Blood, as crimson and wonderful as ever, splattered across Althea's face, a wound skidding across her arm as another dark tentacle had her mind flashing back to the world of the afterlife.

However, this time… this time, she saw a glimpse of a sight that was rather daunting. It looked to be a scene from one of the many horror novels she'd read as a child. The ones that stayed with her days after reading them.

All who sat and stood in that small bunker had their eyes rolled back, their mouths chanting soundless words as a sharp pain had a cry slipping from Althea's own lips.

Althea was strong, she knew that. But this was the force and power of centuries of brutality and lost souls. She may be a God —but this was the power of the Gods' *consequences,* and that alone was very difficult to overcome.

With another frustrated pant, Althea pushed a hand out, and the transcendental light from her palms halted the *shadows-hand* from crashing down on her. Except that didn't seem enough for them, as their wrath continued to rain down on her, leaving

Althea to grind her teeth as she stared up at the beast with venom.

She needed to think of something. To do something —*anything*, that would possibly allow her to take down this cruel darkness once and for all. She'd once had control of this inevitable evil; *why could she no longer find it in her to control it now?*

Althea was strong, she was a God. So why... why was she so horribly weak? Why were her thoughts reminding her of all of the times when her father just simply adored to remind her of her weakness? Didn't her body, her soul, her mind realise that she was trying?

"I don't want this to be true, but I believe you will be my ulti-mate downfall, Althea," her father spoke, and it took everything in Althea's eyes to hold back the tears from falling. *"You have such potential, such miraculous potential... and yet you hold your mother's weak, indecent mindset."*

His gaze on her was sharp, and Althea looked away as she restrained herself from allowing the sob to flow from her lungs.

"Do you know where your mother is, child? Do you know where her life got her? She is dead. Murdered. Killed. Her care-less and reckless nature had her butchered in the night because she refused to accept the gift of our magick."

A silent tear ran down Althea's cheek, and her father reached for it. His hands were calloused. Scarred. It didn't take a scien-tific eye for one to spot the darkness in his veins. It fed off of him as if they were leeches.

Leeches hungry for a feast.

"I do this because I care about you. Because I want you to achieve great things. Your abilities are wonderful. They can do miraculous things—your mother is dead, Althea. I don't want you to end up like her. You can achieve many great things—and merely survive through consuming one's soul and one's emotions. You gain their life, their time, their magick."

"But it goes to you. How does it do anything on my behalf other than build at the guilt in my stomach?"

Her father's eyes darkened, and yet he still dared to answer her. "Do you really believe that I keep it all to myself? Althea, I bless it to you because I love you. Now stop being weak and kill him. I will stand here, but you must do it yourself."

The explosive ringing of a sharp blade swinging through the air had Althea's body flinching as she quickly turned away, sheltering her face from the sound that had the arena quietening. Just a metre away stood Marilla Noxwell, and she was quick to raise a brow whilst lowering the blade covered in black blood. *"Told you,"* she exhaled as she glanced at Althea, the gleam of life heavy on her face. "We are in this together."

The curse didn't wait for Marilla to do anything more than finish her sentence before it was already preparing for the next battle to arise. In rather slow and ragged motions, the darkness covering the floor began to slither back together as if what Marilla had done to it, *them,* the spirits of the dead, hadn't caused any pain. The clumpy shadows took the shape of many spiders and snakes as they scattered away into the depths of the arena, not stopping until all evidence of their presence completely disappeared.

Althea knew that the curse was not *truly* gone, that it hadn't left them to *truly* breathe. It was hiding somewhere in the shadows like a cowering rat. Gathering itself up until it found the perfect moment to strike and slit Althea's throat... or whatever torturous form of death they had in mind for her.

Willix appeared behind his wife, quickly offering Althea a hand which she was tragically quick to take. Except, her attention wasn't fixated on him for long as she eagerly looked towards Kylen Noxwell; the boy was staring ahead with a thousand words in his eyes. He was posed like an old book, one that remembered every mortal who'd once gotten their hands dirty amongst its pages. But then death claimed their hearts and left

the virtue of loneliness to wash upon the cracked spines abandoned in their wake.

Kylen looked as if he had just fallen victim to the curse's
brutality. He looked as if he was peering through the ice of a
frozen lake, watching as every soul he had ever loved sunk
beneath the surface. Ignoring how he did everything in his power
to break them out.

His eyes were wide, his lips slightly parted. He was staring
ahead as if he thought that this was all a mere joke, and when he
shook his head slowly, with a cry escaping from his lips: Althea
knew that that was *exactly* what he was thinking.

Kylen looked like a King who was the last to remain in his
kingdom as war approached it slowly. He looked like a boy,
standing before his childhood home as it burned in flames,
holding onto his one stuffed animal as he waited *and waited* for
his parents and siblings to flee from the burning memory.

He looked like everyone's worst nightmares: the ones you
could never break free from.

Before him, stood two of the people she knew he would've
spent so many long, draining hours thinking about. Kylen
would've spent countless hours crying over their deaths; he
would've spent years mourning for the hearts he could no longer
reach or protect.

Elara and Huntio watched him warily, and the two of them
had silent tears running down their cheeks as they gradually held
their hands up to the barrier as Althea had done so just moments
before. Kylen looked down to their hands, his chest heaving a
heavy cry as he realised just how *real* this was. He looked from
them to his parents, then to Althea with so many questions to his
tears. It didn't take any longer than a splintering second for his
hands to reach for theirs, connecting to the damn barrier, which
was the one thing keeping them apart.

No matter how close they were, it seemed as if there was
always something between them.

Worlds, death, life, Realms.

The enchantment that the curse had left on the barrier sounded to have given way, as Kylen's sob was audible, and a sharp pain had Althea knowing that if she was to ever make it out of this arena with something of her life, she was going to do everything in her power to make sure that they had access to one another.

She would do anything—even if it cost her her life.

She would find a way.

"Oh, my darling, *darling* boy," Marilla whispered as she followed Althea's gaze towards her son, and the expression on her lips was one any child would die for. Any child with loveless parents mourned for. *"Hi, my sweet little boy."*

Kylen looked just about ready to give into the way of the afterlife. His chest heaved another heavy cry that rocked the heavens above, and Uzziah, without a single word leaving his lips, dropped to a bow. He leant on one knee and held his head low, Zaire copying his movements before Atticus, Khatri and Sayah did too.

A sign of respect.

To the glorious leaders that the world grieved for.

Althea looked to her hands as she balled her fists. She *was* going to break the barriers. She *had* to. They deserved to at least hold each other after all this wasted time.

She closed her eyes, and an agonised whimper left Althea's lips as she pushed her hands towards the barriers. There was a pain to her skin, a trembling one, and Althea could feel her bones growing more and more tired by the withering second.

Her magick quivered across her fingertips, an electricity that reached into her bones. It was streaming through her blood, coming alive and rejoicing because she genuinely wanted—*for one of the first times ever*—to embrace it.

Do as I command, and break the barriers; now.

Althea's eyes were horrifically quick to open as a force as

powerful and as lethal as anything rushed through her. Her breath was swift to be taken away as she saw that there was only pure, bright, glistening light warped around her.

Almost like what the abyss of her soul looked like—as well as her magick...

However, that only lasted for a second because as she exhaled and blinked again, her eyes were returned to the bursting barriers before her.

One by one, each barrier holding them captive erupted to Althea's immense surprise, and she'd, fortunately, opened her eyes just in the nick of time to watch as Kylen dove for his siblings with such desperation. He didn't hesitate for another second. No. He dove for them as if he was trying to shelter their bodies from all of the evil they'd *already* come across. His hands clasped at the fabric of their backs, his sobs mangling with theirs as he clutched them with all of his might. Marilla and Willix didn't waste any time either; they ran towards them, too, reaching for the son they had only ever been allowed to watch since that fatal day.

Now they were reuniting after years apart.

Reuniting after death tore a crooked line through their family portrait.

Althea looked away just in time to watch as Zaire ran towards Sayah with tears evidently being fought in their own eyes. They must've gone their own ways or something of the sort, as there appeared to be a reunion happening amongst them too. Sayah leant into Zaire's touch as they reached up to cup her cheeks, their thumb tracing rhythmically against her defined cheekbone. Zaire's touch alone scrubbed a bit of the dirt away, not noticing as it flaked away into the abyss around them as their eyes were solely frozen on the sight before them. "Hi," Sayah whispered, a line of a smile tracing her cheeks. She reached for Zaire's hand before turning it over, pressing a kiss to the top of her palm. Atticus and Uzziah were next to force Sayah into their arms, falling into the enchantment of her sirenix magick as she smiled wider. However, Althea didn't fail to notice how Khatri watched from afar, staring with a ghostly haze in his eyes. He held a similar composer of a cat, one eyeing its prey from the corner of the room before daring to strike.

She would've said something; *she would've*—except her magick was quick to alert her to a presence that reminded her all too well of a time she yearned to forget.

"You shouldn't have come here," a voice snickered from somewhere in the air around them; yet it seemed only as if Althea could hear it, as no one reacted like Althea did. *"You have made a grave mistake, a grave one indeed."*

A sharp rush down her spine had Althea stumbling back several steps. She moved her eyes around the abyss of the arena, only to land on her *own* hands that were beginning to strangely ache.

Her skin was flickering in colour and tone, almost as if she held control of the two 'bodies' that the world had thrown at her. The mental and the *physical*. One felt lighter than the other—and the other… it had a heaviness to it that earned Althea to dig her nails into her bruised flesh in a terribly weak attempt to escape this wrath.

Her hands were normal for a gracious second, yet the next, she found that they held the embodiment of something crueller. She looked like a corpse—living up to what every rumour and every myth said of her *existence*.

Agony swept across Althea's skin, and 'her body' slightly flinched as a throbbing sensation emerged from the middle of her stomach outwards. She looked towards Kylen, panic challenging the delicacy of time to a race. He was weeping in his mother's arms, a mirror image to the boy he once was so long ago. She didn't need to ruin the moment. She didn't need to take Kylen away from his family—not when they had only just reunited.

She could deal with this by herself.

She was strong, was she not?

The murderer her ancestors shaped her to be.

Yet her eyes continuously dropped to her hands as the burning intensified, and as she moved them both slightly back and an inch away from her flesh, she found *fresh crimson blood* covering her palms entirely—*again*. Althea's chest shook with a whimper as she froze, listening to the words that began to send the nausea in the back of her throat skyrocketing. *"You try to save them but at what cost? Would you truly and utterly rather for yourself to be the one to die if they are the ones who get to live?"*

A hand appeared to be clasped onto Althea's shoulder as she turned. Its nails were digging into her flesh, drawing the blood that was slowly dripping down her skin before splattering into the puddle at her feet. Althea gazed up from there, only to find the version of her face that was one she remembered from long ago gazing lustfully down at her.

This girl had black hair.

Deathly pale skin.

Black veins.

Black nails.

The girl she had spent so many sleepless nights dreaming about—wondering if she still existed somewhere; and if that version of her body had found happiness in her agony.

The curse had ruined her entirely, and now Althea felt as if their magick was draining into her blood—poisoning her as she stood frozen in remembrance. The other Althea's expression was calm, *tired*. She looked at Althea as if she was conflicted on what to say or do, on how to act entirely, as Althea watched her with a weary expression.

"I'm sorry, little dove. Please forgive me for what we must do to truly taste the air on our shredded tongue~" While she was the one injecting the cursed magick into her Godly blood, *she*

almost looked sorrowful. Regretful. As if she didn't want to *murder* Althea at all.

"*ALTHEA!*" She heard Elara scream somewhere behind her, except it was no use anymore because the darkness was cold; it was welcoming. It had her head rolling back slightly as her legs gave out from under her.

She was strong, and yet she was weak.

She was burdened, and yet she wanted to live.

Was that so bad?

Her mind was full of such conflict as she hit the ground that everything for an entire moment seemed to silence. *And that was all she wanted.* Just a moment, a splintering second of silence... that way she could feel the cold air enter into her lungs before caressing her burdens away. And she could breathe out, not fearing the pain that haunted her shadow.

Althea had been running from this darkness for so utterly long—and yet the moment she used it to save the ones she *cared* about, it had found a vulnerability to strike, to kill. She was left to scramble to her feet and become the helpless prey the world had always wanted her to be. Althea was becoming one with the darkness yet again. Although she was no longer one of the lucky ones, she no longer held the upper hand in actually controlling this dreadful magick. She was now a victim of it, allowing herself to embrace it because she no longer found it in her power to turn away from it with a blind eye.

TWENTY-FOUR
KYLEN

I f someone was to tell the small boy who knelt at his family's graves with their blood still staining his fingertips that he would be seeing them again one day in the near future—he wouldn't believe an astra of what they had to say. He would roll his eyes and walk away because that was far too cruel for his liking. It was an illusion—a delusion that had his throat drying and his head aching.

Kylen had spent so many long hours kneeling before their graves, wondering how he could ever possibly go on since he was just a boy.

Just a child.

Yet now... *now he was watching as his sister fled from his embrace*, running towards the darkness without a single care in the world because she appeared to want to *help* Althea.

His Althea.

She summoned a sword out of the air around them, slashing it across the darkness's hold on his queen, earning her to fall limp to the ground as *the obsidian blood slowly drained out from her wounds*. He had seen this story before and knew it never ended the way he liked.

"Althea!" Kylen screamed, scattering to his feet like a blind mouse. He glided past his parents as he reached for the girl whose body jolted with a fierce gasp. Her eyes widened as she pushed her chest up, arching her back as if this very world planned to go after her every step—every *breath.*

Althea began to scramble back before she got the chance to even acknowledge what was happening. Fear laced every crevice and scar of her face; a sob melted from her lips as if she had seen into a world he needed to save her from.

"Kylen—" He thought Althea whispered, but nothing was clear as the screams of the curse began to deafen them all. It was terrorizing, like a thousand sirens and a thousand bells were going off in an act of war. Except in a way, it was so much worse, as you could hear the different combination of children and adult voices that strived to make their ears bleed. Althea pushed herself back, continuously gasping down the air whilst she took in the dream-like scene that was playing before her startled eyes. She looked as if she had just emerged from the very depths of the seas, the same fear in her eyes that he had seen when she truly had been *drowning beneath the surface.*

Kylen didn't have to so much as think as he pulled Althea back and away from the threat before them. Her hands wrapped around his arms, grounding and anchoring herself to him as they both watched his family reach his brave sister's side. *An army ready to go to war for their God—when had she gotten so brave?* "I've got you; I've got you," Kylen whispered to Althea as he fully pulled her into his arms. She was so cold, so frightened. Her walls had been blown down, and now she was standing before him with every vulnerability on display; and the last thing he was going to do was going to make her feel *weak* for it. Althea turned into Kylen's neck, burying her face into his shoulder for a delicate second before cowering back towards the monstrous creature that he was going to do everything to keep her away from.

His family had all wielded themselves weapons, but it was when Althea flinched and her Markings started to glow from under her clothes that he realised that they were channelling *off of her*. Her chest rose and dropped drastically as she abruptly inhaled another breath of darling air—except she seemed to choke on it for a simmering second. And if it was possible, Kylen held onto her tighter, looking to her with so many unspoken words to his eyes as he pressed a kiss to her forehead. "*Kylen—Kylen—Kylen—Kylen—*"

One of the words he would forever die to hear her speak.

"I'm right here, my love. I'm right here." *I've always been right here, waiting for you.*

The darkness dove for them after escaping the many hands that were bleeding after it. It came in clouds, forming itself high and into the air before attempting to cave in on them. They didn't get a second to run—they didn't get a second to flee. Kylen was quick to pull Althea back to his chest, sheltering her head with his own as he closed his eyes, practically waiting for the impact that he was sure was going to kill him.

But he didn't care.

He had lost any sense of sanity long ago.

Except a break from this torture never came, and he looked over to find his mother holding the thrashing beast back with a lethal glow highlighting her eyes.

Kylen stumbled several steps back now that he had the luxurious second to do so. His attention was captured by the quickening breaths that left Althea's lungs and skimmed his throat— earning chills to swarm his spine. Did she want to kill him? Because he would happily pass her the blade if that were what she wished. He would do anything for her. Truly. And now that she was in his presence, her eyes connecting with his every few seconds, he felt the sudden need to prove that to her after everything that went wrong the last time.

Althea pulled away slightly as her hand dropped down to

subconsciously hold his. She beckoned him to open the eyes he'd never realised to have closed with a gentle squeeze of her hand, and when he did so, he found her eyes softly watching his before turning away.

On the left of them, Kylen found his mother holding a rather large chain that had somehow weaved its way around the beast's throat. It glistened with the magick holding it in place, and the beast roared with the screams of the lost *victims.*

The screams seemed to intensify every time Kylen heard them, and never once were they enjoyable to hear. They reminded him of the time he had visited *one village* in particular —*one kingdom* that had left scars coating Kylen's palms.

He had gone there on one of his... *missions...* yet the grave-yard that he had found awaiting his presence had been quite daunting.

From the moment Kylen had stepped off of his ship, he had noticed the blood staining the pier, the death that lingered in the air. He had kept his every step cautious, practically hugging his blade in anticipation of what was to come. It hadn't taken him long to follow the scent of the trapped Elemental's. It hadn't taken him long to locate the dungeons they were being kept, tortured, and imprisoned in.

Yet, it had not been their magick to lead him there, nor their secrets or cries, but rather instead their torturous screams that threatened every one of Kylen's *once* sane ideas.

Althea flinched against Kylen's body as another terrible scream burned from the cursed beasts' lips, but Kylen was ready for her, and if she thought that he would let any harm come her way—she was oh so *very* wrong.

On the other side of the beast, Kylen noticed his father was also holding that same chain that held the moulding and quiv-ering darkness in place. "*Marilla—*" Althea gasped, and there was desperation on her features, fear in her eyes. *Just what had happened between Althea and his parents?* Kylen wondered as he looked from Althea to *his* blood. *What had fucking happened?* "Help me up—help me up, *Kye*."

Kye.

That very nickname had Kylen's mind fall silent as he helped Althea to her feet. How he had yearned for this day—if they took away the very evident threat, it was everything he had longed for. Everything he had wished upon every little star for.

His brothers were here.

Sayah was here.

Zaire was here.

His Elara and Huntio were here.

His parents were here.

Althea was here.

It was everything he had pleaded with the gods for.

Everything.

Althea looked to him, and Kylen returned her gaze. He could feel something wondrous brewing. Something beyond any mortal's understanding. Kylen nodded his head, looking towards her as he tucked a strand of hair behind her ear. "What do you need me to do?"

Althea looked to him, and it was clear that she was unsure; her walls were down, and he realised she was content with him seeing her as she was. And he was mesmerized because of that very sight. "I think I need to channel you. You are my anchor, and you do partially have a touch of access to your physical body; therefore, I need to channel you as I kill… *it,* them, all of it," Althea said, rambling every word that was suffocating her mind.

"Will it kill you?" Kylen asked, and he begged for one answer and not the other.

"I don't know."

Kylen had never doubted that Althea had the power of the Gods—*Hel, he was probably the one who believed in her the most*. Yet, as he gazed into the eyes that were staring up at him…

but at the same time down her nose at him, he knew that this was a *God* he was speaking to. A God that would bring the world to peace or burn it all to ash if she so wanted to. This was her world, and Kylen already knew that he'd stretch across every Realm to keep it from paining her *ever again.*

If she wanted an army, he would be the one to walk by her side on the battlefield.

If she wanted to be the Queen of the seven seas, then he would be her king if she'd have him.

There wasn't anything Kylen was afraid of facing if it meant earning the smile that Althea had shed him now. It may have been small, a sly smile if any; but it didn't matter because Althea was physically standing before him, squeezing his hand, and that was more than enough.

One day he would see her true smile again. One day soon.

Kylen nodded, offering her his hand as she slowly turned around and faced the daunting scene before them. By now, the shadowed beast was being held to the ground with several chains that Kylen knew were not ordinary. They had magick from every soul seeping across them, leaving Kylen to wonder how this would damage those who were no longer in the physical Realms.

He looked to his mother and then his father, feeling as his magick began to waltz beneath Althea's electric touch. Would this be the last time he got to see them for a while? At least he knew that they had found peace: they'd found *each other.* That had to mean something; he wanted—begged himself to believe that it did.

Althea shut her eyes, her hand tremoring against his as she slowly stretched her head to either side. Her chest rose slowly, and by the time it fell, her eyes had opened again; and the light that was shining through them was ethereal.

Sayah watched from afar, and he didn't miss the way she looked so undeniably proud at how far the girl had come. *I always knew you had it in you,* she looked to want to say, and

Kylen prayed that there would be a day when Althea would believe her.

The shadowed beast turned its head towards Althea, its makeshift crimson eyes narrowing on her as it dared to try and creep forward. It took Kylen a second to realise that this was it, they were in a war within their shared mind, and he was left to watch as Hel rained down on the *dead...* and the living.

TWENTY-FIVE
ALTHEA

"**W**hy, why, why, why do you repeatedly insist to try and make us burn?" The lie of a girl who knelt before her asked with desperation dripping from their tone. The spirits' hands were clenched against the ground, their nails digging into the abyss beneath them as the sound of a baby crying in the far distance echoed across her skin. Althea could feel Kylen's hand holding hers, as that was the comfort that had her *not* cowering under their severe gaze—so why could she no longer see him? "We have done you no wrong, we have caused you no pain: we only want for you to find the peace and the true happiness of your heart."

Their words were like mockery. A joke shared amongst the ones that were previously wronged and turned away by the Gods.

It dawned on Althea then that she was in another *so-called* vision, glaring into the true soul of the curse that *craved* her death.

The girl before her was that same variation of the one she had seen in her dreams. The one that had *blessed* her the night she got marked with her beloved Markings.

Her Markings now showed her glimpses of all the different trances she was currently trapped in. One could even dare to argue that Althea was nothing more than a mere glimpse across the realms. The scattered ashes of a God.

First, she saw the body of hers that was trapped in the afterlife, sitting on a table with her legs crossed. Vulnerable to all without a blade in hand. Next, she saw the other body of hers that was standing in an arena that she had basically astral projected herself into. Kylen standing before her, prepared to take down whatever dared to cross their path.

And lastly… lastly she was in her *soul,* but not trapped in it as she had been in her mind. She felt the twine that held her to her anchor; she felt the connection that confirmed her freedom.

Althea was in her soul, prepared to rightfully claim what was hers while staring at the possessor of it with the intent to watch whatever makeshift shadowed force it was, bleed.

That particular carriage ride so long ago felt notoriously laughable. Althea remembered how panicky she had felt when she'd woken up, how she'd forced herself into a dramatic escape to flee into the night in an attempt to save herself from this wickedness that she was trapped in now. The *torture* that was unravelling before her very eyes.

The cursed girl took a step towards her before she vanished into a cloud of darkness, leaving nothing more than a hint of a smirk to suffer across Althea's shoulders. The darkness that appeared to be a constant theme whenever the curse was present turned into a mess of one of the memories that had every inch of Althea's mind *captivated.*

One moment, she was in her bedroom in Aeonia; the next, she was in Lorundio; and the next, she was somewhere entirely different. It kept changing, showing her the different perspectives and agonies of her mind. Her *soul.*

What use was this? Did they want to remind her of everything she had 'suffered' through, all the tears that she had shed? Or did they want to remind her of all that she had survived?

All that she had overcome.

If Althea truly did have the abilities of a God, then perhaps she would one day get the chance to open up the doors between life and death. *Do some good for once in her life* and say a big fuck you to all that ever doubted her, ever questioned her.

Because Althea was a God, and she wanted to taste the blood of those who had left scars engraved into her name. She was a God, and she wanted to watch the world burn.

Althea turned her gaze to the left of her, slightly cocking her head as she sensed something that spread a wildfire of tingles across her burning skin. Whether or not she was tilting the head that Kylen could see, she didn't know, nor did she particularly care—there was something before her that she wanted to reach. And she *was* going to reach it.

Althea could feel the way the curse was throwing anything at her that may potentially earn her to spiral and fall victim once again. Except she hadn't gotten this far to become a prisoner. Not again. She was going to be free—and there was nothing that was going to take that eternal yearning from her.

Kylen squeezed the hand of hers that he was holding, a warm tingling sensation rushing across her bones as she squeezed his in response. She blinked once and then twice, and her vision once again revealed to her the cursed Althea that was, for whatever reason, sitting on her father's throne. "Why can't you give up?" the spirits asked her, and Althea struggled with holding back a laugh as she took a cautious step forward.

Deceive, and all will go well. Present yourself with the power you know that they have cowered under before.

"Because I have to believe that there is something more out there, that this has all led to somewhere that will be kind to me," Althea said, watching as the spirits darkened. She had the *upper hand*. A strange, miraculous upper hand. "You have only ever brought pain—don't you yearn for something like closure? Eternal peace?"

The Althea with black hair and pale skin shook her head, a laugh leaving her lungs. Cruel and manacled. For a splinter of a second, a flash of a vision, the true Althea saw several *thousand* bodies consumed by the darkness standing beside them, cluttered together. They varied in age, height, ethnicity.

No two people were the same; all were *different*.

And all were noticeably dead—staring at them—staring at *her*.

One of the younger victims stepped forward, their head slowly tilting back as black blood dripped from their mouth, nose, eyes, and *throat*. They looked no older than the age of ten, and Althea's heart stirred horribly because of that reason alone. There were a thousand stories behind their eyes, and yet none were readable because the curse had poisoned them—leaving a physical corpse left in their wake.

Another soul approached them, and this one was one Althea regrettably recognised.

It was the first soul she had ever murdered: *her* first victim.

He was a guard from the palace of Aeonia, one that had only ever wanted to do the right thing and yet had unfortunately come to work for the wrong king. Althea still remembered that day. She remembered following her father down those steep, broken steps, listening as the rats and cockroaches scattered away while they still had the chance. Her eyes had found the guard sitting on the wooden chair in his cell. He had known what was coming and yet never seemed to fear it. But that was before he realised that Althea would be the one doing the worst deed of them all. He had looked from her to her father, shaking his head and presumably going to say, *"but she's just a child,"* when her father shut his mouth with a wave of dark magick. Sure, Althea had always known that her father was a cruel leader, but she had never accepted it because... well, he was her father… he was meant to be good, loving, and show her the ways of the world.

Althea had looked up to her father then, already pleading for her not to be the one to do such a horrible thing, but he hadn't cared; he said it was time. She still remembered opening the cell and stepping inside, looking towards the stranger that tried to smile at her against all.

When her father couldn't see the guard's face, he'd whispered that it was okay, that he understood that this was what a child had to do to survive in a place where darkness shined.

But the worst thing of all was Althea hadn't ever come to know his name. He was simply referred to as her first victim in her mind, the one she would apologise to every other night for the next several months.

Althea now took a step back, forcing the pictures and memories from her mind to flee as she shook her head. "I want to murder you; I want to murder you like you murdered me." *Don't let them weaken you—you have the upper hand,* Althea sternly reminded herself through the pain, although it all felt like an utter lie.

The darker Althea tilted her head, such sorrowful eyes locking onto her. "But you can't truly ever rid yourself of us, and you know that it would take a sacrifice of more than just yourself to wipe out centuries of such dark magick. You and the ones who made us… *maybe*… could achieve such great things, but you alone… *you alone will die for no reason*, and we will joyously watch as those you seem to care for die too… *care… care, care, care…* your father would be so disappointed to know that you've given into the weak aspect of actually caring."

Althea rolled her eyes and crossed her arms. She'd had this conversation many times with her father, and it seemed as if it miraculously didn't affect her anymore. No matter what she did, she was always deemed as weak. "Then I will just hold the magick of the curse again; I don't mind." *That was a lie, and they both knew it,* although Althea wasn't one to ever admit her vulnerabilities in front of such a threat. "But as if I would ever fall prisoner to your ways again. I would rather we all burn than that ever happen," Althea sneered, holding her head high as she watched the darkness attempt to strike her—however, the cursed girl was again falling to 'her' knees.

Remember what we discussed, Althea. Willix's voice whispered through her mind. *Kill it in any way—any way at all. Just kill it.*

The darkness sprinted for her, and Althea stepped back with a laugh. "You want to dance? Then let's *fucking* dance." Gods, she sounded like bloody Kylen.

The spirits turned on their heel, and Althea grimaced as she noticed how the darkness was starting to bleed from the other 'hers' skin. It truly did look like spiders, and she didn't think that she would ever be at peace after making that grotesque observation.

One of the many hands covered in dark squirming shadows flew for her, although Althea was quick to catch it, to their surprise. She harshly pulled them forwards, feeling as their blood began to merge with *hers* as it splattered kindly across her face. The spirits cocked a brow as they studied her, a rumble of a growl leaving their lips. "You think you are so smart, don't you? We know you, Althea. We know your weaknesses—"

Althea went to bark something cruel in reply, something heartless, but she didn't get a moment to respond as she was being pulled back to the time where she had been confined in that small, *damning* room, and the emotions that were beginning to consume her body and soul had her chest heaving in panic.

For a crackle of a second, Althea was staring at the famous *white walls,* banging her fists against them as her memories were greedily being taken from her reach. Althea's heart began to quicken, her hands shaking at her side as she steadied her breaths.

You're free, Althea heard Marilla say somewhere far. *You're free.*

Althea hadn't known to have wielded a blade before she felt it piercing the chest of the girl before her. She knew it wasn't enough to kill the spirits; however, it was enough to advance on them and allow a moment of vulnerability for Althea to truly butcher the last of its withered soul. They looked at her for a single second before throwing their hands towards Althea's head, their nails already piercing into her 'flesh' and drawing speckles of darling blood. She remembered the last time she had been in a position like this, the last time she was left to stare into the eyes of someone she once recognised whilst plotting their grotesque death in her mind. Yet, she had survived that encounter—no matter the cost of her heart. And she was going to survive this one, too—there were people *counting* on her.

Althea was about to push the blade deeper into their bruised soul when something beyond comprehension had her movements halting, her breaths stifling, and her heart skipping several beats as she physically felt the curse blind her mind.

She was standing in the back of Sayah's room, staring at the bed where a woman she knew quite dreadfully well—*laid*. But, there was another presence in the room, a darker one. This presence didn't wait a second before it was *slitting Sayah's throat,* Althea stumbling back with a gasp fleeing her lungs. "*No*—" The word choked in her throat as she fell into the wall behind her. She couldn't comprehend what she was seeing; she didn't want to comprehend what she saw—none of it made any sense. "NO!"

Blood melted into Sayah's sheets from her throat, and Althea fell to her knees with a body-trembling cry; there was something holding her back that kept her from reaching Sayah and stopping all of this merciless madness. Some type of force that Althea wanted to physically rip to shreds with her bare hands.

The words choked in her sobs, the tears staining her cheeks

as she realised just what had happened and why Sayah had been reuniting with the others earlier.

But she didn't want to believe it.

She truly did not want to believe it.

"Why would you do this? *Why?*" Althea pleaded through her tears. She whipped her head around, seeing the cursed Althea with a blade pierced through 'her' stomach. "WHY?"

"Your siren friend has the power of centuries, and as sirens are becoming weaker and weaker to find, one must rejoice when they do stumble upon such glorious magick."

Althea shook her head, she was going to kill them—but she wanted to do more than that. They have only ever caused her pain through her years, taking advantage of her *time after time* despite her only ever being a *child*. A weak, vulnerable child. All she ever wanted was to see the world—go to the ballet—the shows—the fairs. All she ever wanted to do was plait her hair and go on the adventures that captivated her dreams. Althea pushed the blade deeper into the spirit's abdomen, holding eye contact with the swirling death that appealed to her in so many ways.

"I'm going to make you suffer the same way I've suffered all these months. You will be my prisoner, *my victim.*"

"You wouldn't cope holding the power of both life and death in your hands, child," the spirits said, and Althea shook her head as she blinked away her tears. Her guilt had turned into anger, and anger had always been the one *thing* to fuel her stamina throughout all these torturous years.

"I'm a God. I think I can handle it just fine."

TWENTY-SIX
KYLEN

T he arena had completely filled with shadows that reeked of the death Kylen could still feel swirling around his blood—*despite the fact that it hadn't had that privilege in several months now*. Nothing was visible; nothing was clear. It felt as if one was walking through the fog of the crisp winter mornings in a kingdom where the curse was its one and rightful ruler.

In other words, Aeonia.

Kylen had his hand intertwined with Althea's. The one thing that was driving him to breathe easy as he stared ahead and practically waited for death to claim him at last. He fidgeted on his feet, moving his body and head around as he tried to search for anything at all that would appear to him. Were there threats manoeuvring around the darkness? Tiny, shadowed monsters that were slowly re-killing all that stood in this deceptive arena?

He was going to murder Adonis when he awakened; *that was if Althea didn't beat him to it.* Kylen swallowed the thick paste at the back of his throat, his chest exhaling a sigh as he willed to hear any familiar voice echo through the room. "*Mother*?" It was a strange request, a strange word. It was the word that he had practically sung growing up, as whilst he loved both of his parents evenly, his mother had always been the one to come to his beck and call.

That was until she died. *And he was left to stay silent in the nights.*

It was silent for several seconds as his word echoed through the air. Still, the sweet sound of his mother's breaking voice sounded out, and Kylen closed his eyes for a fatal second, remembering the time where his only worries were sleeping through breakfast. "I'm right here, baby." He could tell that she was holding the tremors back, and that she didn't want to reveal the shared pain he felt. But Kylen couldn't get over how surreal it felt.

He'd spent so many years of his life wondering what his parent's last moments were like. Whether they had thought of him before death claimed him—and he hated himself for wondering such a thing. *Of course, they hadn't thought of him;* they were probably fearing for themselves and their lives; they weren't thinking about him. That was selfish of him to even consider. "I'm right here."

The mist around them began to seep into the air that filled Kylen's chest as he turned to look at Althea. *The girl he had searched for so long and now found.* She was coming back to herself slowly, blinking away the fresh tears that looked to have just recently appeared on her weathered cheeks. There was something about the ghost in her eyes as she opened them, some-thing that had his attention drifting off of his family but solely focussing on her.

"Hi, love," Kylen whispered as a smile caressed his lips, except Althea looked to him with an expression that was damn-ing. *Beyond* damning. Like she had just taken the dagger to kill him but killed herself instead.

"I killed Sayah?" Her question alone had Kylen's heart threatening to wither as he stared at her blankly. All of the other bodies appeared through the clearing shadows, and their eyes were too drifting towards Althea as she stared at Kylen with a haunted, ghostly expression. Sayah took a frail step forward, already shaking her head. Althea, however, looked towards her with a wounded breath leaving her lungs, such fear dripping off the edge of her nose. Almost like she feared herself, the power her hands held. "I... I killed *you*?"

Couldn't she understand that she had not been the one to slit Sayah's throat in two, that she wasn't the one whose soul murdered Sayah's?

"You didn't murder me," Sayah warily said, her eyes beyond sympathetic. She began to walk towards her, taking several quick steps like she knew what Althea was about to do.

Althea raised her hand with a whimper as she shook her head, taking multiple steps back as distress evidently had Althea choking on the air she breathed. "Althea, *please*," Sayah begged. But Kylen knew Althea. She was in her own mind now, not physically, but mentally. She was trapped in a downward spiral that had her face crumbling.

"No," Althea whimpered, and her voice cracked as Kylen's heart throbbed. She didn't deserve this, to suffer because of the curse's actions. Hel, she had been doing this her whole life already—enough was enough. Kylen looked towards his brother, finding that Khatri was staring ahead. It was quite clear that he regretted piling the blame on Althea's wounded shoulders.

She didn't deserve it—for the people to think of her as a monster when she deserved only to be loved.

She had done nothing wrong.

Why was the world blaming her for her very existence?

Kylen turned his eyes back towards her, swallowing the lump in his throat. Althea had both hands placed on her chest, trying to calm herself in the only way she knew how. *By herself.* Sayah walked towards her, ignoring the several signals Althea made that clearly told her not to approach: to run as far as she possibly could. Her nails dug into the flesh of her chest, her breaths skipping several beats as she shook her head. Kylen didn't have to be the smartest man alive to know that she was spiralling, panicking; that every thought in her mind was circling around her, clouding her judgement. "No—no. I didn't mean to. *I didn't even know what I had done—*"

"Of course, you didn't, honey. It wasn't you."

"—But you still died looking up to *my* body—as it slaughtered *you.*"

"Except I also knew that you weren't the darkness that lingered behind those eyes. You are the sweet, calm seas that temporarily become stormy, given very valid reasons," Sayah reasoned as she reached Althea's front, and before she got a single second to argue against that, Sayah pulled her to her chest; holding her, even as she tried to fight her way out. "I don't blame you; I never did. I love and care for you, Althea, and I know that *you aren't bad.* I never blamed you."

Kylen stood watching them, studying how Althea's face crumbled into Sayah's embrace as she heard her speak such delicate words. If he had it his way, that girl would've never known pain. She didn't deserve to. And he would forever loathe himself for what he put her through.

A small tap at his arm had Kylen turning around with his heart threatening to crumble. His sister was standing there, an uncertain smile on her lips as she looked up to Kylen with a small inhale. "*Hi—*" He didn't wait a second. Kylen interrupted her by picking her up into his arms and swinging her around. Just as he used to when he was a small boy, and she was this *same* age. Elara laughed into the crook of his neck, and when he placed her down, Kylen was taken back by the fact that she was actually here, reaching up to his cheeks as he knelt down to her.

"Oh, Lar, it is wonderful to see you, dear sister."

Elara nodded brightly, and Kylen wiped away the few tears that had escaped the war of her eyes. She smiled luminously up at him. He could still see the youth in her future, the light of life in her forever dead eyes. "You too, Kye, you too... *you've grown.*" She sounded so much older. Almost aged... as if time in the afterlife had given her time to grow and learn about the obscurities of the world that she'd had taken from her. Kylen looked past Elara as he noticed a boy walking towards them with his biological parents on either side of him. His mother was swift to quicken her steps, and her arms were so deceptively warm as they wrapped around Kylen's aching frame.

He clasped onto her flesh, breathing in her invisible scent as he closed his eyes against her body. *He wanted this moment to last forever.* While he had grown so used to missing them, he had forgotten how dearly he had *actually missed them.* It had just grown accustomed to him, a thought that didn't take much thinking. He had always known that the further he fell into the spiral of all that he yearned for, it would just end with his eyes staring through his ceiling as the dusk turned into dawn, and the dawn turned into day, *and so on.*

So, he'd found it easier to bury it within him, leading him to forget how he longed for this feeling, how he desired to see his siblings play in the fields again, how he desired to look over and find his parents having their early morning tea together on a little white table that his mother had brought from her homeland. "I missed you," Kylen muttered into his mother's skin, feeling as his father also wrapped his arms around them again. "I missed both of you—all of you so dreadfully much."

Kylen pulled an inch back, and his breath hitched in his lungs. He found both of their tear-filled eyes on him. He couldn't understand that this was real—that they were really here. His mother nodded, except his father was the one who spoke, and Kylen had missed his words of wisdom with everything in him.

"There was never a day where we didn't think of you, where we didn't watch over you," he whispered, and Kylen nodded, clenching his jaw to try and restrain the last of his agony. He couldn't imagine what things would be like if he had been in their position. If he was the one to stare through a glass wall as time moved on for everybody else. It would be agonising, trau-matising. "We are so *proud*, so terribly proud of you, my boy."

Proud.

That was all Kylen had ever wanted.

He wanted to make them proud, to live up to the idea they had of their son.

"One day," his mother replied with a dazzling smile as she tucked a strand of hair behind his ear. "One day, my love," she said, answering the question he liked to ask most nights.

"When I'm King, will you still be around?"

"Well, of course. If I'm alive, I will be watching proudly from the sidelines; but if I've passed on, I'll be watching from within your heart," she answered before waving his fears away. "You will be a great King; I am sure of it. Later in life, once the deci-sion has been made about the timing of when you'll claim the crown, you will work by your father's side. He will teach you just about everything about it as his father did with him. Those are some of your father's most beloved memories, that is. He cher-ishes them to this day."

Kylen smiled at his mother, nodding as he rolled over in his sheets, still facing her. "I'll make you proud," he whispered, earning his mother to chuckle as she tucked a rebellious strand of hair behind his ear.

"Oh, I have no doubt. You already have the heart of a king," she stated. "You show gratitude to your people; you have the desire to not only get to know them but understand them. And as I always say—"

"—The leaders are not the ones who make the kingdom, but

the people are," Kylen finished for her, earning another laugh from his mother's righteous lungs.

"Exactly, my boy, exactly."

Kylen's breath caught in his throat as an undeniable smile caught onto the edges of his lips. He remembered all those chats he'd had with his parents. The ones that either went for hours on end or just a few minutes. His father had always told him that he was welcome to sit in during any of his meetings if he'd liked to; he was always offering to spend time with him... *as if he knew something of what tragedy was crawling just around the corner.* "I only ever wanted to make you proud—*I only ever*—"

"We know," Marilla whispered gently, pressing a kiss to his forehead. He felt her tears drip down onto him, but he welcomed them with a mere sniffle. "We know, baby, we know." His mother's eyes caught onto something past Kylen, and he turned to find Althea standing there. She was facing him while her head rested against Sayah's chest, a silence in her eyes. A horrible, frightening silence.

"I'm going to find a way to open up worlds. I'm going to find a way for the breathing to interact with the dead," Althea firmly stated through the last of her falling tears, and Kylen did not doubt that she would. He moved to look up at Sayah, who nodded towards him with a gentle smile. She was hurting, he could see, but she was suppressing it just as she always did. But the tidal wave was going to come. It always did.

"It's good to see you, darling Sayah," Marilla quipped. "You'll come to stay with us now, will you not?"

Nodding, Sayah smiled, several tears slipping down her cheeks as she whispered, "If only you'll have me."

Elara ran past their parents and towards Sayah, practically leaping into her arms as Althea moved out of the way. She stood tall on her own, but he didn't miss the deathly strong grip she had on her own arms. "*Yes! Yes! Yes!*" the small girl exclaimed eagerly. "Yes!" she added again after a moment's silence, earning a laugh to brush against his lips. However, his attention was still captivated by Althea, and he wanted to hold her—to make things right. She stood with her hands holding her elbows, her eyes on the ground as her chest rose and fell rhythmically.

"I'm glad. I've missed you all terribly," Sayah mused aloud as she looked to Huntio with another gentle nod. "However, I'm afraid we must wrap up this reunion. We are technically feeding off of Althea. If we aren't quick to get her back to the physical Realms, her health can come into question." That's what it was. The troubling haze to her that had Kylen terribly concerned.

Althea looked up then, her cheeks blushing as she shook her head swiftly, almost as if she was embarrassed. "Take your time, *please*," she insisted before turning towards Sayah, but the exhaust was not hidden from her words. The siren had a look of warning on her features. The classic Sayah stare that she had thrown at Kylen for so many years now. "Look," Althea whispered, although it was still audible. She gestured towards Zaire, Khatri, Atticus, and Uzziah, all of whom were watching her with grief in their eyes. "At least spend two minutes saying goodbye. My body took you from this world, but now my soul is going to give you the chance to actually say goodbye."

Sayah's expression softened, but she seemed to realise that Althea was not going to budge; they were both equally as stubborn. With a sigh that was full of many emotions, Sayah approached the others warily.

She stopped in front of Khatri first, giving herself a moment to collect herself before she wrapped her arms around him. It was a sight that had Kylen's lungs tightening and his bones breaking—he couldn't bare to watch the despair trace the features of his brother's face. He couldn't dare to watch as Khatri broke down into tears after being a corpse for so many months.

"Althea?" his father questioned in a quizzical tone, earning Kylen's attention to drift back to the girl who was watching him now. "Come here."

It didn't take much convincing for Althea to walk over. No, she approached them slowly, and Elara took her hand on the way to them. Kylen wanted to know every little thing about their encounter. It was bewildering to him; to even think that his parents had decided to get to know Althea—*his* Althea.

She approached Kylen's side, and he shed her the kindest smile of them all, one that, for a faltering second, had her expression tremoring.

"What happened with the darkness?" his father asked. The question being one on Kylen's mind too. "I know it's not gone since I can sense it, but I also know that it is no longer a threat, so where is it?"

"My prisoner," Althea hesitantly replied with a frail humorous grin nipping against her lips. His mother laughed at that before moving towards her. She pulled Althea into her arms against all odds, and Kylen was again left to watch in awe. Elara joined in too after a moment, and if Sayah was to join in on this group hug, he could say that it was all of his favourite girls.

"That's my girl," Marilla lightly laughed before pressing a kiss to the top of her head. "That's more like you."

A small sparkle appeared in Althea's eyes as they connected with Kylen's, and they held each other's attention for a moment. *A glorious moment in time that both hearts had been waiting for, for so long now.* "Thank you," Kylen mouthed, and Althea furrowed her eyes in question. "*Thank you for it all.*" He knew that she was still confused, but he meant every word, every breath.

He was grateful that she was here, blessing him with her ethereal presence. He was grateful that she had brought Kylen's family back to him, even if it was for a short moment. He was grateful that she had somehow gathered control of the magick, and he already knew that if the time came when she wanted to abolish it completely, he would most definitely help her. He was grateful for every little thing.

But most importantly that she hadn't given up.

Else he wouldn't be watching her now, feeling as his heart truly bled for the first time in months.

Kylen vowed that in the coming days, weeks, months, he would learn every inch that related to the afterlife, *death*. It confused him horribly. How one was dead, alone—but occasionally not? Perhaps Althea would have some answers?

He would find something or another... he had to.

It was about time he actually learnt about what his parents, siblings, Sayah, was up to.

At least he had that comfort.

"It's time," Willix whispered, and his arm that was on Kylen's back pulled him to his chest. "Goodbye, my boy. I have no doubt that Althea will allow us to see each other again, but in the meantime, I want you to know just how proud your mother and I are of you. My boy, you have achieved things beyond comprehension. You have been the ruler I have dreamed of you being—and you... I couldn't have asked for anything more." Watching him, Kylen felt his heart slither up to his throat. Did he know for how long now he has yearned for a conversation like this? To actually come to know just what his parents thought of him. "I am so sorry everything fell into your lap at such an early age, but you have survived wondrously, except now it is time to start *living*. Please just live. We will look after Sayah; she is family, after all, and when we see you again, I expect you to have good stories for us to hear."

Kylen nodded, and he knew that his father had seen the grief in his eyes as he ruffled his hair like he was just a boy again. "I promise." Kylen nodded. "We will see each other again."

"Oh, we know." Marilla smiled. "You'll hold him accountable, won't you, Althea? Make sure he has marvellous entertaining stories to tell us—*but not the type of entertainment that the curse craves.*"

Althea nodded. "Of course."

He could tell from Althea's stare that she was partially afraid of what she would come to find when she'd enter the physical realms, but she should realise by now that he would be there helping her take every step.

He would be there, holding her hand with all the assurance she could ever need.

THE
TETHERED

TWENTY-SEVEN
ALTHEA

"I'm so sorry, Sayah, I truly, truly am," Althea whispered into Sayah's arms, feeling as her warmth spread over Althea's bones like the peace she had desired for so long now. "I'm so sorry. You deserved so much more—you deserved—"

"It's okay, Althea, it's okay," Sayah whispered as she clasped Althea's cheeks, forcing her to look at her, but couldn't she see how cowardly Althea felt right now? She wanted to hide, to find the shadows and cling to them as if tomorrow didn't exist. "It's okay. I forgive you, okay? I forgive you. If forgiveness is what you need to be able to breathe again, then take it. But Althea, sweetheart, I never blamed you. Never. Nor will I ever. I get to reunite with the rest of my family now. Marilla, Willix, Elara, Huntio, Hel, I might even wander around to try and find my Mama and my Papa."

Althea went to look away when Sayah forced her eyes to meet hers again. She loathed eye contact, especially in a confronting situation like this one. "Is there anything I can do for you? I will try to bring you back if you want me to bring you back—I won't rest until I do so."

Sayah shook her head, tucking a strand of white hair behind her ear. She hummed a small sound of disapproval, and Althea wanted to crawl her way into her warmth until utter peace consumed every last piece of her. "You can't do that, my dear. To bring one's soul back from the dead is messing with the order of life. And while you are now the only God to exist, there are things out there that could seriously hurt you if you were to do that."

"But there has to be something that I can do," Althea whispered in such a frail withered voice. "Please." She couldn't live like this. Knowing that Sayah was dead, and it was basically her fault.

Looking over her face in thought, Sayah sighed. "Your mother once dreamt of opening a portal up between worlds," she cooed quietly in reminiscence. "And if you aren't going to achieve actual peace without trying to do something about... all of this, then I'm sure you could spend some of your time researching that—but do not exhaust yourself tirelessly."

Althea furrowed her brows. "How does that work?"

"Well, only the living can visit the dead, and it's essentially what you did before. You used Kylen as an anchor, and you found his soul. If you wanted to visit me, I would be your anchor since I cannot return to the physical Realms, but you can return to death. Does that make sense?" Althea nodded, and Sayah pulled the girl into her arms. "I love you, Althea, please, please, please, actually try to live for once. Find your happiness. Find your eternal love—that can be anything or anyone, even yourself."

Althea closed her eyes, feeling all of the eyes on her and yet she willed herself to focus solely on giving into that strange exhaust as Willix told her to do. She felt as if her body collapsed from underneath her, but somehow, she was also aware that her body in that specific trance had disappeared entirely. *"Goodbye Elara and Huntio, goodbye Marilla and Willix,"* she'd said before, offering them all a hug and vowing that she was going to find something miraculous. She had to. Kylen had been standing beside his two mothers, watching her with such an intimate look that she wanted to melt in. "*Goodbye, Sayah,*" she'd whispered. And with her final goodbye, she'd closed her eyes and allowed her body to finally breathe.

Her body passed through the afterlife with a mere breeze. Althea had known that that specific Realm had been the afterlife as it had the same scent in the air. The same feeling in her soul, the same laughter. Presumably, her unconsciousness had passed through it to collect the remnants of her soul. Picking up the pieces the curse had left scattered across the debt of time.

There was a second of silence where Althea had lost all sense of touch, and fear was quick to weep across her skin. However, that only lasted for a moment or two, as before she knew it, her chest was heaving with a large jolt of her bones.

Althea opened her eyes to a room that she hadn't seen in a long-time, a familiar sensation and scent washing dangerously through her nose. There were tall walls, tall ceilings, and tall windows before her. Yet, all of it, *constantly through her long years and even now,* felt to be caving in on her.

A yelp escaped her lips as she made eye contact with a man from her deepest and darkest nightmares. A man who was practically kneeling over her with a syringe in his hand. Althea punched him before she had the chance to reconsider, but when that chance crossed her mind and Adonis stumbled back, swearing, she didn't regret it one bit.

In fact, in some way, it earned her stomach to feel a little lighter.

As she had felt that punch, she heard his bones crack and tasted the bitter taste that came when one bit their tongue. And it had all been real—not some delusional illusion leaving her perplexed on what to do or how to act.

Althea pushed her hands beneath her, scrambling away from the floor that she had somehow ended up on. In her peripheral vision, Althea noted the black hair that swayed across her shoulders due to her quick movements. *She had actually made it.* She had actually survived—and she no longer could hear the squirming sounds of the curse vibrating across her every touch.

She could feel them—but not hear them... and she took that as a win.

Everything was silent. Nothing was too loud or too daunting. She could actually think.

Althea looked over to the two males who were groaning as they awoke against the walls they were, *for whatever reason* leaning against. Her eyes were first to lock with Kylen's before Adonis' again. *What was he doing here?* Why was he here? Was he here as a gift that Althea could slaughter? How nice of Kylen.

There was blood streaming from Adonis' nose as he looked at her with a sneer. Except it wasn't crimson like she'd expected. Nor was it blue, like a dragon's blood... it was simply black. Pure, glistening darkness.

"You *absolute ass*," Atticus, in this new persona of his, muttered under his breath, rising to his feet. He offered Kylen a hand which he eagerly took, but her *once fiancé* didn't stand still for long, as he was already rushing towards Althea. "You dirty, dirty, *dirty man.*"

"It worked, did it not?" Adonis quipped as Kylen reached for Althea's hand, which she was dreadfully quick to take. He was warm against her touch, his fingers eager to pull her behind him. Althea looked up at him, and it only took a second for Kylen to return her gaze with a soft smile. Reassurance against all. Her body ached as she felt her breaths calm, and with a swift movement of her *black lace dress,* Althea caught sight of the many confronting new wounds that looked to *lace* her skin itself. What had they done to her? What had they put her body through? It was like they had turned her into the curse itself—making her the embodiment of all things horrible.

Adonis dared to step closer, and the laugh Kylen shed him

was anything but nice. Althea looked around as she stood behind him, her eyes unfortunately also catching sight of one of the very large mirrors that stretched across the Aeonian walls. Her father had always been a fanatic for mirrors; he liked to gaze into them and see all that he had *accomplished.*

But Althea didn't see much; she'd always just seen a ghost of a girl who once was.

The sight now was horrible; it had her breaths stilling as Althea let Kylen's hand go.

She had never realised how consuming his touch was until she was drowning alone in the darkness after letting it go... maybe she was one who liked the touch of his.

Subconsciously, Althea turned on her heel and approached the mirror that swept her into the idea of the past. She could feel Kylen's eyes on her, feeling as he protectively watched her every step before nodding for Atticus to watch over her. He said something to Adonis, but Althea didn't hear it. Her mind was too mesmerised by the fact that the girl she was looking at was a complete and utter stranger. She didn't look like the girl she remembered at all.

No.

But then again, Althea had always been the girl who never knew what she looked like. One of the main things she'd always struggled with was the idea that people would remember who she was—what she looked like. It didn't make sense to her how somebody could recognise her.

To her, Althea felt unrecognisable.

Black hair, scarred skin: a ghost of someone who once was.

She reached up for her cheeks, turning her head slightly to the left as she ran her bony finger across her bruised, pale jaw. This wasn't her. She looked like a beast. One horrible, rabid beast.

Althea had never been one to particularly care about how she looked, as she was never seen by anyone other than those she was meant to kill. *Not to mention* that she had been raised being called 'the breath-taking beauty' who could additionally kill. But who was she to say that she was beautiful? She was beginning to think that this was what she had looked like this entire time— even if it wasn't visible to the eyes of those unaffected by the curse.

The throne room doors flew open, and Althea turned around to the abrupt rumbling noise that sent the air tensing. She watched hesitantly as Zaire, Uzziah, and Khatri all hurried into the room, their eyes landing on Kylen and the other two before gliding towards the ruinous sight of Althea Evangeline.

Her breaths appeared to calm when she realised that none of them had the injuries they'd had when Althea first had stumbled out of her subconsciousness, however despite them looking at her for no longer than a single moment, Althea spotted the exact second that their eyes grew wide, and their lips slightly parted at the very sight of her.

She looked like the cursed.

She was the *embodiment* of the *curse*.

She was everything they had ever called her.

"Holy shit," Zaire muttered as they flickered their green eyes over Althea; their expression was wide and quite confronting. That was one of the things she rather liked about Zaire *(no matter the pain it caused her);* they were always honest. Brutally honest even. "Déjà vu much?" they mumbled, turning towards Khatri, who shared that equally as star-struck expression. He was the one who looked to see her as what she truly looked like. There was disgust there, distaste. He took a step back that even had Zaire sending him a strange reevaluating look as they said, "Stop it."

Uzziah didn't pay notice to the other two as he stepped forward. He was alarmed, alert, ready, and eager to go to war. Althea watched as his hand dropped to the sword at his waist before pulling it out and positioning it before him. "What is *he* doing here?" he was quick to ask, although his words came out as a scowl more than anything else.

Atticus turned his nose up at Adonis, a mumble leaving his lips as he rolled his eyes. "He tricked us," he murmured, and Adonis shook his head as a tipsy laugh rolled off his tongue.

Althea wondered how this had all come about. *How in the Realm's name* had they all reunited after the monstrosity of what happened the last time they were all in the same room?

Minus one, of course, since *Althea's body* did murder one of *her first friends*.

One of the first strangers to see her as something more than her father's daughter.

Uzziah stalked forwards, Zaire quickly following behind as they summoned themselves a weapon that defied every odds. A green glow took over their aura, one that twinkled with the energy of death.

"Why did you try to trick us?" Kylen asked. *He was holding the uneasiness back from his voice.* "Why—"

"Trick you?" Adonis retorted with a snort. He was acting as if what Kylen was preaching was propitious, something truly so amusing. "I did anything but trick you. I brought her back, did I not?" There was something to his voice that had Althea's bones unsettling. Something to it that was menacing and cool. Adonis began to walk in a circle around the throne, his dark hands capturing the gleam of death as his cursed magick danced across his palms.

She didn't remember him having possession of the curse?

Atticus shed a small look to Kylen, who exchanged a look with Zaire. "What would you like me to do?" Atticus asked, earning Adonis' brows to furrow with a shake of his head.

Instead of replying with an order that certainly would have been marvellous, Kylen looked to Althea and cocked a brow. "Say the word." His gaze was comforting, easy. He didn't look at her for the curse she held, but instead, he appeared just to see *her*. Althea narrowed her eyes on him, and Kylen nodded, beckoning her to say as she pleased.

He wanted *her* to make the decision.

How was she meant to decide—

Althea looked to Adonis with the craving for death in her stomach. He was another name she had forgotten and yet held the face of one who she'd sadly remembered. She'd sworn death upon his name, practically pleading for the revenge he deserved to suffer. "Lock him up," Althea simply replied, and Atticus, Uzziah and Zaire didn't have to hear her twice.

She was their queen, after all.

They turned towards Adonis, their magick combining together as if this was just another mission for them. Atticus was the one to swoop in on him, Uzziah was the one to make the ground form over his feet, and Zaire was the one to make a mockery of him before his very face. Althea watched them curiously; she was sure that if things had turned out... better than they had all those months ago... she would've seen this performed many times now. Yet she had not. Because she had basically died.

"How are you feeling?" a voice asked from over her shoulder, and Althea turned to find Kylen standing there. His hands were in his pockets, his skin cracked and awfully dirty with blood and grim. How long had she unknowingly waited for this? How long had she desired to find Kylen standing before her, completely unharmed and rather healthy, if anything? Kylen looked down at her with a soothing expression; his eyes were awfully soft. He was cautious with his actions, she could tell. It almost appeared like he didn't want to frighten her but rather instead soak in the moment. That's what she wanted too. More than anything—she couldn't bear to think of the complications of everything. "Do you feel any different?"

Althea shrugged before she crossed her arms. Did she? The only things she had really noticed was how her body ached and throbbed and how she looked nothing like the girl she partially remembered. The girl that had caused so much pain: so much suffering. "I'm alright. Other than the fact that you know... *I look quite different.*"

"You're still beautiful," Kylen was quick to reply with a wink, earning a scoff from Althea. She shrugged her shoulders as she rolled her head back to face his. She'd missed this, and that felt awfully strange to admit considering once upon a time ago, she wanted him dead. "For what it's worth."

Althea cocked a brow. "Still have your charm, I see."

Kylen waved his hand with a shake of his head, "Oh, you should've seen me just a few days ago, *my love,*" he dryly mused, and Althea could honestly admit that she was glad she had not. She liked this version of Kylen. The one that was sweet, kind, caring, and of course, arrogantly charming. It made her ponder on the idea of *their* future if that was even a thing. "I was almost afraid that I had lost my beloved charm." A laugh came from behind him, and Kylen threw his gaze to Atticus, who was walking by. That man had many expressions on his face, but the main one was complete and utter frustration. "Even ask him; I was not my usual self."

"And you are now?" Atticus hummed with a raise of his brow. His voice was strange, his expression one of a stranger. The glance he shed Kylen was one that wasn't necessarily kind nor harsh. It was more so in between, rather condescending.

What had happened between the two?

Althea squirmed at the thought—there were too many questions and too little time.

Kylen shook his head as a rattle of a laugh skimmed his lips. "Nope," he replied with a click of his tongue. "But I'm exhausted, and I can always feel myself slipping away when I am tired." Atticus didn't wait to hear his answer, he had already continued walking as if he didn't care for what Kylen had to say, so Kylen turned to look solely at Althea.

Whilst her curiosity was brimming with ecstatic energy, it was also causing her thoughts to thunder and storm. She wanted to know what had happened; she truly did. But then she was also afraid of what she might find. Kylen looked different now, she'd already made that observation, but he also looked *exhausted*. There was a darkness behind his eyes, one that was both haunting and as cruel as these very palace walls.

Althea swallowed the bile from the back of her throat, turning slightly on her heel as she began to look through the room that felt ancient in her mind. "Is my father here or in Lorundio?"

"In Lorundio," Kylen replied. She could feel his eyes on her; she could feel him assessing her every move. But in honesty, Althea didn't know what to say or do. Was she meant to be frustrated that her father was still alive—what type of daughter did that make her? "What would you like to do?"

"I think I want to go outside."

Kylen didn't wait to hear anything more. He took her hand and began to guide her towards the door that he seemingly knew would lead them to where the fresh air bled. Althea looked towards their intertwined hands, her heart beating unsteadily. She knew that before, when they had been in the trance of her dreams that they had held hands. But this was different. This was her actual hand.

Her actual cursed hand.

And he was still holding it—and whether he knew that he was drawing circles across her knuckles was a mystery to her. Still, it caused her mind to ease and her heart to warmly slow.

They approached the front doors of the palace that Althea had watched people enter through only a small number of times, yet as she passed through them, she felt to be entering into a world that she was a stranger to. "I don't think we will stay inside of the castle tonight," Kylen admitted as they walked down the steps together. Althea's eyes were captivated by the stormy, heavy skies, except the first thing that stood out to her was the fact that she could hear the buzz of people talking and laughing in the distance. Was this even Aeonia? "For one thing, that place majorly gives me the creeps. And secondly, I think it would do us, you, *but us,* some good to actually breathe in the fresh air… even if it is partially flooded with the curse. How does that sound?"

Althea nodded as she took a deep breath, a tremble of a smile stretching across her lips as she felt the first few droplets of rain waltz across her flesh. She knew he was expecting an audible answer, but Althea felt strange to be talking aloud without a consequence following close behind. It felt confronting, in a way.

"Why don't we camp over there? That clearing looks rather… reasonable?"

She hadn't realised that her hand had dropped his until she felt his eyes watch hers intently. Althea was solely focussed on raising both of her palms up and towards the sky that was weeping for all the harm that had crossed it, all the anguish and sorrow that it had been forced to watch the people suffer through all these long years.

Althea crossed her arms as the rain quickened its dance, and her chest rose and fell as she felt her clothes become rather damp.

This was what she had longed for.

To feel the rain caress her skin again.

To breathe in the air that was chilly and awfully daunting.

In the back of her mind, she heard Zaire, Atticus, Uzziah, and Khatri stumble out of the palace, appearing to already know Kylen's intentions of escaping the palace walls.

She turned to him with a small smile and found that he was watching her with a look that no other soul had shed her in her years. His head was slightly cocked to the left, his lips slightly parted as if he was gasping, and his eyes were watching her with a warm aura to them that she wouldn't mind falling asleep to.

He was looking at her as if she was a painting.

And he was just some stranger who would never forget the beauty in the brushstrokes.

TWENTY-EIGHT
KYLEN

For so long, the idea of peace seemed like a joke that was quite unreachable. It seemed like a lie that children were left to pray on because really hope was merely a lost cause in a world like this.

Except Kylen knew as they watched the fire flicker before their very eyes that they were now somewhat closer to peace than they'd ever been before. He knew that peace could be reachable if only he kept striving towards it, no matter how horrific the cost may be.

Kylen knew that for whatever reason, he may not be the one to reach it in the end, Hel, he may end up being the fatal cost... but that was okay because it was these people that deserved to taste peace.

To not have to fear waking up every morning.

Atticus across from him huffed a laugh, and Kylen lifted his gaze over to Uzziah and Zaire, who were telling their stories of the last several months to the busy ears of Atticus and Khatri. While Khatri hadn't said a single thing just yet, it was clear from his open expression that he was curious to find out just what they had been up to.

It was refreshing to hear them speak with kindness to their tones when for months, it had been pure unbreakable anger. It was different, refreshing. He knew they weren't close to forgetting and moving on; however, he also felt as if seeing Sayah one last time had been the closure they had all yearned so earnestly for.

The type of closure that seemed merely impossible to reach.

Not to mention now he knew that his biological family was blissful. He knew that they were safe and sound and living their own variation of life in the afterlife. He was also aware that whilst they could not grow and escape death—they were content. And that's what Kylen had begged all the sleepless nights for.

The rain had parted, and the air around them howled with the cold wind that nipped at all of their aching spines. Though, Kylen now sought the elegance in this cruel weather. It helped him remember and realise that he was no longer in a trance of any type—and that this was real life. *Real, relentless life.*

His gaze wandered over towards the girl who was staring up at the sky that was physically fully clearing for the *first* time in months—years—decades. There were stars sprinkled just about everywhere, as if it was the freckled faces of the lost Gods looking down at them, constellations rejoicing at the sudden freedom they were gifted now that, *for the most part,* the curse was contained.

—To the body of Althea Evangeline... *that was.*

Kylen would almost assume that Althea was dead because of how silent she was, but the slow rise and fall of her chest told him that she was very much alive and simply consumed by her very thoughts. Was it arrogant of him to want to save her from the words in her head? She had already suffered so much; didn't she at least deserve some closure?

He rose without a word leaving his scarred lips, walking around the log that he had sat on earlier this fatal night when the skies were still weeping. Kylen walked towards the clearing where Althea lay, noticing the grace of her presence as she allowed the silence to consume every element of her. Kylen didn't interrupt her thoughts as he sat down, he just laid at her side wordlessly, melting into the cool grass as he muffled his groans. His body ached; every muscle felt torn, and every bone broken beyond repair. But Kylen didn't allow himself to break her silence, he would give her everything he could if it meant keeping her at peace.

Although he knew that they were still a long way from peace itself.

"All these years and I had only ever seen one or two stars occasionally... the curse clouded the sky from all. Now... now I feel like I can see them all; as if at last we have reunited despite never once meeting," Althea mused in a quiet tone.

"It's a nice touch to Aeonia, if I say so myself. It was awfully dark before, and dark Kingdoms have never been my style," Kylen replied as he shed her a quick glance. He was proud to see that there was a curl of a smile caressing the edge of her lips.

Althea nodded, closing her eyes after a ruinous second as she ran a hand through the dark curls of her hair. "Your family is really nice—*your biological one, I mean.* They... really helped me escape all of this, Hel. Don't know why they bothered to do it or what they even got out of it in the end, but I'm glad you got to see them."

From her voice alone, Kylen could tell that it was paining her to recall all that she had survived through during those long months. Almost as if the very memories were stabbing her heart into pieces as she looked away in a weak attempt to try and shelter her pain away from him. Hadn't she realised yet that he would happily take all of her pain, suffering, grief, and emotions that wore her heart to pieces away if he could? There wasn't anything he wouldn't do for her. Nothing at all. "We don't have to talk about it if you aren't ready. We have all the time in the world—"

"*Please take that back quickly,*" Althea was swift to quip as she turned back towards him. She lifted herself up and onto her elbow, looking down at him with a cocked brow. "The last time you said that, I was left to awaken in my subconsciousness without a single thought tracing my mind—only to realise I was *again* imprisoned in a place I could not escape."

Kylen cringed as he shrugged his shoulders; she did have a drastically good point. "Sorry, sorry," he apologised with a laugh. He, too, brought his hand up to his face, running his fingers over the exhaust as he beckoned it away. "I probably should think of something better to say—a new catchphrase of some type."

He found that Althea was looking at him now, really looking at him, watching with the sharpest of eyes as he spoke. "Thank you for... mourning me," she whispered, and the bark of a laugh that left Kylen's lungs had Althea's smile growing—against all beautiful odds.

"Oh, you are so very welcome." Kylen nodded as he crossed his arms. "I've found that I'm quite... skilled at the art of mourning nowadays. Hel, people should hire me because I am just *that talented.*"

"You should add it to your title," Althea noted with a cock of her brows.

"Do you even know what a title is?"

Althea shrugged as she, too, crossed her arms and laid back down. The bliss in her eyes was something that he would die to keep shining.

Kylen grinned a small but certain smile. He looked back towards the night sky as he shook his head. "Oh, you are truly something, Althea Evangeline. Truly something indeed." He could feel Althea's eyes stay on his as he watched the stars waltz up above, and he wondered whether or not she could see him pinching himself to figure out whether this was real life. It felt like a dream—one that, *any second now*, he would wake up from with a terribly heavy heart. "But seriously," he whispered as his eyes fell back to hers, "there was not a day that went by where I didn't think of you. And I don't mean that in a creepy, stalkerish way, but in a way where I am forever sorry for all the wrong that I have caused."

"Oh, shut up," Althea muttered as she shook her head with a roll of her eyes. "Enough tears have been shed already in the last, *however many hours it has been.* I am rather content with keeping the last of them locked away."

A small chuckle escaped Kylen's lips as he took in her every word. She was exactly everything he had ever dreamt of. She was beautiful; even if she did have remnants of the curse scattered across her features, she was still beautiful because he knew that this was *his* Althea.

The one he had fallen in love with the moment her dagger pressed against his throat the day they reunited after all those long torturous years.

Kylen's eyes dropped to her lips before glancing back towards her darling eyes. Did she know how much she meant to him? He would give her the sun and the moons if he could. He would give her every last inch of his soul if it meant seeing her smile in a way that actually met the eyes.

Althea's gaze softened on his, and for a moment, Kylen thought that he'd seen her eyes drop to his lips with a question flashing across her mind. Their eyes met, and the question became evident on both of their tongues as Kylen took in her timeless grace. He looked at her with uncertainty, several strange emotions caressing his cheeks as he leant up and onto his bruised elbow. Kylen reached for the strand of hair that ran wild, and he tucked it behind her ear as he offered her a small laugh.

He had to be dreaming—he just *had* to be.

Kylen looked down at her as if she was his full moon, the only star that would ever matter to him, no matter the galaxy that shone above. "May I?" Kylen whispered gently, but before Althea could utter a single word in response, she had already leant up and met his lips with her own.

And every little thing that had ever caused Kylen agony suddenly didn't seem that bad in the scheme of the universe anymore.

At first, the kiss was small and gentle; it took everything in Kylen not to release a shuddering breath because of her touch alone. *He didn't want to startle her, and she was afraid of what would happen next.* But Althea needed to realise that she didn't need to be afraid. He would never do anything to hurt her ever again.

Althea's lips were soft, everything he had ever imagined. Her hands went up and looped around his throat, holding him to her as if she so stupidly thought that he would abandon her now. Kylen bit back a groan as he returned her force with the force of his own power, and the world went quiet as if they were the only two to ever matter.

Kylen pulled back as he leaned over her, tucking a strand of this new dark hair behind her ear yet again. "Hi," he whispered through a smile, and the smile Althea shed him was everything that he had ever wished for—*he needed to kiss her again.* She was spellbinding and addicting, and because of the constellations in her eyes, he figured that she knew a touch of her own power.

"Hi," Althea replied, and her voice sounded so genuine that Kylen wanted to go to war for her all over again. "How's the view from up there?" she asked with amusement in her lungs. "I would assume it's rather horrendous, if anything."

"Oh, it's the most treacherous thing I have ever seen."

Althea laughed as she pulled on the hem of his shirt, beckoning him down to taste her glorious lips once again. Kylen was thankful for the bushes that were blocking them from view; else, he didn't think he would hear the end of this rather enticing sight. And whilst that wasn't a problem for Kylen in any which way, he figured that since Althea was a rather private person, she would prefer for this to be their little secret.

And if it meant keeping Althea happy, he would keep all of the secrets in the world.

She tasted of everything he had ever longed for. Every little craving and every little dream that he had always presumed to be unreachable. One of his hands dipped down to her cheek as he ran *his* finger over her cheekbone, and his other hand held him up so that he could be as close to her as physically possible.

The kiss was gradual, yet it was passionate.

It vowed for there to be a future no matter all that they had suffered.

He could tell that neither of them were fine, but how could they be after everything? They were both hurting, both mourning. Yet, the best thing they could do was make it known that they were not alone—and Kylen was adamant about doing just that.

Althea pulled back and looked up at him with a sly smirk lining her lips. She tilted her head to the side, almost as if she was assessing him. "I bet you've been wanting to do that for a long time now," she cooed with a wink. Her tone was light, and yet he could tell that she was trying to restrain the pain of the last several months from her voice.

"You have no idea." Kylen beamed gently as he pressed a kiss to her forehead, and he genuinely wished with all of his power that his kiss could take away all of the agony from her mind.

"*Are you guys dead? Or just asleep?*" Atticus' voice asked from somewhere in the distance, and Kylen chuckled into the kiss as a laugh bloomed between the two. "I think they're dead."

A moment passed, and Althea nodded up at him like she knew that the moment was over, and so he offered her a hand to sit up before tucking both strands of loose black hair behind her ears.

There she was.

The girl he had searched for.

"We're okay," Kylen replied as he kept his eyes trained on Althea. "We're okay."

TWENTY-NINE
ALTHEA

I t wasn't that she wanted to keep secrets from them, she truly did *not,* but it was more so that she was afraid of the extra harm that would come their way if she was to open her mouth and spill her plans into their laps.

Althea had already caused so many scars to cross their skin.

She had caused so much blood to be splattered.

And she would not be the one to blame any longer—*plus, she would be back before any of them knew it...*

Well, that was what she told herself as she stared down at the boy asleep at her side. She only needed *some* answers; that was all.

Althea muffled her breaths as she leaned down and pressed a kiss to his cheek, and it truly took all of her stamina not to lie back down at Kylen's side.

He hadn't held her as he once had.

He hadn't touched her as he once had.

Kylen had merely laid at her side, acting as if he knew she could not bear to feel confined any longer.

With one last glance towards the boy who slept peacefully by the sides of those *who cared for him,* Althea began to walk back towards the palace that took everything in her not to *flee* from. It was a daunting sight, a troubling one. It earned the fear to claw at her throat as her slow steps grew closer and closer.

The blood in her veins suddenly felt extraordinarily tight as she calmed her breaths, willing herself not to breathe too loudly in case a monster full of the petrifying screams of the cursed jumped out at her and dared to try and take her life from her hold.

She didn't feel like the girl she had been when she'd left this place in a golden carriage; no, she felt like an imposter.

Someone who was ruined for good.

Althea crept up the steps before slipping behind the closed doors of the place that felt like a graveyard in her mind. Only death was brought to her thoughts as she looked around. It was the only thing that she could clearly remember of this wretched place.

The death of *her* mother.

The death of *her* Eloise.

The death of *her* father.

And the death of *her*.

Had Althea even made it out alive from these walls?

Or was she dead, and this was all a mere nightmare?

The hike down to the dungeons was one that she felt she would be able to perform with her eyes closed. Althea had done it so many times that it felt like second nature to her—no matter the way it earned her skin to burn with the memories of all the lives she'd taken.

The girl who once was returns, returns, returns.

She could hear the boy of dragons' breaths skim the stained floors. He was breathing heavily and yet hollowly, almost as if he was as ill as the cursed were proclaimed to be. "You've come to visit me," he noted as Althea grew near, and there was a comedic tone to his breath, one that had her second-guessing her every step. "How fortunate must I be?"

"You knew I was alive, and yet you never tried to help me."

"In the end, I did. I was the one who helped Kylen Noxwell enter your soul prepared to save your life, *was I not?*" Adonis questioned as Althea reached his cell, and his eyes were awfully venomous as they flickered over her scarred flesh.

Althea shook her head wordlessly, her own bitter laugh trembling off of her lips as her true cravings bent around her fingertips in the midst of the shadowed magick that was now hers to wield. "You tried to poison me so that you could claim my magick. That's what the curse was doing, and I know for a fact that that was what you were trying to do too."

What Kylen had told her had honestly not surprised her in the slightest.

It was given that Adonis would act in favour of the curse; *they* always did.

"So be it. I needed to do whatever I could to get my family back, and still, that got me absolutely nowhere—but surely you cannot *blame* me?" Adonis sneered as he peeled off the skin around his nails, willing Althea's stomach to turn with nausea.

His dark flesh that once held the glimmer of a dragon's scales now reeked with the poison of all who had been wronged.

"I could've helped you with that," Althea said, and Adonis scoffed a laugh that cut her off entirely.

"You were dead, may I remind you. Plus, I would get more from using you than claiming a friendship with you," Adonis uttered as he turned to her with a shake of his head.

"You are quite arrogant, may I note," Althea sourly observed. "Where are your children and husband and whatever, anyway?" she asked, and the shift in Adonis' expression was slightly alarming. "I would've helped you get them back if you asked me to; of course, it would've cost you something, but a deal is a deal."

Adonis shook his head as he rose to his feet, stalking towards the bars that were protected with an enchantment that Atticus had presumably set into place. "It doesn't matter anymore. I have failed." His eyes were solemn, haunted. Catching onto something that was beyond Althea's view. "*I have failed, I have failed, I have failed, I have failed—*"

Before Althea got the slightest chance to question him on whatever it was that he meant, his neck had been sliced into two, and his head fell to the ground seconds before his body followed. He was still twitching a little; his body convulsing as if the curse was taking an extra long time to torture his *corpse*.

Althea gasped, stumbling back, her hand raising to her chest as fear spiked in every corner of her soul. The dark blood splattered across her body, but she figured that that didn't quite make the difference since she was unfortunately already decorated in it from head to toe.

Hands that were as sharp and calloused as anything she had ever known clasped around her head, using her moment of pure disastrous shock to *their* merciless advantage. Althea turned in her clasp only to find a man that looked something similar to the ghost of Erwin, the man who'd led Althea to Kylen in the first place last year, looking down at her with white eyes. Although, she knew that this was not him—but perhaps the brother she had always heard the heavy rumours of.

"Hello, Your Highness," he seethed through his clenched jaw, his spit flying at her through the holes of his yellow teeth.

"*Kylen*—" Althea went to whisper, except whatever cursed magick had lingered in both the spit and blood that now covered her whole, made Althea not able to move nor utter a single word.

She was frozen.

Completely frozen in the eyes of death.

THIRTY
KYLEN

The sun, or whatever Kylen should call it in a shadowed Kingdom like this, slowly urged him to awaken from his slumber. His body ached as he whimpered through a yawn, every muscle and bone feeling as if they had been torn from his flesh and stabbed ninety thousand times.

"What time is it?" Kylen heard Uzziah ask as he grumbled himself awake, and with a narrowing of his eyes, Kylen found that he had no true idea himself. Perhaps it was afternoon... evening... or even morning.

Kylen stretched out his arms before him, shrugging in his throbbing shoulders before he dared to gaze over to where Althea had lied just the night before—but now... now she was *gone?*

Missing.

The ghost of her leaving not a trace in sight.

"Althea?" Kylen whispered as he scrambled to his feet, his eyes gliding through the air before landing on the last of his family. "Where is she?"

Atticus shook his head as he ran a hand through his hair. It was clear that he had just awoken, but Kylen didn't exactly have a second to dwell on the misfortune of that catastrophe. "*Adonis*—" Atticus breathed, and Kylen's eyes flew to the castle that had several thousand crows resting atop it.

Kylen didn't give himself a chance to hear what any of them said next. He began to run towards the cursed palace, his stomach filled with the worst type of dread.

The halls felt colder as he entered them, a type of darkness that was known to him waltzing across the cracked floorboards. That darkness only seemed to thicken as Kylen, and his family crept below—and when the sight of Adonis' lone rotting head came into view, everything seemed to freeze entirely.

"What the Hel," Zaire whispered as Kylen approached the bars of the cell that flourished in a cruelty that burned his flesh. "Do you think she did this?"

Khatri shook his head as he reached Kylen's side, his face tense as if he had been the one to perform such a treacherous act. "It's a magick of the darker arts. It uses the curse—but not the curse that we know of. Whoever did this has the ability to draw on the *original ability* of the curse, the pure, unrelenting, and merciless version of the curse before it got divided and shared amongst fatal leaders."

"Erwin?" Uzziah questioned, and Khatri shrugged his shoulders in response, but the look on his features was the most troubling thing of them all.

"Possibly…" he muttered as he ran a hand through his hair. "But I'm thinking more so his brother."

☾

He knew sleeping had been a bad idea at a time like this. It was stupid of him—idiotic. Kylen should've stayed awake and protected Althea from all the horror of the world.

At least then, that would've prevented this horrific journey to a land that had remained untouched and whispered with the lives of the past for centuries now.

Kylen looked towards Zaire, who sat cross-legged on the other side of the carriage that had a rather complicated spell to conceal it from any prying eyes. What was the spell? Kylen had no idea, but he trusted Khatri enough to know that the magick that was being channelled off of all of them was being put to good use.

Zaire's hands were resting against their knees; their eyes shut as they muttered several words of a different language under their bloodthirsty breath. "I wasn't aware that the King of the East was Erwin's brother," they mumbled after several seconds, leaving Kylen to exchange a quizzical glance with Atticus.

He hadn't been aware of that either.

"He's not," Atticus replied in a rather puzzled tone.

"Hate to be the one to say it, but I think you are wrong, *dearest Atticus.*"

Atticus looked over his shoulder at Kylen, and he knew that his brother was confused about whatever it was that Zaire was exactly doing inside that mind of theirs. He had never really understood the extent of their abilities.

If Kylen had the will to explain to him, he would; instead, he could only look to Uzziah and beckon him through a silent plea to do it for him.

"Z is gathering every piece of information ever written about the originality of the curse. Of course, as we and the world know, the curse formed because of two wronged but greedy brothers; however, only one in the marvel of time has ever been revealed... *Erwin,*" Uzziah explained, and Atticus slowly nodded. "As well as that, I am presuming that Z here is also *going against Khatri's wishes* and trying to put themselves back into the beginning of time... in an attempt to watch the birth of the curse through the third-dimensional aspect... to get to the basics of... *everything*."

Now Kylen could tell that his dearest brother was desperately horribly confused.

A bump in the road had Kylen's grip tightening on the blade in his hand, and he looked towards the window that showed him the land that no one had dared to journey across for centuries now. Not since the great war.

It was dark, haunted. All the trees were burnt, and the land was all dead. Kylen could spot pieces of history that had been crumbled and broken down to look as if it hadn't existed at all; however, that stirred his stomach horribly.

For a while, the past few hours, the lot of them had used Khatri's magick to jump across time and land in order to try and reach Althea far more quickly. Nauseating but efficient. They were ultimately jumping from Realm to Realm, from sea to sea, until Khatri's magick became of no use because of the strange current that filtered its way through the air—it felt like he was back inside the trance of the curse... except this was real life.

Sure, Kylen had somewhat known and heard of the rumours that there were lands out there where the magick of one's soul was nothing in the eyes of death... but he hadn't actually believed that *there were Realms out there where magick was limited and pathetic.*

It felt... awfully confusing and rather conflicting to wrap his head around.

Everything felt confusing now.

But he didn't have time to dwell on that; he was busy making sure that the little magick Khatri could use to his advantage was following the scent of Althea—and trying to prevent her from harm... but Kylen spotted every time Khatri's face flinched. And he swore that that was because he could *feel* what was happening to Althea.

"But why does Erwin's brother—or the King of the East want Althea?" Atticus asked with a shake of his head.

"Because she is a God, Atty. And someone as power-hungry as that is going to do anything and everything in their power to gain more of it... think of our past experiences with Erwin, for instance. Remember how delightful that was?" Zaire hummed as they opened their eyes. They shut them for a second time with a furrow of their brows, except just as quickly they opened them. "I just lost connection with *that* element of magick; however, I can confirm the fact that Erwin's brother is the nameless King of the East, and he does want to do whatever he can to devour the souls of the Gods."

"Like Hel, we are letting that happen," Kylen sneered under his breath, and Khatri looked at him with his own wordless gaze.

His eyes looked strange as he stared at him, words floating through them as if they were doing everything in their power to escape Khatri's tongue. "I owe you an apology," Khatri noted after a crackling second, and tension began to build in the silent carriage.

Kylen shook his head as he looked away, but Khatri kept his gaze steady.

"I'm sorry for being a dick."

"I was as much as a dick as you were—plus you were grieving, you still are," Kylen simply muttered as he rolled his gaze back to his. He didn't want to have this conversation, to relive past events. He was merely just glad that they were all back together again and not dead.

"You were grieving too," Khatri pinpointed with a raise of his brows. "I should've been more considerate."

Kylen didn't reply; he couldn't will himself to. His past felt like a terrible drunken blur. One that was intoxicating with the stench of corpses left to fend their way to the afterlife. He looked away from Khatri as he sent him a half-hearted smile. He just wanted this mess to be over—to be able to breathe again without worrying about the lives of the ones he loved becoming ripped from his clasp.

"We are entering the inner borders of the King of the East's castle," Uzziah noted as he exhaled a deep and heavy sigh. "It's time to park this baby and tread on foot."

THIRTY-ONE
ALTHEA

Althea shook her head as a sob rocked her chest into two. The slithers of the curse tightened on her hands and wrists, and with everything in her, she wished that the cold marbled floor beneath her would swallow her whole. "*No* —" she went to whisper; however, the moment her words parted with the answer he didn't want: another wave of brutality had a scream piercing from the depths of her soul.

This wasn't meant to happen.

She simply meant to go to Erwin and demand answers before returning to the small, little campsite and sleep the rest of her nightmares away.

"I don't want to keep playing this game with you, Althea." The king scowled as he stalked around her frozen body that lay shuddering against the floor. Her blood was splattered everywhere, her clothes torn from where the curse had punctured into her flesh. "But I need you to give me your magick."

It pained her, but Althea shook her head as she looked at him with bloodshot eyes. She expected that now that she had the possession of both the curse and her Elemental magick, that she would be the one to hold the advantage—but she was sourly mistaken.

This man was the enemy of the curse.

The enemy of all magick.

And the enemy of the Gods.

"I would rather die," Althea spat as the curse tightened on her once again, and her eyes fell shut in a fatal sob as she felt her flesh split into two. Her face crumbled as several more tentacles of the curse entered into her blood. She just wanted the pain to stop; she wanted everything to go back to how they were when she was a baby, and she had no clue about the brutality of this world.

Althea tried to look away, except a hand that was sharp and calloused had her face turning back to face the King's. And despite the king being blind, his face was aligned with hers as he leant over her. "Then I will cut it out of your corpse."

She was tired.

So horribly tired.

As she shook her head against his grip, several cries left Althea's lungs. She just wanted this to stop—she just wanted it to stop. And yet she knew that she could not give up and give it to him because then they would all end up dead... and Althea hadn't made it this far for that to happen.

She wasn't aware when the king had left her to suffer silently in her own blood; she had only opened her aching eyes to find that she was in his throne room alone. Left to gaze up at the high ceilings and tall walls as the bile met with her lips.

Everything was blurred and distorted, sending several waves of nausea to attack her throat as the world blamed her for simply existing.

She knew he would return soon; he always did.

And Althea didn't think that she could fight him off any longer.

THIRTY-TWO
KYLEN

I t was foolish of him to think of Aeonia as the worst kingdom of them all when the Kingdom of the East stood tall in all of its eerie misery. Everything was different shades of dark green, blue, and black—the scent of death slithering over Kylen's bones as he slowly and silently hiked towards the decaying castle walls that he could feel Althea's magick suffering within.

The water thrashed below the cliff they were hiking across. Kylen looked towards it with an uneasiness suffocating his stomach. He could hear the screams the dead were shedding him, and he could practically hear the sanity of his mind begging him to turn around no matter the cost. *But his heart was in control now, and he was going to get what he wanted.*

Kylen didn't have a good feeling about this whatsoever—not as he looked towards his family, who were all prepared to go to war for their queen that wasn't even *their* queen.

He had only just gotten her back… and yet he'd already lost her again.

Uzziah met his gaze with a nod of his head, and Kylen

returned it with a nod of his own. Silent words of reassurance going unspoken that he knew they both needed.

He was worried about what he was going to find on the other side of these palace walls, especially since they could all hear the faint murmur of the curse's victims screams through the air... warning them of the time when they dared to wander such treacherous trails, and how now their bodies were forever missing alongside the purities of their souls.

However, every single one of those fears were quick to silence in his mind when he heard a scream that had the blood of his heart curdling with a rage that vowed death upon all of those that dared cross his path. Because it was an ear-piercing scream that left the lungs of Althea Evangeline—*his* Althea Evangeline.

And now Kylen was rather eager to watch the blood spill.

He didn't wait to hear what the others at his side were going to do next as they all abruptly halted their steps. No, he *couldn't*. He wouldn't stand here, wasting time, whilst he knew Althea was being tortured for something that *she never even wanted in the first place.*

Like Hel, Kylen wasn't going to do something about it.

His grip tightened on the blade in his hand, and he began to sprint towards the castle walls that flashed with the horrifying sight of crows. Except these birds weren't lively in any way... *no*... they were made up of pure bones and rotting skin.

Kylen spotted a grey window that he was rather eager to smash his way through when a hand was quick to pull him back before he even got a chance to do so. "*Kylen*—" Khatri was quick to breathe as he tugged on his arm, but Kylen wasn't going to let his brother slow him down—not when he knew *her* blood was being spilled. "No—*stop.*"

"Let me go. *I need to get to her*—"

"Yeah, and nobody's stopping you. But if you go in there and he spots you—or he feels you, you are dead. This man is a myth, a legend. S-*Sayah* and I were fanatics of his rumours despite never once knowing that he was actually real—*Hel, who were we* to realise that the boring King of the East, who had only been spotted once or twice, was actually the mythical legend of *the brother?*" Khatri whispered as the others reached their sides. Kylen tugged his arm out of his reach. He didn't want to hear any of Khatri's useless stories of the past in times as fatal and lethal as this. "Right now, there is a blanket of all of our magick's covering each other, but the moment one of us gets too far—or gets out of reach, the bubble disappears... and we all die."

Kylen's jaw tensed as he looked away. *He didn't want them to die—but he didn't want her to die either.* He was about to say something when Zaire's head shot up with a heave of their chest. Their eyes wavered with a vigorous green wave of their magick, and Uzziah clasped onto them to stop them from fainting. "He's left her."

"*What?*"

"She's alone—this is our time to reach her and fucking escape this miserable excuse of a place."

"Where has he gone?" Khatri quickly asked as he looked around. The storms were brewing above, lightning threatening to strike any second now.

And Kylen hoped that it wasn't because the curse had just claimed another Godly soul.

Zaire shrugged with a shake of their head as they fully, at last, came back to their senses. "I don't know. I can only do so much with my magick now that we are here, and I asked it to tell me when he leaves the room Althea is in. So, I suggest we get our bloody move on if we want to save her—"

Kylen didn't have to hear them twice. He began to walk towards the window that he planned on probably *idiotically* smashing when Khatri's hand *once again* held him back.

He didn't get the chance to ask his dearest brother what it was that he was doing, as Khatri's magick had already thrown him through the now transparent wall and into one of the many unnerving rooms of this palace that appeared to be quite literally frozen in time.

Not a single sound had occurred from his entrance.

Nicely done.

One by one, Zaire, Atticus, Uzziah, and Khatri all entered into the same room without a sound, and Kylen's heart was becoming extraordinarily loud in the back of his mind as he stalked towards the open doorway. He prayed that she wasn't going to be dead when he found her—that she wouldn't be mere skin and bones after all this time of yearning.

He just needed her to be okay.

To not be dead.

This palace was like a maze, and every corner they turned only seemed to be leading them further into the trap *Kylen had no doubt* the king had set.

Because they were focussing on keeping their cover sealed and away from the prying eyes of death, they had lost their connection to Althea; but what use was tiptoeing through a warzone if the girl they were there to collect was already drowning in her own blood?

A small, scattered whimper had Kylen's feet freezing a mere metre away from a door that was half shut with a dark whisper to it. It was strange how this castle had doors, and yet there was no furniture to lace the halls in any way. Almost as if the king knew that there were already too many lost souls suffocating the air.

The others stopped at his side, and he knew that they had heard the same heart-shattering cry. He only hoped that it had not come from *her* lungs. They exchanged a weary look as Kylen took a step forward, and that was when the sight of *her* wounded body came into view. A sight that had Atticus reaching for Khatri as a gasp audibly left his lips.

Althea was sprawled across the large empty floor, her body chained to the ground with the curse slithered across every inch of her skin. Her eyes were shut, the only sign of life appearing through the way her chest convulsed every time she took a single breath.

Kylen hadn't even noticed that he'd started to run towards her—he hadn't noticed that he was now on his knees, reaching for her cheeks as his hands silently shook.

He was too focussed on the fact that this looked like the exact same scene he had found himself in the last time they were in this position—and he'd basically lost Althea for good then, even *if things had turned out slightly... alright... in the end.*

"Lift her head up," Khatri demanded through a single breath, and Kylen was quick to comply. Her head felt so loose in his hands, rolling to the side because of his very touch. What had *he* done to her? He was going to pay with his existence—Kylen vowed that much.

Zaire pushed their hands out to hover above her chest, presumably feeling and trying to contact the exact troubling beats of her heart. Since they held more of the fairy gene in their blood than Uzziah did, they were able to bend and mould blood to their will.

A rare art that had been long ago banished.

But Zaire never once followed the—*his* rules.

And it was in moments like these that he was forever thankful for that.

"Her heart is weak, failing."

Khatri shook his head, glancing up at Kylen before moving his distressing gaze to Zaire. "Gods don't need hearts," he sighed as he reached for the pulse of her throat, and Kylen remembered those few pieces of text that had told him the exact same thing. "Even if her heart gives out, she will still live—and her magick will be able to be claimed."

"We need to get her out of here," Uzziah uttered as Kylen noticed how cold her skin felt—she *felt* and *looked* like a *corpse* now, and Kylen didn't know what to do... how to react.

"Help her," he pleaded, and for the first time in a long time, he didn't care how weak and vulnerable his voice sounded. "Please—help her. I cannot *lose* her again."

Khatri's expression shifted slightly as he nodded. "I will. Kylen, *I will.*"

Kylen dropped his eyes to the girl in his hand, slowly tucking the damp curls of hair behind her blood-stained ears. It was then that he noticed that Atticus had been working on burning the curses away from their clasp on her skin. Using the vengeance of his magick to torture the dark, shadowed tentacles that were actively eating at her flesh as he watched—however, Kylen seemed to realise something before his brother did...

As Atticus didn't seem to understand yet that those tentacles were extended hands and arms of the old, withered king himself.

Meaning that the King of the East now knew that they were here.

THIRTY-THREE

ALTHEA

Consciousness, as cruel and malicious as it was, warped across Althea's mind as she beckoned her eyes to open. Her head throbbed as she tossed, a sharp pain flashing against the back of her mind as her chest seized with an ache that was terribly painful. "Althea—" Her name was soft as it left the lips of someone she recognised, almost as if they thought she could do no wrong. Was she imprisoned in her subconsciousness again? "My love, it's okay, *you are —and you will be... okay.*"

Althea narrowed her eyes as her vision began to clear from the blurred, strange haze that it was, and she noticed the pained outline of a face that wasn't cruel as it looked down at hers.

Was this death?

Was he here to take her away to the sweetness of the afterlife?

She hoped so.

That seemed so much easier than opening her eyes and allowing her life to go on and suffer through the brutality like normal.

THIRTY-FOUR
KYLEN

K ylen didn't get a second to warn the others of the emerging beast before the door had opened. His old, manacled body stood there as several bolts of lightning struck inches before the windows. "I see you have graced my lonesome self with some visitors," the King of the East uttered through a deep inhale. "If only you would've told me sooner; this is terribly embarrassing for me, but it seems I have forgotten to furnish the place."

Swiftly, Khatri looked up from where he was helping push Althea's limp body into Kylen's arms. The deadly *panic* that seeped over his expression was horrifyingly daunting. Never once did his brother present himself with fear. Yet, that was the one physical expression on his lips that Kylen could recognise.

"What a pity indeed."

Kylen had no idea what the old bastard was going on about, but he didn't quite exactly have the darling second to care. He could feel Althea slowly coming back to herself as Zaire pumped her blood to her heart, except he doubted that she would want to remain conscious for long when the sight before them was one that was appallingly petrifying. Kylen looked down at her as he rose to his feet, Althea in his arms as well as a sword in one of his hands.

He was leaving here with her, he was sure.

"Leave us be," Khatri carefully said as he stepped forward, his arms raised as if the old king had the eyes to see him acting seemingly *innocent*. "We are just here to collect our Queen."

The King laughed, his chest rattling like a rattlesnake. "She is no Queen—especially no Queen of *yours*."

"She is our Queen, and we are returning her home," Zaire breathed like they also wanted to pick a fight with the dearest man who controlled the lightning that bled. They stepped forward and in line with Khatri, giving Kylen a vulnerable second to step back. Althea released a breath that had her lungs choking, and she coughed into his chest as his hold on her tightened. Like Hel he was going to let her go after everything this man had put her through in the last few hours alone.

"And where exactly is that home... for the *young* maiden?" the King asked with a raise of his brow—sending a few more hairs upon his head and brows to decay in the process. "That girl has no—"

"Lorundio," Uzziah laughed as if it was the most humorous thing to leave his tongue. "And you are quite idiotic if you think we aren't going to bring her home after all that she—"

"Has done?" the King said, finishing Uzziah's sentence for him. "You mean, try to kill Mr Noxwell, then try to kill you all—then actually killing one of the seas children? What was her name? ...Sayah?"

Kylen's jaw tensed as his eyes flickered to Khatri, although his stare remained unwavering. That was the first time he'd seen the male not react to the mention of Sayah's death—the first time where he didn't look to want to fall victim to those very words.

Perhaps they were closer to closure than they'd presumed.

"*Kylen?*" the word was small, a mere whisper against the eyes of the God. Kylen looked down to Althea with furrowed brows, his jaw tensing even harder now that he knew that she was going to have to witness all of the blood that was about to spill. "You came—"

"Of course, I did. I told you, did I not? I would always come for you—no matter how far you lay," his words were soft, near silent, beckoning Althea's ears to be the only ones to hear them. Althea tried to say something more in response, although her tongue failed at the exhaust lingered upon her fingertips. Her eyes shut once again, but the small shake of her head told her that she was still conscious.

"I *remember* my first love," the old man laughed with cruelty to his tone. Slowly, very slowly, the darkness that stood tall in every corner of the room began to form into physical bodies that appeared similar to the *one* Kylen had faced in the curse's subconsciousness. They were all scarred, wounded with pleads and sorrow dripping from their butchered tongues. They began to surround them, and Kylen watched as each surviving member of his court began to stretch around him with weapons in hand.

They may be his friends, *his family*...

But they were also his finest guards.

And they were all *bloody good* at spilling blood.

Especially the curses.

"It was too bad though..." the king reminisced as darkness flickered across the whites of his eyes, "her skin was rather quick to rot after our first kiss." He shook his head, wiping away the words from his tongue as he took a slight step back. "I would tell you to give her back to me... but fortunately, I have found that my... children... have grown rather hungry. And what father would I be if I denied such a wonderful feast?"

A silent wave of electricity streamed through the air as the thunder echoed in the near distance. The curse began staggering towards them, taking the cruel shapes of creatures that were unspeakable.

Althea gasped as Kylen quickly took a step back, and her

eyes only seemed to widen as she realised just what was happening. "Kylen—" she whimpered with a shake of her head, her fingers balling onto the material of his shirt.

She was afraid.

She was actually afraid—

"It's okay—*It's okay.*"

Zaire slid on their knees as their sword flew through the air. The cursed soldier before them sliced in half—however, this was the consequence of the Gods, and it was going to take something more than just a mere blade to slaughter it away. Atticus looked out for Khatri's back as he leant off of him. He ducked into a roll as his sword went flying through the air, and Kylen felt as Althea began to squirm in a weak attempt to land on her feet.

"Althea—"

"Kylen, let me fight."

"Althea, *sweetheart*—"

Althea shook her head in his arms, and he wondered whether she was aware that a small, agonised cry had left her lips the moment she tried to move. "I can fight; I'm a good fighter." For a second, her eyes threatened to roll back, yet her whole face pursed as she fought herself to stay awake.

"I know, darling," Kylen breathed as he dodged a slither of the curse that flew through the air aiming for their souls. "You are the best of the best—"

"Kylen, you need to get her out of here!" Khatri yelled over the loud screeches of the lost spirits, and Kylen's eyes whipped to his as he quickly shook his head. "Now!"

Was he delusional? "I am not leaving you," Kylen seethed in response. Despite the old king no longer being visible to Kylen's selective eyes, he could feel the mockery of his laugh crawl over his bones. He probably assumed that Kylen was weak—mad —*insane*—but Kylen knew that he was anything but. He was *loyal*. "I won't—"

Zaire's face appeared before him, and the expression coating their lips was one that had his words halting. It was sorrowful yet accepting? "You have to." Their tone was quiet, almost as if they were fearful of the words themselves. "It's *she* that he wants; *her* magick, *her* power. You need to get her out of here before he gets the chance to kill us all."

Kylen shook his head the same moment a cry left Althea's lips, and that had his gaze drifting there. He wasn't oblivious. Kylen knew what would happen if the curse was to gain every last inch of Althea's magick. All would be left to die, and Kylen would be left knowing that he was the reason why.

"I can't leave you," Kylen whispered as his eyes held Zaire's, and their own gaze was the strongest he had ever seen it. "I *can't.*"

"The curse has tried to kill me so many times now, Kye, and yet you still are reluctant to believe that I am a survivor. I won't let it kill me or those stupid brothers of yours."

Whilst the words didn't leave their lips, he felt Zaire speak to him through the blood oath of their minds. *'The King's specific curse cannot devour the souls of mortals who have previously won his battles. Because we have outrun the curse in the past, and it has just skimmed our souls... now we don't need to worry about this variation of it killing us. The most he can do is lock us up in another Realm but guess what, Kye, your girl is a God. She can get us back if she's in a good mood—and alive. So, go. Don't worry about us, please.'*

What had happened to the small fairy that Kylen had found so intriguing? What had happened to the small child that reminded Kylen of both of his biological siblings in such peculiar ways?

They still had that lively sparkle to their eyes—except now it looked stronger, *braver.*

And if there was one thing that Kylen had learnt in all of his years, was that he should always (if the situation is right) trust Zaire.

No matter how painful it was.

Kylen looked towards his brothers, watching as they fought for their lives as Kylen's chest heaved a scattered sigh. Zaire was right, and he knew that—and that was the worst part of it all.

Another scream of one of the curses soldiers echoed through the thickening air, and Zaire nodded towards the window he had briefly seen when entering the room in that *frantic manner.* He knew that the restless seas laid thrashing below, and he heard as Zaire whispered, '*Jump, and I will do the rest.*'

If he'd had the chance to reconsider or dwell on the decision any longer, he knew that he would make the wrong one… His love and loyalty to his family would blind him, and the world would be left to falter beneath his very touch… so Kylen didn't give himself that fatal second.

He simply ran.

Zaire had already opened the window for him, and with Althea in his arms, he darted towards it. The spirits began to reach for him—taking the shapes of claws that punctured his arm and left blood in their wake.

He could hear the King roar with the realisation of what he was doing—beckoning the lost souls to reach him before he reached the seas, but they were too late, as with one last glance, Kylen had already jumped…

With Althea in his arms.

Leaving the ones he had spent so many years loving behind.

The air was quick to warp around them, and Kylen had been in this position *one too many times* to know that Zaire's magick was wrapping around the two and sending them to a Realm somewhere far. Zaire was gifting him with their trick of Realm warping, the act of visiting the in-between Realms before landing at one's desired location.

And it seemed now Zaire wished for them to be as far and as unreachable as possible.

"Hold onto me~"

The icy water swallowed them whole. The seas thrashed as Althea and Kylen sank beneath the surface of somewhere in the Sommsia Realms. For a second, he wondered what would happen if he allowed himself to sink; if he allowed the water to take away his pain and bless him with the fate of meeting with his family on the other side...

But then he saw a glimpse of Althea's struggling, drowning face, and he couldn't will himself to be selfish just this once.

Kylen's hand struck out for Althea's, pulling her body towards his as he quickly swam them both up to the glistening surface. In sync, they both gasped as if their lives depended on it; and Althea clung to Kylen's chest as if she knew something of all the monsters that lingered in the depths below.

He held her with a firm grip, pulling away a mere inch to make sure that she was alright; and that she was safe.

"Kylen—" Althea whispered as she looked around, and he knew just what it was that she was realising.

The others were gone.

He had left them—

"We're okay," he replied as he began to swim towards the beach that was only a few metres away. There were no souls that lingered upon these Western sands—no souls that might've seen the waves wash away the sins of their blood. "We're okay."

Althea didn't respond until she felt the sand melt against her feet, but even then, she waited for him to say anything at all.

But what could he say?

He had left them there...

He had left them for *dead*.

Kylen looked to her with his heart in his throat, wholly suffocating him from the inside out. His hands shook on either side of him as he watched Althea study him with careful eyes, the water of the seas dripping down her face without even the slightest of reactions. Could she see through him? Did she know now that he was a failure?

"Oh, Kylen..."

He didn't get the chance to utter a single word, as Althea's hands had already wrapped around him, and she'd pulled him to her soaking chest. Her hands combed throughout his hair, and she held him tightly as a sob emerged from his throat at last.

Kylen didn't regret saving her—he would do it *again,* and *again,* and *again,* if that was what he had to do to keep her heart beating... He loved Althea, and that was one of the truest things that he had realised in these last unrighteous months.

However, it was the fact that *they* were enduring the punishment on his behalf that had his life wanting to never resurface above the daunting waves.

It was his fate as king to endure the pain so that his people could live without a care caressing their minds. And it was his destiny to gift Althea with the life that she deserved after all that she had suffered through because of him...

Except despite what one may delicately think, destiny and fate were two very different things... though, they both were equally as cruel.

EPILOGUE
THE GOD OF BLOOD AND FIRE

T he sound of war cries had the kingdom silencing; not a single soul dared to declare their location to the death that was out for their throats. Their eyes sought the Queen, that was, even the Princess, who was nothing more than a child. They sought them all—looking and searching for whoever would dare to fight and *stand* by their sides.

Mothers hugged their children; fathers hugged their families. Parents of all different nature positioned themselves at the front, holding their torches and makeshift weapons in a memorable attempt to protect those they loved.

And protect the homes they helped make.

"I'm scared," the small child with brown braids whispered. Her breath alone sent the mice fleeing to somewhere far. "*Please* —please don't go." She had been one of the few who couldn't leave her home, as her mother was ill, holding her back from being able to run.

The woman who appeared to be the child's mother smiled, except sorrow dripped from it like one of the waterfalls on the edge of the island in the north. "It is okay to be afraid, my little love. It shows your humanity, your heart."

"What good is a heart in the eyes of tomorrow? The curse is here, the—"

"Do not speak that word out loud; they can hear it and your fear."

Several tears dripped off the girl's cheeks as she looked away. She narrowed her eyes on the small gap in her curtains, looking towards the blood fire that lit up the dark skies with a strange orange aura. "I thought you said the Queen will save us."

"She will, in time."

The girl looked back to her mother with a shake of her head, her tears quickening as they drowned into her sheets. "Then where is she? Why is she—"

Something loud and earth-shattering had the Realm beneath their feet trembling, and the mother grabbed her child just in the nick of time before the ceilings came down on them. Forever erasing the memory of what was.

Murdering the love, the hope, the fair, and the determination of the people of Harlia.

It was only a week before crimson wildflowers bloomed in their wake. And it was only a month before the barrier formed from their spirits—murdering all of those who dared to cross onto the Harlian soil without the blood of Harlia running through their veins.

Where was the Queen? Why hadn't she come for them?

They were the words, the questions, the shock that twisted through the air from their graves. Anguish to their tone as if they believed that the Queen had not been doing everything in her power to try and save them—

She may be the Gods in their physical form, but this sorcery, this magick, this consequence… was everything she feared.

The only enemy of the Gods that could defy them.

The only enemy of the Gods that had the Queen pleading for her daughter's life because she knew something that they did not.

That Althea Evangeline was the God who would revenge, and she was the God of blood and fire—the only soul who actually had the power of both the curse and the Gods on her side.

Meaning that she was the only one to pull the roots of the curse out and watch it suffer.

Acknowledgments

If you are reading this, then I must apologise for the torment and utter heartbreak, I have put you through over the last four-hundred or so pages. If you continue to follow me on this journey, I vow that book three will be a different experience altogether now that Althea and Kylen have finally reunited. As for Zaire, Atticus, Khatri, and Uzziah…? Well, you'll see.

Firstly, I would like to thank two people who helped bring this story to life: my editor Alex Halverson and my cover designer Miriam Schwardt. Without you both, this series wouldn't be what it is today, so I thank you both endlessly.

No words can describe how eternally grateful I am for the family and friends that have supported me since I began this series. From the early mornings of writing before school, to the late-nights brainstorming. To the weekends, where my beloved sister, Indi, would get me to tell her the tales of Althea and Kylen's adventures. To you Indi, I promise to always be your knight in shining armour, ready to stand by your side, hand in hand, when you need me most. To my brothers, thank you for giving me the space to write. I am aware you don't know anything about what I'm writing, but I hope that one day you find yourself lost in these fantastical worlds.

Now, to the person who this book is dedicated too. My grandmother, Glenys Jones, a courageous, kind-hearted and strong-willed woman. I have always looked up to you and treasure all the moments we have spent together. I love reflecting on my childhood and the times spent at your house, rummaging through your bits and bobs and playing alongside your darling dog Plugger. I love you grandma.

To my parents, thank you for your love and support. Everything that you have done for me means the world and no amount of words could capture my gratitude. Thank you and I love you.

To my friends, new and old, I appreciate your support and all your ongoing words of encouragement.

And to you, my beautiful readers, know that I will be the one who shows up for you amidst the storm of life, whether you want me to or not.

Love always, Sienna xoxo

www.ingramcontent.com/pod-product-compliance
Lightning Source LLC
Chambersburg PA
CBHW020250120726
47904CB00001B/149